LOST SOULS

JAMES QUINN
BOOK 2

D.P. JOHNSON

PINE CONE BOOKS

AUTHOR'S NOTE

Lost Souls is the second novel in the James Quinn series. It follows on from *Stolen Lives*, where the story really begins. Although *Lost Souls* can be enjoyed on its own I would recommend that you read *Stolen Lives* at some point to fully understand the history between the main characters.

In my novels I always try to use factual locations, but to better suit the plot I sometimes take the liberty of creating a few fictitious establishments and localities. I hope you don't mind too much.

And talking of fact and fiction, *Lost Souls* was written at a time when extensive COVID-19 restrictions were in place. I believe fiction should be an escape, so I banished the pandemic from the book.

For Grandad
In loving memory

ONE

FIFTEEN YEARS AGO

IT ALL HAPPENED SO QUICKLY, she could barely take it in.

One minute, Urtė had been asleep in the back seat, dreaming happy dreams about the new life awaiting them at their journey's end in London. The next minute, a hulking man snatched her from the car and bundled her, kicking and screaming, into a waiting van.

He threw her down, slamming her spine-first onto the bare, ribbed metal floor. Pain rippled through her. He climbed inside and slammed the door, shutting out the driving rain.

As she struggled to a sitting position, Urtė registered the presence of two more men in the van. One moved to stand over her and shoved her hard in the chest, sending her head crashing to the floor.

He tore strips of tape from a reel; bound her hands and ankles, then gagged her mouth.

The cold, humid air was laced with the stinking fusion of sweat, beer and cannabis.

One of her abductors banged on the solid partition

with his fist, and in response, the driver beyond crunched the van into gear and set off.

The interior light went out, and Urtė lay there, squirming and groaning in the dark. She felt every bump and dip on the rough, winding road. She heard the dull drone of the engine; the throb of rock music; the metallic drumbeat of rain.

The men, seated on the bench in the back, swigged beer, one can after another, discarding their empties on the floor. They were acting as if she wasn't even there, laughing and joking. Urtė couldn't be sure where they were from, only that it was somewhere in the East, like her. She recognised a few words, but not enough to discern their conversations. Maybe that was for the best.

Even though it was pitch black, she closed her eyes and tried to process her predicament. Where were they taking her? Why had they separated her from Rūta? What was going to happen to her? Would she ever see her again?

Every so often, the light would come back on. At first, it terrified her, until Urtė realised they needed the light to play their card games.

Each time the light came on, it would take a few moments for her eyes to adjust. When they did, she would furtively study her abductors' features. There might come a time, she prayed, when she had to describe them to the police.

The guy who had hustled her into the van had sharp features and deep set eyes. One of his canine teeth was missing, so she named him Gappy. The second was heavier set with a round face. He had a habit of blinking, so, of course, in her mind, he was Blinky. The third guy intrigued her the most. He was much younger; smaller; quieter. She didn't need to invent a name for him because Gappy and Blinky did that for her. They called him Shortcake.

2

Shortcake would look away whenever he noticed her looking at him, which meant Urtė could study him for longer. She soon learned that he wasn't drinking his beer as quickly as the others and that he made little contribution to the banter. Indeed, the jokes were often at his expense. He would laugh, but it was obviously forced.

It was when the light came on for perhaps the fourth or fifth time that things escalated.

Her eyes had barely adjusted when Gappy moved from the bench to squat astride her. He gripped her chin and ripped the tape from her mouth, then he squeezed her lips apart to pour a vile, bitter liquid inside. It immediately hit the back of her throat, making her gag. She spat it out, and he slapped her hard about the cheek. Blinky moved to grip her by the hair, yanking back her head so that Gappy could try again with the liquid. She had no choice but to swallow.

They moved back to the bench. Blinky shouted something to Shortcake and slapped his back.

Shortcake rose reluctantly to stand over her, hunched under the low roof.

Gappy and Blinky thumped their thighs and chanted.

As the chanting became more frenzied, Shortcake fumbled with his belt. His hands shook so much that she was surprised when he managed to unbuckle himself. His trousers and boxers dropped to his ankles. Embarrassed hands shielded his groin.

'No, *please!*' she pleaded, trying to engage his eyes. But he wouldn't look at her.

The van went over a hard bump and Shortcake's head crunched into the tin roof. His hands shot up to brace himself, exposing his limp penis.

Gappy and Blinky roared with laughter.

Her efforts to kick out were hopeless.

Whatever drug they'd made her drink was starting to take effect. It was like she was physically separating from her body; like she was floating up to the ceiling to look down with a detached interest.

Shortcake was banished to the corner. Gappy took his place and pulled down her denims; her panties. Untethered her ankles.

Later, much later, Urtė would look back on the journey almost as if she were remembering a dream. Strangely, the primary emotion conjured by the recollection was never pain or humiliation or fear. It was *pity*. Pity for Shortcake cowering in the corner, his head bowed, elbows on his knees, palms pressed to his ears. What was his story? Why was he there? Was it some kind of initiation test? A rite of passage? She would never find out, but she would never forget him.

Overcome by the effects of the liquid, she soon lost track of time and place, only registering that it was dark and that it was no longer raining when the van finally stopped and the rear door burst open.

Gappy and Blinky took her by the upper arms and dragged her from the van. Shortcake and the driver remained inside.

Urtė looked about her. A dilapidated old fuel station. In the distance, she could hear the dull roar of traffic and saw a trail of lights. A motorway, she guessed.

Her legs were so weak, the men practically carried her towards another vehicle—a black Mercedes. Two huge men emerged from the vehicle, one carrying a sports bag. They were so alike that they had to be brothers.

The brother without the bag swaggered towards her. He regarded her like a farmer inspecting a specimen at a cattle market, probing every inch of her with his dark eyes. Eventually, his mouth split into a grin. He turned to his brother and gave him a nod. The brother opened the bag and brought out bundles of cash, which he handed to Blinky.

It was much later when Urtė discovered how much they'd paid for her.

Twenty thousand pounds.

TWO

ONE YEAR AGO

THINK OF THE MONEY, she told herself yet again. *Think of what you can spend it on*. A new outfit? Perfume? More make-up? A girl can never have too much make-up…

A sliver of sunlight burst through the flimsy bedroom curtains, jolting her from her thoughts. She closed her eyes and savoured the glorious warmth on her face.

A heatwave in autumn. What a treat.

Beneath her, Simon writhed and groaned.

Alexia smiled coolly. He was going nowhere. Not while he was bound to the wooden bedposts and pinioned under her taut, leather-clad thighs.

Of course, he was lying about the name. This man wasn't called "Simon". Not that she cared. Her real name wasn't "Alexia", either.

They'd been acquainted for twenty minutes at most. The first time they'd met was when he'd opened the door and invited her into his elegant Notting Hill mews house. He was not an unattractive man, she supposed. Mid fifties. Reasonably trim. A typical English gentleman: posh accent; foppish fringe; a gold sovereign ring on his pinky finger. And so effortlessly superior.

Now, as he lay trapped beneath her in his dotted silk boxers, fighting for breath, *she* was the one enjoying superiority.

How long had it been? Thirty seconds? Sixty? Evgeni had told her that most people lose consciousness after two minutes without oxygen. Or was it three? No matter. The job would soon be done.

Her mind started to drift again, and she wondered if she'd have time to squeeze in a trip to Harvey Nichols afterwards. She had her eye on a gorgeous Vivienne Westwood handbag: black leather; gold orb; matching purse. Beautiful. Window shopping only, of course.

No, she'd head straight home. She couldn't risk upsetting Evgeni twice in one week.

Her thoughts lurched back to the present as Simon let out a muffled howl and arched his back, throwing her off kilter.

As she clambered back astride him, Alexia noticed his cheeks were threaded with tiny purple blood vessels. *Are they new?*

His cold blue eyes bulged and bore into hers.

Probably time, then.

She took a firm pinch of one corner of the silver tape covering his mouth and nostrils, closed her eyes and pulled hard. The awful ripping noise sent a cold shiver through her. She cautiously opened one eye to ensure his skin was still intact. No damage. Despite appearances, she was no sadist. She was just doing what she was paid to do.

While Simon gasped and spluttered and fought for breath, she lowered her head until her lips were almost touching his and calmly asked again, 'Where are the blueprints?'

He said nothing, so she slapped his cheek with the back of her hand—and again, harder, for effect. 'I said, *where are the blueprints?*'

Fighting between laboured breaths, he stammered, 'I shan't tell you … I won't … I will never betray … my country!'

Alexia swallowed an urge to smile at the way he pronounced the letter "r" as "w". She had to stay focused on the job; to see it through to completion. 'You have five seconds,' she sneered in an exaggerated Slavic accent.

Simon shook his head furiously. 'No!'

'One … two … three …'

'*Never!*'

'Four …'

'Go to hell, bitch!'

'*Five!*'

Simon squeezed his eyes shut and jerked his head away in anticipation of dread.

Alexia reached to the other side of the bed and slid her hand under the pillow. Her fingers scrabbled around, trying to locate the gun.

It wasn't there.

She cast her eyes around the bedroom in blind panic. Where could she have left it? She could be such a scatter-brain sometimes!

Simon half-opened one eye, then his head snapped back to face her.

She brazenly chanced a smile, but he saw through it.

'Whatever is it, woman?' he demanded huffily.

THREE

THE ENSUITE! She'd left it in the damned ensuite!

'I'm so sorry, I've forgotten the gun. I will get it. Give me a minute.'

Alexia scrambled off him, off the bed, and made for the ensuite, her killer heels sinking noiselessly into the deep pile carpet.

'Eyes!' the client barked.

She stopped in her tracks. 'What?'

'The tape, woman!'

'Yes, of course. Sorry.' She hurried back to blindfold him, pressing down the edges of the tape to ensure there were no gaps.

'And stop saying sorry, for Christ's sake! What kind of Russian assassin ever apologises?'

I don't know, she wanted to say. *This domination shit is Roxie's speciality. I'm just filling in for her while she's sick.*

But Alexia couldn't tell the truth, or betray her inexperience. So, channelling her best dominatrix voice, she commanded, *'Quiet!'*

The client's mouth split into a smile. 'Better.'

She dashed to the ensuite, closing the louvred door quietly behind her, threw back her head and took a deep breath. She knew that if she messed up this gig, she could lose Andric and Evgeni their best paying client. Then there would be hell to pay. She exhaled slowly. Panic wouldn't help anyone.

Calmer now, she knelt to the floor and raked through her tote bag, quickly locating the grip of the gun amongst her everyday clothes. God, she longed to get out of Roxie's ridiculous catsuit! It was making her clammy and itchy, and it was completely the wrong size. Roxie had the figure of a supermodel: tall and slim, small-breasted, whereas Alexia was busty and curvaceous.

She pulled out the gun, Evgeni's pride and joy. She couldn't quite believe he'd entrusted her with it. Alexia had never handled a gun before; had never wanted to. Why had the client insisted on it being *real*? She would have been *so* much more at ease with a fake.

She was panicking again, her hand trembling.

At least the weapon wasn't loaded. All she had to do was go back out there and get the dirty rich pervert back in the zone; whip him into a sado-erotic frenzy. She would tease him with the gun for a few moments—perhaps run the cold metal over his hairy nipples, press it into his sweaty groin—then shunt the barrel into his mouth and lean across to whisper "*hasta la vista*" into his ear. And then … *Click*.

Simple. Five hundred quid in crisp new fifties, thank you very much.

'What are you doing, woman? Where are you? Don't you know how busy I am!' The client's bellow made her jump.

Alexia leapt to her feet and turned to grab the door handle.

Without warning, a loud, banging noise made her pause. She peered through the slats to see the bedroom door burst open. A man dressed in dark clothing entered the room. He wore a balaclava and held a gun. Alexia's gut lurched. What the hell was happening?

She held her breath.

The intruder stole a quick look around the room, then edged towards the bed, pointing his weapon at the client.

Alexia smiled and allowed herself to breathe. This had to be part of the plan, didn't it? The client must have arranged it, for extra kicks. A threesome. Alexia found herself giggling at the prospect. What was she supposed to do now? Await her cue to join in?

The intruder paused again and looked about him, his eyes briefly flicking in the direction of the ensuite. His gaze flickered between the client, the window, the wardrobe and the ensuite. Was he looking for her? Was she expected to be out there?

Then Simon called out, 'Hey! What's the hold-up? Get on with it! I've got a bloody Select Committee to attend in an hour!'

Alexia didn't have a clue what that meant.

This did get the intruder's attention, however, and he swivelled back to face the client. He approached tentatively, edging around the side of the bed, before stopping and pressing the barrel against the client's temple.

'Ooh, yes … that's it,' Simon groaned, arching his back with pleasure.

Ha! It was clearly a game. Alexia felt the tension melting away.

The intruder paused for a moment, as if nervous or unsure of what to do, then he traced the pistol over the contours of Simon's face, over his nose and top lip, before poking the barrel into his compliant mouth.

Was Alexia supposed to join in for this bit? She didn't understand. Evgeni hadn't explained this part. Or had he, and she just hadn't listened properly? It wouldn't be the first time.

BANG!

Alexia's eyes snapped shut in unconscious response to the deafening sound of gunfire.

It had to be a blank. It had to be.

She slowly opened her eyes and looked out into the bedroom again.

O Dieve!

Blood was spattered everywhere, and Simon lay, deathly still.

The man in the balaclava just stood there, looking down at the client, as if in surprise. Or shock. Was it a terrible accident?

With the noise of the gunshot reverberating in her ears, Alexia brought a hand to her mouth. Suddenly unsteady, she stumbled, and grabbed the door frame.

The noise snapped the intruder out of his trance and he turned to face the ensuite, levelling his gun at her and advancing in her direction.

Alexia backed up, retreating further into the ensuite. One step, then another … until she struck the sink basin with a jolt. Her desperate hand groped around the granite surface, seeking something useful to grab hold of—a heavy object, *anything*, that she could use to defend herself.

Her fumbling hand struck an object, and it fell to the floor, smashing on the tiles.

Alexia looked feverishly around her. There was no window; no means of escape at all. Could she somehow block his entry? There was nothing she could use as a barricade, only her own body, and the intruder could easily just shoot her through the door.

What was happening? Who was he? What did he want?

Alexia dared to look towards the door. His frame loomed. There was a *click*, and the door handle turned.

This was it, then.

'What do you want?' she screamed.

The man didn't answer. Didn't say a word.

The door creaked open.

Her hand located an object, and her fingers curled around it. Thin and plasticky, Alexia realised what it was and sighed. Arming herself with an electric toothbrush against a madman with a gun. It was so ridiculous, she almost laughed.

The gun! Evgeni's gun!

Alexia held the dull pistol in her other hand. Stupid woman! She just needed to convince the man that it was loaded and she was prepared to use it. There was nothing to lose now.

She dropped the toothbrush and raised the pistol, gripping it tightly in both hands, trying to suppress the tremors.

The intruder was standing in front of her now, not speaking a word.

They each had their gun trained on the other.

Alexia could see the whites of his eyes, the tremble of his gloved hands; could hear his ragged breathing.

'What do you want?' she said.

No response.

'Why don't you just go? Leave,' she begged. 'I don't know who you are. I won't say anything.'

Nothing.

'Please!'

The man took a step forward.

'I'll shoot!' she said.

He raised his free hand and placed it on the barrel of her gun, forcing her to lower her arm.

He knew she was bluffing.

Slowly, the man raised his gun to her temple, pressing it hard against her skin.

'*Please!*' she begged. 'I don't want to die.'

She squeezed her eyes shut and held her breath.

Then there was a sound from the road out the front: a car's idling engine.

The pressure in her temple suddenly released, and Alexia dared to open her eyes—

To see the intruder turning his back and fleeing the scene.

FOUR

OH, sweet Jesus.

Alexia looked down at the client's body in horror. At the deep burgundy stain flowering on the pillowcase. At the little clumps of flesh, singed hair and spots of blood spattered about the room—over the furniture; the walls; the curtains. Everywhere.

The sickly, metallic smell was making her gag.

She brought up a hand to cover her mouth and nostrils. Her other hand, quivering against her thigh, held the dead weight of Evgeni's pistol.

What should she do?

Call the police? No, she'd be as good as dead the minute she dialled the number. No police. Ever. That was the rule. And, besides, they'd never believe her in a million years.

Clear all traces of her presence from the house? Impossible!

No, she needed to get out—fast. Think of a plan later. Act now, worry later; that had always been her mantra.

Alexia went into mental overdrive. She grabbed her

tote bag from the ensuite, lobbed the gun inside, threw on her long ankle-length summer coat to conceal the catsuit and then fled back through the bedroom and out onto the landing.

There was an open sash window to her left, and she paused to poke her head through. A neat courtyard garden below. Neighbouring gardens beyond. A drainpipe leading to the ground, just outside the window. She wondered if this was how the intruder had entered and escaped.

Come on! No time to lose!

Alexia turned and made for the stairs, then stopped herself. *Wait!* There had to be a better option. What if she pretended everything had gone according to plan? What if she didn't mention the masked man to Evgeni? The murder, too? The police would later work out there had been an intruder, and they'd find his DNA. Wouldn't they?

O Dieve! she imagined her future self saying as Evgeni told her the news. *It must have happened right after I left!*

But for the plan to work, Alexia needed to collect the fee. Where was the cash? She dashed back to the bedroom and rifled through the pockets of the client's suit, which lay crumpled on the floor, next to the bed. She found his wallet, but there was no cash inside; just a collection of credit cards.

The bureau under the window? Framed photographs covered its surface, splattered with blood. A stash of unopened letters. A leather-bound day planner. The client's gold watch—a Rolex. Must be worth thousands, not that Alexia would ever contemplate stealing it. She still had a moral compass, despite everything.

The fee, though, was rightly hers. She'd completed the job, after all. Sort of. She pulled open the drawers and raked through their contents. More correspondence. Receipts. Cufflinks. Pens. At the back of one drawer, she located a brown envelope, stuffed with cash. She pulled it out and quickly leafed through the notes, did the maths. There had to be about five hundred there. In the bag it went.

Alexis looked about her—at the ransacked bureau; her footprints in the bloodied carpet. She thought of her fingerprints everywhere.

Get the hell out.

She barely touched the stairs, jumping three or four treads at a time, only grabbing the rail as it turned at the dogleg and using it to slingshot herself around the corner.

As she drew near to the bottom, a shadow loomed in the glass of the front door. Alexia stopped abruptly. Held her breath.

A key turned in the lock.

Shit!

She glanced back up the stairs, contemplating retreat. Perhaps she could escape through the landing window? Clamber down the drainpipe?

But what if she fell and broke her neck? What if …? What if …?

Paralysed by indecision, Alexia turned back to face the front door. As it opened, she caught the rich, powdery scent of perfume. The client's wife, maybe?

Alexia's hand rummaged through the bag, quickly locating the gun. She curled her fingers around its grip, inhaled deeply to steady her nerves and pushed herself against the wall.

A woman entered the hallway: small and dumpy; old; shoulder-length black hair; olive complexion; a lived-in face that no amount of make-up was ever going to fix. At a guess, Alexia would have said she was Spanish or Portuguese. South American, perhaps. The woman carried a large bag of groceries. The cleaner? Housekeeper? Maid?

The woman, oblivious to Alexia's presence, dropped the bag to the floor, then turned to close the front door.

Knowing it wouldn't belong before she was noticed, Alexia needed to take the initiative. So she took out the gun, pointed it at the woman, counted to three in her head and then bellowed: '*Freeze!*'

It was a perfect imitation of the movies she'd seen with the female FBI lead.

The woman gasped and turned slowly around to face Alexia. Her expression changed from bewilderment to shock and then fear. The poor woman's stumpy little arms flew above her head in surrender.

'Move against the wall!' Alexia commanded, gesturing with the gun as she stepped down onto the tiled floor and edged towards the woman.

The woman pressed her back to the wall, where a large gold-framed mirror hung at her side.

Alexia, emboldened by a sudden and unexpected sense of power, strode confidently towards the woman. Keeping the gun trained on her, she said in her best *Terminator*-style voice: 'Call the police and I kill you. Okay?'

A small part of her was enjoying this. The remaining part was sick with terror.

The woman—her wide eyes darting—nodded her silent assent.

Alexia caught sight of herself in the mirror. The gun, the hair braided into the stupid ponytail snaking over one shoulder, the make up—all at the dead client's request— reminded her of a low-rent Lara Croft.

She threw the maid woman one last menacing glare, then lurched for the door and fled out into the cobbled street, where she steadied herself against a wall and took a relieving gulp of air.

The street was lined with pretty, pastel-coloured mews houses, Narnia lampposts, neatly trimmed plants standing in cube containers and narrow balconies adorned with flower displays.

It was eerily calm, despite being the middle of the day. The residents would be at work, Alexia supposed, toiling away in the city—bankers, lawyers, media executives. She didn't know what her client's occupation was, only that he was a *very important person*. Evgeni's words. She gulped. A very important *dead* person, now.

Time to get moving. It was only a matter of time before the maid discovered the body and called the police.

Before all hell broke loose.

To her left, she saw that the road came to a dead end. Only one option, then: head the other way towards the busy Bayswater Road and merge with the hordes.

A small object on the front of a salmon pink house opposite caught her eye; a curious little black-and-white cube above the door. She stared inquisitively at it for a few moments before the realisation struck. A security camera! And she was still holding the damn pistol! How could she be so stupid?

Turning quickly away from the camera, she tucked the gun into her bag and ran down the street, the clatter of heels striking the cobbles echoing around the empty street.

In Hyde Park, a brisk, thirty-minute walk later, Alexia found a deserted spot in a thick copse of trees at the edge of the Serpentine. Sweating from the heat, it was a relief to shed her coat and peel herself out of the catsuit. She kicked off her heels and changed into a pair of skinny

jeans, an oversized Zara sweatshirt and, to her consider-
able relief, a pair of ballet flats. She removed the clips from
her ponytail and shook loose her brunette locks.

Then, paying scant regard to the merits of the action
she was about to take, she hurled Evgeni's Glock 17 into
the water, followed swiftly by the catsuit, the heels and the
hairclips.

As the catsuit finally sank and the ripples on the surface
of the water faded, Alexia soberly assessed the day thus far:
she was in the frame for the murder of a dead client, and
Evgeni's expensive gun was now lying at the bottom of a
lake.

This was going to take some explaining.

Lucky then that Evgeni was only a cold-blooded, socio-
pathic maniac!

Their flat in Camden Town was perhaps another hour
away on foot. Alexia didn't dare risk public transport and
all the security cameras. No, she needed to get back to the
flat and explain everything to Evgeni.

He'd know what to do.

She just prayed he was in a good mood.

With a mounting sense of trepidation, she resumed her
journey, traversing the enormous expanse of Hyde Park,
criss-crossing her way through the prosperous streets of
Marylebone, skirting Regent's Park and weaving through
the crowds of bohemian Camden.

They'd been living in the flat for nearly three months; a
basement hovel of a once-grand old building that now
stood almost derelict, accessed by a reeking alleyway.

At the front door, Alexia stole a deep breath, turned
the key in the lock and stepped into the living room.

She dropped her bag to the floor and was immediately
struck by the cloying, skunky scent of a recently smoked
joint.

The huge wall-mounted flatscreen was on at high volume, tuned to a football game. The sofa was unoccupied, but the imprint of Evgeni's colossal, gym-honed frame was visible in the seat cushions. Amongst the detritus on the coffee table—rolling papers, roach clips, tin foil, straws, a cracked mirror, some razorblades, a hunting knife—she found the TV remote and muted the football match.

'Evgeni?' she called, her voice cracking. 'Where are you?'

No response.

It wasn't unusual for him to spend the daylight hours either slumped on the sofa or sleeping in bed. He was a creature of the night, after all.

He wasn't in the bedroom.

'Evgeni?'

There was no sound except for the ever-present *thud, thud* of bass that travelled through the fabric of the building from an indeterminate flat above.

The bathroom door was closed and she rapped lightly on it. 'You in there?'

Pressing her ear to the door, Alexia heard nothing, so she turned the handle and pushed open the door.

Sweet Jesus!

There he was, slumped on the toilet, his chin resting against his bare, muscular chest, his arms—threaded with prominent bodybuilder veins—hanging limply against his splayed thighs. His black jeans were crumpled around his milk-white ankles, and the his studded belt lay limp at his feet, like a coiled snake.

Her gut lurched. Was he dead?

She put her hand gingerly under his nose, but felt no breath.

She tapped him on the shoulder. 'Evgeni!'

Shook his arm. 'Evgeni!'

Slapped his cheek. '*Evgeni!*'

She was aware her voice was becoming steadily more hysterical.

What should she do?

Call for an ambulance and then run? No, to hell with the ambulance. Alexia didn't owe him any favours. She just needed to run. But where to?

The memory of her last escape attempt slid to the surface. It had been three years ago, but Alexia could remember it like it was yesterday. She'd only got as far as the Regent's Canal in Hoxton before he'd found her. She could see the dark figure as if he were in the room now, emerging from the shadows to block her path. She could hear his manic laughter; could feel him dragging her into the cold, wet bushes and the hot pain of his hunting knife slicing through her skin like it was paper. In unconscious response, she traced a finger along the ridge of rigid scar tissue stretching from the crook of her elbow to her wrist.

She turned to face the door.

This was it, then. Her chance at freedom.

Mentally, she was already there, lying on the yacht's waxed deck, the white sails fluttering in the gentlest breeze, her face turned to the hot sun, drifting noiselessly across a vast, turquoise sea, the sky impossibly blue.

As quickly as the image had formed, it dissolved back into her dirty reality. Alexia had nowhere to go; no passport; no friends on the outside; and no money, except for the cash in the envelope she'd taken from the client's house. How long could she make that last?

Act now, worry later.

She snatched up her bag and dashed to the bedroom. Flinging open the wardrobe, she tore the items within from their hangers—shirts, sweaters, *anything*—and stuffed them into her bag, as much as she could squeeze in.

The phone! Her secret phone! Alexia went over to the side of the bed, pushed aside the nightstand and crouched to the floor. Digging her fingernails into the gap between the wall and the ventilation grille, she prised it open and grabbed the phone she'd stashed behind it.

The floorboard creaked behind her.

'What the *fuck's* going on, bitch?'

O Dieve.

Alexia stood and turned, her fingers curling around the phone. Evgeni's huge frame filled the doorway.

Just at the point she registered his total nakedness, he smashed the weight of his fist into her collarbone.

Pain shot through her body and she fell to the floor, losing her grip on the phone.

She tried to scrabble away from him, but it was no good. Evgeni grabbed her ankles, and dragged her across the floor like a sack of potatoes, towards the living room, her sweater riding up her torso. The friction against the bedroom carpet burned her skin as she desperately threw her good arm about her, trying to find something to grab: the bed; a heavy object; anything.

She found a shoe: a six-inch steel spike heel with detachable ankle strap.

Evgeni dragged her further into the living room, across the sticky laminated floor, stopping at the coffee table.

She twisted onto her side and felt for the edge of the table so she could get to her feet.

He kicked her hard in the kidney.

'Stay still, bitch.'

Alexia curled herself into a foetal ball, howling in pain.

'You ungrateful whore!'

'I … I …' She turned to look at him. His eyes blazed with murderous intent.

Then she saw the knife, clasped in his hand.

'I'm sorry, Evgeni. Sorry! Please don't hurt me.'

A cruel smile pierced his lips, revealing his teeth, the upper row of which were gold and glistening with saliva.

Alexia turned away, curling her fingers tighter around the shoe.

'Look at me, bitch!'

With his free hand, he grabbed her upper arm, twisting her onto her back, before dropping his weight onto her thighs and forcing her to face him.

His gaze shifted to the stiletto in her hand, then back at her.

He laughed, and before she had time to react, he snatched the shoe from her grasp and hurled it across the room. It hit the TV, smashing the screen.

'You know,' he said, running the tip of his forefinger down the blade of the knife, 'clients don't like whores with scar face.'

He examined his bloodied finger with great interest, then brought it down to her face, calmly tracing it from the top of her forehead, down her nose, her lips, her chin …

'Evgeni, *don't!*' she wheezed. 'Please!'

She smelled his rancid breath as his fat pink tongue emerged from his mouth. She screwed her eyes shut, then felt the hot, wet muscle make contact with her skin and slither haphazardly over her face. He squeezed her cheeks, forcing her mouth to open, allowing his tongue the freedom to circle her lips and probe her mouth.

Fear gripped her heart.

Alexia opened her eyes, her vision clouded by the dark, blurry shape of his face.

Then, channelling years of pent-up hatred, she clamped his tongue between her teeth and bit down as hard as she could.

Evgeni wrenched himself free, howling in agony, and

his hands snapped to his mouth. The knife fell, clattering on the laminate floor beside her head. Blood streamed through his fingers and cascaded down his arms.

'*Bitch!*' he grunted, barely able to form the word.

Exploiting the opportunity, Alexia reached to grab the knife, swung back her arm and then plunged the blade deep into Evgeni's chest.

There was an awful moment—probably only seconds, but it felt like much longer—where nothing seemed to happen. Then Evgeni's face turned ashen. His hands felt limply for the knife handle, but he was too weak to gain a purchase.

He slumped sideways to the floor, relieving the pressure on Alexia's legs.

She watched, numb with disbelief, as he squirmed and twitched. Evgeni tried to speak, but he was choking. Another sound: a gurgle, a rattle.

And then nothing.

FIVE

PRESENT DAY

HE WAS HOPPING about pathetically on the little patch of front garden below her, attempting to insert a foot into the leg of his jeans, when she hurled the second size 10 at him.

Molly Tindall had been aiming for the glistening dome of Justin's buzz cut head, but his arm flew up to briskly deflect the shoe.

'Molly, please! I can explain!'

'Don't tell me,' Molly screeched; 'you just *forgot* to mention it? I know how easy it is to forget sometimes. I mean, I popped to the Co-op the other day for a bag of onions and only came back with a copy of *Cosmopolitan* and a pint of semi-skimmed milk! But I *think* I'd remember bloody being *married*!'

'Molly! Come on!' he pleaded. 'Let me back in, will you, darling?'

'Don't you "darling" me, you lying *turd!*' She turned and retreated into the bedroom.

His shirt lay crumpled on the carpet at the base of the bed and she bent to pick it up, ready to jettison. Scrunching the smooth cotton fabric in her fist, Molly took a deep, consolatory sniff and savoured the heady, masculine scent.

She sighed ruefully. Bloody Lucy at the dating agency! It was all her fault; another one of her legendary cock-ups.

'Got a great one here for you, Molly,' Lucy had gushed. 'Justin Blakemore. He's a barrister, and—oh my goodness! —he must *really* work out.'

'A *barrister*, you say, Luce?' Molly had said, her interest piqued. She could so easily picture herself hobnobbing with the great and good of the legal world. 'Send him my way!'

She should have smelled a rat the moment Justin pitched up at their restaurant date in a clapped-out Punto and a cheap suit. *No matter*, she'd thought, guessing that he must be one of those legal aid types, an altruistic, do-gooder in it for the idealism, the noble pursuit of justice, not the dosh.

'*Pro bono?*' she enquired, half distracted by the delightful wine list.

'Can't say I'm a great fan of *U2*, no,' he'd replied dryly.

Molly had hooted with laughter. A barrister *and* a rapier's wit! Where had this one been hiding? 'I think you and I are going to get along just fine, Justin,' she'd said. 'How about a 2019 *Pouilly-Fumé*? That float your boat?'

Not once did Justin disabuse her of the notion he was a lawyer, despite the multiple opportunities he'd had to fess up. 'Let's not talk shop, hey?' he'd said, when, over breakfast one fine morning, she'd enquired about his greatest court victory to date. Molly hadn't appreciated the literal nature of Justin's turn of phrase until, several weeks later, after a work appointment in St Albans, she'd popped into a Caffè Nero for an urgent espresso. And who had it been behind the counter to serve her? None other than Justin *bloody* Blackmore, standing there all sheepish in his pec-hugging black t-shirt.

A bloody *barista*, for crying out loud! With the benefit of hindsight, Molly should have ended things there and then; told the good-for-nothing toerag to sling his hook. But, *by God*, those pert buttocks of his were capable of cracking walnuts …

Molly turned and hurled the shirt out of the window, watching as it fluttered down to land in the pyracantha hedge. The fabric snagged as Justin tugged it free from the thorns, and she smiled at the satisfying sound of the material ripping.

Something in the corner of her eye caught Molly's attention, and she looked across the street to catch Gloria Shepherd, the nosey cow from number six, the self-styled doyenne of Datchworth, snapping her head away to feign sudden interest in the nearest lamppost. She held the lead of that silly little dog of hers while it sniffed at Mr. Foskett's front gate. The dog was one of those ludicrous mop-head breeds that served no purpose other than to look pretty.

Jemima, she'd named it. Gloria treated Jemima like the child she'd never had (imagine!). The woman had even plaited the poor creature's hair in two symmetrical ponytails and tied the bottoms with little green bows, for crying out loud.

'Nothing to see here, Gloria!' Molly yelled.

Gloria, flustered and pretending not to have heard, turned on her heel and attempted to tug the stupid mutt up the road, but the dog steadfastly refused to budge while it cocked its leg and took aim at Mr. Foskett's fence.

Molly returned her attention to Justin, who was now fully trousered. He clamped his palms together as if in prayer. 'Please, Molly. Just one last chance?'

After a nanosecond's contemplation, she gave him the

middle finger and slammed the window shut.

Molly took herself to the bathroom for a long, hot shower in an attempt to cleanse the lying bastard from her soul. After the shower, she felt the need to dress in something black—who was she, Queen Victoria in mourning? —then made her way to the back bedroom and switched on the computer.

Working from home a couple of days a week was a godsend: no long commute into London and a respite from the constant interruptions of her gossipy colleagues at the *Chronicle*. Mind you, she wasn't averse to indulging in a bit of gossip herself …

As she waited for the computer to fire up, Freddy, her British Shorthair cat, jumped up onto the desk. He sniffed suspiciously at the computer mouse, then nudged it with his paw, but when the mouse didn't want to play, Freddy mewled for Molly's attention instead. She obliged with a tickle under his chin and then ran her hand down his velvety grey back. Freddy arched his spine and purred with pleasure.

'Another one bites the dust, hey, Freds? I got out of that one *Justin* time.'

Molly snorted at her own joke, then sank her chin into her hands. 'Why do men have to be so shit?'

The cat turned to her and blinked.

'Not you, mate, obviously. I'm thinking of becoming a nun. Or a lesbian. Perhaps both. What do you reckon?'

Freddy cocked his head inquisitively, as if he were making an effort to understand what she was saying.

The computer elicited the little jingle to announce it was ready. 'Off you pop, sweetheart,' she said to the cat, picking him up and dropping him to the carpet. 'I've got work to do.'

At least work would help to take her mind off the

disaster zone that was her love life. For weeks now, Molly had been immersed in a "cash for access" investigation, the latest in a long line of lobbying scandals to afflict Westminster. A couple of her colleagues at the *Chronicle*, posing as Chinese investors, had caught three senior politicians on hidden camera accepting offers of cash in exchange for access to senior members of the Cabinet. When would they *ever* learn? The corrupt bastards!

Further meetings were planned, and the editor held out hope that more politicians would be ensnared in the scandal. If that happened, there was the distinct possibility that the government itself, with its fragile majority, could fall, triggering a general election. Molly found the prospect thrilling. What power her typing fingers wielded!

She knew she really ought to be cracking on with her draft report, but first a bit of procrastination was needed to help settle her mind. She scanned the major news websites (nothing terribly exciting) and logged on to her bank to check her balance (she *really* needed to cut down on her spending). She checked her emails and found her inbox clogged with the usual crap: an invitation to leaving drinks for someone she'd never heard of (*delete*); yet another reminder from security to lock unattended computer screens (*delete)*; an email advising that the women's loos in the office were out of action again, due to "ongoing blockage issues" (what *were* people stuffing down the bogs, for God's sake? *Delete!*). Another email notified her that she'd received a message on Facebook. Now wasn't the time for social media; she'd log on at lunchtime, and check out Twitter, too. No, bugger that—it would just gnaw away at her all morning. Who was it? What did they want?

'Well, blow me down,' Molly said, bemused, when she discovered the answers to those questions. She slumped in her chair. '*This* is a turn-up for the books!'

SIX

RYAN LOMAX THRASHED about on the floor like a wounded fish, leaving thick red smears among the shards of shattered glass surrounding him.

From his covert position metres away, James Quinn retrieved his iPhone from his pocket and snapped a couple of high-resolution photographs.

Ryan was attempting to speak, but the sounds that came out were guttural and indistinct. He arched his back and grimaced.

A woman—in her forties, smart trouser suit, in a hurry, a bottle of expensive red in her hand—rounded the corner, clapped eyes on the wounded man and let out a yelp of horror. The bottle slipped from her grasp and fell to the ground, shattering at her feet and splattering her shoes and lower legs with wine.

Ryan howled.

It was a scene of utter carnage.

James smiled.

Behind him came the sounds of rapidly approaching

footfalls, a crackly radio receiver, urgent instructions being conveyed.

'My back! My back!' Ryan Lomax groaned.

'Don't move, sir!' a suited man shouted breathlessly as he drew closer.

James's phone buzzed and he looked down at the screen. Molly. She'd always had a knack for bad timing. He rolled his eyes and accepted her call. 'You're spoiling my fun!' he complained.

'What?'

'Doesn't matter. I hope this is urgent. Can you make it quick?'

'Those charm school lessons really are paying off, aren't they?'

'Yeah, yeah. Whatever. What do you want? I'm kind of busy here …'

'Well, you're not going to believe this—'

'My back!' Ryan hollered. 'I think it's broken!'

'Where are you, exactly?' Molly asked.

'Sainsbury's, Letchworth. Pasta sauce aisle.'

'Of course! Silly me for asking.'

'We're calling an ambulance, sir. Just stay still,' the suited man said reassuringly.

'That *fucking* display nearly killed me! I'm gonna sue your fucking arse!'

'So,' James said, addressing Molly, 'you were saying?'

Ryan Lomax grabbed a low shelf and tried to scrabble into a seated position despite the protests of the duty manager. The shelf gave out and a stack of tins clattered down, smashing into Ryan's face.

The duty manager's hands flew to his mouth in horror.

'Just wait a minute, Molly. Won't be a tick.'

James walked over and placed a calming hand on the

LOST SOULS

duty manager's forearm. The manager turned towards him, his face ashen. James noted the name badge: Philip Heckington.

'It's okay, Philip, relax. Thing's aren't quite what they seem. Isn't that right, Ryan?'

Ryan Lomax twisted to face James. 'Huh?'

'Bit accident-prone, aren't you, Ryan?' James pointed to his phone. 'Don't worry, I've captured your little pratfall on camera. A career in slapstick comedy awaits you, if all else fails.'

Resignation fell across Ryan's face.

James dug into his pocket to retrieve his business card and handed it to Philip, who studied it with puzzled interest.

'I've been engaged by an insurance company to investigate young Mr. Lomax, here. Seems he has a habit of making vexatious personal injury claims.'

'Ahh,' Philip said, catching on.

'Up you get, Ryan. Why don't you give Mr. Heckington a hand clearing up this mess? You never know—the court might take good behaviour into account.'

Philip Heckington smiled uncomfortably, and James patted him reassuringly on the shoulder. 'Have a good day,' he said, walking away from the carnage.

He pressed the phone to his ear. 'You still there?'

'You never cease to amaze me, Jimbo.'

'I aim to please. Now, what was it you were going to say?'

'Look, it might be nothing … probably is nothing, a bit fanciful, really, but …'

'Spit it out!'

'Remember Sir Geoffrey Fitzroy-Fergusson?'

'Minister at the Foreign Office, assassinated by a

woman posing as a dominatrix? Kind of hard to forget, Moll!'

'Well, what would you say if I told you the assassin might have been Urtė?'

James had reached the fruit and veg section. He steadied himself against a chiller cabinet where an elderly lady was earnestly pressing her thumbs into one end of a honeydew melon. Urtė had been best friends with James's deceased wife, Ruth. She'd been abducted shortly after their arrival in the UK from Lithuania, fifteen years ago.

James had never been able to escape the bitter sense of irony; both women had come here in search of a better life, and both had had it taken from them.

'*What?*'

'I've received an email in response to that Facebook appeal we've been running. Apparently, it's from a woman who says she was Geoffrey's housekeeper at his Notting Hill pad. On the day of the murder, she came back to the house after a trip to the shops. As she entered, the assassin was there in the hall; threatened her with a gun. Swears blind it was Urtė.'

James paused for a moment, trying to take the information in. It all sounded utterly ludicrous. 'There's *no way* it can be her. It's totally out of character. Ruth told me Urtė was a sweet-natured woman. Wouldn't harm a fly.'

'I'm sure you're right, Jimbo, but what if it *was* her? You can't ignore it.'

His brain was whirring. 'Suppose …'

'And besides, there's a chance you could crack a high-profile murder case here. Surely that beats pursuing insurance fraudsters in small-town supermarkets?'

The old woman next to James brought the melon to her ear and started to shake it vigorously.

'What's the housekeeper's name?'

'Gabriela Rodríguez.'

'Think I'll pay her a visit. Text me her number, will you?'

SEVEN

Rosa sat, absently twirling a lock of her red hair, surveying her neon fiefdom. All around her, the unremitting machines bleeped and flashed and whirled and pulsated.

If she closed her eyes and breathed in the heady, citrus-scented surface polish, she could almost be in Vegas, at the roulette table in Caesar's Palace. She imagined herself dressed in a Versace ruffle trim pleated midi dress and matching Naplak pumps, her hand looped through the arm of a tuxedoed, cigar-chewing property magnate as he blithely bet all his chips on red.

But Rosa wasn't in Vegas. She was working the change booth of a down-at-heel amusement arcade in Great Yarmouth.

Rosa wasn't her real name, either. It was the latest in a long roll call of fake identities. She collected them like some women collected shoes. In fact, settling in to a new identity was, in many ways, like breaking in a new pair of shoes: they might rub the little toes for a few days, chafe at the heel, but before you know it, your feet feel like they're being cosseted by old friends.

It hadn't been part of the plan, though—all these identities, the horrors, the rollercoaster ride of the last fifteen years in England. All she'd ever wanted was to marry into the aristocracy; was that too much to ask? She quite fancied herself as a duchess, countess or marchioness—the exact title didn't much matter; didn't really know what they each meant, to be honest. The appeal for her was the idea of gliding majestically around some great stately home with manicured gardens, haughtily dispensing instructions to the staff. Rosa pictured the sweeping staircase, the dazzling chandeliers, the society balls …

The reality of her present life couldn't be more different. It was late September, the tourists had largely gone, and the arcade was virtually empty. A group of teenage boys—truanting, probably—were huddled around one of the motorcycle simulators, noisily cheering on the rider as he lurched this way, then that. A middle-aged man, underdressed for the weather in shorts, t-shirt and sandals, stood at a coin pusher machine, his pot of change resting on his belly, earnestly shoving ten-pence pieces down the ramp in pursuit of a piece of worthless tat. A crab-themed fridge magnet; a plastic kiddies' bracelet; a miniature packet of *Love Hearts*. That kind of crap.

A sudden blast of cold air made Rosa shift her gaze to the automatic entry doors, where an elderly man was pulling down the hood of his blue cagoule and shaking off the rain. He started towards her, and as he drew closer, she recognised him. Red of cheek; a milky glint in his eye; a spring in his geriatric step. Norman Price—one of her regulars.

That word—*regular*—carried a whole new meaning now. Rosa smiled at the thought.

Most customers used the automated change machines dotted about the arcade. Those who came for change at the booth were, in Rosa's experience, typically elderly. Or perverts. Often both.

Like Norman Price. Old, lonely and smelling of wet dog and cheap biscuits.

But customers were customers, so Rosa straightened her back and put on her best smile. 'Morning, Norman. The usual?'

'Yes, please, sweetheart,' he replied, shoving a crisp twenty through the hole in the Perspex screen.

His fingers brushed against hers as she took the note. She deposited it in the secure drawer and leaned forward. Norman's mouth dropped as his gaze shifted to her cleavage.

Rosa had no misgivings about weaponising her greatest assets. The low-cut button-up stretchy t-shirt was no casual clothing choice.

While Norman was otherwise engaged, she counted out eighteen pounds in his desired denominations, putting the remaining two pounds to one side. It wasn't theft, she told herself; it was payment for services rendered. Commission. Bonus. Service charge. Call it what you like, just not stealing. Rosa would never dream of stealing. And, besides, it was only two pounds! To think, only a year ago, her commission as an escort would have been anything up to fifty pounds per job after Evgeni and Andric had taken their cut. And the agency, of course. On a busy night, she'd seen six or seven clients. Most were married men. Some were rich. Others were lonely, like Norman, who just wanted to talk.

And a few were *monsters*.

Rosa shook away the memory and pushed the change towards Norman in neat piles. 'Good luck, Norman!'

He wiped a slither of drool from his chin with the back of his hand, then scooped the change into one of the plastic pots. 'Thank you, sweetheart,' he said and turned to walk away.

Now, in Norman's place, stood another of her regulars: Nancy Patterson. Quite possibly the oldest person she'd ever met. Tiny, hunched, skin creased into a thousand wrinkles. Clouded grey eyes. Thin strands of white hair sprouting from beneath a plastic rain hood, which was tied with a neat bow under her chin. She had that stale, acrid, old-person smell. 'How did you get there, Miss Patterson!'

The old lady, gripping the handle of her tartan walker-cum-shopping trolley, seemed transfixed by Norman Price as he walked over to the coin pusher machines. She turned back to Rosa, narrowed her eyes and said in a conspiratorial tone, 'Is he a fifth-columnist?'

'Sorry?'

'A fascist sympathiser?'

Rosa had no clue as to what the woman was talking about. 'I-I don't—'

'A traitor? Quisling?'

'I don't think so.'

'Must be a Jerry, then.'

Despite having lived in England for years, the subtleties of the English language and the eccentricities of its speakers constantly perplexed Rosa. 'No. He's just Norman,' she ventured hesitantly.

The old woman was seemingly lost in thought for a few moments, then, with a sudden flash of steel in her eyes, she said, 'Never trust a Jerry, Daisy!'

She passed Rosa a five-pound note she's been clutching in her gnarled, arthritic fingers.

Rosa substituted the note for twenty-pence pieces,

supplementing it with an extra five coins, courtesy of the "commission" pile.

'Thank you, Daisy,' Miss Patterson said as Rosa counted out the money into the proffered pot. The old woman then cautiously placed the pot on the lid of her shopping trolley.

Miss Patterson had always called Rosa "Daisy", for some reason, and she'd never had the heart to correct her. Besides, what difference did one more identity make in the grand scheme of things?

Rosa dropped her chin into her hands and watched the old lady trundle over to the grabber machine. The routine was always the same. Same day of the week (pension day); same time; same machine; same quantity of money exchanged; same success rate (zero). The prizes in the grabber machine—hideous sequinned cuddly toys— couldn't have been worth more than a pound or two each. Rosa had once offered to give Nancy one of the toys, to save her the expense and effort, but the old woman had had none of it. There was something simultaneously sad and uplifting about the woman. Rosa couldn't quite put her finger on the reason why.

A girl lurking near the machines beyond Nancy Patterson grabbed Rosa's attention. Stick thin. Long, straight jet black hair. Panda eyes. Piercings everywhere. Pinched, undernourished look to her porcelain face. Black coat and fishnet tights. Chunky boots. Rosa guessed she was about fourteen.

Something in her gut told her this girl was trouble.

Sure enough, the girl slouched about the arcade, casting occasional furtive glances. Eventually, her attention alighted on Nancy Patterson's trolley and her pot of coins, and the girl crept stealthily towards the old woman.

But Rosa was an expert in stealth. A black belt. She quietly slipped out of the change booth to manoeuvre her way, Pac-Man style, through the maze of machines, emerging beside the girl just as she was dunking her thieving hand into the old woman's treasure trove.

Rosa pounced, grabbing the girl by the wrist. 'Got you!'

The girl spun around, twisting and squirming, struggling to free herself. Rosa held firm.

'Stealing from old ladies? You should be ashamed!'

The girl snarled.

Nancy Patterson, unaware of the fracas, had one hand pressed to the glass of the grabber machine, the other clasping the little red joystick, as she shakily manoeuvred the claw.

'Is the cat biting your tongue?' Rosa said to the girl. Somehow, she knew the phrase wasn't quite right.

The girl continued to stare for a beat or two, then, oddly, bared her teeth and hissed like a wild animal. Catching sight of the little silver stud in the centre of the girl's tongue, Rosa found herself momentarily lost in thought as she tried to rationalise why anyone would voluntarily inflict such pain upon themselves.

As if sensing Rosa's guard was lowered, the girl spat in her face.

Rosa recoiled in disgust, and the girl, taking full advantage of Rosa's loosened grip, wrenched herself free, turned on her heel and fled from the arcade.

'Don't come back! Ever!' Rosa shouted as she cleared the spittle with the back of her hand. 'You are banned!'

Nancy Patterson casually retrieved a coin from her pot and popped it into the grabber machine's slot, then turned to Rosa and said, 'I told you, didn't I, Daisy? *Trouble!*'

Rosa smiled and watched for a few moments as Nancy returned her attention to the machine and became seemingly lost in her own little world.

EIGHT

SEPTEMBER 1939

NANCY PATTERSON WAS in her favourite place—propped up on her bed with a book—when her mother's shrill voice pierced her quiet sanctuary.

'*Nancy Patterson!* Come downstairs, at once!'

What now?

Nancy sighed and threw down her book in frustration. She supposed her mother had yet *another* tedious chore lined up for her. She'd already hung out the washing and dusted the house from top to bottom. Was she not entitled to a few moments of peace?

Nancy thudded down the stairs of their modest Plaistow terrace. She might have been a petite, young-for-sixteen girl, but she was quite capable of making her presence known.

In the parlour, she found her mother and father huddled around the wireless. Mother—a duster in one hand—turned to Nancy and made a *'shh'* gesture with the forefinger of her other.

Father twisted the tuning dial, causing squeals of static.

'Oh, hurry up, Ralph,' Mother chided.

'Stop nagging, Frances. It's very sensitive. You have to get it just right.'

Grandma Ada was in her armchair in the bay window, as usual, knitting furiously.

There was a final crackle from the wireless, and then the clipped tones of Neville Chamberlain rang out.

'This morning,' he announced …

Click-clack.

'… the British Ambassador in Berlin handed the German government a final note, stating that, unless we heard from them by eleven o'clock …'

Click-clack.

'… that they were prepared, at once, to withdraw their troops from Poland, a state of war would exist between us.'

Click-clack.

Mother and father exchanged anxious glances. Then father turned to Grandma and said, 'Put a bloody sock in it, woman. I can barely hear myself think!'

Mother responded with one of her stern looks. Grandma, seemingly nonplussed, simply carried on with her knitting, staring blankly ahead.

Despite the gravity of the situation, Nancy struggled to suppress a giggle.

'I have to tell you now,' the Prime Minister continued, 'that no such undertaking has been received, and that, consequently, this country is at war with Germany.'

Father switched off the wireless. There were a few moments of awful silence; even though everyone had known that war was coming, the actual declaration still came as a shock.

Nancy had the feeling that nothing was ever going to be quite the same again.

Grandma Ada dropped her knitting into her lap and said, 'Bugger.'

Nancy brought a hand to her mouth. It wasn't the swearing that shocked her; it was the fact that Ada had spoken at all. In all of Nancy's life, she'd never once heard her maternal grandmother utter a single word. Her father had once told Nancy that Ada had last spoken on the cold April day in 1915 when she'd received the telegram informing her that her only son, Billy, had been killed in action in France, two days shy of his seventeenth birthday.

'Well, that's it, then, I suppose …' Father sighed matter-of-factly, before silently making his way to the back garden.

Mother—avoiding eye contact with Nancy—said, 'I'd best check on the potatoes. See if those sheets are dry, will you?'

Grandma resumed her knitting.

Nancy sidled past her mother as she tended to the potatoes boiling on the stove and went through the back door into the garden. It was a sunny morning, with barely a cloud in the sky. She cursorily ran her hand across a bedsheet on the washing line, which was stretched across the width of their narrow plot. Then she pushed through a gap and found Father smoking a woodbine as he paced up and down the path that ran alongside their small vegetable patch. Potatoes, onions, parsnips, carrots, marrows— Nancy had helped sow the seeds in the spring. In light of the news from the wireless, it suddenly seemed like a life-time ago.

She glanced at the Anderson shelter at the far end of the garden, then back at her father. 'Is Hitler going to invade, then?'

He took a beat too long before he replied with a fake smile, 'Of course not. The bugger will have to back down eventually. Britannia rules the waves, and all that.'

'Will you be called up to fight?'

Her father looked up to the sky, drew deeply on his cigarette, then said, 'It's only a matter of time, love.'

'Take me with you.'

He smiled, then nodded in the direction of the house. 'Those two fruitcakes will need you right here. You'll be the only sane one in the house!'

Nancy contemplated that prospect for a moment. 'I don't think I could bear it!' She thought enviously of her brothers, Albert and Harry, who had been evacuated to Norfolk earlier in the summer. She imagined they were having a whale of a time, away from their mother's incessant nagging and life-draining strictures.

Father dragged deeply on his Woodbine, then extinguished it on the path and pocketed the end in his trouser pocket. Mother *hated* him making any kind of a mess.

He rummaged in his breast pocket. 'There's something I want you to have.'

'What is it?'

Before he could answer, the caterwaul of the air raid siren started up, making Nancy jump.

She hurriedly scanned the flawless London sky. 'Surely they're not coming already?'

Concern flashed across Father's ruggedly handsome face, weathered by years of working outdoors as a bricklayer. 'Best get in the shelter, love. I'll go and collect the rabble. Your Mother will be flapping around like a bloody headless chicken in there!'

A strange calm washed over Nancy; she didn't feel remotely scared. Numb with shock, she supposed. The calm before the storm.

As she continued to scan the sky for any hint of the Luftwaffe, she heard a commotion next door. Nancy looked across the low wire fence to see Mrs. Tungate shepherding her brood towards their own shelter. Couldn't bear to send her young ones off to the countryside, apparently. She looked comical in her gas mask, as did the baby, totally enveloped in the mask, which looked to Nancy like a deep-sea diving helmet. The two girls were holding hands as they scurried up the path. Then there was Jack, the eldest, bringing up the rear, grinning and nonchalantly swinging his gas mask.

'He's a rogue, that one,' Mother had once said of him. 'You watch yourself around him. He's no good, mark my words!'

Jack was a year or two older than Nancy, with a mop of wavy dark hair, piercing blue eyes, and an impish grin. He always looked tanned, for some reason, lending him an exotic, Mediterranean appearance. Or perhaps it was just ground-in dirt.

Jack turned to Nancy and flashed her a toothy smile. Her cheeks started to flush, and she jerked her head away, then scurried to the shelter.

The Anderson shelter was cold and damp, and an unpleasant, stagnant smell loomed beneath the sheet metal.

Whatever would it be like if the war was still going in winter?

Mother arrived next, fussing about all manner of trivial things: potatoes, bedsheets, important paperwork. Father manhandled Grandma into the shelter, then pulled the tin door tightly shut. Mother let out an apprehensive whelp at the sudden darkness, only calming down once her eyes had adjusted.

The three generations of the Patterson family sat in silence on the long bench for a few minutes, furtively focusing on the arching metal above their heads, before Grandma resumed her knitting. As far as Nancy was concerned, it was a complete mystery as to what her grandmother was making and where the fruits of her labour ever went—the bin, probably, knowing her mother. *If ever I end up an old woman who does nothing but knit*, she thought to herself, *I want my nearest and dearest to shoot me. Put me out of my misery.*

'Should I fetch us some tea?' Mother said, her voice quavering with nerves.

'Not now, woman!' Father said sternly. 'Expect it's either a false alarm or a test, but we should wait in here till the all-clear sounds.'

Mother fell silent, and soon, Grandma's knitting needles began to clack an eerie beat inside their tin cage.

Nancy turned to her father. 'You said you had something for me?'

'Ah, yes, love.' He pulled an object from his breast pocket and handed it to Nancy.

She recognised it in an instant: Grandpa Joe's cigarette case, its silver surface tarnished and scratched.

'Saw your Grandfather safely through the Great War, that did,' Father said proudly.

Nancy fingered the indentation created by the German bullet that had otherwise been destined for Granpa's heart.

Mother tutted. 'You and your damn superstitions, Ralph!'

'I can't take it,' Nancy said to her father. 'You'll need it more than me.'

Father wrapped his hand around Nancy's skinny fingers. 'I'll be fine, love. Mr. Hitler wouldn't dare do me any harm. He'd have *you* to deal with!'

A tear rolled down Nancy's cheek as she nestled herself into her father's shoulder.

After a while, Father said, 'Suppose we'd better put these gas masks on, then.' He flicked his head towards Grandma. 'Who's volunteering to help the Queen of Sheba into hers?'

NINE

GABRIELA RODRÍGUEZ HAILED FROM COLOMBIA, but her current home was a poky, claustrophobia-inducing council flat in a rough part of Islington.

James Quinn stood in her living room, examining a kitsch pink plastic cuckoo clock. An entire wall was covered in novelty clocks, thirty or forty of the things. There was one in the style of a fried egg, with a knife and fork forming the hands; a Wallace and Gromit clock; one fashioned from a slice of sawn log; and another displaying the visage of a young Elvis Presley.

'Milk and sugar?'

He turned round and, for a moment, thought he was looking at another novelty clock, but it was, in fact, the plump head of Gabriela Rodríguez framed by the service hatch.

'No, just black, thank you.'

When she returned to the living room with the coffees, James had finished perusing the clocks and was inspecting a framed photograph that sat proudly on a lamp table beside a porcelain figurine of the Virgin Mary. The photograph, yellowed with time, showed the Disney World castle in the background. In the foreground, Gabriela stood next to a much taller man. Her hands rested proudly on the shoulders of a stocky young boy, perhaps five or six years old, sporting a pair of Mickey Mouse ears.

Gabriela handed James a cute kitty novelty mug. 'That's me and husband, Diego, and our son, Santiago.'

James took a sip of coffee as Gabriela continued. 'Diego left me for a …' She pursed her lips and waved a hand about her chest, searching for the word.

'Model?' James ventured.

'No! Erm … how you say in English? … *El travestido* … Drag queen?'

'Oh.'

'*Bastardo!*'

'I see. And what about your boy?'

'Santiago?' Gabriela clamped her hands to her bosom and smiled. 'He such a good boy.' She brought a finger to her lips and nodded at a closed door. '*Shh!* He sleeping.'

James frowned. 'How old is he now?'

'Thirty-six.'

'Right. Of course.'

'Please, sit.' Gabriela gestured to an armchair.

There was a black cushion on the chair, emblazoned with silver sequins that spelled out: "World's Best Mum!". He moved the cushion to one side and sat down.

Gabriela flopped inelegantly onto the sofa opposite.

'So,' James said, keen to get down to business. He set his mug down on a nearby lamp table, then took out a photocopied picture of Urtė from his jacket pocket and handed it to Gabriela. After briefly explaining his connection, he said, 'I understand you recognise this woman as the person who murdered your former employer, Geoffrey Fitzroy-Fergusson?'

Gabriela took the picture, inspected it for a moment or two, then contorted her face. 'Yes. *Definitivamente!*' She made a pistol shape with her hand and pointed it at James. 'She hold gun to my head. *Crazy woman!* I never forget faces. She look like Sandra Bollock, no?'

James smiled. 'You mean Bullock?'

Gabriela cupped her hands around her breasts and raised a suggestive eyebrow. '*Tetas grandes!*'

James's interest was piqued. Ruth had once told him that her best friend also bore a degree of resemblance to the Hollywood actress, but he had never been able to see it himself.

There was nothing in the elderly woman's tone or expression to suggest she was anything other than genuine in her belief. Eccentric? Yes. But a liar, a fantasist? James didn't think so.

'Will you hunt her down?' she said, leaning towards James, her eyes fixed in a fierce glare. '*Kill* her?'

'I'm afraid that's not how we do things, Mrs. Rodríguez. I'm a private detective, not a trained assassin. If I find her, it will be for the police to pursue any charges.'

Gabriela sank back in her chair and gave a look that suggested disappointment.

'Talk me through that day of the murder,' James said, steering the conversation back on course.

Gabriela sighed extravagantly, then raised a hand to stroke her crucifix pendant. 'Well, where to start? *Señor* Geoffrey was working that morning, at the House of Commoners—'

'Commons, you mean?'

'Whatever,' Gabriela said, swatting away James's correction. 'I was at the house in Notting Hill, cleaning, you know, getting everything … How you say? … "*Span and spick*". *Señor* Geoffrey like things *just so*, you know? Anyway, he phone me. Say he coming to the house at lunchtime for important business meeting. Tell me to get out of house, go shopping for food.'

'This business meeting? Do you think he'd arranged a … you know … a—'

'Session with dirty hooker?'

James smiled. 'Yes.'

Gabriela shrugged. 'I suppose.'

'He had form, didn't he? You know, caught in that tabloid sting—'

'*Sting?* I no understand.'

'You remember? He got caught exchanging messages with a journalist posing as a sex worker. Lost his job.'

'Yes, I remember.' Gabriela tutted.

'So why would he risk everything after he'd been given a second chance?'

'Because he is rich and think he can do anything he like,' Gabriela scoffed. 'But, really, is none of my business what he do. I just clean up afterwards. You know, I once found a *profiláctico* under the bed when I was doing the vacuum.' Gabriela's face puckered in disgust. 'I squirt it with the bleach and throw it down toilet with salad tongs.'

'Lovely. Do you know if this particular girl was a regular? Had you seen her at the house before?'

'No.'

'Do you know how he made arrangements to see her? Through an agency, maybe?'

She shook her head. 'No, sorry.'

'Anything in the house at all? A note, letter, business card?'

'No. I already tell police everything I know.'

'Okay. Take me back to the day of the murder again. You returned to the house from the shops?'

'Waitrose. *Señor* Geoffrey like good food. Steak, seafood,

er … *langosta* … He ask me to get so much stuff, I had to get taxi. Geoffrey pay, of course.'

'That's good to know,' James said, masking his impatience. 'Anyway, you walked into the house and …?'

'She was there—your missing *bitch*. Hold gun to my head. She smiling. *Crazy woman!* Tell me she kill me if I call police. Then she leave.' Gabriela clutched her chest. 'Nearly have heart attack!'

'Then what?'

'I look around house. Go into *Señor* Geoffrey's bedroom and— *¡Ay, Dios!*—there he is.' The elderly woman looked to the ceiling and gestured the Catholic sign of the cross with her forefinger. 'Dead.' She poked two fingers into her mouth. '*Pfft.* Blood everywhere.' She flapped her hand about in the air as if she was dispersing thick smoke.

'Must have been a big shock. Might I ask, how long you were employed by Sir Fitzroy-Fergusson?'

Gabriela sucked her teeth in concentration. 'Twelve, maybe thirteen years? A long time.'

'And what was he like?'

'What you mean?'

'As an employer. Did he treat you well?'

'Yes, of course. Very generous man. Very kind.' She narrowed her eyes. 'Unlike his wife.'

'Oh?'

'She is *bitch*. I am no surprise he use hookers with wife like her! She sack me after Geoffrey die. She lives in big house in the country. With horses.' Wrinkling her nose disdainfully, Gabriela added, '*Very* rich.'

'What's her name?'

'Felicity.'

Felicity Fitzroy-Fergusson. James appreciated the alliteration. 'Were you aware of anything suspicious? Anyone who wanted to harm Geoffrey?'

Gabriela shook her head. 'No. I suppose he very important person, being a politician. Easy to make enemies, no?'

Behind James, the wall suddenly came to life with a cacophony of bells and gongs, whistles and cuckoo sounds.

He couldn't resist. 'Don't suppose you know the time, do you, Gabriela?'

'*Qué?*'

'Only joking. I'd better get going. Call me if you think of anything else that might be useful.' He got up and handed over his business card, which the woman studied with keen interest before showing him out.

As Gabriela opened the front door, James caught sight of a photograph on the wall. An attractive woman; thirties; blonde hair; green eyes; sumptuous lips parted into a smile that hinted at mischief.

'My sister,' Gabriela explained, following his gaze.

'Really?' James said, before realising how rude that probably sounded. There was no familial resemblance at all. Perhaps they were stepsisters?

'She's very sick, back home in Colombia. Needs big operation. But very expensive.'

'Well, I'm very sorry to hear that.'

'We try to raise money from friends, family, but it's difficult. Everybody is … How you say …?'

'Tight-fisted?'

'Poor,' Gabriela said firmly. She brought her hands to her chin, her fingers laced, and went all doe-eyed on him. 'Will you make a donation, *señor?*'

How could he say no? 'Sure,' James said, reaching for his wallet. He had three crisp twenties inside and gave her the lot.

Gabriela took the cash with gratitude, and as he departed, she called out, 'I hope you find *la cabrona*!'

.   .   .

James left the flat and dashed to the communal car park, mentally crossing his fingers. Against his better judgement, he'd left his Audi there, a sitting duck amongst the rusting Fiestas and clapped-out Corollas.

Phew! She was still there. And she wasn't propped up on bricks or daubed in graffiti. The windows weren't smashed in. The wiper blades weren't bent out of shape …

Just as he'd about exhausted his mental checklist of council estate clichés, a bicycle-riding youth arrived on the scene and proceeded to encircle the car. He wore the expected ensemble: baggy tracksuit, gleaming white trainers, back-to-front baseball cap. An invisible cloud of skunk hung about him.

'Nice wheels, bro,' the youth smirked.

James regarded the youth's cycle: one of those ridiculous BMX things with a low seat, oversized handlebars and fat tyres. 'Hmm, thanks.'

The youth blithely cycled off, showing the waistband of his underpants, and James went around to the driver's side and pressed the key fob. As he reached for the door handle, he noticed a deep scratch, an inch or so in length, above the wheel arch.

'*Hey!*' he shouted at the youth. 'Did you do this?'

The youth raised his middle finger above his head and disappeared.

'Arsehole!' James yelled as he climbed into the car, slamming the door shut. *Time to get the hell out of Dodge.*

Twenty minutes later, he was merging onto the A1 and trying to get hold of Molly on hands-free.

'And?' Molly said when she eventually picked up. 'Anything promising from the Rodríguez woman?'

'Mad as a box of frogs, but she genuinely believes that the woman she saw that day is Urtė. Not a moment's hesitation when I showed her the photo. I'm less sceptical now.'

'*Ooh*, exciting! So, what's next?'

'I'm on my way to check out the wife. Called her just now. Sounds like there might have been some friction there. Lives in a country house in Suffolk. Fancy joining me?'

'This afternoon? No can do, I'm afraid. Up to my eyeballs.'

'Not got yourself into hot water again with that libel issue, have you?'

'No, you cheeky sod! That was all a misunderstanding! All cleared up now. No, I'm meeting one of my MP contacts. Hoping to gain some traction with this lobbying scandal.'

'Well, good luck.'

'May be worth sounding him out for any information on Fitzroy-Fergusson. You never know?'

'Worth a try, I guess. Well, I'd best get going …'

'Hey, Jimbo?'

He'd long given up protesting against her annoying nickname for him. 'What?'

'How's it feel to be back in the game?'

Half a smile tugged at his lips. He changed into a lower gear and floored the accelerator, pushing himself into his seat, and the thoughts of the scratched wheel arch melted away. The Audi glided across the tarmac, slick from recent rain, into the fast lane. A watery sun poked through the murky clouds, dazzling him momentarily.

'Feels good, Molly,' James replied, slipping on his aviators. 'Catch you later.'

TEN

THEY WERE DINING at *Il Basilico*, a gorgeous little trattoria off the beaten track in Mayfair. Just the two of them: Molly and Edward Littlejohn, a Parliamentary Private Secretary in the Department for Communities and Local Government.

Try saying that after a few glasses of Sicilian Syrah!

'Cheers, Edward,' Molly said, clinking glasses. 'Good to see you again.'

She took a deep lungful of the red's intoxicating aroma and attempted to identify the component parts: cherries, blackberries, pepper, dry herbs …

On occasions like this, Molly sometimes had to pinch herself that this was her *actual* life and not a pipe dream. It wasn't that many moons ago when a meet-up at a greasy spoon with PC Plod of Herts Constabulary counted as a rare treat, tapping him up with an all-day breakfast and a sugary tea in the hope of wringing out titbits for the front page of the *Herald*. An arrest for drink-driving here, a suburban drug bust there. *Bor-ing!*

This was a totally different league, mixing with politicians. The legislators. People whose decisions could impact the lives of millions, good or bad. In her view, politics and journalism went hand in glove. Both were a game of *quid pro quo*: you scratch my back, I'll scratch yours.

Their agendas were as transparent as the jug of cucumber water on the table: she wanted names of MPs who might be susceptible to lobbying and Edward Littlejohn wanted his profile raised in the national press. He knew that; she knew that. So, where was the harm?

Mind you, Molly was conscious of not deluding herself that she'd hit the big time. It wasn't like she was hobnobbing with prime ministers and presidents. A "Parliamentary Private Secretary"—PPS, for short—may well sound grand on paper, but the reality of the job was somewhat different. "Bag carriers", they were known as in the trade. No additional financial perks beyond a basic MP's salary. A good PPS serves as the eyes and ears of their master, reporting back on all the gossip people are saying about their boss in the bars and cafés of Westminster. But all careers have to start somewhere, and for any member of parliament harbouring governmental ambitions, the bottom rung was serving as a PPS.

And, *boy*, was Edward Littlejohn ambitious. He had the classic background: scholarship to Eton; PPE at Oxford; made a fortune in merchant banking in the City. Why, then, would he give it up for the relatively paltry salary of an MP and all the shit and public opprobrium that goes with that territory?

The answer was simple.

Power. The ultimate aphrodisiac.

Oysters came a close second, in Molly's humble opinion. A memory struck her of that get-away-from-it-all break in Corfu, way back. She was dining alone under a grapevine-tangled pergola at a lovely seafood shack, to the accompaniment of Greek folk music and the rhythmic *whumping* of the Adriatic against the shingle beach. The waiter was being *ever so* attentive. Now, what was his name, again? Christos! Flawless Mediterranean complexion; luscious jet black hair; neat goatee; sultry hazel eyes. He plied her with so much ouzo that if someone struck a match anywhere near her, they'd hear the explosion in Athens! By the end of the night, he was whispering sweet nothings in her ear and she was scribbling the name of her hotel on a paper napkin. And the memory of that moonlit skinny dip would stay with her forever …

'Earth to Molly?'

The image of her Greek Adonis dissolved, and she was left with the divergent features of Edward Littlejohn in all his oily, Anglo-Saxon, ruddy-cheeked glory. A man who looked like he'd spent a lifetime keenly cultivating gout and a high cholesterol count.

'Oh, sorry, Edward. Away with the fairies. Must be this delicious wine?'

'Gorgeous, isn't it? Plenty more where that came from.'

He clicked his corpulent fingers and bellowed to the waiter, who was serving a couple at the far end of the room.

'Giovanni?' Littlejohn boomed, raising his empty glass. 'Another bottle of Syrah when you're ready, old chap.'

He gestured to where Molly's notebook lay on the crisp white linen tablecloth to the side of her plate. 'As I was saying, you may wish to make a note of what the Permanent Secretary said about me the other day: "Edward Littlejohn has a *very firm grip* on planning policy."'

Playing the game, Molly picked up her pen, opened the

notebook and started to scrawl. 'Very … firm … grip …' she repeated, trying to stifle a giggle.

'Perhaps you might want to add—and I don't mean to be putting words in your mouth here—something like: "One to watch for the future?"'

'I'm sure I can find some suitable words, Edward.'

The waiter appeared with another bottle and poured a small amount for Edward to sample. The PPS performed an extravagant sniff-and-swill routine with the glass, then knocked back its contents.

'*Grazie*, Giovanni!' he said in an excruciating Italian accent. 'Fill her up!'

The waiter attentively poured the wine, topping up Molly's glass.

'Thank you,' she said.

The waiter reciprocated with a warm smile, then disappeared.

Edward Littlejohn leaned in towards Molly, and she caught a waft of stale sweat. 'Have you heard the latest about poor old Tommy McBraid?'

Thomas McBraid, Minister of State in the Department for Digital, Culture, Media & Sport. An earnest, humourless fellow. 'No? What's the story?'

'The poor chap's having a torrid time of it with his wife and the divorce. The frightful old crone is taking him to the cleaners. She's after all his property *and* his investments!'

'Oh?'

'There's no way the man—*any* man—can concentrate on his departmental portfolio with all that extracurricular business hanging over his head.' Littlejohn drained his wine glass. 'And if there's ever a department that's in need of a "firm grip on policy", it's the Department for Culture, wouldn't you agree, Molly?'

He tapped a finger against the side of his bulbous nose. 'I catch your drift, Edward.'

There was something else on Molly's mind that she had been waiting for an opportunity to raise. No time like the present, she supposed.

'I hear you were at Eton with Geoffrey Fitzroy-Fergusson?' (*Wikipedia. What* would *we do without it?*)

Littlejohn raised a quizzical brow. 'Geoffrey? What made you think of him?'

'Well, it's been a year since the murder, and the police never caught the culprit …'

The portly politician took a large mouthful of tuna tartare and rolled it around his mouth contemplatively.

'We were *acquaintances*, I suppose. Played a bit of rugger, both members of the debating society, that sort of thing.'

'Any theories as to why he was killed?'

'Who knows? In politics, one tends to acquire enemies. An occupational hazard, one might say. Take Twitter, for instance. You only have to make one seemingly innocuous remark and, in the blink of an eye, the mob descends on you, making malicious threats. Anyway, who's to say it was an assassination? Nobody knows. Perhaps it was an accident?'

Littlejohn's use of the word "assassination" was telling. Despite his intention to play down the killing, his choice of words completely undermined his statement. Still, Molly decided there was no harm in playing along. 'What, like some kind of sex game gone wrong?'

Littlejohn shrugged. 'Perhaps?'

'Was it common knowledge—you know, before the tabloids stung him—that he had a fondness for … domination?'

'Oh, yes! As Freud might say, you only need look at a

man's relationship with his mother to work out how he ticks. And poor Geoffrey's mother was a *dragon.* Had him packed off to boarding school before he'd even uttered his first word.'

'Wasn't that the same for you?'

'Yes, I suppose you're right. Hey! You're not going to start psychoanalysing *me*, are you, Molly?' Littlejohn gave a deep, guttural laugh. 'That was never part of the agenda!'

'*Ha*, no!' Molly took a bite of her Caesar salad—figure to watch, and all that—and, feigning innocence, said, 'You know, how would you even go about *finding* someone who performs those sorts of *services*? The mind boggles!'

The politician threw back his head and laughed. 'Come on, Molly! Don't pretend to be so naive.'

He stole a glance about him to check he wasn't in earshot of anyone else, then reached behind him to the jacket draped over his chair and rummaged in the pocket. 'You're a woman of the world, aren't you?'

'What's that supposed to mean?'

He brought out a grey business card and pushed it across the table towards Molly.

She looked at the card, then back at him, puzzled. 'Dry cleaners, Edward?'

'Let's just say that if Mrs. Littlejohn were ever to root through my clothes … *this* little card would never raise any suspicions.'

He tapped his nose again and winked theatrically.

'*Edward!*' Molly said, fabricating surprise. 'Well, I never!'

'It's just a bit of harmless fun.'

A sudden, grotesque image formed in Molly's mind: Edward Littlejohn in a gimp costume, a dog chain around his neck, crawling along the floor.

"Littlejohn". Just how literal *is that surname?* ...

The PPS snatched back the business card and returned it to his jacket pocket.

Molly smiled and took a sip of wine, blinking away the gimp image and all thoughts of microscopic penises. 'And,' she ventured, 'just out of interest, Edward, did Sir Geoffrey happen to send his suits to be cleaned at the same establishment?'

Littlejohn raised a brow, then glanced at her wine glass. 'You're running low, Molly. *Giovanni!* The lady needs topping up!'

Ten minutes later, Littlejohn had stumbled to the loo to expunge the copious amounts of booze he'd consumed. Molly knew she wouldn't need to wait long for her opportunity. She dabbed the corner of her mouth with her napkin, glanced over her shoulder, then went around to his side of the table to retrieve the dry cleaner's card from his pocket. She quickly copied down the address and telephone number in her notebook.

As she went to return the card, she noticed there was something written on the back in pencil: "*Six inches off the hem.*"

She smiled, returned to her seat and awaited Edward Littlejohn's return.

Later, Molly stood, propped against the side of a bus shelter, smoking a Marlboro Light, hopeful that the nicotine would take the edge off her wine-induced headache.

She'd been watching the comings and going at the dry cleaners on the opposite side of the road for five minutes or so. It certainly *looked* like a legitimate dry cleaning business. The shop sign—black with gold text—read:

"GLADES OF BLOOMSBURY." And, in cursive text underneath: "*Satisfaction guaranteed*."

Brazen!

A double-decker swooshed by on the wet road, sending up a wave of water that crashed in front of her, narrowly missing her tan leather pumps.

'*Arsehole!*' she hollered at the bus.

Since her arrival, Molly had clocked three customers at Glades: two women and a man. The women had dropped off garments, and the man had collected. There was nothing obviously suspicious—she couldn't clearly see from this distance—but, of course, she'd let her imagination run riot. It was hardly a scientific sample, but still, why were the women dropping off and the men collecting? What kind of garments were they? What sort of *stains* were involved? How, exactly, did you clean leather? Were the garments decoys?

There was a grey door to the right of the shop entrance, which she assumed served domestic flats above. The curtains were drawn on all three windows on the first floor. Mid-afternoon; *that* was suspicious, surely? Should she go and investigate?

Molly took the notebook from her handbag and flicked to the earmarked page. She stared for a moment at the telephone number she'd jotted down in *Il Basilico*, then glanced back at Glades. A man—mid forties; well dressed; real sense of purpose about him—walked into the shop.

And the idea just popped into her head.

Her mouth split into a demonic smile. *Oh, Molly, you shouldn't. You really, really shouldn't.*

She raised her head to the sky and exhaled a plume of smoke, then dropped the cigarette to the pavement and extinguished it underfoot. She took out her phone and dialled the number. A woman answered the call after two rings. 'Glades. Can I help you?'

'Oh, hello. I'd like to make an appointment.'

'I'm sorry?'

'To have six inches taken off the hem of my brother's trousers.'

'Oh, I see, madam. Putting you through now.'

ELEVEN

WILSHAM HALL. An attractive Elizabethan manor, built by the Wilsham family in 1588, promising two hundred acres of parkland, a walled rose garden, and wide lawns hedged by yews. Regularly hosts events such as open-air opera, theatre performances and an estimable country fair.

Or so Google said, anyway.

When James arrived, he was told by some poor lackey that Felicity Fitzroy-Fergusson—"her ladyship"—was in the stable block.

He found her there, shovelling horse shit into a wheelbarrow.

James had never understood the appeal of horses; such gormless, disproportionately small-brained creatures, and so unjustifiably twitchy and nervous, in his humble opinion. *What exactly do they* do, he mused, *other than consume vast quantities of hay and churn out mound upon steaming mound of manure?* It seemed like such an extravagant, over-engineered endeavour to transform hay into fertiliser when you could just so easily pop to the garden centre for a bag or two of compost.

He didn't think much of horsey people, either. Princess Anne. Jilly Cooper. Claire Balding. All the same to him: their appearance; their manner of speaking; Somehow their entire character seemed to be defined by their obsession with horses.

The pervasive stench of horse was making his nose twitch, so he clicked out several Smints from the little blue container he kept in his trouser pocket and threw them into his mouth.

'Lady Fitzroy-Fergusson?' he called out, trying to make his voice heard above the din of whinnying and the sound of metal scraping across concrete.

There was no response, so he coughed loudly.

The lady of the house turned to him and straightened her spine. She rested her knuckles against her hips and raised her brow, regarding him with breezy, upper-class condescension. She wore a green quilted gilet, a tweed skirt and Hunter wellies. Her greying hair was tied in a loose bun, and she had the weathered look of an outdoorsy type. 'Yes?'

'James Quinn. Here to speak with you about your late husband?'

'Ah, Mr. Quinn,' she said officiously. She wiped her palm down her skirt and came over to him with an outstretched hand.

He paused for a beat or two, trying to block out the thought of what she'd been touching, then lightly shook her hand.

She fixed him with a pitying glare. 'Want to know what my dead father always used to say?'

'Do tell?'

'*A man with a limp handshake is weak of mind and loose of morals. Almost certainly homosexual.*'

'Is that right?'

'I'll have no truck with homophobia myself, you understand, Mr. Quinn. What you do in the privacy of your own home is *entirely* a matter for your own conscience …'

'Can we just—'

'See my head gardener over there?' She gestured towards a man emerging from a distant greenhouse. 'Mr. Winters. He *bats for the other side*, as it were. I couldn't give two hoots. All that matters to me is that he keeps my lawns free of dandelions and my roses pruned to perfection.'

James smiled weakly. He raised the back of his hand to his nostrils. 'Is there somewhere … more convenient we can talk?'

'I can see you're not a chap who's comfortable in the country, Mr. Quinn. Or perhaps it's your own *skin* that you're uncomfortable inhabiting?'

She left the question hanging for a few beats, then started towards the house. 'Come. We'll go to the kitchen. You have fifteen minutes of my time, no more. The needs of my horses take priority.'

The kitchen was an enormous, dishevelled place: high ceilings; copper pans hanging from oak beams; shelves overloaded with mismatched pots and bottles and trinkets; bouquets of dried flowers tied to a length of rope that stretched across one window; an old Aga in a magnificent stone alcove; baskets full of leafy, freshly harvested vegetables …

Felicity thrust a plate under his nose. 'Cake?' The plate contained what he could only describe as roughly formed beige balls dotted with burnt raisins.

'No, I won't, if you don't mind.'

'Wise choice,' she said. 'We have a new cook. Bloody atrocious. Please, take a seat.'

They sat down at an enormous old pine table, and Felicity pulled back her sleeve to examine her watch. 'So,

Mr. Quinn. What would you like to know about my husband?'

James slid the photograph of Urtė across the table to Felicity, then quickly explained his endeavours to find his wife's best friend. 'The housekeeper is convinced this woman murdered your husband.'

Felicity lifted her gaze from the photograph and snorted with derision. 'That Rodríguez woman! I have no idea why my husband chose to employ that *lunatic*.'

James recalled a sudden image of the clock collection. He smiled.

'Whenever I went down to London,' Felicity continued, 'which was seldom, I might add—I *detest* the city, the people, the pollution—that woman would make me feel like an uninvited guest. In my own *bloody* home, for Christ's sake! Once, I politely pointed out to her that there was room for improvement in the manner in which she pressed the bed linen. After that, I was forever in fear that she would stir arsenic into my Darjeeling. It was *such* a relief to dispense with her services and sell the house, I can tell you. I always thought Geoffrey was such a humourless kind of a fellow, but it turns out I was mistaken. Humour is the *only* explanation as to why he would have employed such a *ghastly* woman. Funny, isn't it, how one thinks one has the measure of a man?'

'Do you believe the assassination theory?' James asked.

'Well, I can quite understand why someone might have wanted Geoffrey dead, but I struggle with the far-fetched theories peddled in the press that this woman'—she jabbed at Urtė's picture and laughed—'was an agent of the Russian state.'

'How so?'

'Well, how can I put this? A title, a public school educa-tion and fine elocution can mask a man's intellectual deficiencies. Without them, there is no way that Geoffrey would ever have got as far as he did in politics. Think of all the people he fooled on his way up; the selection committees, the whips, the party managers, the permanent secretaries, the MPs with superior intellects but inferior educations, overlooked for promotion. Even the prime ministers he served. Being taken for a fool must create a festering resentment, don't you think, Mr. Quinn? But as far as the Russians go, they wouldn't have been fooled. Geoffrey was no threat to them.'

'I see. Can you think of anyone in particular who might have wanted him dead?'

She shrugged her shoulders and sighed extravagantly. 'There's no one in particular. I've been over all this with Scotland Yard, Detective.'

'Forgive me, but you don't seem too concerned that justice hasn't been served?'

Felicity Fitzroy-Fergusson threw back her head and laughed. 'Mr. Quinn,' she said eventually, 'justice has *already* been served. My husband is *dead.*'

There was a chill in her voice, and James was momentarily taken aback. 'I imagine it must have been difficult—humiliating, even—seeing all that stuff about his private life splashed over the front pages? Especially a second time, after he'd vowed to stop. The allegations of sexual misbehaviour, the use of prostitutes—'

'Let me stop you right there, Mr. Quinn. You appear to be implying that *I* am one of the people Geoffrey fooled? Well, you are quite wrong. I was *perfectly* aware of his pathetic weaknesses; his need for *attention*. I was not prepared to attend to his needs, and, in a way, I suppose, I was content for those needs to be attended to by others.'

Felicity looked down at James's hand, and he realised he was subconsciously rubbing his wedding ring.

'I'm sensing that you and I may have different views about marriage, Detective. In my opinion, it's an overrated institution, but it does confer certain advantages. Taxation, asset ownership, and so on and so forth.'

'Romantic,' James said absently. He'd intended to voice that thought only in his head.

Felicity looked at her watch and got to her feet. 'Time's up! I must return to my horses. Such *loyal* creatures. I can't let them down.'

TWELVE

Freddy was perched on the windowsill in her home office, snoozing contentedly, while Molly was tapping away at the keyboard.

Her phone buzzed. Nandita, calling from the office. Bloody good journalist, Nandita: cool head, keen brain, as energetic as the Duracell Bunny. And gorgeous skin; as smooth and blemish-free as a baby's bottom. *The cow!*

'Hi, Nands.'

'Hi, Molly. Great news! You were *so* right about Thomas McBraid; he's taken the bait! We've got him on camera offering access to the Home Secretary for fifty thousand. Can you believe it?'

'Well, I never! Great work, mate! Time for a celebration soon, don't you think, once we've published?'

'Absolutely, Moll. Catch you in the office tomorrow?'

'Sure thing. See ya there.'

Molly ended the call and sat back in her chair, savouring the satisfaction that warmed her skin like a tropical sojourn. She raised an imaginary glass to that slimeball, Edward Littlejohn. Or Edward *Tinycock*, as she'd childishly taken to calling him since their last meeting.

Downstairs, the letterbox clattered, stirring Freddy from his slumber and prompting an extravagant yawn.

Out of nowhere, Molly felt a sudden yearning for cheese on toast. She checked her watch. Barely eleven o'clock. Ho hum, she'd just call it an early lunch. 'Fancy a bite to eat, mate?' she said to the cat, who was stretching his front legs.

The cat licked his lips and mewled enthusiastically. He dropped to the floor and sidled over to Molly to rub himself affectionately against her shins.

Molly and Freddy went down the stairs in unison. Bills and junk mail covered the mat at the bottom.

She'd have to speak to the postman about the junk mail. Again! *Such a colossal waste of trees*, Molly mused. Just like her old rag, *the Hertfordshire Evening Herald. Ha!*

She scooped up the mail and rifled through each piece of crap in turn.

FANCY A PIZZA? GO LARGE AND GET ONE FREE! *Rip*.

RUBBISH BINS PONGING? CONTACT US FOR A NO OBLIGATION QUOTE! *Rip*.

WEEKEND MEDITATION RETREAT. HALF PRICE SALE NOW ON!

Molly hesitated for a moment, the flyer stirring up old memories. Many moons ago, after a particularly painful break-up, a despondent Molly had booked herself on a last-minute journey of self-discovery through South America. She hadn't managed to find herself, but she did happen upon a fraudulent Benedictine monk who'd sweet-talked her into a one-night stand in the foothills of the Chilean Andes. She'd come back with chlamydia and her savings wiped out. All in all, more self-loathing than self-discovery. Never again.

Rip. Rip.

Finally, there was an envelope embossed with: "NEWMAN, SIMS AND REYNOLDS SOLICITORS."

'*Ooh!* What's this, Freddy?

She opened the envelope, took out the letter and read it to him, putting on an affected posh accent. "*Dear Miss Tindall, I wonder if you would you be so kind as to contact my secretary, Mrs. Deavers, to make an appointment at your earliest convenience regarding a confidential and important matter. Yours sincerely, Cecil G. Sims, Partner, Wills & Probate.*"

This Cecil G. chap was clearly a man of few words; couldn't even be bothered to spell out his full middle name, for goodness' sake. She wondered what it might be. Gary? Gilbert? Gordon? Perhaps he was embarrassed? A name unsuited to the legal system? Gavin? Greg? Gus?

In any case, how frustratingly mysterious! Molly studied the letter again. '*Wills and Probate*, Freddy? What do we reckon this is about?'

The cat showed no interest. He sat on the bottom tread, licking himself with great fervour.

A thought struck her. God, what if it had something to do with *her*? Molly looked up to the ceiling, imagining her mother, up there in the afterlife, rocking back and forth in her chair, cackling like a demented witch.

Molly's relationship with Joyce Tindall had been fraught for as long as she could remember. Nevertheless, she'd dutifully nursed her over those long, winter months while she'd slowly succumbed to the cancer. Joyce had expressed her posthumous gratitude by bequeathing her entire estate to the Cats Protection League. Molly had had the last laugh, though, successfully contesting the will on the basis that her mother hadn't been of sound mind at the time she'd made it.

Surely, this couldn't have been her handiwork? Not after all this time? And someone or something would have had to come out of the woodwork, in that case. Who? What?

Why?

Molly looked down at the cat, as if the answer might be on his tongue. Unfortunately, what was on Freddy's tongue was Freddy's moistened scrotum.

'Come on, mate,' she said. 'Let's get you some proper sustenance. How'd ya fancy a tin of tuna in jelly?'

Curiosity didn't kill the cat, but it *did* get Molly an appointment with Cecil G. Sims at four fifteen that very afternoon.

'So,' she said, taking a seat at the old mahogany meeting table, 'what does the "G." stand for?'

'I'm sorry?'

'Your name—"Cecil G." I'm intrigued.'

'*Gaylord!* Isn't that right, Mr. Sims?'

This outburst erupted from Mrs. Deavers, who whisked into the room with a tray containing two coffees, a milk jug, a sugar bowl and a plate of assorted biscuits.

She was a large, graceless kind of a woman, but seemingly good humoured.

'It is "*Gaillard*", Mrs. Deavers,' Mr. Sims said wearily. 'The name originated in the sixteenth century. It means *brave, spirited … cheerful,*' he added, with precious little cheer.

'Well, I guess that's your specialist subject for *Mastermind* sorted, hey? Onomatology?' Molly said. 'You know, origins of names?'

Mr. Sims arched his bushy monobrow, tilted his head

towards Molly and looked down at her over his half-moon glasses. It was the look of a headteacher who was receiving a child and their scathing end-of-term report. Molly remembered *that* look well.

Molly's fingers danced indecisively over the biscuit selection for a few moments before she eventually opted for a custard cream. She took a bite.

'I'll leave you both to it,' the secretary announced. 'Shout if you need anything else, won't you?'

'Thank you, Mrs. Deavers.' Mr. Sims said.

Looking at the jaded decor and Mr. Sims in his three-piece brown suit, Molly felt like she'd been transported back to the seventies—the decade that taste forgot. It reminded her of that sitcom with Leonard Rossiter, *The Fall and Rise of Reginald Perrin.*

'So, shall we get down to business?' Mr. Sims asked, reaching for a large envelope at his side.

'Please!' Molly managed through a mouthful of biscuit.

The solicitor ran a finger under the sealed flap.

Molly beat a drum roll on the table. 'And the Oscar for best actor goes to …'

He gave her another headteacher look.

'Sorry. Nerves,' she admitted, dropping her hands into her lap. 'They make me do silly things.'

He removed a single sheet of paper from the envelope and handed it to Molly.

She quickly scanned the page. Her eyes alighted on a sum of money. A *very large* sum of money. Three hundred and forty seven thousand pounds, to be precise.

Molly handed back the letter. 'I'm not giving it to the bloody cat charity!'

'I'm sorry?'

'My mother. That's where she wanted her money to go.

But I inherited it fair and square. I went through a proper process.'

'You've not read the letter properly, Miss Tindall. This has nothing to do with your mother's estate.'

'Oh? Then who else could possibly be demanding that sort of money from me?'

'It's not a demand, Miss Tindall. It's an inheritance.'

'*Inheritance?*' she said, almost laughing. 'There's got to be some kind of mistake … There's no one left in my family for me to inherit from.'

'It's your father.'

Molly's stomach lurched.

'My father? You mean … he's dead? Wait. Don't answer that, Cecil. Rhetorical question.' She continued, feeling strangely numb. 'I haven't seen or heard from him in years. Since I was a small child. My mother drove him out of the house. When I left home, I tried to find him, but it was hopeless. Nobody would help me. There were no records. It was like he'd vanished into thin air. My mother, she—'

'Miss Tindall,' Mr. Sims said firmly, placing a hand on her arm. His voice had acquired a new, moderately sympathetic tone. 'I know this a lot for you to take in. Please, take the letter and read it carefully in your own time. I'm sure you must have many questions.'

'*Many questions?* That's the understatement of the century! I can think of a few, like, er, why did he disappear without trace? Where did he live? Who did he live with? Did he remarry? Have any other kids—'

Mr. Sims opened his mouth, but Molly wasn't finished.

'And why the f—lipping heck did he never bother to contact me when he was alive?'

'I can well understand your frustration, Miss Tindall.'

'Call me Molly, for God's sake, man! We're in the twenty-first century now.'

'Right, *Molly*,' Mr. Sims acquiesced. 'I'm afraid I'm not at liberty to answer many of your questions. All I can tell you at this stage is that your father died, after a short illness, just over a year ago.'

He had to be joking! 'A *year* ago, Cecil! A *year*?'

'Yes, that's right. There were specific instructions written that you were only to be contacted after his assets were liquidated, the creditors were settled and provided at least twelve months had passed.'

'*Specific instructions?*'

'My understanding is that your father *desperately* wanted to see you again, but it just wasn't possible.'

'Not possible? What is that supposed to mean?'

'Your father lived under a different identity.'

Molly opened her mouth to speak, but no words came out. The news that her father was dead wasn't the big revelation; she'd kind of operated on that assumption for years. It was all the other stuff—the secrecy, the stuffy formality, this *identity* business—that was poleaxing her. It didn't sound like the father she remembered at all. She remembered him as such a straightforward man: kind; gentle; loving. Worked nine to five as an electrical engineer. Enjoyed a pint or two on a Friday night with his pals. Read her bedtime stories. Sat at the end of her bed until she'd drifted off into a deep, worry-free sleep.

Or were they false memories? Something she *wanted* to believe?

'I think I've already said too much, Molly,' the solicitor continued. 'My advice to you is, read the letter, take the money and move on with your life.'

'Don't you try to fob me off, Cecil!' Molly erupted. 'I'm not having it! Was it my mother? Did *she* have something to do with this? It certainly sounds like her *modus operandi*.'

'No.'

Cecil G. Sims stole a look at his watch.

'What is it, then? I don't understand. Why couldn't he see me? Why did he have a new identity? Was he a criminal? Was he under a witness protection programme? Was he on the run from the mafia? Wait! Why that specific twelve-month thing? It sounds like something out of a bloody James Bond movie!'

The solicitor's eyebrow twitched slightly.

'No! *No way.* He wasn't some kind of spy, was he? An MI6 agent? A *double* agent?'

Molly was starting to conjure an image of her father in an Aston Martin, tearing through the cobbled streets of some ancient Eastern European city, trying to shake off a dogged KGB agent.

'Miss Tindall, *please*!'

'It's *Molly!*'

The solicitor got to his feet and gestured towards the door. 'I have another meeting starting soon, I'm afraid. I must prepare for it.'

'Sit down, Cecil!' she growled. 'You're a high-street solicitor in a dead-end town with an office over a branch of *Ryman*'s. It's hardly Rumpole of the pissing Bailey! I *need* to know, and I need to know *now*!'

Cecil G. Sims sighed and reluctantly flopped back into his seat.

'Look,' he said, his tone emollient, 'I might find myself in a world of trouble for this, but there is one surviving relative of your father's left in this country, as far as I'm aware. I've never met her, but she may be able to provide some of the details you crave about your father.'

'A relative? Who?'

'Your father has an aunt on his mother's side. Were you aware?'

'No!'

'Her name is Nancy Patterson. She received a very small bequest from your father's estate, which is how I came to know of her. She's extremely elderly.'

'Where does she live? Can I call her?'

'I will ask Mrs. Deavers to provide you with the details. Miss Patterson grew up in the East End of London and lost most of her family during the war, as I understand it. She now lives in Great Yarmouth. There was an anti-aircraft station outside the town, where she served in the Auxiliary Territorial Service. That's how she wound up there.'

Molly's hand flew to her chest. 'She was an Ack Ack girl?'

'Correct.'

'She sounds like my kind of relative! I *have* to meet her.'

THIRTEEN

SEPTEMBER 1940

NANCY WAS in her poky bedroom, lying on the patchwork quilt, her hands tucked behind her head, contemplating life and the future.

Father had been in Libya for months, fighting the Italians, and Nancy was missing him terribly. He sent infrequent letters, all of which she stowed neatly in a shoebox under her bed. She would read them over and over under the covers by torchlight, long into the early hours when sleep had the habit of evading her. His world sounded so *exciting*!

Life in Chesterton Terrace was drearier than ever. It was a strange time, knowing there was a war on, but nothing dire seemed to be happening. The air raid precautions that punctuated daily life were becoming tedious, and people were showing resentment towards the AR wardens who enforced the blackout and exhorted people to carry their gas masks everywhere they went. Mother was given to complaining that ARP was an appalling waste of public money; that thousands of pounds had been wasted on useless equipment to deal with a gas bombardment that had never materialised. Nancy supposed her mother had read about it in the newspapers or picked it up during the exchange of gossip on her grocery errands. Mother wasn't known for forming original opinions about current affairs —or much else, for that matter.

Nancy had taken a part-time job at Mr. Thorpe's bakery shop, five minutes' walk from home. The work was dull and repetitive, and her days were filled with humdrum interactions with folk—mostly women much like her mother—complaining about their meagre rations, the weather, their lot in life, and so on. Mother forced Nancy to hand over the majority of her fifteen-shillings-a-week earnings, but at least she had some kind of freedom. Left her with enough for the odd trip to the cinema or to the shops in the West End. It was an escape, of sorts.

Nancy sighed wistfully. She had a clear sense of what she *didn't* want to be once the war was over: a shop worker, a nurse, a typist. Certainly not a housewife—that would be dreadful! But she only had a vague sense of what she *did* want. She wanted action; she wanted to *achieve* something, to actually make a difference. But doing what, exactly?

Her thoughts were interrupted by a distant rumble, and moments later, the wail of the air raid warning— "Moaning Minnie", as it had become known. Nancy scrambled off the bed, switched off her little lamp and made her way to the window, parting the thick blackout curtains. The window, like all the others in the house—the street, too—was criss-crossed with brown tape that Mr. Elmswick, the warden, had insisted upon, much to her mother's chagrin. ('If a bomb goes off, you don't want to be cut to shreds by shattered glass,' he'd warned. 'But how am I supposed to keep them *clean*, covered in that ugly brown tape?' Mother had replied testily).

Nancy's bedroom faced south, towards the docks. The

sky was a deep orange, and, for a moment, she thought it was a vivid sunset, before she realised that couldn't be the case. It was the wrong direction; the wrong time.

The docks were ablaze!

Searchlights poked their long, inquisitive fingers into the night. Nancy could make out a cluster of black dots blinking in and out of existence in the shifting light; were they the German bombers?

Her bedroom door flung open, and she turned to see her mother standing in the doorway, white with panic.

'Nancy! Are you deaf? We need to get to the shelter. Come on!'

Nancy took out Grandpa Joe's cigarette case from her desk drawer, pocketed it, then followed her mother downstairs. Grandma Ada was fast asleep on her chair, and Mother got into quite the flap trying to raise her from the dead. 'How on earth can you sleep through *this* racket?' she fumed, poking Grandma's fat stomach and slapping her about the cheek. 'You and Nancy are going to be the death of me!'

Nancy found herself chuckling at the sight.

Then there was a weird whistling from outside that lasted for several seconds, followed by a flash that exploited the cracks in the curtains, infiltrating the gloom of the front room. There was a deep *boom*; the ground heaved under them, and the glass in the windows shook.

Grandma finally spluttered into life.

Grandma huffed and puffed down the garden path, and Mother pushed and tutted and prodded from behind, like she was herding cattle.

Nancy surveyed the sky: searchlights; livid flashes of orange and purple; billows of black smoke. The ack-ack guns fired incessantly—*crack-crack-crack*—their shells bursting overhead.

A small dagger of fear jabbed at Nancy's stomach. But there was something else, too: a competing feeling that, at last, the war had finally become *thrilling*. A ripple of excitement went through her.

Eventually, Mother managed to hustle Grandma into the Anderson shelter and turned to beckon Nancy inside.

The three women sat on the bench, mute, rapt by the dull, menacing crunches; the whining; the reverberations and the almost comical accompaniment of Grandma's knitting needles. Nancy didn't feel particularly cold, but her mother was shaking and rubbing her arms frantically.

Grandma had soon dropped off to sleep and was snoring like an old dog, her head propped against the cold, corrugated walls.

An awful rapping at the door made Mother jump out of her skin. 'You don't think it's a *German*, do you?' she said, half hysterical.

Nancy laughed. 'Don't be so ridiculous! I'll see who it is.'

'Be careful!' her mother shrieked.

Nancy sighed inwardly. The war was turning her mother mad. Well, madder than she already was.

Nancy opened the door to discover it was Jack from next door. He smiled warmly at Nancy, then pushed past her to address Mother. 'Have you got room for a small one, Mrs. Patterson? We're crammed in like sardines next door, and the baby's bawling his eyes out. It's doing my head right in.'

'Certainly not, you insolent young man,' Mother admonished, putting on her silly posh accent. *Ideas above her station*, Nancy could hear her father muttering under his breath. 'You should get back to your family at once; they need you. Nancy, shut the door!'

'But Mother–'

'But nothing, Nancy! Good*night*, Jack.'

'No problem, Mrs. Patterson. Sorry to have bothered you.' Jack turned to Nancy, flashing her one of his cheeky grins that made her stomach flutter.

Nancy watched him scurry back down the path. Just as soon as he leapt over the fence, a terrific thunderclap boomed in the sky, and Jack dropped to the ground.

'Door, Nancy!'

Nancy stared out fretfully for a few moments while Jack got to his feet and scarpered from her view, then she pulled the door firmly shut.

She rejoined her mother on the bench, reached into her pocket to run her fingers over the cigarette case and sank into a deep depression.

FOURTEEN

When Rosa finished her shift at seven o'clock, it was already starting to get dark. The nights were drawing in, fast, and the prospect of spending another bleak winter in this godforsaken place thoroughly depressed her. Rosa wished there was an alternative, but she had nowhere near enough money to fund a move somewhere better. A ten-hour shift at the arcade earned her seventy pounds cash in hand, plus "commission", which, on a good day, might top her up to a hundred. Take away the costs of living and she didn't have much left to stash in her getaway fund.

She was heading back, along the promenade, to the caravan; a journey that took no more than ten minutes. A gust of wind, whipping off the grey sea, cut through her like an icy blade. She turned up the collar on her coat and trudged onwards.

In the distance, there was a shelter, and, within it, she could make out the shapes of a couple sitting on the bright orange bench. Above the shelter, seagulls squabbled bois-terously.

As Rosa drew closer, she saw that it was an elderly

couple, seated perhaps half a metre apart, with a bag of chips in the gap between them. The woman wore a clear plastic rain hood and a blue coat, buttoned up to the collar. The man's attire comprised a beige mac, grey trousers and a flat cap. The couple were pecking at the bag of chips with their little wooden forks, staring into the distance while they chewed.

The absurdity of the English at the seaside never ceased to amaze Rosa.

The woman suddenly looked across to Rosa and flashed a warm, toothless smile. Feeling slightly embarrassed for staring, Rosa gave a little wave, then looked away.

Farther along, she was startled to see a boy—couldn't be more than four or five—arms aloft, hands gripping the handles of a child's buggy, fighting to shove it up the steep path that linked the beach to the promenade. In the buggy was a tiny child: a girl, red cheeks, face smeared with food, bawling her eyes out. The pushchair was laden with stuff: buckets; spades; carrier bags hanging from the handle bars. The boy was dressed in nothing more than a thin Superman t-shirt, red shorts and sandals. His skinny legs were blue with cold, the poor little mite.

Where were the parents? Rosa immediately began to feel sick with worry.

Right on cue, a couple emerged, trailing the kids by several metres. A mismatched couple, if ever she saw one. The woman, wearing a white singlet and denim skirt, was as thin as a rake and sported bottle blonde hair, with just about every part of her exposed skin covered in tattoos. She was licking an enormous ice cream. The man was huge, his blubbery stomach hanging over his shorts. He wore an England football shirt, and he was swigging a can of lager. Both of them were impervious to the cold, it seemed.

Rosa knew she was staring again, but she couldn't help herself.

A crashing noise returned her attention to the buggy. She whelped in horror when she saw that it had toppled onto its back, the little girl strapped into it thrashing her legs helplessly in the air and screaming blue murder.

The woman shrieked, dropped her ice cream to the ground and ran up the slope, quickly righting the buggy. 'What are you doing, you fucking idiot!' she hollered at the boy. Then, with one hand on the buggy, she slapped him with the other, hard, on the back of his legs. The sound cut through Rosa like a scythe.

The boy started sniffing, trying not to cry.

How could she be so horrible to her child? Poor little thing. It broke Rosa's heart. She would never hurt a child in a million years.

She'd been pregnant once. Tried to keep it secret. But of course, you can't keep something like *that* secret for long. The baby had lived for nearly four months inside her, snug as a bug, before Evgeni had made her have the abortion. The "procedure" was done in a dirty room behind a printing shop in King's Cross. It had been over as quick as a flash, but the pain still lingered. It was for the best, of course. The poor kid wouldn't have stood a chance.

If things had been different, Rosa might have had a family around her now. A pretty daughter clinging to her with one hand, cautiously patting a friendly dog with the other. A bonny boy running into the sea, whooping with delight. Daddy building a castle in the sand …

Rosa quickened her pace. There was no point looking backwards. *Face the future, Rosa. There's nothing for you to fear.*

· · ·

Once inside the caravan, Rosa locked the door behind her and switched on the light, casting the tired interior in a dim, jaundiced glow. Outside, beyond the thin walls, the wind whistled and growled.

She shucked off her coat and hung it on the wall hook, then flicked on the little plastic kettle and made her way into the tiny living area.

The furniture—a corner sofa; a wall unit housing the television; a very old Hi-Fi system; a tiny, faux wood table —was all fixed in place. It reminded Rosa of a prison cell, but at least here, she was free to come and go as she pleased. She sometimes wondered why she didn't feel more grateful for that freedom. So many years had passed since she'd last had it, after all.

The sofa was constructed from a wooden frame, and the thin cushioned seat was hinged, providing access to additional storage space underneath. A valuable commodity in a home so small, she supposed, but she had little need for storage. Contained within were various items left in place by the landlord—some blankets; pillows; a collection of tattered board games—a legacy of when he'd rented it out to holidaymakers.

And there was her getaway cash, stashed inside, of course.

Rosa lifted the seat and took out the old biscuit tin, setting it down on the table to prise open the lid. She took out the folded notes from the back pocket of her jeans and peeled off two ten-pound notes, adding them to the stash. There was over a thousand pounds in there now. She reckoned she needed at least five to make a fresh start: plastic surgery on her face; a fake passport; a one-way plane ticket. She didn't have a specific destination in mind; didn't much care, so long as it was hot and sunny.

The kettle clicked, making Rosa jump.

She quickly stowed the tin back under the sofa seat and returned to the kitchenette to make herself a milky, sugary coffee. She was spooning instant from the jar when there was a sudden rapping on the door, behind her. Startled, the jar fell from her grip, smashing on the laminate worktop and scattering the granules all over the place.

What was making her so jumpy today? She'd lived in the caravan for a year now. Surely, if Andric or one of his gang was going to track her down, he would have done so by now?

She turned to face the door. Through the frosted glass, she could make out the unmistakeable shape of her landlord, Clifford. She breathed a sigh of relief, put on her best smile and unlocked the door.

'Cliffy! How are you?'

Clifford was a timid sort of a man, tall and slim; well into his fifties, Rosa guessed. Never married; lived alone in a caravan on the other side of the park. He'd invited her inside on a few occasions, but she'd always politely declined.

Despite the cold, he wore only a thin, brown zigzag-patterned pullover sporting a white stain on the shoulder, which Rosa knew was ground-in bird shit. There was the usual smell of bad personal hygiene about him.

'S-s-s-sorry to bother you, Rosa,' he said in his reedy voice. His gaze shifted momentarily to the floor, at the spilt coffee granules. 'I was wondering,' he continued, 'what the situation was, you know, with the rent? You're several weeks behind and—'

'Aw, *Cliffy*,' Rosa said, fluttering her eyelashes and puffing out her chest. 'I'm so sorry! Peter is having problems at the arcade and hasn't been able to pay me. But he promises me soon, okay? Maybe next week?'

His focus shifted from her eyes to her chest, then back to her eyes.

'I r-really d-don't think I can wait—'

'Tell you what, Cliffy—how about we do deal? If I pay you half rent this week, then we go back to normal next week? That will help me get back on my legs. What you say?'

'Well, Rosa, I really can't afford— '

She put on her best puppy dog eyes. '*Please*, Cliffy?'

'I-I-I …' he stammered.

She reached out with her finger and made light contact with his cold, pallid forehead, tracing the edge of her finger slowly, seductively, around his eye socket, across his check, and down to his bottom lip, which hung slack and moist. Clifford's breathing grew heavy, carrying the phlegmy quality that gave her the creeps. '*Pretty please?*'

She pushed her fingertip into his mouth, feeling his tongue retreat. She drew her finger out, then pushed it back in again, repeating the action several times. His eyes darted to one side, then the other, and he garbled something too indistinct to discern.

Rosa had him right where she wanted him. Easy peasy. She withdrew her finger from his mouth, then pushed her hand into her back pocket and expertly peeled away two twenty-pound notes. 'This is all the money I have. In the whole wide world. Until Peter pays me. I won't be able to eat until he does, but hey, you're the most important thing …' She pushed the money into his hands. 'Take it, Cliffy.'

Clifford sighed in resignation. 'I can't take it, Rosa. I'm not a heartless monster. Let's call it quits. Wipe the slate clean. Start again afresh next week, eh?'

'No, Cliffy. You take it.'

'Keep it, Rosa. Please.'

'Well, if you are sure, yes?'

He nodded.

Rosa returned the cash to her trouser pocket, smiling inwardly. Rosa, one; Clifford, nil.

'You are good man,' she said, and she clasped her hands around his ears and planted a soft kiss on his forehead, feeling his hot, moist breath on her neck.

'Bye, Cliffy,' she said, closing the door on the man while he stood there, slack-jawed and wide-eyed.

Later that evening, Rosa was slumped on the sofa, a blanket over her shoulders and a large bag of corn chips on her lap, casually flicking through the measly selection of channels on the TV set. It was on old portable model with a coat hanger-type aerial sticking out of the top and the reception was terrible, no matter how she configured the aerial.

A twenty-four-hour news channel. *Click*.

A cookery show. *Click*.

A programme about people being treated in a hospital accident and emergency department. *Click*.

Where were the feel-good dramas? The old black-and-white romance movies?

She sighed and turned off the TV. A long, lonely night stretched ahead of her.

Beyond the flimsy wall of her tiny home, the wind had dropped, and the night was eerily quiet. Rosa parted the curtains to steal a look outside. Only a handful of caravans had their lights on; the majority stood dark and empty, now the summer tourist season was over. It was just the permanent residents and some hardy holidaymakers taking advantage of off-peak prices who remained. And it was only going to get worse.

Rosa pulled the blanket tighter around herself. Perhaps

she should just crawl into bed? No, it was far too early. Early nights were for old people and losers; people with nothing to look forward to other than death's sweet embrace. She was a sociable creature at heart.

Rosa could feel herself sinking into one of her black moods—the sort that needed alcohol to fix—so she went to the kitchen and opened the cupboard over the sink. The large, half-full bottle of cheap vodka inside winked at her. She grabbed the bottle and a tumbler from the draining board and filled the glass, almost to the brim.

As she brought the drink to her lips, she caught sight of her reflection in the blackness of the small kitchen window. It looked like someone else, someone she didn't recognise: a bitter old spinster with stupid dyed red hair, drowning her sorrows.

Rosa took a large mouthful of vodka and gulped it down. The liquid burned her throat, and she gasped. Then she carefully poured the remainder of the glass back into the bottle.

It was time to stop the self-pity. It was time to grab life by the balls again.

FIFTEEN

She perched herself, cross-legged, on a barstool and set her clutch bag on the counter. Full make-up, and dressed to kill. Metaphorically speaking, of course. Her objective tonight was fun, not slaughter.

Summer of '69 was playing on the jukebox, and Rosa started to tap along to its beat with the steel toe of her stiletto.

'What can I get you, darlin'?' the barman said. He wasn't exactly Tom Cruise in *Cocktail*; more like Tom Hanks in *Forest Gump*, only with less hair and more stomach. Still, what more could she have expected? This was the Coach & Horses in Great Yarmouth, after all.

There was a sign on the bar that said: "STELLA ARTOIS. 2-FOR-1."

'Do you have vodka?'

'Of course, love.'

'Make it double. No ice.'

A voice to her side said, 'Let me get it.'

Rosa turned towards the voice, to find that it belonged to a young man standing farther along the bar, brandishing a twenty-pound note. He had short, spiky hair, slick with gel, and a gold stud earring. Dressed in a polo shirt, black skinny jeans and gleaming white trainers, she guessed he was in his early twenties. A mere boy. His eyes travelled up and down the length of her body, then his mouth split into a cocky smile. The sickly-sweet scent of his aftershave tickled her nose.

'Thanks,' Rosa said, returning a sweet smile.

The barman set down her drink in front of her. She took it, and, turning her head to the lad, raised it to her mouth and rolled the glass slowly back and forth across her bottom lip. She threw back her head and downed the drink in one. It burned her throat, but she wasn't going to let on.

'*Wow*,' the boy mouthed. 'Another?' he ventured hesitantly.

'Why not?' Rosa said. It saved her from spending her own cash.

The barman poured her another drink. She decided she was going to savour this one.

'Do you … want to join us for a game of pool?' the boy asked.

Rosa could hear the sound of clinking pool balls and animated chatter from the other end of the pub, but she didn't look.

Staring straight ahead while she sipped her vodka, she said, 'I don't play children's games.'

'Right, okay.'

While the barman served the young man with several pints of lager, Rosa's thoughts slid back to her own youth, to the time when she would have willingly got it on with lads like him. Back then, it was just harmless fun. Over a few drinks—okay, *many* drinks—they would engage in inane conversations about pop music and TV programmes. And after that, they'd go for a late-night pizza, then back to his place for casual, forgettable sex. It was a pattern she'd repeated countless times as a young, carefree girl back in Lithuania, much to the disapproval of her straight-laced friend, Rūta.

Her best friend. Her soulmate. Not a day went by when Rosa didn't think of her. What had really happened to her? Evgeni had told her she died, but Rosa always suspected that was because he wanted her to stop asking questions.

Rosa felt her eyes brimming with tears.

'You okay, love?'

'Yes, I am fine,' she said, looking up at the barman. He was drying a pint glass with a cloth. She wiped her eyes with the back of her hand. 'Allergy,' she explained. She smiled at him and drained her drink. Pushing the empty glass to him, she said, 'Another, please?'

'Of course.'

They talked for a while. Well, *he* talked; she listened. She learned that his name was Michael and he had a young wife, Tiffany, and a two-year old daughter, Elsie. He had pictures of them both in his wallet, and Rosa could tell by the look on his face and the pride in his voice that he loved them with all his heart. He had aspirations of buying his own pub one day; a family pub with nice, wholesome food and a children's play area in the garden.

It had been a long time since Rosa had met a lovely, kind, genuine man like Michael. 'Tiffany is lucky lady,' she said.

But Michael didn't hear; he'd gone to serve a customer at the far end of the bar.

Behind her, things were getting rowdy. Rosa glanced over her shoulder at the pool table. Three lads loitered beside it, all dressed in similar attire to the youth who had bought her vodkas, laughing and taking huge gulps of beer. There was a girl, too: a skinny, black-haired creature bent over the pool table, lining up a shot. Two lads whooped their encouragement while the third, who stood behind her, tongue poking from the corner of his mouth, crudely simulated doggy-style intercourse. The girl took her shot, and missed. The lads commiserated with a chorus of *ooh*s.

The girl stood up, handing her cue to the sex-simulation guy, now acting virtuous, and took her pint from the table. It was then that Rosa saw the pallid face, the piercings, the make-up, the surly expression, and realised who it was. Goth Girl, from the arcade. The wannabe thief. And to think that Rosa had been feeling sympathetic towards her!

Rosa turned back to the bar and contemplated snitching on the girl, who was clearly underage. She thought better of it. *She* was hardly in a position to moralise about underage drinking when she'd committed far worse crimes herself.

'Another vodka, Rosa?' Michael asked.

She felt the start of a headache coming on.

'Just water, please.'

The rest of the evening in the pub was uneventful yet pleasant. Rosa talked more with Michael; he told her more of his life story and she offered up tiny, sanitised snippets of hers.

Goth Girl and co. had long since staggered drunkenly from the pub, and the place was almost empty when Michael rang the bell, calling time.

'It was lovely to meet you, Rosa,' he said as she put on her coat. 'You'll come again, won't you?'

'Sure,' she said. And meant it.

She'd always dreamed of marrying an aristocrat: a man with a title, money, land and connections. But perhaps

D.P. JOHNSON

all she needed was a man with a warm smile and a kind heart? A man like Michael.

She stepped out of the pub into the cold night. The sky was full of stars, and the sea shimmered with a million winking diamonds. The pier, in the distance, jutted confidently into the water. In her head, she heard the *twit twoo* of an owl, which somehow seemed a fitting soundtrack for the panorama before her.

Then she heard the scream.

The sound was no figment of her imagination. It was the awful, piercing scream of a woman in desperate trouble. Rosa had heard the sound countless times before. Thought she'd left it in her past.

Another scream, even louder.

Without much more thought, she ran towards the source of the sound: a shelter, in the middle distance, at the far end of a large expanse of grass. She stumbled, slid, limped and lurched her way across the wet grass, regretting her decision to wear the ridiculous stilettos. As she approached, she saw the gang from the pub. The girl was standing amongst them, make-up mixed with tears streaming down her face, her forearms drawn protectively against her chest. Her thin, strappy top had ridden up her torso, exposing her bra. Her coat lay crumpled at her feet.

The boys, surrounding her, chanted, '*Get it off! Get it off! Get it off!*'

'Hey!' Rosa yelled.

The boys snapped their heads in her direction.

One of them—the leader, she assumed—peeled himself away from the group and walked towards her, adopting a drunken, alpha male swagger. He looked Rosa up and down, then sniffed. 'Fancy a piece of the action, bae?'

'Leave her alone!' Rosa hollered at the other lads, one

of whom now had his hand clamped around the girl's upper arm while she squirmed and shrieked.

Alpha laughed. 'Or what?'

Keeping her gaze fixed firmly on his, Rosa walked slowly towards him, hitching up her coat sleeve.

'See this?' she said, revealing the long scar that ran along the underside of her forearm. 'My last boyfriend did to me.' She spoke in an exaggerated Slavic accent. 'And now he's dead. I kill him with hunting knife. He was proper man, not silly boy.'

Alpha's gaze shifted to the scar and back again. He tried to mask the panic the scar provoked, but she spotted it. Fear was bubbling in her own heart, but there was no way she was going to expose it to this idiot. 'Want to see the knife, boy?' she said, opening up her clutch bag and hoping to God he would cave. All it contained was random bag junk.

The boy glanced over his shoulder, seeking reinforcements. The girl had broken free and was running away; the spiky-haired boy giving chase.

'Reece!' Alpha yelled. 'Leave it!'

Obediently, Reece stopped. The girl continued to flee in the direction of the pier.

'Thank you,' Rosa said.

Alpha's lips curled into a contemptuous grimace. 'Skanky *bitch!*'

Rosa took that as a compliment and smiled sweetly.

The boys regrouped, and Rosa watched while they skulked away, tails between their legs.

Her thoughts turned to the girl, hoping she was okay, not too damaged. The poor thing. She scanned the horizon and saw her: a tiny black figure, running, running, running. Too far away now to shout out to her, to tell her things would be okay.

Rosa sighed and picked up the girl's coat from the ground. It felt heavy, like it was laden. It felt wrong, intrusive, but she checked the pockets. A mobile phone, sheathed in a black case studied with little silver skulls; a set of keys; a bank card; a dark purple lipstick; a ten-pound note; some loose change; and a packet of condoms.

She looked to the horizon, flushed with fresh concern. After stashing the items back inside the coat, she ran after the girl.

Rosa soon found her at the far end of the deserted pier, standing on the ledge, clinging to the handrail behind her with nothing between her and the swell below. In the cold glow of a streetlamp, Rosa could see the goosebumps stippling the girl's skinny arms. The wind, which seemed to have arrived from nowhere, was whipping the girl's gothic fringe into a quiff.

'Don't jump!' Rosa pleaded, but her words were carried away by the wind.

She inched towards the girl, not wanting to cause any panic. 'It's okay, it's okay,' she repeated, drawing closer. 'Please don't jump.'

She got to the girl's side and leaned briefly over the railings to look at the black waves slapping against the stanchions below.

'It will be colder in the water,' Rosa said. 'Much colder.' She could sense the girl watching her warily, as if she might make a sudden move to grab her.

'I have your coat,' Rosa said, and she calmly placed it over the girl's shoulders. The girl remained passive, staring out into the darkness, her fingers gripping the handrail tightly.

'Life sucks sometimes, hey?'

Rosa placed her hand gently on the girl's. It was cold to the touch, and her teeth were chattering. A single tear fell from her eye, to be quickly banished by the wind.

'What is your name, darling?'

The girl whispered her reply. 'Kayleigh.' As if triggered by speech, something gave within the girl and she started to sob.

'That is nice name. I am Rosa. Why don't we go somewhere warm, hey, Kayleigh? You can tell me all about it. If you want to?'

Kayleigh nodded almost imperceptibly.

'Come on, sweetheart, let me help you back over this side. You can do this.'

SIXTEEN

While Kayleigh took a hot shower, Rosa switched on the electric storage heater in the caravan. It had been so long since she'd last used it that it gave off the smell of burning dust. Ordinarily, she tried to only put it on for short bursts when it got *really* cold, in the depths of winter. Money spent on heating meant less money in the getaway fund. And less money in the getaway fund meant longer in the caravan. But now Rosa had a guest, and it was important to make her feel welcome.

She contemplated giving the room a dusting and running the vacuum cleaner over the carpet. It was the first time she'd had a proper guest in the van and she felt an irrational need to make it as comfortable and welcoming as she could. Like this poor girl would notice—or care.

Twenty minutes or so later, Kayleigh came through to the lounge wrapped in Rosa's pink towelling bathrobe. Stripped of her make-up, she was pretty as anything; nothing short of a porcelain doll. Rosa felt a sudden twitch of anxiety. Kayleigh was so young, and it struck her that there was probably a frantic mother out there, somewhere, pacing about the house, sick with worry that something awful had happened to her daughter. She looked at the clock. Nearly one a.m.

'Do you want to call your mum? Tell her you are fine?'

'I don't have a mum. Have you got any food?'

'A dad?'

Kayleigh scoffed. '*He* doesn't care. Won't even notice I'm not there.' Her eyes flitted to the kitchen. 'I'm starving.'

Rosa looked at the gaunt girl and wondered when she'd last eaten a hot, nutritious meal. 'I can make you something. Pasta?' she offered, but Kayleigh wasn't listening; she was already rooting through the cupboards.

Moments later, Kayleigh was sitting next to Rosa with a packet of plain biscuits in her lap and a glass of milk in her hand, enquiring whether there were any decent films on TV. She took a long drink of milk and smacked her lips with satisfaction.

Rosa couldn't quite reconcile in her mind the girl who had been on the cusp of throwing herself into the sea barely an hour ago with the one who was sitting next to her now. Part of her wondered whether she'd been duped; whether this was all some kind of elaborate ploy. To what end, though?

She immediately thought of the money under the seat. Cash. Was that what Kayleigh was after? But how would she know about it? Had she been stalking her? Perhaps the girl was lying about living with her father. Was she homeless? That would explain the thieving; her appearance; the hunger. No, she had a phone; a bank card; house keys.

Rosa's brain was jamming with all the questions. Eventually, she turned to Kayleigh and asked, 'So, where do you live?'

Kayleigh didn't answer; she'd fallen fast asleep. Her

glass had fallen over, spilling the remains of her milk over the seat.

But Rosa didn't mind. She didn't mind one bit.

Rosa had taken herself to bed, but she couldn't sleep. Couldn't take her mind off the girl in the lounge. She'd left her asleep on the sofa, having gently manoeuvred her into a laying position and covering her with a blanket. She'd then crept from the room and switched off the light.

Something was telling her that it wasn't right for the girl to be staying here. Rosa wasn't one hundred percent sure the girl was being completely honest. But what if she was genuine? What if she really was suicidal? Rosa was no expert, but Kayleigh might have a mental health condition. Bipolar? Schizophrenia?

There was a maternal instinct within Rosa, lying dormant, just under the surface, waiting for an opportunity to leap into action. To be the mother she had craved for herself. To nurture and fret, worry and fuss and nag and smother with love.

But Kayleigh had told her she had a parent already; a father. A father whose daughter hadn't returned home. A young, pretty, vulnerable daughter. She'd said he didn't care about her. Could that really be true? What if he was out of his mind, thinking the worst? Perhaps he'd already reported her missing to the police? Perhaps a search party was already out there, trawling the dark streets, combing the undergrowth with sniffer dogs …

Oh, God! The girl's phone! The police could trace a person's location using their phone signal, couldn't they? They'd find her in no time. And what if they did and Kayleigh kicked up a fuss, made out Rosa was harbouring her against her will? They'd arrest her for kidnapping.

Take her fingerprints. A DNA sample. Then it would only be a matter of time before they linked her to the murders and charged her.

No, that was the last thing Rosa needed: the police turning up on her doorstep. She needed to stay firmly under the radar until she could put her escape plan into action. And Kayleigh being here wasn't helping one bit. She had to get her out of the caravan. Get her back home, for both their sakes.

Rosa got dressed and returned to the lounge.

'Kayleigh?' she whispered.

She pulled back the blanket a little and lightly shook the girl's arm.

'Kayleigh, darling?'

The girl opened a drowsy eye.

'We should get you home. You cannot stay here. Your father will worry. Come on.'

The girl murmured something, then her eye snapped shut.

'Come, now.'

Kayleigh stirred. 'Let me stay,' she said groggily.

'No. It is not right.'

'Just one night? Please?'

'No.'

The girl grunted and shifted position, turning away from Rosa.

'I will call police if you do not go,' Rosa said assertively. It was an empty threat; she didn't even have a damn phone.

Kayleigh groaned and got to her feet. The blanket fell to the floor. '*Fine!* This place is a fucking dump, anyway.'

. . .

The night had turned bitterly cold. As they walked through the deserted streets, Rosa tried to hook her hand through Kayleigh's arm, but the girl shrugged her off.

They were in a part of town Rosa didn't recognise, perhaps a kilometre or so from the caravan. 'Is your house far, Kayleigh?'

'No,' she grunted.

'The boys. Do you know them well? Or did you just meet them today?'

'None of your business.'

'Did they hurt you?'

Kayleigh shrugged. 'What do you care?'

'You should report them to police.'

The girl snorted derisively. 'The police? Are you having a laugh?'

Rosa persisted. 'You could tell your dad? You cannot let them off the fishes' hook.'

Kayleigh smirked at Rosa's turn of phrase. 'If I told my dad, he'd kill them, as simple as that.'

'That is because he care for his daughter. Does not want you hurt. You say he does not care. I do not believe you.'

Rosa had never known her father. Didn't even know his name. She wasn't even sure if her mother had known for definite who her father was. In any case, she'd been sent to a children's home because her mother had been too young to look after her. Soon after, she'd completely lost touch with her mother.

Kayleigh grunted and picked up speed. Rosa struggled to keep up.

They turned into a street lined with smart, semi-detached houses, all in darkness.

'That's mine,' Kayleigh said, pointing to a house with a flashy car parked out front. 'Bye, then.'

'I will wait until you go in.'

Kayleigh rolled her eyes. 'Do you think I'm seven or something?'

'I just want you to be safe.'

'Fine. I'll go through the back door. Wait here. Dad'll go mad if we make a noise and wake him up.'

'Okay.'

Kayleigh sauntered around the side and went through a gate, closing it quietly behind her.

Rosa waited for a minute or two until a light came on in the house. She sighed, turned up her coat collar and headed back to the caravan.

The girl had only been in the van for a couple of hours at the most, but her distinctive smell—a hint of coconut mixed with notes of cigarette smoke—was the first thing Rosa noticed when she got back and flicked on the light.

Then the awful silence.

Her senses heightened, Rosa soon realised it wasn't silent at all. The refrigerator hummed. The ceiling light fizzed. The wall clock ticked. The sounds grew louder and started to gnaw at her, like tinnitus.

She switched on the TV, tuning it to the twenty-four-hour news channel, to block out the other sounds. And to make it feel like she wasn't so alone.

There was no point going to bed—she was far too uptight for sleep—so Rosa poured herself a large glass of vodka and returned to the lounge, slumping on the sofa. She looked at the milk stain and ran her hand over the fabric of the seat cushion where Kayleigh had slept. The space was cold to the touch now. She took a swig of vodka.

The woman reading the news had a lovely voice: measured and soothing, almost hypnotic. Rosa closed her eyes and listened to it, registering random words but not taking in the sentences, just letting the lilt and rhythm of the woman's voice wash over her.

Theft.

The word caught Rosa's attention, and she opened her eyes. There was a banner at the bottom of the screen: "BRITAIN SEES RECORD RISE IN REPORTED BURGLARIES."

She sat bolt upright.

The cash!

What if Kayleigh had been pretending to sleep while Rosa had been fretting in her bedroom? She could easily have found the stash and stuffed the notes into her coat pockets.

Rosa hurriedly opened the hinged seat to retrieve the tin. She checked inside and sighed in relief. It was all there, so far as she could tell. Of course that would be the case; if Kayleigh *had* found the cash, she would have scarpered with it. Stupid Rosa for thinking that; for assuming the worst when it came to the girl's motives.

She stowed the tin away. As she closed the seat, Rosa saw Kayleigh's phone, almost camouflaged in the dark carpet. She picked it up and pressed the circular button at the bottom, but nothing happened. Out of battery, she guessed, smiling wryly. Teenagers seemed to be surgically attached to their phones these days; Kayleigh would no doubt be distraught when she woke up and couldn't find it.

Rosa smiled. She'd return it to her first thing in the morning.

SEVENTEEN

HE'D BEEN LETTING his standards slip recently—taking long lie-ins; going days without shaving; living off too many takeaways. The search for Urtė was going nowhere, and the insurance fraud work had pretty much dried up. Money wasn't the issue; James could live quite comfortably on his ill heath police pension. The issue was needing to keep busy.

He'd given himself a stern talking-to in the bathroom mirror that morning. It was time to buck up his ideas. Stop wallowing in self-pity. Face the future.

So, to kick start his new regime, he'd come to the barbers for a short back and sides. Nice and early, when it wouldn't be busy.

The shop was the old-fashioned type: inexpensive; efficient; no nonsense. Here, you could safely rely on the conversation comprising nothing more than a polite "How you doing?" and "The usual, mate?"

But not today.

There was a new barber in town, and this one was a

talker. Said his name was Jason. Or was it Jayden? Too late to ask now, not that it mattered.

Jason/Jayden was a young, undernourished guy. Tattoos, piercings. The works. His hair was sculpted into a bizarre multi-coloured wave; less a haircut, more a work of abstract art. He was constantly bouncing on his feet while he scissored James's hair, his effete pinkie jutting out. Said he'd moved down from the North East for a fresh start.

Jason/Jayden pulled a face as he tugged at the stubborn tuft around James's crown that always stood proud no matter how much it was brushed. 'What shall I do with this, pet?' he said, conducting the conversation via the mirror.

Pet?

'Just cut it short.'

'Don't fancy growing it long on top for a change? That'd sort it.'

'No.'

'Summat a bit more radical?'

'No.'

'Like mine, mebbies?'

'No!'

'Whatever ye say, pet.'

'Thank you.'

There was a short period of silence, which James used to examine the clumps of hair falling onto his cape. It was more grey than brown now. Only a matter of time before all vestiges of youth were expunged. He was nearer to fifty now than forty, after all.

'D'ye ever have any recurring dreams, pet?' Jason/Jayden enquired out of nowhere.

'What?'

'Oneirology,' he said. 'I'm well into it. Ye know, the study of dreams. Fascinating stuff.'

'Fascinating,' James echoed, deadpan.

'So, d'ye have any?'

James hesitated for a few seconds, then said, 'I have a recurring dream that I'm in a car, hurtling towards a brick wall, and there's nothing I can do about it.'

'Ooh, I think I know what that means!'

'Enlighten me.'

'It means ye've been avoiding a confrontation. That dream is your subconscious allowing ye to have one safely.'

'I don't think that's right.'

'Been passed over for promotion recently?'

'No.'

'Got yersel into a spot of bother with ye finances?'

'Nope.'

'Wrestling with the consequences of a messy breakup?'

James met the barber's eyes in the reflection of the mirror. 'My wife died in a car crash and I've never got over it.'

Jason/Jayden flushed and softly cleared his throat. 'That'll be it, pet.'

'Yes.'

'Should I run some product through the top? A bit of wax? Gel? Putty?'

'No, thank you.'

'Whatever ye say, pet.'

After several minutes of blissful commentary-free scissoring, the phone in James's pocket began to buzz. He left it. If it was important, they'd call again.

The phone buzzed again. He reached into his pocket and brought out his mobile from under the cape. It was Molly. 'Mind if I get this?'

'Be my guest, pet.'

'Molly. What is it?'

'Hey, Jimbo. Busy?'

'Up to my neck in it. Can you make it quick?'

'How you fixed for Thursday afternoon, two o'clock?'

He didn't need to consult a diary to know that he had nothing on. He sucked his teeth. 'Too short notice, sorry.'

'What if I told you I've found someone who may be acquainted with Urtė? Emphasis on the *may*.'

'I'd say you're probably deluded. Who is it?'

'Her name's Roxie. Doubt very much it's her real name. Intrigued?'

'How did you find her?'

'Remember I met that sleazebag MP the other day?'

'And?'

'Turns out the filthy pervert shares a similar hobby with Fitzroy-Fergusson.'

'What? The …'

'Domination shit? Yeah, exactly that. Anyway, I called the agency he uses, and guess what?

'Tell me.'

'I've got an appointment for you with Roxie.'

'When you say "appointment", what exactly do you mean?'

'Promise you won't be mad with me?'

'No, I won't promise. In fact, I can probably promise the exact opposite.'

'Well, as I'm sure you can appreciate, I couldn't exactly tell them you're a detective, a former copper …'

'Molly?'

'Look, as far as Roxie's concerned, it's your birthday on Thursday. You're lonely and you need cheering up. I told them you've not been having much fun since your wife died. I said the pair of you used to be into all that kinky stuff. You know, whips, chains. Nothing too erotic. A bit of harmless, common or garden bondage.'

'Bondage? For fuck's sake, Moll!'

Jason/Jayden suddenly stopped scissoring and his mouth fell. James glared at him and motioned for him to butt out.

'Look, don't worry, Jimbo, I told them you're shy. And a bit rusty. You might need some limbering up, as it were. She'll go easy on you. Besides, it's only a thirty-minute appointment. It's all I could afford. You should see their prices! And that's before they add travel expenses.'

'*Travel expenses?*'

'Yeah. Anything outside the M25, they whack on mileage. She's coming to your house.'

'For Christ's sake! You gave out my home address?'

'What would you have preferred? A seedy motel on the A1? A disused car park? A dank alleyway?'

He was too annoyed, too shocked, to speak.

'Look, all you have to do is go along with it for a bit, get her relaxed, press her buttons. Then find a natural segue to Urtė.'

His lips moved, but no words formed.

'Or should I just cancel the whole thing, Jimbo? Kiss goodbye to the best lead you've had in years?'

Nothing.

'Thought not. Let me know how you get on.'

He shook his head.

'Jimbo? You still there?'

'You … *bastard*.'

'Catch you later, birthday boy,' she said and hung up.

As he returned the phone to his pocket, Jason/Jayden enquired, 'Everything okay, pet?'

'Couldn't be better,' James snarled, then added, '*pet*.'

EIGHTEEN

Rosa got to Kayleigh's house just after nine. In the cold light of day, the street looked different; far scruffier. The majority of the gardens were a mess of overgrown weeds, but this house had a freshly painted fence and a tidy front garden with a square patch of lawn and neatly tended shrubbery.

Rosa pushed the doorbell and waited. Nobody came. She tried again, pressing her thumb on the bell and keeping it there.

Eventually, the door was opened by a middle-aged woman in a dressing gown, her hair up in curlers. Rosa wasn't expecting a woman. Kayleigh's grandmother, perhaps? Although she couldn't see any familial resemblance.

'Well?' the woman sneered, looking Rosa up and down with a sneering look.

Rosa took the phone from her pocket and held it out to the woman. 'It is Kayleigh's. She leave it behind.'

'Who?'

Maybe Kayleigh had lied about her name?

'Skinny, black hair, lots of piercings. Fourteen, fifteen years old … Your granddaughter, maybe?'

'How *dare* you! I'm not old enough to be a *grandmother*.'

'I do not understand,' Rosa said. She checked her bearings. This was definitely the street. The same pretentious car was parked in front, she was sure of it. 'Kayleigh say she live here. I drop her home last night. She went round the back, through the gate.'

The woman's hand flew to her chest. '*What?*' She turned back into the house and hollered, 'Ted! Get down here!'

'I am sorry,' Rosa said. 'I think I make terrible mistake. This must be wrong address.'

The woman calmed. 'Well, I'm sorry, too. For my tone. Perhaps I've overreacted. We were burgled the other night, you see. While we were asleep. Can you believe it? They made such a mess. It's not like anything was worth a great deal. Some jewellery, ornaments, that kind of stuff. But it's the sentimental value, isn't it? And the *worst* thing is the invasion of your own private sanctuary. I don't think I'm ever going to feel safe again. I've barely slept since. My husband, on the other hand, he can sleep for England …'

'You called, dear?'

The voice belonged to a dishevelled-looking man, now standing behind the woman.

'False alarm, Ted. I thought for a horrible moment that our burglar friend might have returned last night, through the side gate. The gate I've told you *time and time again* to secure with a decent lock.'

The man started to stammer apologetically.

The woman sighed. 'It doesn't matter. Go back to your golf or whatever it is you're watching on that box.' She shooed him away, as if he were a bothersome fly.

'I'm sorry I disturb you,' Rosa said.

The woman shot her eyes to the sky. 'Men! Who'd have 'em!' she said as she closed the door.

'Daisy?'

Rosa heard the name, but it didn't register as anything relevant to her. She was too deep in thought, her mind in knots about Kayleigh, as she made her way back to the caravan. What was she up to? What game was she playing?

'Daisy?'

This time, she turned towards the croaky old voice.

'Oh, hello, Nancy. I did not realise. How are you?'

Nancy Patterson stood, stooped and slightly breathless, at an open gate. Behind her, at the end of a long, over-grown garden path, stood a three-storey, ramshackle house. It was weatherboarded, with dormer windows in the roof. Totally different to anything else in the street. To Rosa, it brought to mind all those American horror films she'd watched as a teenager and the tropes of the genre: rocking horse in the attic; creepy portraits; rickety staircase …

'Is this your house?' Rosa had pictured a little bunga-low, or a retirement apartment, or an old people's home.

'Of course it is. Whose else would it be?'

Rosa smiled to herself.

'Daisy, dear, will you help me open this damn box, please? My fingers have gone all stiff.'

'Sure.'

Nancy opened her palm to reveal a tiny key. Rosa took it and used it to turn the lock in the mailbox. The small space was stuffed to capacity; it clearly hadn't been emptied in a long time.

'Are there any letters?' Nancy asked. There was excitable hope in the old woman's rheumy eyes. 'I check every day.'

Rosa rifled through the mail. 'There is many junk mails … some bills … Wait! What is this?'

A handwritten envelope.

Nancy clasped her hands together. 'Will you open it for me, dear?'

'Okay.'

Rosa opened the envelope and pulled out the letter. She held it out for Nancy.

Nancy raised her palm. 'Will you read it to me? I've left my reading glasses in the house somewhere.'

'Okay. If you are sure?'

'It's from Father, isn't it?'

'*Your* father?'

'He's fighting the Italians in North Africa. Don't you remember *anything* I tell you, Daisy?'

Rosa offered a plaintive smile. 'Of course. Silly me. I forget.'

'I haven't heard from him in such a long time. I check every day to see if he's written.'

Rosa looked at the letter. Her reading ability in English was poor and the handwriting was elaborate. She recognised some of the words, but struggled to piece them together to form coherent meaning. For a moment, she contemplated humouring Nancy and pretending the letter *was* from her father, but that seemed unnecessarily cruel and, besides, Rosa lacked the mental agility. She scanned the letter, taking in the signatory. 'I am very sorry, but it is not from your father, Miss Patterson.'

'Oh?'

'It is from someone called Molly Tindall.'

'Molly Tindall? Never heard of her!' Nancy turned and started back towards the house.

Rosa watched, feeling both pity and respect, while the old woman made her laborious journey along the path, each tiny shuffle a monumental human effort. 'Have a nice day!' she called out. Nancy didn't respond. Then Rosa realised she was still clutching the letter. 'Miss Patterson!' she shouted, waving it above her head. 'Your mail!'

Nancy took an age to turn around. 'My mail? What mail?'

'This.'

'You're late, postman! Put it in the box where it belongs!' Nancy turned and resumed her epic trek. 'It can wait till tomorrow. It won't be anything important.'

NINETEEN
OCTOBER 1940

I⊤ WAS GONE three in the morning, barely five minutes since the all-clear, yet Mother was out in the front yard, dressed in nothing but her peach cotton nightgown, sweeping the debris from the path like a woman possessed.

Nancy stood, propped against the wall, numb, surveying the scene. On the opposite side of the street, there was a gap in the terrace where only an hour ago two houses—numbers thirteen and fifteen—had stood. Both had been reduced to rubble now, not even a piece of furniture visible; only piles of earth, loose bricks and broken timber beams. Number eleven—old Mrs Prentice's—was ablaze, sparks and burning embers spitting out onto the road. An AFS unit was tending to the fire, their hoses carpeting the street, and a stretcher party scrambled over the rubble. A strong smell of gas hung in the air, and the acidic stench of powdered brick and cordite stung Nancy's lungs.

The omens weren't good, but Nancy prayed they'd all be rescued. She didn't know the occupants of the obliterated house particularly well. The woman from number thirteen —*unlucky for some*, Nancy shuddered—was as pretty as a picture; never seen with so much as a hair out of place; always smiling. The sort to say a cheery hello whenever they passed in the street.

'Are you just going to stand there gawping, or will you help me out here?' Mother complained. 'The place is in *such* a state.'

'Shouldn't you get some sleep, Mum? All this will still be here in the morning.'

Mother shifted her gaze to the rubble across the street, then back to Nancy. She raised her brow and said sceptically, 'Will it?'

Right then, as if in response, Moaning Minnie began to wail.

Mother sighed and shook her head in despair. 'I should finish up here. You get to the shelter, Nancy.'

The discordant noises of war were upon them once more: the undulating drone of the German bombers; the ack-ack barrage; the screams of falling bombs; the rumbles and reverberations of distant explosions.

'Come on, Mother!' Nancy shouted to be heard. 'I'm not leaving you here.'

A whistle blew, and Mr. Elmswick's voice boomed: 'Get to your shelter, *quickly!*'

Mother seemed not to notice or care. She just continued to sweep, muttering unintelligibly under her breath.

Nancy leapt towards her mother and grabbed the broom, but Mother refused to relinquish her grip.

The sight of two women fighting over a broom would have looked such a spectacle to any onlookers as the incendiary bombs rained down about them.

'*Shelter!*' Mr. Elmswick hollered.

Eventually, Mother relented, throwing the broom to

the ground. 'Fine! Have it your way. Like always!' She turned on her heel and headed back into the house. Nancy followed, keeping her distance.

They marched through the parlour, ignoring Grandma in her armchair, knitting away blissfully. Weeks ago, she'd set out her stall in her own mute and steadfast way. Nancy supposed her grandmother was reconciled to whatever fate God had in store for her. Like many people in the East End, her grandmother had decided that if she was going to be killed, it might as well be in the comfort of her own home.

When Mother and Nancy stepped out the back door, incendiaries were clattering down the slate tiles, hitting the ground around them, bursting and showering the garden with white magnesium fire. '*Hurry, Mum!*' Nancy urged, starting to panic.

In the scramble to the shelter, Mother's nightdress suddenly went up in flames in a great *whoosh*. She screamed blue murder and started to frantically run around in circles, patting herself to no great effect.

Nancy had to do something. But what? She was paralysed by indecision. Just as she was about to turn and head back out to the street to seek help from the AFS crew, Jack vaulted over the fence with a pail of water. Absurdly, the nursery rhyme *Jack and Jill* flashed through Nancy's mind.

Jack hurled the contents of the pail over Mother, extinguishing her at once. He wrapped his arm around her and helped her to the Anderson shelter.

Mother's screams subsided to distressed whimpers as she sipped from the flask of tea Jack had retrieved in a heroic dash to his house.

Nancy raked through the first aid kit—nothing more

than an assortment of odds and ends stowed in a battered old biscuit tin—and found a tube of ointment. Lacking a label, Nancy had no clue what it was for, but she supposed it couldn't do much harm, so she smeared it liberally over the burns on her mother's legs and hands. Mother flinched slightly, but otherwise didn't complain. That wasn't a good sign, however; her mother could complain for England.

'Why don't you have a lie-down, Mrs. Patterson, till this raid is over?' Jack encouraged, motioning towards the lower bunk. Mother had had a couple of men come round a few weeks back to help build the shelter's new bed. It had thin, narrow mattresses and scratchy, damp blankets, but it was infinitely more comfortable than sitting for hours on end on the hard bench with a sore behind.

Mother smiled weakly, groaned, then flopped onto the mattress. Jack tenderly lifted her legs and pulled the blanket over her, up to her neck.

'Suppose I'd better be going, then,' Jack said.

Mother remained silent, her eyelids drooping.

The ground rumbled beneath Nancy's feet and, outside, she heard the distant sounds of bombs wreaking their havoc. 'Stay, please?' she asked meekly.

She hugged her arms, trying to generate some heat. The makeshift candle-in-a-pot heater was hopeless. The thought of the Blitz continuing through the winter was almost too much to bear.

'Well, if you insist.'

Nancy smiled inwardly. 'Mind if I get into my bunk? I'm freezing.'

Jack's eyes glistened in the dancing candlelight. 'Want a hand?'

'I think I can manage,' Nancy said, clambering up the little wooden ladder. She snuggled under the blanket. 'Sorry, we don't have any spare covers.'

'It's okay, I don't feel the cold. Ma says I've got hot blood running through my veins. Take after my old man.'

They listened in silence to the booms, whistles and grumbles outside. Then, when there was a moment of relative quiet, Nancy enquired, 'How much longer do you think the Huns are going to be bombing us for?'

'I dunno, but I reckon Mr. Churchill will send them packing before long. Wish I was old enough to fight.'

'Me, too,' Nancy said.

Jack laughed. 'You're not a typical girl, are you?'

'Suppose not.' She heard the faint sound of her mother snoring and leaned over the edge of the bed to steal a look. 'Can't believe she's flat out. Must be the shock.'

'Or these,' Jack said, brandishing a brown pill bottle and grinning from ear to ear.

'What are they? Where did you get them?'

'They're Ma's. She gets 'em from a man on Fenton Street. Barbiturates. They help her nerves. Reckon they could knock out a rhino!'

Nancy giggled. 'Your mother couldn't get me a year's supply, could she? I fancy a bit of peace and quiet!'

'You're a funny one, Nancy.'

'Funny *ha-ha* or funny weird?'

'*Ha-ha*, I mean.' Jack smiled, then cocked his head to one side. 'You're pretty, too.'

Nancy felt herself blushing. 'Bet you say that to all the girls.'

'You're the first, and that's the God's honest truth.' He brought his hand up to his chest. 'Cross my heart and hope to die, Nance.'

'Don't say that!'

'What? *Nance?*'

'No! *Die*, you idiot!'

Outside, there was an almighty *crack*, as if the sky had

split in two, followed by the dull thud of something or other falling onto the thin layer of earth above their heads.

Jack's smile dropped, and Nancy saw that his teeth were chattering. His breath was fogging in the cold, damp air. 'You can stop the tough man act. I can see you're freezing.' A new confidence fizzed in her veins, and she raised her blanket with one arm and shuffled to the back edge of the bed. 'Why don't you join me up here?' God, her mother would kill her, if only she wasn't out like a light …

Jack didn't need to be told twice. Before she'd had time to blink, he had sprung from the bench, scrambled up the ladder and nestled in alongside her, his face inches from hers. She felt a sudden warmth.

A thought flashed into her head. *What if this has been his plan all along?*

She smiled to herself and wagged a finger at him. 'No funny business, okay?'

'Cross my heart, Nance.'

TWENTY

APRIL 1941

IT WAS A BEAUTIFUL EVENING; biting cold, but clear and still. A new moon gleamed bright and clean in vivid contrast to the filth of the city. The sky was disturbingly quiet.

After almost two years at war, the quiet felt unnatural.

By the time Nancy and Jack arrived at the bomb site, all the expected parties were already there: bomb disposal; the rescue squad; the stretcher team; an AFS unit; a pair of mortuary vans.

They'd been told that an aerial torpedo had hit Whitwell Road, wiping out several houses and the hairdressers on the corner. Chunks of masonry and sections of iron railings were strewn haphazardly all around them. The bomb had fractured the main water pipe in the road and water was cascading everywhere.

They dropped their bicycles on the pavement in front of what remained of the hairdressers, now a mound of rubble. Jack raced ahead, clambering across the debris, and Nancy followed.

Officially, they were lowly messengers, but in reality,

they threw themselves into whatever task the circumstances demanded: searching for survivors; administering first aid; chasing off looters; consoling the bereaved. All hands on deck.

A few yards ahead of Nancy, Jack started digging with his bare hands among the cracked mirrors, glass fragments and wreckage.

'Found something?' Nancy shouted.

Jack pulled out an object and, as she drew up behind him, the rubble shifting underfoot, he turned to her, brandishing the decapitated head of an auburn-haired woman in his outstretched hand.

Nancy's hand flew to her mouth, stifling a squeal of horror. It wasn't the sight of a severed head that had caused the reaction. She'd long since grown inured to the carnage of war: dead babies; mutilated bodies; torsos stripped of their limbs and clothing by the sheer force of the bombs. It was the fact the poor woman bore a wide, toothy, red lipstick smile.

Jack started to laugh mischievously.

It took Nancy several beats to realise that the head belonged to a wax mannequin.

She slapped him hard on the arm. 'You *pig!*'

Then she heard something that sent a shudder through her; above the noise of the crews working at the far end of the street: the furious yapping of a dog. She turned, training her ear to locate it.

'There!' she said, pointing to a badly damaged house over the road. 'Let's take a look.'

The front door lay on the ground, blown off its hinges. They stepped over it, into a dark hallway smothered in white dust. The stench of gas was overwhelming.

'Hello?' Nancy hollered into the darkness. 'Anyone home?'

No response.

While Jack disappeared into the front room, Nancy followed the sound of the dog.

She soon found the animal, filthy but unhurt in the kitchen, where an electric light bulb fizzed and flickered. Water dripped from the ceiling. The dog was a little scrap of a thing—wiry, matted fur—running around in circles in the tiny room.

The dog had done its business on the tiled floor and the smell of it, combined with the gas, made Nancy's stomach churn. She would see if the dog wanted a drink of water; the poor thing's throat must have been dry and sore from all the dust and the incessant barking.

But first Nancy opened up the back door to let in some fresh air. That was perhaps a mistake, because as soon as she did so, the dog took its opportunity to sprint off into the night. Maybe the dog would find its owners, wherever they might be? Nancy hoped so.

She was switching off the gas when Jack came into the kitchen, grinning. 'No one here,' he said, slightly breathless. 'I've checked every room.' The flickering bulb illuminated his dirty face, contrasting with the white of his teeth. He looked like he'd returned from a long day in the coal mine. 'Nance,' he said, digging into his trouser pocket, 'close your eyes and hold out your hand.'

'Not now, Jack!'

'Please—just do it. Won't take a tick.'

Nancy sighed and closed her eyes, humouring him. He took her hand, and she felt him slip something over her finger. *Oh, God*, she thought. *I hope this isn't what I think it is …*

'You can open them now,' Jack said, a hint of mischief in his voice.

As she'd feared, he'd slipped a ring on her finger: an

awful faux emerald costume piece, many sizes too big for her. She conjured an image of its owner: a matronly middle-aged woman; rouged cheeks; limp hair.

'What do you think you're playing at, you daft bugger? Don't you know there's a war on?' She took off the ring and handed it back. 'And put the bloody thing back where you found it!'

'So, Nance, do you fancy getting hitched, then? After the war?'

'Not sure what Mother would have to say about that! And, besides, you'd best learn which one's the bloody wedding finger first, cloth head!'

'Come here, Mrs. Tungate!' Jack said, grabbing Nancy by the waist and pulling her towards him. Her back arched, and she found herself staring up into his face. He started to kiss her passionately: first her lips, then her neck. She closed her eyes, transporting herself to an imagined future, after the war: a beach all to themselves, its white sand dotted with fallen coconuts; blue sky; bath-warm sea; palm trees swaying in the tropical breeze. She'd fallen for him, hook, line and sinker.

A sudden noise from the floor above snapped her back to the present: a creaking sound that grew steadily louder, into an arcing groan. The house began to shake, dust falling from the ceiling.

Jack's smile dropped, and he grabbed Nancy's hand. 'We need to get out! Now!'

They hotfooted from the house and out into the road just as the building collapsed with a tremendous *whump*, sending a mushroom cloud of dust into the sky.

Jack, panting from the adrenaline rush, dropped his hands to his thighs. 'Close shave, Nance!'

Nancy sank her hand into the pocket of her overalls and found the cigarette case. Was Father right? Was it a talisman? Would it really see her safely through the war? *Where is Father now?* she wondered, looking up into the sky and half expecting to see his face among the stars, smiling down on her.

A thought struck her: Father loved dogs, and he'd always tried to convince Mother to get one. Nothing too big or troublesome; a Jack Russell, perhaps. Mother had had none of it, of course. *'Over my dead body! Damn dirty creatures!'* Had he somehow intervened to see to it that the dog was rescued? *Don't be so bloody daft, Nancy!* The war was addling her rational brain. Lack of sleep, that would be it. It really was the devil.

'Oi, love birds!' Mr. Hibbs, the sector leader, called from farther up the street, frantically waving his hands above his head. 'Get up here, now! Casualties!'

They started to run towards him, when, all of a sudden, Mr. Hibbs began pointing to the sky behind them. Nancy became aware of the drone of a passing plane, and she turned to see it looming overhead: hardly any clearance from the rooftops. The drone quickly grew to an ear-splitting roar.

She paused, momentarily transfixed; she could make out the German insignia. How had it appeared from nowhere, without any warning?

Sudden violent bursts of machine gun fire rang out.

'*Take cover!*' Mr. Hibbs bellowed.

Nancy turned back to see that he'd thrown himself to the ground.

A hailstorm of bullets pitched all around them, ricocheting off the tarmac.

She dashed into the cover of a doorway, turning to see Jack barrelling towards her, even now grinning like a Cheshire Cat. Had he no fear at all? He paused, took something from his back pocket and pointed it at the sky.

When he let out a volley of gunshots, she realised he was holding a revolver. Had he stolen it from the house? The bullets were soon spent, and he dashed in her direction.

The plane roared overhead and was gone, as quickly as it had arrived.

Jack collapsed breathlessly into her arms, the gun clattering to the ground. Nancy struggled to avoid buckling under his weight. 'Get off me,' she wheezed. 'You're hurting me. And you need to return that gun. You can't just go stealing everything in sight!'

Jack didn't respond. Instead, he sank to his knees, his head flopping backwards. There was the ghost of a grin. Out of the corner of his mouth, a trickle of blood emerged and dribbled down his chin.

Nancy watched—mute, numb, disbelieving—as Jack slowly turned a deathly pale. He gurgled and gasped, trying to tell her something.

Before the light went from his eyes forever.

TWENTY-ONE

SHATTERED YET TOO fretful to sleep, Rosa sat at the table in the caravan with a strong coffee, mindlessly drumming her fingernails on the laminated surface and staring at Kayleigh's mobile phone.

There was something about the girl that had got under Rosa's skin, and she kept replaying the scenes from the previous night, after she'd left the pub. She wondered whether the Coach and Horses would be open now. She could ask Michael if he knew anything about Kayleigh; perhaps he might know where she really lived. Then she could use returning the phone as a pretext to set her mind at rest that the girl was safe and well.

Rosa checked the clock; just gone noon. There was enough time before her 2pm shift at the arcade started. She finished her coffee and dumped the mug on the drainer, grabbed her keys and threw on her coat.

As she opened the door, the wall calendar caught her eye: today's date, circled in red pen. *O Dieve!* It had completely slipped her mind—she was supposed to have called Roxie this morning!

They'd agreed the date and time the last time they spoke, a month ago. Each knew how dangerous it was to maintain a line of communication, but they were careful. They stuck to a rigid plan. Roxie kept the existence of her mobile phone from Andric, stashing it in a secret place, always switched off. Rosa didn't possess a phone now; she was paranoid that if she did, Andric would somehow track her down. She'd heard the term "triangulation" used on TV shows. She had no idea what triangulation involved or how it worked, or even whether it was actually possible in real life, but she had no intention of putting it to the test.

Rosa locked the caravan door behind her and set off for the pub at pace. She was sure Michael would let her use his landline. She'd learned the trick that if you added the digits "141" before the number, to withhold your identity. Hopefully, Roxie would keep her phone turned on for a while longer.

Rosa's heart sank as she rounded a corner and saw Clifford Snell, busying himself with some kind of foul-smelling maintenance work. He was on his knees, his sleeve rolled up to his upper arm, poking a stick into an open drain.

With luck, he wouldn't notice her sidling past. Quiet as a mouse, Rosa scurried across the grass. The last thing she needed was to get trapped in a boring conversation about—

'Rosa!'

Dėl Dievo meilės!

Sighing, she turned around. There he was, holding aloft the stick, matted at one end with a clump of some-thing disgusting. Brown liquid sluiced from the object, running down his fingers and forearm, before slopping to the ground.

'Wet wipes,' he said, shaking his head sadly. 'I wish

people wouldn't flush them down the toilets. They cause such t-t-terrible blockages.'

Rosa's nose twitched. She threw a thumb over her shoulder. 'Sorry, Cliffy. I am in rush. I need to make phone call.'

His eyes lit up, sensing an opportunity. 'You can use my phone. In the van.'

'It's okay,' she said, feigning gratitude. 'I don't want to be trouble, and a nice walk to town will—'

'It's no trouble, Rosa. Come on.'

Clifford threw the stick and the attached clump of wet wipes to the ground and quickly replaced the drain cover.

'Well, okay,' she replied cautiously. The Coach and Horses was a good ten minutes away, if she walked briskly. Was there really any harm in going to his van?

'Excuse the m-m-mess,' he said as he turned the key and led her inside. 'We weren't anticipating guests.'

Rosa frowned. '*We?*'

'Newton and I.'

A *screech* from the corner alerted Rosa to the presence of his grey parrot, in its cage.

Clifford, wiping his hands on a dirty towel, asked, 'Can I get you something to drink?'

'No, thank you.' Rosa looked about the squalid interior. 'Where is phone?'

He pointed to the table. 'Please, help yourself.'

The table was covered with old newspapers, foil containers, mugs, and takeaway litter. She nudged aside a plastic box filled with chopped peach pieces to reveal the phone.

She put the receiver to her ear and turned to see Clifford opening the bird cage. The parrot flew onto his shoulder. As they came over to the table, the parrot bobbed excitedly on his shoulder. '*Rosa! Rosa! Rosa!*' it chanted.

'How does he know my name?' she asked.

Clifford blinked a couple of times. 'Newton knows all the residents' names. He's very clever. Such a fast learner.'

'*Clever boy! Clever boy!*' the parrot screeched immodestly.

'That's why I called him Newton, after the great man himself.'

'Who?' Rosa said impatiently. She was beginning to regret accepting his offer.

'Sir Isaac Newton. You must have heard of him? Formulated the three laws of motion, the basic p-p-principles of modern physics …'

'Clifford!' she said, irritated, then stopped herself. She couldn't be angry with him. She was indebted. Swallowing her annoyance, she smiled sweetly. 'Cliffy, please. I really need to make call.'

'Yes, of course. Please—go ahead.'

Rosa turned her back and started to punch in the number she'd long since committed to memory, just in case. She turned to see Clifford feed Newton a piece of fruit, which the bird held in its claw and gnawed at messily, fragments flying everywhere.

The parrot tilted his head to one side and glared at Rosa. Unnerved, she switched her attention to Clifford. 'The call is private,' she said assertively.

'Oh, yes … Sure … I'll just go and … d-do some paperwork out the back. Come on, Newton.'

Rosa waited for the internal door to close, then finished dialling the number. She tapped her foot as she waited for the ring tone, but instead she got the message: "*The person you are trying to reach is unavailable.*"

'*Fuck!*' she shouted at the phone.

She dropped the receiver onto the cradle and scarpered from the caravan, slamming the door behind her.

She was so annoyed. With herself. With Clifford. With the bloody parrot. Roxie was her best friend. Her *only* friend, really. Keeping in touch, if only with a snatched five-minute conversation once a month, meant the world to Rosa.

O Dieve. A horrible thought struck her. Had she remembered to dial 141 before inputting Roxie's number? She started to panic, before realising that it didn't matter. Roxie's phone was switched off, so it wouldn't record the details of the caller.

'Rosa?'

God, she hoped Roxie was okay. Andric could be so hot-tempered. So cruel. So irrational. Hopefully, she was worrying over nothing. That Roxie had simply turned off the phone and she was fine. Yes, of course. *Stop worrying*.

'Rosa?'

But Roxie must be worrying about Rosa. Thinking the worst when she hadn't called at the agreed time? She'd never forgotten before, not once.

'*Rosa!*'

She turned to see Clifford standing on the step of his caravan. 'Everything okay?' he asked.

'Fine,' she said.

'Would you like to stay for lunch?'

'No, thank you.'

'I have a lasagne in the freezer. It won't take me long to defrost it.'

'I say no, Cliff.'

'It's Sainsbury's Taste the Difference. I've been saving it for a special occasion …'

'*Uzsipisk*, creep!' she yelled. *Go fuck yourself!* She turned on her heel and fled the caravan park.

TWENTY-TWO

By the time she got to the Coach and Horses, Rosa was feeling terrible about how she'd treated Clifford. Yes, she was stressed and anxious, but that was no excuse. Clifford was a good man; so sweet-natured. He was just lonely and wanting some human company. She, of all people, should have shown sympathy. Would it have been too much trouble to stay with him for an hour and have a bite to eat?

She resolved to make it up to him later. For now, she had to put him to the back of her mind and concentrate on tracking down Kayleigh.

The pub was quiet. Michael was wiping the bar when she entered. He looked up and smile. 'Hey, Rosa! Nice to see you again.'

'You remember me?' Rosa said, touched.

'Of course. How could I forget? What can I get you, darlin'? Vodka?'

'*Ha!* No! It is too early for drink. I am here to ask about someone.'

'Sure thing.'

'You remember the guys in here, playing pool, the other night? There was girl with them.'

Michael rolled his eyes.

'You know her?'

'*Everyone* knows Kayleigh Bridger. Why do you ask?'

'It is long story, but I have her phone. I need to give it back to her. Do you know where she lives?'

'Yeah, I do, as it goes. She lives with her father, Dean, on Fairview Road, on the other side of town. Do you know it?'

'No.'

'It's a very rough area. Hey, why don't you leave the phone here with me? I can give it to Dean when he's next in. He's a regular.'

'Thank you, but I want to take it. I want to see she is all right.'

Michael laughed. 'She can look after herself, that one! She'll be fine.'

'I think she might be mentally ill. Maybe depressed?'

'Well, she's mental, all right.' He twirled his finger about his temple.

'Then why you let her drink when she is under the age?'

Michael sighed deeply. 'If it was up to me, and this was my pub, I wouldn't let her. The problem is the landlord, my boss.' He leaned in and lowered his voice. 'Between you and me, a few months back, he was in trouble—up to his eyeballs in debt. At one point, he even thought he was going to have to shut this place down. Dean offered to help out with a loan. The banks wouldn't touch this place with a barge pole, you see. Dean's money has helped keep this place afloat. The trouble is, the loan came with a price—and I don't just mean the exorbitant rate of interest. Free supply of drink for Dean and turning a blind eye to his daughter's underage drinking …'

'Dean does not sound like very nice man.'

'He's a nasty piece of work. Are you sure you don't want to leave the phone here?'

'I am sure. Do you have the house number?'

'No, I don't, but you won't need it.' Michael smiled. 'You'll know which house is his, trust me.'

Rosa found Fairview Road, courtesy of a battered old A-Z she'd retrieved from the kitchen drawer in the caravan.

It was an awful, rubbish-strewn street lined with narrow terraced houses, the front doors abutting the pavements. Cars were parked nose to tail and half on the pavement, making it awkward for pedestrians to squeeze past. An old washing machine had been dumped outside one house, together with a busted mattress and some black bin liners filled with God knows what, completely blocking the path and forcing Rosa to walk on the road.

Now, what had Michael meant when he said she'd recognise the house? She scanned the terraces on either side. Each little house looked barely distinguishable from its neighbour. She was cutting it fine now it she was to get to work for 2pm.

She rounded a bend and saw it, on the opposite side: a house painted with a huge mural of a shark, made to look like it was bursting out of the brickwork.

Rosa chuckled to herself. *That will be it.*

She crossed the road, hearing music spilling out of the house as she got closer. The music—something with a throbbing bass beat Rosa didn't recognise—grew louder when, after several increasingly loud knocks, the door was finally opened by a large man, who was naked except for a small white towel wrapped around his ample waist. His torso and arms were covered with tattoos. He was dripping wet; just emerged from the shower, she guessed.

'Mr. Bridger?'

The man's eyes narrowed as he looked at her with barely concealed disgust. 'Who's asking?' His voice was deep and rough.

'I have something for your daughter, Kayleigh. She left it behind at my home ...' Rosa took the phone out of her pocket.

Dean Bridger's gaze switched to the phone, then back to Rosa, and his face crumpled into a snarl. 'Kayleigh? Left behind?' He stepped forward onto the street to stand inches from her and screamed into her face, 'You're that fucking *dyke* she's shacked up with, ent ya?' He looked up and down the road. 'Where is she?'

Rosa took a step back. 'I thought she live here? That's why I come ...'

'Don't give me that shit! She sent you here to fucking wind me up, didn't she? To rub my nose in it.' He jabbed an angry finger at her. 'Where is she? I'll rip her fucking throat out!'

'I-I-think I make a mistake,' Rosa said and made to leave.

'Not so fast, dyke!'

Dean lurched and grabbed her wrist. Before she could fully process what was happening, he bundled her into the house and kicked the door shut behind him.

Rosa squirmed and wriggled, but she was no match for the man's brute strength. Gripping her tighter and covering her mouth, he pulled her along the hallway. The phone fell from her grip and she heard it clatter on the floor.

He dragged her into a small living room and threw her facedown onto a black leather sofa.

The music stopped abruptly.

Rosa scrambled to turn herself onto her back, to find him standing before her, naked and aroused.

It had happened so quickly that she wondered whether he'd somehow managed to drug her and she'd just come round. But that thought was absurd! She knew she shouldn't really be surprised by the violence men were capable of.

Her mind drifted briefly to the day she'd killed Evgeni. Why did she keep ending up in these situations? What had she done to the gods to make them so angry? Or was it just fate?

A strange calmness washed over her, almost as if she was floating out of her body and watching remotely.

The illusion snapped as he edged towards her. 'I'll show you what you're missing, dyke!'

Rosa scrambled to a sitting position. She cast her eyes about the room, contemplating her options. She quickly realised they boiled down to two: submit or fight.

It was obvious what she had to do.

Inside, she was a mess, but she forced herself to visibly relax. Arranging her mouth into a seductive smile, she beckoned him with a *come-to-me* finger gesture. 'I am ready!' she whispered.

His expression changed. The rage, the frenzy, fell away, to be replaced by bewilderment.

She glanced at his pathetic pencil dick and feigned delight. 'Do not be shy,' she said, hamming up the Slavic accent. 'Alexia does not bite.'

He edged further towards her, until he was just inches away. Licked his lips.

'Ready, big man?'

His face lit up with hunger. 'You dirty, dirty bitch!' He laughed and clasped his hands around the back of her head, pulling her towards him.

'Wait!' she said, resisting. She could feel the awful, clammy warmth radiating from his flesh. 'Be patient!'

Dean relaxed his grip slightly and she took hold of his buttocks, digging her fingernails into the blubbery flesh. He arched his back and groaned with pleasure.

She moved her hand to his knee and traced a nail, the lightest touch, slowly up the outside of his fat, hairy thigh.

'Ready?' she said.

'Yes!' he howled.

She gently cupped her hand around his balls.

'*God!*' he cried.

And with that, she squeezed with all her might. Twisted, for good measure.

'*Pervert!*' she screamed and jumped to her feet.

Dean dropped to his knees, then fell onto his side, writhing in agony. For a few seconds, he couldn't speak, but then he managed to spit out the words, 'I'll fucking … *kill* you …'

Rosa kicked him, again and again, at the base of his spine. '*Shudas*!' *Piece of shit!*

She hurried to the front door, only stopping to pick up Kayleigh's phone.

Outside, in the cool air, Rosa ran into the road and threw up in the gutter.

TWENTY-THREE

WHAT TO WEAR for an appointment with a dominatrix? The question had occupied him all day.

In the end, James settled for smart casual, in the form of a blue shirt and a pair of cream chinos, creased down the front. *You don't crease chinos, Jay!* Ruth had always said it made him look like an old fogey.

Guilty as charged.

He stood at the front window, awaiting the call girl's arrival, nervously fastening and unfastening the top button of his shirt on endless repeat.

Bloody Molly! He could swing for the woman. Why the hell had he agreed to go through with this charade?

He looked at his watch. One fifty-nine.

Urtė's framed photograph sat on the windowsill, her pretty face smiling sweetly. Ruth had brought the picture back from Lithuania after one of many desperate and futile trips she'd made to her home country to track down her friend. James had always tried and always failed to stop her wasting her money on flights and accommodation. The picture had been taken at a dance class they'd attended. Urtė wore a figure-hugging green sequinned ballgown. She had a hand on her hip and was smiling like she didn't have a care in the world.

James picked up the photograph and looked at her face close up. No matter how hard he tried, he still couldn't see the resemblance to Sandra Bullock.

The rumble of a car engine shook him from his thoughts, and he looked out to see a grey Chevrolet parking farther up the road. The glass was tinted, and, in any case, the car was too far away to discern the features of the occupants.

A striking blonde woman stepped out from the passenger side. Tall, slim; long black coat down to her ankles. She carried a black holdall.

James set Urtė's photograph on the sill and retreated from the window to await the doorbell. When it chimed, he took a deep breath before heading to the hallway.

Opening the door, he arranged his face into the most natural smile he could manage and offered his hand. 'James,' he said nervously. His nose twitched at the powerful aroma of sweet perfume. 'And you must be Roxie?'

'Yeah, Roxie,' the woman said coolly, ignoring his hand.

He stepped back and invited her inside. After stealing several furtive glances outside, he shut the door and turned to see Roxie halfway up the stairs.

He cleared his throat. 'Shall we … start in the living room, perhaps?'

Roxie shrugged and came back downstairs.

James showed her into the living room, where Roxie took in the beige and grey decor. *How many suburban three-bed semis does she encounter in her line of work?* he mused. She turned to give him a look that suggested the interior decorating wasn't her cup of tea, then set down the leather holdall on the coffee table, next to his neatly stacked pile of back issue *Runners World* magazines.

Christ. He gulped. *What's in the bag?*

He rubbed his sweaty hands down the sides of his trousers. This wasn't his scene at all. He had no taste for the erotic. James was your archetypal repressed, socially awkward Englishman. To his mind, sexual adventure was best left to the French or the Italians.

'Can I get you a drink?' James asked, abashed. 'Tea? Coffee?'

The look the sex worker gave him bordered on contempt. 'Roxie only drinks champagne,' she snarled.

'Right. Afraid I don't have any in.' He jerked a thumb in the direction of the kitchen. 'Might have a bottle of white in the fridge. Shall I go and check?'

'No!' she said with such assertion that James physically flinched.

Roxie unzipped her long coat to reveal the outfit beneath: black plunging V-neck corset; leather skirt; stockings; knee-high stiletto boots. He swallowed and felt the uncomfortable dry bob of his Adam's apple.

Roxie threw her coat over the DFS three-seater, placed her hands on her hips and looked him up and down. 'So, we do it here?'

James, rubbing his thumb over the opposing palm, glanced over her shoulder to the window. The neighbours were in for a shock if they happened to pass by.

Roxie's eyes—an icy blue—bore into his. The blue was so vivid that James wondered whether it was natural. Perhaps she wore contacts. In any case, he couldn't bear their scrutiny, so he shifted his gaze elsewhere.

And alighted on her cleavage. She'd applied some kind

of make-up—bronzer, he guessed—to make her small breasts appear bigger than they were.

'Look at Roxie,' she commanded. James obliged, flushed with fresh embarrassment, and Roxie continued. 'Your sister say you are nervous. First time. It's okay. Relax. Roxie doesn't bite.'

Well, *that's a positive, at least.*

He cleared his throat. 'Look. Can we just … talk?'

Roxie reacted to his request first with suspicion, then shrugged a disinterested acceptance. 'Talk? Really? Fine. What do you want to *talk* about?'

He motioned for her to sit down on the sofa.

The sex worker shifted her coat to one side and sat down, crossing one long slender leg over the other to the sound of creaking leather. James couldn't be sure if it was the boots or the corset.

He took the armchair opposite and leaned forward, elbows on knees, kneading his hands. How to start a conversation? After a long pause, he asked, 'So, Roxie. Been to Hertfordshire before?'

'No.'

'You're not missing much.' He gave a nervous chuckle. 'Weather could be better, don't you think?'

Roxie had no interest in his line of questioning and started to examine her scarlet fingernails. She yawned, making only a cursory attempt to disguise it.

'Look,' James said, shifting uncomfortably and running a hand through his hair, 'this is silly. I've no interest in this'—he circled his finger in the direction of her holdall— '*stuff*. And it's not my birthday.'

The sudden outburst of honesty felt good, like the release of trapped wind. The tension fell from his shoulders, but it had the opposite effect on Roxie. She stiffened and switched her attention from her nails back to James.

'I should explain,' James said. 'My sister—well, she's not actually my sister, but that's not really the point—got you here under false pretences.'

Roxie's eyes flitted nervously about the room, like she was tracking a trapped fly. Her hand moved to her coat.

'It's okay. It's nothing untoward. I'm looking for a missing woman.'

Roxie grabbed her coat and got to her feet. 'You tricked me. I leave.'

She went to snatch the holdall, but James, leaping up, clasped her wrist. She looked down at his hand and, trying to pull her arm away, said, 'You hurting me. Let go or I scream.'

James immediately released his grip and apologised. 'Hear me out, please. Her name is Urtė Cuda. Do you know her?'

Roxie shook her head. 'I leave now.'

'Wait!'

He dashed over to the window for Urtė's photograph and then showed it to Roxie. 'Do you recognise her? This was taken many years ago. She was my wife's best friend. They travelled to this country from Lithuania in search of a new life, but they were trafficked into the sex industry against their will. Separated on the day they arrived. Urtė hasn't been seen since.'

Roxie dropped her coat to the sofa and took the photograph. As she studied the picture, James noticed the faintest twitch of recognition. He knew she was lying when she handed him back the photograph and said, 'I don't know her. I can't help.' She went over to the window and peered out to the grey Chevrolet. 'I must go now.'

'*Please!*' James begged. 'You may not know her as "Urtė". Did you work with her? What was the name you knew her as? Where is she? Have you spoken to her?'

She turned to face him. 'Is this trick?'

'No!'

James took his wallet from his pocket and opened it, to show the woman the passport photo of Ruth. 'This is my wife. Her name was Rūta, which she changed to Ruth to fit in. She died in a car accident, and I made a solemn promise as she lay dying that I would find her best friend. Please help me.'

Roxie regarded Ruth's picture, chewing her lip. Eventually, she looked up at James. 'Are you policeman?'

'No,' he said, choosing not to embellish that answer. 'You're only asking me that question because you know something, don't you?'

'I go now. Time is up.'

Roxie went to push past James, but he held his ground, barring her exit. 'Look at this,' he said, taking out another image from his wallet. 'This is an ultrasound scan. Ruth was pregnant when she died. She was coming home from the clinic when she crashed the car.'

The woman paused, then stole a look at the image.

'It was a girl. She'd be three years old now. You know Urtė, don't you?'

Roxie nodded, almost imperceptibly.

'Where is she now?'

'I … I don't know.'

'Please. I'll make sure she's safe, I promise. That's my job.'

'No.'

'*Please*.'

Roxie hesitated for a moment before her shoulders dropped and her demeanour completely changed. She spoke softly, in almost a whisper. 'I know her as Alexia, not Urtė. I haven't seen her for a year. We speak on phone about once a month—'

'Do you have her number?'

'No. She calls me from different places. Holds back the number.'

'So, she's in hiding?'

Roxie stayed silent.

'It's okay. I know about her involvement with Geoffrey Fitzroy-Fergusson.'

Panic flashed across Roxie's features, and she shook her head furiously.

'Why does she call you, Roxie?'

The sex worker didn't respond, but her eyes were brimming with tears.

'She's scared, isn't she? She's alone in this world, and you're her only friend. Where is she, Roxie? Where is Alexia hiding?'

'I say too much already. I must go.'

'You know where she is, don't you? Tell me, and I can help her.'

'If he finds her, he will kill her,' she said flatly.

'Who? *Who* will kill her?'

Roxie's gaze shifted briefly to the window and then back to James. 'I don't know where she is. And that's the truth. All she say is she is in caravan. At seaside. I must go now. Time up.'

'The seaside? This country? Do you know where, precisely?'

'No. Sorry.'

There was the sudden noise of a car horn, and the woman visibly jumped. She wiped her eyes with the back of her hand and quickly gathered her belongings.

James followed as she rushed to the front door. 'What's your real name, sweetheart?' he asked as she grabbed the door handle.

'My name's Roxie. I already tell you.'

'You know, it doesn't have to be like this. You have options if you want to get out of your … *situation*.' He pressed a business card into her hand. 'Call me, please. If ever you need my help.'

She regarded the card for a beat or two, then shoved it deep into her coat pocket.

'Bye,' she said and fled from the house.

James watched at the window as the Chevrolet travelled up the road, repeating the registration number in his head. When it turned the corner, he went to the kitchen for a notebook and pen.

TWENTY-FOUR

THERE WERE SOME—NOT many, admittedly—advantages to being an ex-copper. One of them was having a little black book brimming with old contacts to tap up.

A quick call to a friendly young constable at Herts Constabulary quickly yielded the registered keeper of the grey Chevrolet: a Milush Kulik of 53 Whitehurst Road, Ashford.

Unfortunately, it took James the best part of a day, dozens of phone calls and a round trip to Ashford to establish that the name and address were fake.

So, he was back to square one. All he had to go on was the belief that Urtė was residing in a caravan someone on the coast. Perfect. Only thirty thousand kilometres to explore, then. Should keep him out of mischief for a while.

There was, however, another contact in his little black book that was worth a shot. Nothing to lose, after all.

The visitor's room at Her Majesty's Prison Blackford gave James the shudders every time he came here.

He sat with his elbows propped on the table, twiddling his thumbs, while he waited. The table, like the hard plastic chair he was sitting on, was fixed to the floor. The room was filling up fast, and loud chatter reverberated around the stark surfaces. He felt a headache brewing.

By rights, James should never have agreed to keep in touch. He could have forgotten all about Ian Murdoch; easily left him to rot in jail. His former superintendent was serving fifteen years after pleading guilty to a list of crimes as long as your arm: corruption; money laundering; perverting the course of justice; accessory after the fact to manslaughter … You name it, Ian Murdoch had done it.

But James was a charitable kind of fellow. He believed in the concepts of rehabilitation, redemption and second chances. And Murdoch wasn't one of these rotten-to-the-core types. A bit of moderate greed here, misguided loyalty there, a taste for the good things in life that could never be satisfied by a superintendent's salary, and he somehow found himself embroiled in covering up a manslaughter and framing an innocent man for the crime. That said, the "innocent" man was Troy Perkins, James's erstwhile tormentor. The wannabe serial killer had stolen his happiness, caused the death of his wife and wrecked his career. James had put the bastard six feet under after he'd abducted Molly and choked her to the brink of death.

At a table against the far wall, an auburn-haired woman—tall, attractive face, heavily pregnant—was engaged in conversation with a con. She took his hand and guided it gently over her bump, and the con smiled with obvious pride. James couldn't help wondering whether the kid's future was already blighted before it was even born. Naturally, James's mind drifted to the memory of Ruth and the fateful day of her car accident. How could he have been so pig-headed, so insensitive to her needs, so wrapped up in his work? He'd asked himself those same questions every day since. Driven himself to the brink of madness, thinking how different things would have been if he'd driven her to the clinic instead of letting her go alone. The reminders were everywhere.

Stop it. There's no point in living a life of what ifs *and if* onlys.

'You okay, James?'

Ian Murdoch, dressed in a prison-issue grey sweatshirt and jogging bottoms, stood before him.

'Yeah, sorry, Ian. Miles away. How's retirement working out?'

Murdoch smiled and sat down. The "retirement" thing was a running joke. 'Oh, wonderful. It's nonstop. Not sure how I ever managed squeeze in work, you know. And you? Keeping yourself busy?'

'Mustn't grumble.'

The small talk quickly petered out. Back in the day, Superintendent Ian Murdoch had been capable of talking for England. He was many things that James wasn't: collegiate; avuncular; a keen participant in office banter; larger than life.

But now, he was hugely diminished, and not just physically.

'Actually, there's a reason for my visit, Ian.'

Murdoch raised a sardonic brow. 'You surprise me.'

James explained the situation with Urtė and the possible link to Geoffrey Fitzroy-Fergusson's death.

'No way?' Murdoch said, confounded.

'I know. Sounds totally ridiculous, doesn't it? I was doubtful myself, but now I think there might be something in it.'

'So, how can I help?'

'Can you speak with Jack Tomkin?'

Murdoch grimaced. 'We're not exactly best pals, James. I tend to steer clear of him, for obvious reasons.'

There was no night and day with Tomkin; he was a proper bad apple—a despicable gangster. Last year, James and his team had rescued several trafficked women from an illegal brothel in Stevenage. After the brothel was busted and following a new lead, Murdoch had authorised a raid on Tomkin's premises, a recruitment agency in Peterborough. The agency operated ostensibly to recruit eager young workers from Eastern Europe to do the type of menial jobs lazy Brits turned their noses up at: fruit picking; vegetable packing; working the production lines in meat processing plants. But there was a more lucrative side to Tomkin's business: luring vulnerable young women into the sex industry against their will. During the raid, Murdoch's team had discovered a horde of passports belonging to the women rescued from the brothel, which proved Tomkin's complicity and sent the bastard down for ten years.

James was convinced, but had never been able to prove, that Tomkin was the guy who'd lured Rūta and Urtė to the UK fifteen years ago with the promise of work in the hospitality industry in London. The pair had landed at Robin Hood Airport, Doncaster, and a driver had picked them up and taken the girls to a remote spot where Urtė was snatched and bundled into a van, never to be seen again. Rūta, meanwhile, was drugged and taken to a derelict building in Letchworth, Hertfordshire, that had been operating as an illegal brothel.

James, then a lowly uniformed officer, had been part of the team assigned to bust the brothel. Thankfully, they'd rescued Rūta before the gang holding her had had chance to 'initiate' her. The thought of what might have been still sent shivers down his spine.

'I have no expectations he'll talk, but it's worth a shot. Can you have a go? Dangle the possibility of a favourable parole hearing if he provides information that leads to an arrest. He won't give a shit about the personal consequences for Urtė.'

'But *you* don't want her arrested, surely?'

'I want to *find* her, Ian. See what she has to say. If she's guilty, then, of course, I want her to pay for her crime.'

'That's what I've always admired in you, James: integrity. Shame there aren't more like you.'

'So, will you do it?'

'Leave it with me.'

'There's one more thing …'

'Which is?'

'Can you ask around and see if the name "Milush Kulik" means anything to anyone?'

After the visit, James felt the need to go to the gym, to expunge the stench of prison.

It was a cheap and cheerful place, occupying the first floor above a B&M store in his home town.

He'd joined, reluctantly, on his doctor's advice. His off-peak membership was cheap and meant he never needed to wait for any machine, but he rarely went. It was a reminder that he had too much spare time and too little work. And it was a reminder of his heart attack. His doctor had advised aerobic exercise—gentle, steady and regular—combined with strength exercises to rebuild his stamina and stretching to increase flexibility.

The advice rankled. The fact he'd even had a near fatal cardiac arrest rankled. It wasn't like James had been the typical heart attack candidate. He wasn't obese, a heavy smoker or a couch potato. He blamed it on stress;

overwork; the loss of his mother. And, of course, Troy Perkins.

There was no one else in the gym, which was unusually quiet. No thumping music, only the sounds of a muttering television and the clank of his barbell dropping into place.

After the weights session, James moved on to star jumps and burpee repeats. He watched himself in the mirror, watched his t-shirt rise as he jumped, exposing a stomach that had grown flabby on a diet of too many takeaways.

Ab crunches next.

Then the treadmill. He didn't want to think about Ruth, so he thought about Urtė, but then he didn't want to think about the search because it had frustratingly yielded so little. He dialled up the speed to fourteen kilometres per hour and let the exertion absolve him of the need to think about anything at all.

He was towelling himself down in the changing room after a long, hot shower when his phone buzzed within his sports bag. He pulled out the iPhone to see it was a with-held number calling. 'Hello?'

'Mr. Quinn?'

'Yes?'

'HMP Blackford. Are you okay to take a call from prisoner Ian Murdoch?'

Well, well. 'Yes. Put him through.' He paused for a moment. 'Ian?'

'James. I'll be quick, as I know you like to get straight to the point. That name you gave me—I mentioned it to Tomkin. He says he can't promise you anything, but—you know how it goes—he knows someone who knows someone who may know something.'

'And?'

'I've got a name for you: Alf Kealy.'

TWENTY-FIVE

JAMES PULLED up in the forecourt of Kealy Crash Repairs, got out of the Audi and zapped the central locking.

The garage was one of a number of businesses nestled in the arches of the viaduct. It felt like he'd pitched up on the set of *Eastenders*, and he half expected that bald Cockney thug with the gravelly voice to emerge from the shadows any second with a wrench in his hand and a maniacal glint in his eye.

Before setting off, James had taken the precaution of running a Disclosure and Barring Service check on Alf Kealy. He came back clean—no unspent or spent convictions, cautions, reprimands or warnings in existence on the Police National Computer—but that was no reason for James to lower his guard. Who really knew what the guy was capable of, or what Tomkin's true motive was for supplying Kealy's name?

His trepidation outweighed by intrigue, James started towards the workshop. *In for a penny, in for a pound*, he heard his mother's voice say.

He'd barely taken a step when a noise made him stop and turn.

It began as a low hum, soon a distant rumble and then, within seconds, a monstrous roar. The forces of hell breaking loose. Hunkering instinctively, a high-speed train thundered over the viaduct.

The train was gone in the blink of an eye, but the ringing in his ears lingered. How could anyone work in these conditions?

Right on cue to answer that question, a mechanic materialised next to the Audi. A slip of a lad—fifteen, sixteen, perhaps; dirty overalls hanging off his bony shoulders; face smeared with grease. The skinny lad looked down at the Audi's wheel arch, fingered the scratch, sucked his teeth, then said to James, 'Want us to fix that, mate? We'll have it looking like new in no time.'

'No, ta. Is your boss around?' James was here to do business with the organ grinder, not the grease monkey.

'Yeah, he's in there,' the lad said, flicking his head in the direction of the workshop.

James stepped through the wicket door entrance into a cavernous, echoey space. The high arched ceiling, the exposed brickwork, the pneumatic power tools, the radio at full blast, all conspired to create an atrocious din.

A disembodied voice from beneath the chassis of a classic Lotus was murdering the chorus of an Oasis hit.

'Mr. Kealy?' James shouted to a man at the rear of the workshop. He was well into his sixties, James guessed; short, trim for his age; tanned. He was smartly attired in a shirt and tie and clutched a clipboard with clean hands; all clues which screamed: "gaffer."

The man smiled and came over. He walked with a terrible limp, and as he got closer, James noticed a jagged scar etched on the side of his face. 'Call me Alf,' he said and shook James's hand with expansive good cheer. 'And you must be Little Bo Peep?'

'I'm sorry?' James replied, nonplussed.

'A little bird tells me you've lost a sheep and don't know where to find her.'

A middle-aged Cockney crook, speaking in riddles. His favourite kind. James feigned a smile. 'That's right.'

'Sheep, eh?' Alf Kealy said, rolling his eyes. 'Who'd have 'em?' He set the clipboard down on a workbench, then shouted down into the inspection pit. 'Hey, Malc? Turn that shit off, for Christ's sake. How's a man supposed to bloody think?'

Quite, James thought. Then a train roared overhead, triggering a chain reaction. Everything that wasn't screwed down—engine parts; tools; jars and tins—shook and clinked and rattled, like an earthquake had struck.

Once the noise had subsided, Alf Kealy said, 'Come into my office, Bo. Let's see what we can do about your sheep.'

He led James through to a small room at the back of the building and slammed the metal office door, muffling the din from the workshop. 'Take a seat,' he said, gesturing to a plastic chair.

James obliged while Alf Kealy perched himself on the edge of a large desk, strewn with mess: loose papers; dirty coffee mugs; stationery; box folders. James wondered what treasures lurked within the small, windowless room. Dodgy VAT returns? Fake invoices? Dead body encased in the concrete floor?

Not my concern anymore. Leave it.

'Drink, Bo?'

'I'm okay, thanks.'

'Nonsense. I'll get my secretary to bring you a coffee. It's no trouble.'

Alf Kealy got out his phone and tapped the screen. He held the phone to his ear for several seconds without taking his gaze from James. 'Malc. Bring our guest a coffee, will ya?' He covered the mouthpiece and looked down at James. 'How do you take it, Bo?'

'Black, no sugar.'

'She takes it black, no sugar. Make mine the usual. Cheers, Malc.'

James wasn't sure he had the patience for this nonsense. 'Look, I don't know what games you're playing here, Alf, and I'm not here to cause any trouble. I just want to find this woman.' He reached into his pocket for Urtė's photograph.

'*Games*, Bo?' Alf said, opening his arms in a gesture of innocence. 'We're mechanics. We fix smashed-up cars. We've got work coming out of our ears. I ain't got time for no games.'

James took a few beats to consider whether the double negatives in that sentence carried any deliberate meaning. He handed over the photo. Alf Kealy screwed his eyes and brought the picture close to his face, then regarded it at arm's length. 'Can't see a bleeding thing, Bo. Now, where are my specs? To think, it wasn't many moons ago that I had twenty-twenty vision.'

His glasses lay atop a copy of the *Express*, opened at the puzzle pages. James noticed a half-finished crossword. 'Never get old, Bo, that's my advice,' Kealy said, picking up the glasses. He shook out the temples with a flick of the wrist and fogged the lenses, then rubbed them slowly with the end of his tie. 'Now, where were we?'

Alf put on the glasses and scrutinised the photograph for a few moments. Stroked his chin. Took an exaggerated intake of breath. Then he shook his head and set the photograph down. 'The trouble with sheep, Bo, is they all look the bloody same. I suppose that's why farmers have to brand 'em? Tag their ears, or whatever it is they do.'

Right then, the door opened with a rusty squeak that made James flinch. The man who entered was so tall, he needed to duck through the doorway. Not a good sign. In one hand, he held two brimming enamel mugs, clinking against one another.

'Ah, refreshments,' Alf said. 'Cheers, Malc.'

Malc was enormous. In all directions. And completely bald. In fact, James noticed, he was *utterly* hairless: no eyebrows; no lashes; no stubble. Nothing. He handed out the coffees, first to Alf, then to James.

Alf took a noisy slurp from his mug, then set it down on the table. On the photograph.

James brought his mug to his lips, noticing that it was covered in greasy fingerprints. He sipped, blinked and shuddered.

'That good, Bo?' Alf enquired, looking over the top of his glasses.

'It's got a lovely note of engine oil. Castrol GTX?'

'Tesco's finest,' Alf said with a chuckle, before motioning to his colleague. 'Malc, check's Bo's pockets, will ya?'

'Righto, boss.'

James jumped to his feet. 'For Christ's sake! What's with this charade?'

Alf smiled. 'Relax, Bo. It's just a precautionary measure. I'm sure you understand?'

There's a third mug in this room, James mused. *Me*. 'I've got no interest in setting you up. All I want to know is where I might find Urtė Cuda. That's it. Straight down the line.'

'Malc?' Alf said, flicking his thumb at James. 'Do the honours, son.'

James figured he didn't have much choice but to

consent to a vigorous frisking. Malc found his phone, car keys, business card holder, wallet and his collection of assorted mint packets and threw them onto the table. Then he stepped back and stood with his arms folded, blocking the exit.

Alf Kealy took James's phone from the table and switched it off. He took a business card from the holder and made a fuss of examining it before smirking and throwing it to one side. After regarding the mints for a moment, he said to James, 'That's a lot of mints, Bo. Halitosis?'

'No. I've got an extreme sensitivity to smells. Hyperosmia. The mints help.'

'Smells, eh, Bo? Lucky for you, Malc's given himself a good squirt of Lynx Africa today. Between you and me, his natural odour is like being downwind of a landfill site.' Alf teased an Extra Strong mint from its packet and popped it on his tongue. 'Sit down, Bo,' he said, rolling the mint around his mouth. 'Take the weight off.'

James obliged begrudgingly.

Alf Kealy moved his mug away from Urtė's photograph, then turned the picture facedown. He raked through the crap on the desk and found a pen; a silver retractable ballpoint. He clicked out the nib and scribbled something down, then handed James the photograph. 'Check out an old associate of mine, Bo. We fell out many moons ago. Can't even remember what about now. Something out of nothing, probably. He might speak with you. Just don't tell him it was me who gave you his name, will ya?'

James looked at the photograph. On the back, Alf had scrawled: "ERROL FOSAND. CANTERBURY TIMBER LTD, UNIT 13, FALCON COURT INDUSTRIAL ESTATE. HEMEL HEMPSTEAD."

'Now, if you don't mind, Bo, Malc and I need to get back to work.' He winked at James. 'Good luck finding your sheep.'

James walked back to the car, seething at allowing himself to be patronized by a middle-aged crook and his hench-man. He should at least feel grateful, he supposed, not to have been castrated with an adjustable spanner.

As he reached into his pocket for his keys, the teenage mechanic intercepted him. The lad held a rag in his hand and a grin on his dirty face.

James looked down at the wheel arch. The scratch had gone; no trace of it whatsoever.

'Told you I'd have it like new, mister.'

'Well, thanks. But I did ask you not to …'

The boy sunk his hands into the pockets of his overalls, lifted himself onto the balls of his feet, then back down again. Chewed his lip.

James sighed. 'How much?'

'Ah, cheers, mate. Whatever you think is right.'

James retrieved his wallet and thumbed through the notes. 'Ten? Twenty?'

'I was thinking something like … I don't know … Forty?'

'Jesus Christ! It was only an inch-long scratch!'

'Workmanship like that don't come cheap, mate.'

James thrust two twenties at the boy, begrudgingly conceding defeat. 'Ever considered a career in the City, son? You'd make a bloody killing.'

A light rain fell as he trudged around Falcon Court Industrial Estate.

JR Scaffolding. Screwfix. Enterprise Rent-a-Car. Toolstation. He couldn't find Unit 13 for love nor money.

'Can I help you, mate?'

James turned to see a man sitting on a wall outside the front of Toolstation, puffing a cigarette. 'I'm looking for Unit 13. Canterbury Timber?'

The man took a long drag on his cigarette, then exhaled smoke into the sky. It swirled above his head. 'Unit 13, mate? You won't find it. There hasn't been a Unit 13 for three years. The timber merchants burnt to the ground, then they went into liquidation. The owner hadn't paid his insurance premiums. Or at least that's what I heard, anyway.'

'Oh?'

'One cigarette. That's all it took, apparently.' The man looked at his fag hand and smirked, then motioned to the scaffolding firm opposite. 'They've been there for the last year or so. It was renamed Unit 12A. Who'd want to rent 13 after what happened?'

James sighed. He took Urtė's photograph out of his pocket and turned it over. 'The guy who owned the timber merchants—was his name "Errol Fosand?"'

'Nah, mate. The guv'nor was a man called Alf Kealy.'

James felt the awful sensation of someone who'd just been made a fool of. His fingers curled into a fist.

'What's up, mate?' the man asked.

'I've just driven forty miles under false pretences, that's all.'

'Shame. Tell you what? We've got some great offers on impact drivers. Fancy taking a look?'

'No, you're all right.'

'Suit yourself, mate.' The guy dropped down from the wall and extinguished his cigarette underfoot. 'Catch you later.'

James looked down at the back of the photograph, staring at the name for a moment or so. Errol Fosand.

Then he remembered the half-finished crossword puzzle on Alf Kealy's desk and realisation dawned.

'For Christ's sake!' he hollered and kicked the wall.

TWENTY-SIX

THEY'D AGREED to meet at a "child-friendly" café in town.

Mel was tucking into a huge wedge of cake with great fervour whilst simultaneously bouncing the baby on her knee. The kid's big chocolate eyes bored into James, unnerving him. He fashioned his face into a smile. The kid's lip started to tremble, then the baby burst into tears, wailing like a banshee.

How could a person so small produce a sound so loud? James cast his eyes about the café, embarrassed, but no one else was batting an eyelid. Which is what "child-friendly" means, he supposed.

Mel calmly dunked a finger into her cake and shoved it into the baby's mouth, bringing instant pleasure to the kid and relief to James.

Were you supposed to feed cake to kids that age? He had no idea.

'So,' he said, after a forkful of brownie, 'how's life with …' He circled his finger at the baby.

'Harriet, guv. Your goddaughter, remember?'

'Yeah, of course. It was on the tip of my tongue. You know me and names.'

Mel rolled her eyes and smiled knowingly. She was more acquainted with his foibles than anyone currently alive. They'd worked together at Herts Constabulary for more than five years. His favourite detective by a country mile; not that he'd ever tell her, of course. Sweet of her to still call him "guv", though. Or perhaps it was just habit.

Mel nestled her mouth into the baby's thick nest of brown hair and gave her a noisy kiss. 'Wouldn't be without her. But, boy, is she tiring! Looking forward to getting back to work for a bloody rest! How about you? Busy?'

'Yeah, plenty of assignments to keep me occupied,' he lied. 'And now I have this new lead on Urtė, of course.'

'Exciting, hey? But do you think it's really her?'

'Maybe. I'm just following wherever the evidence takes me.' James looked at his watch. 'What's keeping Luke?'

Luke, now Mel's husband, was second on James's list of top detectives he'd worked with. They'd got off to an inauspicious start on the first case they worked together, breaking a sex-trafficking syndicate. James had assumed Luke was laddish and lazy, but Luke had quickly confounded his low expectations. Made him reassess his tendency to judge people on first impressions. But above everything else, James owed him an enormous debt of gratitude for saving his life after the heart attack.

'He's on his way from HQ now. Shouldn't be too much longer,' Mel said. 'No matter,' she deadpanned, 'we can just talk babies while we're waiting, hey?'

Horror flashed through James.

Mel laughed. 'Kidding!'

The child shoved two sticky fingers into Mel's cake, then brought them up to her face, smearing brown mess all over her nose, her cheeks, her hair, her ears, before eventually locating the intended orifice. When she finished, she let out a contented burp.

Mel sucked the kid's fingers clean and then demolished the rest of her cake.

James looked down at his half-finished brownie, turned up his nose and shoved the plate away.

'Don't judge,' Mel warned, dabbing the corner of her mouth with a paper napkin.

'Wouldn't dream of it.'

The waitress came over with their coffees and collected Mel's plate. 'Fancy another slice?'

'No, thanks. I'm on a diet. I shouldn't. Oh—go on, then. What the hell!'

Harriet giggled and slammed her fist on the table, depositing a brown print.

The bell over the door jangled and Luke strode into the café with his usual confident male swagger. He smiled when he caught James's eye.

'All right, guv? How's it going?' Luke kissed Harriet's head, then Mel's and sat down, placing a buff A4 document folder on the table.

The waitress came over with Mel's second portion of cake.

'That for sharing?' Luke enquired of his wife.

'Bugger off. Get your own.'

'Guess I'll have a slice, then,' he said to the waitress. 'And a tea. Earl Grey?'

'No problem. Be right back.'

James looked at the folder. 'So, what have you got for me?'

Luke pointed at the discarded brownie. 'Don't you want that, guv?'

'Be my guest.'

He snatched the plate and ate the brownie in two

mouthfuls before sliding the folder across to James. 'Take a look. I've only had chance to flick through it myself. The Met are happy to share this with you. It's not necessarily the full file. Obviously, they're keen for you to offer anything new; any alternative theories. They've been scratching their heads for months.'

The folder contained a bundle of papers, perhaps an inch or so thick. James thumbed through the contents, stopping at a black-and-white photograph. He pulled it out for further scrutiny: a grainy picture of a woman in a full-length coat, standing in a cobbled street, looking straight at the camera. She had a bag slung over her shoulder and what looked to be a pistol in her hand. James recognised it as the same picture posted by the press at the time of the murder.

He handed the photograph to Luke. 'Tell me, do you think she looks anything like Sandra Bullock?'

'*Sandra Bullock*?' Luke repeated, puzzled. He examined the picture for a few moments. 'Maybe. Difficult to tell. Why do you ask?'

'The housekeeper said that's who she reminded her of.'

Luke shared the picture with Mel.

'I can't really see it,' she said.

'Me neither,' James agreed. He then took out the copy of his own photograph of Urtė in the green dance outfit.

'What about this? See any resemblance between the two? Bear in mind they're taken fifteen years apart. The funny thing is, Ruth used to say Urtė looked a bit like Sandra Bullock, too. It can't be a coincidence, right?'

While Mel chewed her lip in concentration, the waitress came over with Luke's cake and tea.

'Ooh, lovely!' he said, rubbing his hands together with glee.

'Here,' Mel said to the waitress. 'Would you say she looks like Sandra Bullock?'

'What, from that film, *Miss Congeniality*?'

'I preferred her in *Speed*,' Luke added.

'*Two Weeks Notice*, all the way for me,' Mel said. 'What about you, guv? Favourite Sandra Bullock film?'

James sighed and addressed the waitress. 'Well, do you think she looks like her?'

The waitress shrugged. 'Maybe. There is something about the cheekbones, I guess. And the eyes. Any more for any more?'

'No, thank you,' James said.

The waitress cooed and fussed over the baby for a few moments, then left them all to it.

'So,' Luke asked, 'have you found anything useful so far?'

'Well, I've spoken to a woman who knew Urtė. Worked with her.'

'*Worked*? In what sense?'

James lowered his voice. 'She was a dominatrix.'

Luke's face lit up. '*Dominatrix*?' he echoed indiscreetly.

'Put your tongue in, Porter,' Mel said. 'This is a respectable establishment.'

James decided not to embellish the nature of his meeting with Roxie. 'The only thing she was able to tell me was that Urtė, if it is her, is living in a caravan, somewhere on the coast.'

'Which coast?' Mel enquired.

James shrugged. 'Dunno.'

'Well, *that* narrows it down …'

'Quite.'

'Anything else?'

James sighed. 'You know I see Ian Murdoch every now and then?'

'Yup. Don't know why you bother with that scumbag.'

'I sometimes wonder myself. Anyway, he squeezed a name out of Jack Tomkin. Alf Kealy. Runs a crash repair centre out near Milton Keynes.' James quickly relayed the story of his visit and the false lead, missing out the part about Alf Kealy having fooled him.

'I'd offer to dig for some dirt for you, guv,' Luke said, 'but you know how it is. No just cause.'

'Cheers, Luke. I understand. I did a basic background check on him, but nothing cropped up. Might do a little research myself—into his businesses, his public connections, that kind of stuff.'

Mel let out a big sigh and held Harriet out to Luke. 'Take her for a bit, will you? She's given me a dead leg.' She turned to James. 'So, if I was to summarise where you're at, you've basically got diddly squat to go on?'

James tapped the case file. 'Well, that's where I'm hoping this will come in useful. You never know, there might be something in here that's been overlooked. Perhaps a link to a coastal town?'

Mel raised a sceptical brow. 'What about the wife? What was her name? Felicity? I remember seeing her on the telly. As cold as ice. Didn't exactly seem the grieving widow.'

'I've been to see her.'

'What was she like in the flesh?'

'Princess Anne.'

'Stiff upper lip? Calls it as she sees it? Prefers horses to humans?'

'Yep. That just about sums her up.'

'Knew it! So, do you reckon she could have had a hand in it?'

'Seems a bit far-fetched. What's the motive?'

'Humiliated by her husband. Embarrassed by his

170

antics. She'd stood by him after the tabloid sting. He promised to behave himself. Then he did it all over again. If Luke *ever* did something similar, I'd hang him out to dry. A woman scorned, and all that …'

'Why would I want to even *look* at another woman when I've got you, my sweetness and light?' Luke said with a grin.

'Yeah, I get the theory,' James said, 'but the woman seemed pretty thick-skinned. Knew perfectly well what he was like; what he got up to.'

'Sounds very liberal!' Luke added.

Mel shot him a look, then returned her attention to the cake, attacking it with gusto, all the while absently twirling Urtė's photograph in the fingers of her other hand. She stopped when she noticed Alf Kealy's handwritten note on the back.

She frowned for a moment, then smiled. '*Errol Fosand*, guv? Seriously? Tell me you didn't fall for that?'

'Well …'

'What?' Luke said through a mouthful of cake.

Mel showed him the scribbled note.

'Oh, yeah,' he said, smiling.

'*Fool's Errand!*' Mel and Luke said in unison.

James could feel his cheeks flushing.

'It's bloody obvious, guv,' Mel said. 'Never watched *Countdown*? The conundrum at the end?'

Luke started to hum the theme tune while Mel used her cake fork to gesture the second hand of a clock, ticking down.

Of course he'd seen the programme, now he had oodles of spare time.

'*Hilarious*, you two! Don't suppose you've got some needle and thread so I can stitch my sides back up?'

Baby Harriet started to laugh, then her expression

changed to wide-eyed surprise, followed rapidly by concerted effort. Her face reddened, and there was a gurgling noise from her stomach before she created a stench of utter foulness. James's hand flew to cover his nostrils.

'Has she just done a …?'

'Bowels like her father,' Mel said. She rummaged in the bag under the table and threw a disposable nappy at Luke. 'Your turn to change her, big man.'

James snatched the case file, got to his feet and dropped a tenner onto the table. 'Right, I'm gonna have to love you and leave you … Got work to do.'

'Course you do, guv,' Mel said, unconvinced, handing him back the photograph. 'Catch you around?'

TWENTY-SEVEN

THE NEXT MORNING had dawned gloriously sunny, but James's mood was anything but.

In fact, the sun was bringing on a headache, so he pulled down the blind and switched on the desk lamp.

Better.

He took a sip of strong black coffee and sighed, then set down the mug atop the Fitzroy-Fergusson file. He'd already combed through it three times, and it was a pretty comprehensive dossier, so far as he could tell: witness statements; interview notes; crime scene photographs; forensics reports; telephone records—the lot. Frustratingly, there were no apparent holes in the Met investigation; no obvious leads they'd failed to follow; no alibis that hadn't checked out. And nothing hinting at a coastal location where he might find Urtė.

James took another look at the still taken from the CCTV footage, squinting at the blurred and grainy image. He really couldn't tell if it was her, nor could he make out the manufacturer and model of the weapon, which was a pity, as he'd developed quite an extensive knowledge of firearms from his stint as a sergeant, many years ago, in Organised Crime.

The image of the woman would certainly never hold up in court. The Met had spoken to the owners of the camera, the house opposite Fitzroy-Fergusson, and had obtained the recorded footage they'd stored on their home computer, which amounted to two external cameras—front and rear—after they'd suffered a burglary several weeks' prior. The footage, according to the police report, showed Fitzroy-Fergusson's arrival on foot at 11:47 a.m., then him greeting the suspect, who'd also arrived on foot, at 12:02 p.m. The next significant event was a taxi pulling up out front at 12:27 p.m. and a short female passenger climbing out carrying several bags of shopping at 12:28 p.m. This was consistent with Gabriela Rodríguez's statement that she'd been instructed to collect shopping at Fitzroy-Fergusson's request. Two minutes later, the suspect emerged from the house, noticed the camera, then seemingly fled on foot. Police were unable to identify the suspect on any other CCTV cameras in the vicinity. Only two other individuals had been present in the street at the time of the incident and neither had reported anything suspicious prior to, during, or after the incident.

Forensics had identified seven DNA profiles from trace evidence found at the crime scene. Four of the profiles matched, respectively, Mr. and Mrs. Fitzroy-Fergusson, their housekeeper, Gabriela, and her son Santiago, who, it seemed, frequently attended the property to carry out routine repair and maintenance tasks. Of the three remaining profiles, one was female and two were male. None matched the national DNA database and were never linked to specific individuals.

After another sip of coffee, his thoughts returned to Alf Kealy and Jack Tomkin. He'd been stewing about them all night, picturing them laughing at his expense, congratu-lating each other on the genius of their prank. God, he hated being made a fool of.

And he hated not having the police databases at his fingertips. Digging for dirt on Google was like cutting the lawn with nail scissors.

The keyboard, as usual, bore the brunt of his frustra-tion. James never had mastered the art of touch typing. Mel frequently used to mock his technique—a one-fingered jab—which, she said, was like watching a game of whack-a-mole.

He searched for any apparent connections between Kealy and Tomkin. Nothing. Although he found nothing to indicate Kealy had ever been arrested or questioned by the police, he did discover several online news articles covering the fire at the timber merchants. He was about to click on one when another headline grabbed his attention. He clicked the link to the article.

WOMAN DIES IN HORROR CRASH ON A508 AFTER BRAKE FAILURE

Jackie Kealy, 56 was travelling back home from a concert in Northampton with her husband when they crashed at 60mph near Yardley Gobion.

Jackie, who was driving, died instantly. Her husband, well-known businessman Alf Kealy, 58, suffered facial injuries after the airbags deployed, broken ribs, a smashed pelvis and a ruptured spleen.

The road was closed for several hours while emergency services worked at the scene. It reopened in the early hours of this morning.

Police believe that the crash occurred due to brake failure. No additional comment was provided.

. . .

That explains the scar and the limp, then.

After reading the article, James began to see Alf Kealy in a more sympathetic light. He knew too well the pain of losing a spouse in a car accident. He did wonder, though, if the brakes had been tampered with by someone who wanted to cause the Kealys harm. Frustratingly, Google yielded no further commentary on the outcome of the investigation.

James continued his search for useful intel on Kealy. He had no social media profiles, so far as he could tell. A search on the Companies House website revealed Kealy was the director of several businesses—mostly dissolved—including the defunct timber merchants in Hemel Hempstead. James made handwritten notes of each of the businesses, their addresses and the names of their other directors.

Next, he returned to the plethora of news articles covering the fire at the Hemel timber merchants. He clicked one at random and scanned the content to establish the key facts.

The fire crew had responded to an emergency call at 2:15 a.m. on the morning of Friday, April 19, three years ago. By the time the blaze was brought under control, the building was almost totally destroyed. The investigation team had established that the fire had started in the staff room. The only person present in the building that night had been a Mr. Hudson Loftus, a warehouse operative who had been working a night shift. Mr. Loftus had admitted to smoking during his break, and the investigation concluded that the cause of the fire was consistent with a cigarette not being properly extinguished. There had been nothing to suggest foul play and the police were not asked to investigate.

Mr. Alf Kealy, joint owner, was interviewed at the time,

and he'd stated that, unfortunately, the insurance policy had lapsed and the business would therefore have to be dissolved with immediate effect. His partner, Mr. Eric Pitcairn, had not been available for comment.

James smelled a rat.

A lowly warehouse operative on his Jack in the middle of the night? A conveniently lapsed insurance policy? Nothing to suggest foul play?

Pull the other one.

He typed *Hudson Loftus* into Google. Couldn't be many of them in this world, surely? Correct, he soon discovered. Google threw up a link to a Facebook profile, which James clicked on. A picture of a man flashed up on screen. He wore a red cap and a big grin, and in his outstretched hands was a huge fish. James guessed it was a carp, but the species of the fish was of no real interest.

Unlike the happy angler.

It was the chap he'd met outside Toolstation.

He dashed back to Hemel and burst into the store. Hudson Loftus looked up from behind the counter.

'Mr. Loftus?'

'Who's asking?'

'Remember me from the other day?' James jerked his thumb over his shoulder. 'I was enquiring about Unit 13. The timber merchants.'

Hudson Loftus smiled as the recognition dawned. 'Oh, yeah. Alright, mate?'

The smile reminded James of the Facebook profile picture. 'I was wondering if I could have a word? Somewhere private.'

The smile fell away, immediately suspicious. 'Why? You're not police, are you?'

'No,' James said. 'I'm looking for a missing woman, and I'm hoping you can help.'

'I don't know anything about any missing woman.'

'This won't take long, then. Please?'

Loftus hesitated for a moment, then shouted over his shoulder to an unseen colleague in the warehouse, asking him to hold the fort. He raised the counter hatch and led James through to a small, windowless office. James declined the offer of a drink and sat down at the round table, motioning for Loftus to join him. 'I understand you used to work at the timber merchants?' James asked.

'That's right.'

'And you were the only one in the building on the night of the fire?'

Loftus's gaze darted to the door, to the ceiling, to James. 'You said this was about a missing woman? What's the fire got to do with it?'

James took out Urtė's photograph and passed it to him. 'Her name's Urtė Cuda. She's been missing for over fifteen years. Recognise her at all?'

Loftus studied the photo for a few moments, then shook his head.

'Look,' James said, holding up his palms to face Loftus. 'I can tell you're apprehensive about my motives, so I'll just tell it to you straight. Urtė was my late wife's best friend, and I made a solemn vow that I would find her, whatever it took. I've no idea whether she's dead or alive. I just need to find out which. That's it. My enquiries have led me here. All I know is, there is some connection between the fire and Urtė. I don't know *what* that connection is, but I'm hoping you can help.'

'I ... I'm sorry. I don't think I can.'

'Are you married, son?'

'Yes. Five years.'

'Kids?'

'Yes. A boy and a girl.'

'Lovely. You'd go to the ends of the earth to keep them safe, to protect them, wouldn't you?'

He nodded.

'Thought so. You're a good man, Hudson. Now, tell me what happened on the night of the fire.'

Loftus shifted uncomfortably in his chair for a moment, then he spoke. 'It's like I said at the time, I was there to do a night shift. We had a big shipment come in from a supplier in Spain, and Alf asked me to get it ready for one of our major customers to collect the next morning. I'd been working four, five hours straight and I was desperate for a smoke. It was pissing it down outside, so I had a sneaky fag in the office. That's how the fire started.'

'And the insurance policy had lapsed, right?'

'Yes. Which is why Alf had to shut the business. The cost of replacing everything was too high. He had other businesses to fall back on, and, lucky for me, there was a vacancy here …'

James smiled. 'Lucky,' he repeated. 'Because a man like Alf Kealy certainly wouldn't want someone so untrustworthy, so reckless, working for him any longer, would he? How much did that cigarette cost him? A hundred grand? Half a million? He must have been pretty damn angry with you, hey?'

Loftus moved to get up. 'Sorry, I've not got much else I can tell you.'

James motioned for him to stay seated. 'Bear with me. I won't keep you long.' He leaned back in his chair and continued. 'Something doesn't ring true with me about the fire, Hudson. Mr. Kealy, so far as I can tell, is a very clever fellow. A highly successful businessman. Irons in many fires. I can't believe he'd allow an insurance policy to lapse, not with a business where its value is tied up in stock and premises.'

Loftus looked away, trying to settle his gaze on something, anything, rather than James.

James left the silence to gnaw at the man's conscience. Sure enough, Loftus eventually looked up to ask, 'Where are you going with this?'

'It definitely *was* an accident, wasn't it, Hudson? The cigarette? You only snatched a minute or two for a quick hit of nicotine. You were keen to get back to work. That's why you didn't stub it out fully. A bit of paper caught alight. So easily done. Bet you constantly relive that night, don't you? Ask yourself the same questions, over and over. *If only I'd given up smoking. If only it hadn't been raining. If only I'd been more careful extinguishing my fag.* That about right?'

Loftus frowned. James nodded his head slowly, prompting him to copy.

'Well, we all make mistakes. No point crying over spilt milk, as my old mum would say. But tell me this—was there an *upside* for Alf Kealy when the place burned down?'

Loftus shifted position in his seat and looked down at his restless hands.

'Come on,' James said softly, 'you'll feel a whole lot better after you've told me. What did Kealy have to gain from losing his business in that way?'

Loftus drew a deep breath, looked James in the eye, and began. 'If this all comes back to bite me, I'll deny everything. You got me?'

'Go on.'

'Understand that I don't know all the details. I was just a lowly warehouse operative. Alf was a good boss; he looked after his workers, paid us above the going rate. But he was involved in … dodgy dealings.'

'Such as?'

'Drugs. Cocaine. The shipments came in three, four times a year, to be stored in the warehouse. *Huge* quantities of the stuff. It was basically a distribution centre disguised as a timber merchants. The timber business turned a decent profit, but the real money was in the drugs. I didn't like it one bit, but what could I do?'

'So, what happened? Had Kealy got wind of a planned raid by the NCA?'

Loftus laughed nervously. 'No. He wanted out. Said he was getting too old for the game; wanted a simpler life. But the smugglers were having none of it. They told him he couldn't pull out of the deal.'

'I see,' James said. 'So, the fire provided an opportune way out. Shame about the insurance policy lapsing, though. Mind you,' he added wryly, 'at least no one was ever going to accuse him of insurance fraud!'

Loftus smiled awkwardly.

'Don't happen to know the names of these smugglers, do you?' James continued.

Loftus shook his head. 'I've already said too much …'

James got out his notebook and thumbed through its pages. 'Milush Kulik,' he said. 'Does the name ring any bells?'

There was a flicker of recognition on Loftus's face.

Again, James allowed the silence to do the work. 'That's an alias for one of them,' Loftus said resignedly.

'"*One* of them?"'

'The Panchenko brothers. Andric and Evgeni.'

'Mind if I make notes? I'm not good at remembering names.'

Loftus shrugged. While James scrawled the names, he asked, 'How did these guys react after their shipment went up in smoke?'

'No idea.'

'Imagine they were pretty cross with Mr. Kealy?'

'I guess …'

'Don't suppose you know if these guys smuggled anything else, do you?'

'Like what?'

'*Women*, for instance?'

Loftus shook his head, then looked at his watch. 'Sorry, I really must be getting back.'

'Of course,' James said, snapping his notebook shut and pocketing it.

They rose from the table and walked back through the warehouse.

The morning had turned out far better than James had imagined.

The radio was on, the sun was out and the visor was down. James tapped the catchy beat of an Aerosmith number on the Audi's steering wheel, mentally formulating a plan for the minute he got home.

He stole a glance at the box on the passenger seat. It contained a DeWalt cordless impact driver replete with two batteries and a twenty-five-piece combination bit set. He had no idea what he was going to use it for, but it had seemed like a genuine bargain and he was sure it would come in handy at some point.

The phone started to ring. A mobile number he didn't recognise.

He turned off the radio and engaged the hands-free. 'Hello?' he said with uncharacteristic cheer.

'Bo!' the caller said. 'Alf Kealy. Okay to talk?'

James's smile dropped. 'What is it?'

'Had any luck finding your sheep?'

'Is this urgent? I'm driving.'

'Won't keep you, Bo. I understand you've just been speaking to an acquaintance of mine. Hope he gave you a good deal on that DeWalt? It's an absolute belter! You won't be disappointed. Sorry about all the merry-go-round; Tomkin told me you were a tenacious little bugger, and you just proved him right.'

James started to fume. 'Get to the point, Kealy.'

'Fair play, Bo. Let me be crystal and spell out the deal …'

'I'm not making any deals.'

'Oh, I think you will. Thanks to me, you now know who stole your sheep, and it's only natural that you'll want to thank me. I'm not talking flowers or chocolates, Bo. Not my scene.'

'What do you want?'

'It's simple, really. I want you to bring me the bastards who killed my wife.'

TWENTY-EIGHT

ALF KEALY TOLD James to check out an old associate of
his, a man called Harold Whittaker.

As it turned out, Harold Whittaker was a recently
retired former detective inspector at Scotland Yard.

James had arranged to meet him at his home, deep in
the Essex countryside: a tidy bungalow sitting on an expansive and well-tended plot.

A cold front had brought torrential rain, making yesterday's sunshine seem like a distant memory.

'James?' Whittaker said genially when he opened the
door. 'Come in.'

James shook off the rain, wiped his feet on the mat and
hung his jacket on the coat stand.

Harold Whittaker had the air of a man who'd lived a
life of hard knocks. He was in his late fifties, with thinning
grey hair and crumpled grey skin. The bags under his eyes
were so pronounced, they looked almost prosthetic. The
faint whiff of whisky didn't surprise James, but the heavy
Yorkshire accent did.

He was led through to a room at the back of the

bungalow. The broody sky and the rain pounding the window conspired to make the room feel dark and unwelcoming.

'So, Alf Kealy sent you my way, did he?' Whittaker commented wryly. 'How is the old toerag?'

'He told me the pair of you have history. But when I did a background check on him, it came out clean.'

Whittaker gave a knowing smile. 'Do you know what we called him at the Yard? Teflon Kealy. Nothing ever stuck. The sly old dog knew exactly how to play the system. Expensive lawyers. Friends in high places. Evidence trails that always led to someone other than him. Guess you know the type?'

James smiled wryly.

'Can I get you a brew, James? Or maybe summat stronger? I know it's only eleven, but hey, who's counting?'

'Black coffee, please. If it's no bother.'

'Take a seat, pal. Won't be a tick.'

James sat at the large table, before a huge, partly finished jigsaw puzzle. The puzzle box lid showed a scene of lush hills and mirrored lakes. Beside it was a magnifying glass, a pair of reading glasses and a folded newspaper.

James teased the lid from the box and plucked a random jigsaw piece from the jumble inside. It looked to be uniformly green, so he examined it with the magnifying glass for any distinguishing marks. Nothing. Intrigued, he tried to see if he could find its place in the incomplete picture.

He'd got nowhere when the former DI came through and set down the drinks.

'Been doing that wretched thing for months now,' Whittaker said. 'The wife bought me several of the buggers off Amazon. Thinks they'll keep me out of mischief. Look at it! It's just a mass of greens and blues!

Hundreds of near identical pieces. I'll get it done, though. Won't let it beat me. You a puzzle man, James?'

James threw the piece back into the box. 'Not really.'

Whittaker dropped into a chair opposite and took a sip from his mug. 'You'd think it would be satisfying, wouldn't you, completing a five-thousand piecer? All that effort; the painstaking work; the tantalising promise of elation when the final piece slots into place. But in the end, it's not like that at all. In fact, it's a bloody anti-climax. You sit there and ask yourself, "why did I go to all the bother?" A bit like police work, eh?'

James masked his irritation with the tortured metaphor and smiled agreeably. 'So, you were in the Flying Squad?'

'Thirty years, pal. And you used to be a DCI?'

'Correct. Major Crimes, Hertfordshire.'

'And now you're a PI?'

To James, it sounded more of an accusation than a question. Or maybe it was just him being paranoid. 'Yes. Well, kind of. I do the odd assignment. Insurance fraud, debt recovery, that kind of thing.'

'Interesting career choice. Much money in it?'

'I'm not in it for the money. Mind if we get down to business?'

'Not at all.' Whittaker leaned back in his chair and laced his fingers across his stomach. The posture reminded James of Ian Murdoch, back in the day.

'Tell me about the Panchenko brothers.'

Whittaker's eyebrows furrowed. 'They're identical twins. A right pair of hard bastards. Imagine the Kray brothers—the awful violence, the dangerous charisma. Well, take away the charisma and … You get the picture. Armed robbery. Drug smuggling. Fraud—'

'Human trafficking?'

'Not as far as I'm aware, but I wouldn't put it past 'em.'

'With that charge sheet, why aren't they already inside?'

Whittaker smiled. 'Good question. Despite our best efforts, we were only ever able to pin relatively minor offences on them. Petty theft. Personal drug use. Assault. Most they ever got was two years, and even then, they were released early for good behaviour. The bloody irony! Anyway, a couple of years back, we were confident of getting them put away for life after an armed raid on a jewellers in Clapham. But—in one of life's little mysteries —the key witness disappeared and the case collapsed before it got to court.'

'Where are they now?'

'Well, they kept their heads down; slipped off our radar. They've always moved about, never staying in one location for very long. You know how the game works. Anyway, we were pretty confident they were living in the Camden area, so when a member of the public reported a group of men bundling a suspicious item into a van outside a block of flats in Kentish Town three months later, we took an interest. And when I say suspicious, I mean a body, of course.'

Whittaker paused to drink, then continued. 'The property—a basement flat—had been stripped bare and cleaned when uniform got to the scene. Neighbours said a couple had lived there for a few months. Kept themselves to themselves. The landlord was interviewed, but the tenants' names and details turned out to be fakes. But the description he gave matched Evgeni Panchenko.'

'If the brothers are identical, how can you be so sure?'

Whittaker chuckled. 'It's fairly easy to tell them apart when one has a scar across the eyebrow and the other has two fingers missing from his left hand.'

'I see. Don't suppose the fake name was Milush Kulik?'

'I wouldn't remember something like that, pal. I'm not great with names.'

James smiled. 'You and me both! Was a body found?'

'No. Nothing. And there was no effort made to look for one, either. No one was ever officially reported missing, and who's to say it wasn't a roll of sodding carpet they'd thrown into the van?'

'And when was this?'

'It'll have been about twelve months back, give or take. Not long before I retired.'

James showed Whittaker's Urtė's photograph. 'Recognise her at all?'

Whittaker put on his reading glasses and studied the picture with great interest. 'She's a belter, all right. But no, she's not ringing any bells. You think she's somehow involved with the Panchenkos?'

'It's looking that way. If I email you a copy of the picture, could I ask you to send it to your former colleagues in the Met for me? See if anyone recognises her?'

'Sure thing. I'll give you my email address.'

'One more thing, Harold. Did the Panchenkos ever come up in the context of the Fitzroy-Fergusson investigation?'

Whittaker shifted his glasses to sit atop his head. 'No,' he said. 'Not as far as I know. Murder investigations weren't exactly my wheelhouse, but given our experience with the Panchenkos, the Flying Squad would have been drafted in as extra bodies on the footwork if they'd been involved. Why? You got summat to connect 'em? My colleagues would be *very* pleased to hear about that!'

'Well,' James said. 'Let me tell you what I know …'

TWENTY-NINE

MOLLY WAS at her desk at HQ, watching YouTube and listening through her earphones.

The Daily Chronicle occupied the top three floors of a gleaming twelve-storey, glass and steel building in South-wark, on the bank of the Thames. From her desk, Molly had a glorious view of London's finest sights: Tower Bridge; the Shard; Tate Modern; City Hall; the Millennium Bridge. What a contrast to the *Hertfordshire Evening Herald!* Her erstwhile workplace was on the second floor of an out-of-town concrete monstrosity, earmarked for demolition. There, if you stood at the window on tiptoes and squinted hard enough, you could just about make out the Pets at Home superstore on the far side of the busy dual carriageway—and nothing much else.

Occasionally, Molly's mind would slip back to her time as Chief Crime Reporter (what a joke that title was; she'd been the *only* crime reporter!) She still missed some of her old colleagues; Kelvin, in particular. What a darling. She kept in touch via email and the occasional text message. That aside, she didn't miss the paltry pay and certainly not that prick of an editor, Brian. Last she'd heard, he'd taken early retirement to indulge his hobby of life drawing. Molly pictured the poor, unsuspecting model: a Rubenesque grandmother in her sixties, disrobing her size 18 gown and reclining in the chaise longue to present her every fold and crease to the scrutiny of that pervert and his quivering charcoal stick. Molly shuddered at the very thought.

No, she'd *definitely* made the right move in leaving. Should have done it years ago. Yes, the work was tough and the hours were long, but she loved it. Investigative journalism was her calling in life, even if it did feel, at times, like she had imposter syndrome. So many of her new colleagues came from far more privileged backgrounds; plummy private school accents and double-barrelled surnames abounded. Everyone to a tee was possessed with an inner self-confidence—or so it seemed. Molly was superficially confident; her self-assuredness was really just a front, a bold and brash shell she'd constructed over the course of her life to stop others from seeing through to the wreckage of insecurity, self-doubt and loathing that bubbled inside. She blamed her mother, of course.

Molly had taken the opportunity of a lull in the cash-for-access investigation to conduct some research on Nancy Patterson, the great aunt she'd never heard of until good old Cecil G. had revealed her existence. A few minutes of judicious googling had unearthed a veritable treasure trove. Molly was staggered to discover that Nancy had been a feminist trailblazer, smashing through numerous glass ceilings as she forged a successful career in the male-dominated fields of intelligence and scientific research.

Molly learnt this from a regional television interview she was now watching for the second time. Conducted way back in the eighties, as Nancy approached retirement, the interview had now been uploaded onto YouTube for posterity.

Nancy was a somewhat reluctant interviewee, publicity shy and self-effacing; someone who preferred to let her work speak for herself. (*'I've always held the view that it is better to want to* do *something than to* be *someone.'*) Elegantly dressed and smartly made up, Nancy spoke in a crisp, cultivated accent; her tone was warm and engaging. A casual observer would never had guessed that she had grown up in a working class environment in London's East End. She had lived through the Blitz and, shockingly, had lost just about every member of her family. After narrowly escaping death herself on more than one occasion, Nancy had joined the Women's Voluntary Service as soon as she was old enough. And, later still, she had been stationed at an anti-aircraft battery outside Great Yarmouth.

She'd never married or had children. '*It wasn't to be,*' she said to the interviewer, without any hint of bitterness. '*I suppose I just threw myself into my work. After everything that happened during the war, you realise how precious life is. You can't waste a moment.*'

After the war came a decade-long stint at MI5. Of course, she declined an invitation to divulge any interesting titbits. After MI5, she'd trained as a scientist and had gone on to work in cutting-edge research on childhood diseases, spearheading an Anglo-German joint venture that had made medical breakthroughs and saved countless lives. The interviewer suggested to Nancy that she was entitled to harbour a grudge against Germans, given the devastating loss she'd suffered during the war. Nancy gave short shrift. '*My gripe was with the Nazi regime, never the German people, who I invariably find are polite, industrious and conscientious.*'

Molly slumped in her seat and pulled out her earphones. 'What a woman!'

'Talking about me again, Molly?'

Molly spun around in her chair to see Nandita standing there in her coat, her handbag slung over a shoulder. Immaculate hair. Flawless skin. Effortlessly gorgeous. They'd struck up a friendship in the smoking area not long after Molly had joined the *Chronicle* and had been joined at the hip ever since. Unlike Molly, Nandita's skin showed no sign of smoking damage. *Bloody cow!*

'*Nands!* You startled me!'

'Ready?'

'For what?'

'Lunch, of course. Everything okay, Moll?'

Molly looked at her watch. 'Is it that time already? Sorry, Nands, bloody miles away.'

They were heading for a well-earned lunch at Wagamama's, five minutes up the road, to celebrate the success of the cash-for-access investigation. She locked her computer screen, snatched her handbag and pushed herself out of her chair. 'Let's do this.'

Moments later, they were walking along traffic-clogged Dock Street when an ATM caught Molly's eye. 'Give us a minute,' she said, stopping abruptly. She wanted to check if the inheritance had come through. It was supposed to clear today, but there was no sign of it when she'd logged onto her online account first thing this morning. She wasn't going to let herself believe it was true until she saw it in black and white.

She put her bank card in the slot and entered her PIN, then requested a printed balance. Tapping her fingers impatiently, it seemed an age before the slip finally came out. When she read it, she had to blink. Yep: over three hundred grand. She looked around to check if anyone could have observed her, then quickly stuffed the slip in her handbag and returned to Nandita.

Nandita looked concerned. 'What's wrong?' she asked. 'You're shaking like a leaf.'

'Tell you later, mate.'

Molly's brain was doing somersaults as they carried on along the road, thinking about the money; her father; Nancy; family secrets. She tried to calm herself by composing a mental checklist of what she could do with the cash. Pay off the mortgage; the car loan. A nice holiday somewhere. Squirrel some away for a rainy day. Treat herself and her friends.

Yes, she'd start right now. 'How about we scrap Waga-mama's and go to Methuselah's instead?'

Methuselah's was, by common consent, the best champagne bar in town. Located in the converted cellar of an old Grade I listed building on Pall Mall, it oozed raffish charm with its vaulted ceilings, exposed brickwork, plush velvet seating and long, wood-topped bar.

Molly carried the drinks over to Nandita, who had nabbed a small round table in a cosy corner. Nandita took her flute of Bolly with gratitude and raised it to her lips. After an obviously satisfying sip, she said, 'Coco Chanel famously professed to drinking champagne on only two occasions: when she was in love, and when she wasn't.'

Nandita was fond of peppering conversation with quotations.

'And very wise, too,' Molly said, taking her seat and raising her glass. 'To Coco!'

'To Coco!' Nandita echoed, and they clinked glasses. She took another sip, then enquired, 'So, are you in or out of love at the moment? I can't keep up.'

Molly mockingly blanched. 'I've taken a vow of

chastity, you know, after what happened with He Who Shan't Be Named.'

'*Pah!*' Nandita scoffed, almost spitting out her drink. 'I don't believe *that* for a second!'

'It's true! I mean it. I've had it up to here with men.'

'What about that detective friend of yours? You're always on about him. He's still single, isn't he?'

Her glass barely an inch from her mouth, Molly almost sprayed the table with Bollinger. 'James? You're having a bloody giraffe! Don't get me wrong, I love him to bits, but this table's more capable of expressing its feelings.'

Nandita laughed. 'And what about the dating agency? Still on their books?'

'Lucy? Binned her. Utterly bloody useless.'

'You should try Tinder. Drag yourself into the twenty-first century, Moll! That's how I met my Rocco.'

'I told you,' Molly said, 'I've had it with men. Now, can we please change the subject?'

Nandita glanced briefly over Molly's shoulder, then leaned closer and lowered her voice. 'Don't look, but there's a chap in the corner who can't stop staring at you. He is, like, seriously *hot*.'

'Really? No. You're pulling my leg.' Molly tucked a strand of hair behind her ear, sucked in her tummy, pushed out her tits, then stole a surreptitious look to the corner. The table was unoccupied.

She turned back to find Nandita smiling. 'Chastity, my arse, Molly.'

When Molly flashed her an unimpressed look, Nandita was contrite. 'Hey! I'm sorry for being so insensitive. Your luck will change soon. I just know it.'

Molly sighed and drained her drink. 'Shall we get a bottle?'

'Well … I've got a couple of meetings this afternoon … and I really ought to be making a start on—'

'Get a bloody grip, woman!'

Molly raised an assertive hand and quickly caught the attention of the sommelier; a gorgeous, black-haired man, immaculately attired in a shirt and waistcoat combo. He had a sun-kissed, southern European look about him. About twenty years her junior, damn it.

He swiftly came over to their table, flashing an attentive white-toothed smile.

'A bottle of your finest Dom Pérignon, if you please, kind sir,' Molly said, putting on an exaggeratedly posh accent.

The sommelier gave a little bow of his head. 'Certainly, madam.'

As he turned towards the bar, Molly placed a hand on his arm. 'In fact, make it a magnum.'

'*Molly!*' Nandita protested. 'I can't go splashing the cash like this.'

'Don't worry, Nands, this is on me. I've come into a little windfall, you see.'

'*Ooh!* Tell me more!'

Molly rifled through her handbag until she located the balance slip and slid it across the table to Nandita, then watched her jaw drop.

'Bloody hell, Moll! Have you won the lottery?'

'Wish it was that simple. No, it's an unexpected inheritance. From my estranged father.'

'Oh, sorry, I didn't even know.'

At that moment, the sommelier returned, brandishing the champagne and an ice bucket. He placed the bucket on the table and, after performing an elaborate cork removing routine, filled their glasses, then stowed the bottle in the bucket and waited for Molly to give her nod of approval before departing.

Molly swallowed half a glass, then proceeded to regale Nandita with the story about her father, the inheritance and the revelation that she had a semi-famous great aunt living on the Norfolk coast. As she spoke, she realised how fanciful the tale sounded. 'There's clearly some huge family secret,' she confided. 'I always thought my mother drove him from our home and never allowed me any contact because she was a nasty, manipulative bitch. I resented her for the rest of her life. But I'm starting to think it was something altogether more complex. That she was protecting me from the truth. Why would he be living under a new identity? He was meant to be an *electrician*, for Christ's sake!'

Nandita's hand flew to her chest. 'God! You don't think he was a paedophile, do you? Maybe after he served his sentence, the authorities had to give him a new identity; sent him into hiding to protect him from being lynched?'

Molly looked aghast. '*Nands!*'

'Sorry. You know me and my overactive imagination.'

'To be honest,' Molly said after another sip of champagne, 'the thought has crossed my mind. I couldn't *bear* it if that turned out to be the truth.'

Nandita took Molly's hand in hers. 'Might not be?'

'I've also wondered if he was in the intelligence services. The whole electrician thing might have just been a charade; a cover. Kind of makes sense now I've found out Nancy Patterson worked for MI5. Maybe it's in the Tindall genes? It certainly aligns with me being a journalist. You know, a desperate yearning to expose the truth …'

'And the solicitor can't tell you more?'

'Oh, believe me, I've tried. Says he's bound by confidentiality.'

'Other family members?'

'No one. They're either dead or moved overseas decades ago.'

'*Hmm*,' Nandita mused. 'If you want my advice, go and see the old woman. Even if it turns out your old man was a kiddy fiddler—'

'*Nands!*'

'Sorry! What I mean is, I always think it's better to regret something we *did* than to regret something we *didn't*.'

'Very sage.'

'Not my words. Sydney J. Harris.' She paused, then added, '*Chicago Daily News*.'

'Niche. I suppose he's right. Think I'll chew on it. Talking of chewing, do you think we ought to get some olives to line our stomachs?'

Nandita grimaced. 'Olives? Can't stand them.'

'Me neither.'

They both laughed. Molly lifted her glass to her lips, and Nandita said, 'There comes a time in every woman's life when the only thing that helps is a glass of champagne.'

Molly raised a quizzical brow.

'Bette Davis,' Nandita clarified.

THIRTY

SOMETHING WOKE HIM.

It took James several seconds to realise that it was his phone. He fumbled for it on the nightstand and forced one eye open to see who it was.

No Caller ID.

Who the bloody hell was calling at this time? Two in the pissing morning!

He accepted the call. 'Hello?' he grunted.

No one answered. The only sound was the crackle of a bad connection. He should have just left it, but now he was annoyed and wanted to give whoever was calling a piece of his mind. Probably a nuisance call from overseas. 'Who is it?' he demanded. 'Don't you know what time it is?'

A tiny, distant voice answered, the words unintelligible.

'I can't hear you!' James barked.

'Mr. Quinn?' The voice was louder this time. A woman with a heavy accent.

'Who's asking?'

'Roxie. Remember me?'

Roxie? Roxie? Oh, yes! Suddenly alert, he sat upright and

switched on the bedside lamp. 'What is it? Where are you? Are you in danger?'

'I think something's wrong. With Alexia.' Roxie spoke quickly. 'I've been worrying for days. She didn't call. She always call. I should have tell you but—'

'Slow down please, Roxie. You need to give me more information. I can't do anything unless you tell me where I can find her.'

'I don't know. That is truth.'

'Then how can I help her? Let me come to you so we can speak. Tell me where I can find you.'

'*No!* That is not possible. I have number. You might trace her with it. It was the first time she call me, after she escape from London, after she kill ... no, after ... I mean—'

'Fitzroy-Fergusson? So, she *did* kill him. Why?'

'*No!*' Roxie said assertively. 'The newspapers get it wrong. Alexia didn't ... It wasn't ... I can't ...'

For the sake of clarity, James tried to help. 'You mean it was an accident? Or was she acting under the instructions of somebody else? Come on, you can tell me.'

'No! I *can't.*'

'Please, Roxie. This is really important. Tell me *everything.*'

He heard a background noise on the line and Roxie started to speak hurriedly. 'I can't talk now,' she said. 'I give you number. It's—'

'Wait!' He raked through the nightstand drawer for a pen. 'Go on.'

Roxie reeled off the number, which he scribbled down. A landline. The dialling code was 01493; not one he recognised.

'Find her, please,' Roxie pleaded.

And hung up.

THIRTY-ONE

THE NUMBER ROXIE gave him belonged to a pub called the Sailor's Tavern in Great Yarmouth. When James called later that morning, at eight, a cleaner answered. He reeled off the names Urtė and Alexia and gave a description, but the woman said it meant nothing to her and hung up before he could ask any more questions.

He should have called back and persisted. Instead, he spent the rest of the morning producing a batch of missing person flyers and packing a small suitcase for a mini-break on the east coast of Norfolk.

It was late afternoon by the time he arrived at the Sailor's Tavern. The pub was situated in the dockland area on the south side of town, an area which looked well past its heyday, if, indeed, it ever had one. There was a sign outside that said: "GOOD FOOD SERVED HERE". That usually signified traditional pub grub cooked from frozen: scampi and chips; lasagne; meat pie. The sort of fare his late mother had served at the Royal Oak, in times long past.

Biker types—studded leather garb; beards dangling at

mid chest; beer guts—hovered around in groups out front, smoking, guzzling pints and conversing at an unnecessarily high volume. Music blared from inside.

As James stepped through the door, the music stopped. The bar fell silent, and the patrons all turned in unison to stare down the stranger in their midst. Well, not exactly, but it was that kind of place.

James stood at the bar, patiently waiting his turn to be served. The barmaid was a hardened blonde; the type of woman who would take on any man in an arm-wrestling contest and win without even breaking a sweat.

After fleeing London Urtė had, for whatever reason, come to Great Yarmouth and had then called her friend to let her know she was safe.

James scanned the room for any sign of a telephone. Nothing in the public bar. He peered through a doorway into a hallway behind the bar. Nothing there, either. Perhaps it was in the flat above the pub?

His mind fired questions faster than the bikers could rev their choppers outside. Why did she call from here? Why risk giving away her location? Maybe she didn't realise she was? Was she desperate, not thinking straight? In fear for her life? Why this particular pub? It wasn't close to anywhere in particular, like a railway station or a coach stop. Perhaps that was the point. Was she working here at that time? Living here? *Looking* for work? Why had she come to Great Yarmouth, of all places? How did she get here? How long had she been here before calling Roxie? Was the plan to board a boat and flee to the continent? Had something gone wrong?

The more unanswerable questions he asked himself, the more they multiplied.

Finally, the barmaid turned to him and disrupted his frenzied train of thought. 'What can I get you, love?'

At last, a question he could answer. 'Pint of Guinness, please.'

'Haven't seen you before,' the woman commented as she pulled the pump. 'New in town?'

'Just visiting.'

'I'm Trudie.'

'James.'

'What brings you here, James?'

He took out one of the flyers from his pocket and showed it to Trudie. 'Do you recognise her?'

She squinted at the picture. 'Can't say I do, love. Who is she?'

James explained the story as succinctly as he could, without giving reference to the murder. 'Some people say she looks like Sandra Bullock,' he added.

Trudie shook her head. 'Sorry, love. It's not ringing any bells. Do you want me to ask around for you? You never know.'

'Thanks. I'd appreciate it. Perhaps you could put up the flyer at the bar?'

He gave her his business card for good measure.

'*Ooh*,' she clucked. 'A private detective. I've never met one of those before.'

'Do you have a landline in the pub?'

'In a room at the back.' Trudie held up his business card. 'How am I going to call you if you haven't got your own phone?'

'It's not that. I believe the girl used it to call a friend. She would have been distressed.'

Trudie gave James his pint. She chewed her lip for a few moments, then said, 'The landlord, Vince … He might know something. Bet he'd remember a pretty face like hers.'

'Good. Is Vince around? Can I speak to him?'

'Afraid not. He's in hospital. I'm visiting him tomorrow. I can ask him then, if you like?'

'Thanks. I appreciate it.'

'He's having treatment for cancer. Liver. Occupational hazard, I guess!'

'Sorry to hear that.'

'He'll pull through. He's a stubborn sod.'

'Married?'

'*Ha!* No! There's no woman desperate enough to have him. Why do you ask?'

'It would be really useful to get permission to release his phone records. It's a long story, but it'd help to identify the number the girl called.'

James hoped he didn't have to explain further. Luckily, Trudie seemed the trusting type. 'I can do better than that, love,' she said. 'Vince keeps every scrap of paperwork. He has itemised bills. Credit card statements. Receipts. Goes through everything with a fine-tooth comb. He's as tight as a duck's arse. When I get a quiet moment, I'll go and dig out the paperwork for you. Vince won't mind. Well, he won't know—cos I won't tell him!'

'If you're sure?'

Trudie frowned and cocked her head to one side. 'You're not one of those con men, are you?'

James smiled warmly. 'I can assure you I'm not. I was a police officer for twenty years. Hertfordshire Constabulary. Major Crime Unit. I can prove it, if you like?'

Trudie waved her hand and smiled. 'You're all right, love. I'm only teasing. I can tell you're the honest type. Call it female intuition.'

A door to the side of the bar opened and a young girl came through, carrying a tray of food. He caught a pleasant waft of hot, salty chips as she hurried past.

'Couldn't order some food, could I?'

'Of course, love. Make yourself comfy and I'll get you a menu.'

'Trudie!' an impatient voice hollered from the other end of the bar. One of the fat bikers, brandishing an empty pint glass.

'Keep your wig on, Flash!' Trudie said. 'I'll be with you in a minute.'

'*Flash*?' James queried.

Trudie leaned in and said through the corner of her mouth, 'His real name's Desmond, but keep that one to yourself, love.'

After a hearty meal that far exceeded his expectations, James made his way to the bed and breakfast he'd booked over the phone with the landlady, Mrs. Elliott. Three nights for the price of two. Eighty quid, in total, including a full English.

Hillcroft House was freshly painted in mint green and adorned with attractive hanging baskets on either side of the entrance. It was, like its neighbours, five stories from basement to attic. Most of the neighbouring properties were also guesthouses, but none were a match for Hillcroft House's neatness. He imagined his houseproud mother in the afterlife, nodding her approval.

The small car park to the rear, was accessed by a long, narrow gravel track. There was just enough manoeuvring space for him to reverse the Audi into a gap between a knackered old Mondeo and a Renault people carrier. He grabbed his suitcase from the boot and made for the B&B.

He pushed open the door and stepped into the potpourri-scented hallway, where a wiry woman stood behind the front desk. Mrs. Elliott, he presumed. She wore an old-fashioned floral dress and spectacles attached to a chain. A radio was playing in the small back office. She was busily scrawling on a piece of paper; too engrossed to register his arrival, it seemed. Or perhaps she was hard of hearing.

James cleared his throat.

Mrs. Elliott gave a sideward glance at the reception bell, which bore a sign that said: "RING FOR ATTENTION". She returned her own attention to the piece of paper. A shopping list, he realised.

Bemused, he jabbed his palm at the bell. Twice. Very satisfying. Immediately, Mrs. Elliott put down her pen and looked at him over her spectacles. 'May I help you?'

'I'm here to check in.'

She reached under the counter and brought out a red ring binder. 'Your name?' she said, leafing through the binder.

'James Quinn.'

'You said you'd be here by five.'

He looked at his watch. Six thirty. 'That was just an educated guess. The traffic was awful. Does it matter?'

'I see. And you're using the car parking facilities, yes?'

'Correct.'

'In which case, may I take the registration number and a copy of your driving licence?'

'Really?'

The woman peered over her glasses and smiled thinly. 'Insurance,' she said, by way of explanation.

James relayed the Audi's registration number and then reluctantly handed over his licence, which she took into the office. 'Follow me,' she said once she emerged. His protest that he was perfectly capable of finding his way to the room went ignored.

He was led through the hall, where a table displayed an assortment of leaflets about local tourist attractions. Off the hall was the breakfast room, where he could see tables set for the morning. Three steep flights of stairs took him to a stuffy attic room. The room was clean and tidy but austere: a double bed; a small corner wardrobe; a cast iron fireplace with a vase of dried flowers inside; a nightstand and lamp; a chest of drawers with a kettle and bowl of assortments on top; and a solitary picture hanging on the wall. He could see through to a tiny bathroom with an avocado loo and basin and a short bath replete with shower attachment.

'Is everything to your satisfaction?' Mrs. Elliott enquired.

'Perfect,' he said. Would he dare say anything different?

She handed him the keys, which were attached to an enormous plastic key fob bearing the name and address of Hillcroft House. 'I bolt the front door on the inside at eleven p.m. sharp,' she said crisply. 'So, don't even think about returning late.'

James put on his best smile.

'Breakfast is served at eight o'clock. Any particular food intolerances I should be aware of?'

He was surprised to be offered the choice. 'No eggs, please.' His nose twitched at the very thought.

'As you wish,' Mrs. Elliott said, and she left the room, closing the door behind her.

James set his backpack down on the bed, then opened the sash window to let in some fresh air. There was a metal fire escape just outside. An option, he mused, to bypass Mrs. Elliott's curfew, or, even better, to bypass Mrs. Elliott altogether.

There was no view to speak of; only rooftops peppered with satellite dishes and television aerials. Below, he could see into the small, tatty gardens of neighbouring properties. Seagulls were squabbling yobbishly overhead in the fast fading evening light.

He filled the kettle with water from the bathroom tap, flicked on the switch, then set about emptying his suitcase. He'd brought a few changes of clothes—enough to last beyond the three nights he'd booked. Hopefully, he wouldn't have to extend his stay, but it was difficult to estimate how long he might need. And, of course, there was no pressing need to get home quickly.

He divided his clothes between the wardrobe and the chest of drawers and put his washbag and medication on the glass shelf above the bathroom basin. He took his phone and several packets of mints from his pocket and set them neatly on the nightstand. Then he retrieved the Fitzroy-Fergusson case file and the Ordnance Survey map he'd purchased, setting them down on the bed. On the map, he'd circled all the local caravan parks in black marker pen and assigned a number against each one—the order in which he'd visit them, starting tomorrow morning.

The kettle clicked, and James made himself a black coffee. He took a sip, then set the mug down on the nightstand and settled himself on the bed, ready to study the police file for the umpteenth time. He found the photographs of the crime scene and pulled out a particularly grisly picture of Fitzroy-Fergusson's corpse splayed on the bed.

Fitzroy-Fergusson had been bound to the bedposts and was naked save for a pair of underpants and a blindfold fashioned from a pair of stockings. There was no indication of a struggle nor evidence of a break-in, so the working assumption had been that he'd voluntarily consented to the activity. Given the MP's well-known interest in the erotic, it wasn't really all that surprising.

Forensics had established that the cause of death had

been one bullet fired at point blank range from a pistol in his mouth. The majority of his brain and the rear of his skull had been destroyed. Toxicology reports had found traces of cocaine in his blood.

What the hell had happened? Roxie had said Alexia hadn't murdered him. Did she mean it was an accident? A sex game gone wrong? A trick? Had she been led to believe the gun was empty, but someone had loaded it? Who tricked her? One of the Panchenkos? Were they acting on behalf of another party? Was it a politically motivated assassination, after all? He desperately needed to speak to Roxie again. She knew the truth. Trudie at the Sailor's Tavern had found the likely number from the landlord's records. She'd told him she'd spent a good hour trawling through the records, bless her. When he'd tried the number, he was frustrated to find the phone was switched off. He tried calling the number again. Same result.

He threw the iPhone back on the nightstand and returned his attention to the case file. There had to be something in here that the police had missed. Well, there *was* one thing: Fitzroy-Fergusson's telephone records. Amongst the outgoing calls from his landline was the number for the dry cleaning business—the front for the sex agency. Molly had discovered it almost effortlessly, yet the Met had failed to uncover the connection. James allowed himself a grudging smile at the thought of Molly outwitting the cops.

He casually flicked through the contents of the case file. As much as he tried to convince himself that he was a loner and self-motivated, James missed having a trusted colleague to chew the cud with—to poke at the evidence; test hypotheses; play devil's advocate. *Mel?* He checked his watch. No, it wasn't fair; she and Luke would have their hands full with the kid (*Hannah? Hilary? Harriet!*) and the bedtime routine. Which really left only one choice.

He sighed, picked up the phone and called her. It rang for ages, then, just as he was anticipating it going through to voicemail, the line opened.

'Molly?'

'Jimbo.'

She sounded strange, like he'd woken her.

'Good to talk?'

'Not really, but go on.'

'I can call another time …'

'Are you watching *Cockleshell Bay* on the telly?'

'What?'

'The seagulls.'

James got to his feet and shut the sash window to quieten the racket. 'I'm in Yarmouth.'

'What? As in *Great* Yarmouth?'

'Yes. Although there's nothing particularly great about it. The trail's led me here.'

'You serious?'

'Why would I joke about that?'

'That's bloody *uncanny*, Jimbo.'

'What?'

Molly relayed a long and unlikely tale about her estranged father, inheriting his estate and an ancient aunt she knew nothing about, living in Yarmouth. 'I've written to the old dear, asking if I can visit, but she hasn't responded.'

'Perhaps she's still only on page forty-three? I know how verbose you journos can be. Why write one word when a thousand will do?'

'Good one.' Molly let out a small groan, then said, 'I think my father might have been a spy.'

James laughed. 'A *spy?*'

'That's my best guess. What else explains all the mystery? I was hoping to discover more from this aunt. She was a big thing after the war, you know.'

'Course she was.' Sensing an opportunity to quell his loneliness, he ventured, 'Why don't you just come out here and pay her a visit? Since when has a small matter like consent ever stopped you?' James could hear nothing but her heavy breathing. 'Molly?'

'I'm thinking about it.'

'Right.'

'Okay. I've thought about it. I'll come tomorrow.'

'That's great. You can help me with my search. I've got a plan to cover fourteen caravan parks.'

'Sounds *thrilling*, Jimbo. I'm one lucky girl. Is that what you called me for? To rope me into the world's shittest magical mystery tour?'

'No. I've been thinking about the Fitzroy-Fergusson murder.'

Molly let out a pained gasp.

'You okay?' he enquired.

'*Ooh*, yes, Sergio. Right there! Get those knots out. You can be as rough as you like.'

'Where are you?'

'Treating myself to a freestyle deep tissue massage. Dad's money's come through, so why not? Can't use my hands right now, so I've got you on speakerphone.'

'Oh, that's just *perfect*.'

'Don't worry, Sergio's very discreet.'

'I'll call at a better time.'

'Sergio, couldn't be a sweetie, could you, and fetch me an iced tea? Slice of lemon? Actually, bugger it—make it a gin and tonic! And tell them to go easy on the tonic. Thank you, darling.' Then, after a pause: 'Go on, Jimbo. All clear. Shoot.'

'*O-kay.*' He cleared his throat. 'There's something I'm struggling to get my head around.'

'What's that? The meaning of life? The point of our existence? I wrestle with that question every day …'

'If you wouldn't mind getting off the subject of *you* for a minute …'

'Rude bugger.'

'It's about the circumstances surrounding the murder. Fitzroy-Fergusson. He was … tied up … Seemed like he was voluntarily consenting to … you know …'

'Sadomasochism. Bondage. Domination. Say it as it is, Jimbo. Don't be shy.'

'Whatever. He was blindfolded. There was no sign of a struggle. Having someone pop a gun in your mouth—is that even a *thing*?'

'Who's to say he thought it was a gun? Could have been anything. A finger. A cigar. A pen. A d—'

'Okay, I get the picture.'

'Want to know my theory?'

'Go on.'

'Suicide.'

'Eh?'

'Easy. He arranges the rendezvous. Tells the poor girl he wants to simulate being held up at gunpoint. Gives her a gun; tells her not to worry, it's fake. She thinks, "*whatever mate, no sweat, easy money*". Beats the "walking across a bloke's naked body in high heels" thing, hands down. So, she just pulls the trigger and, hey presto, blows his brains out. She thinks, "*holy shit! I've just committed murder*", realises her prints are all over the gun, DNA's everywhere, so she panics and scarpers.'

'It's a bit far-fetched, don't you think? And if someone was suicidal, why would they make it so elaborate?'

'Fitzroy-Fergusson was a politician. Different breed. Say no more.'

'*Hmm.*'

'Got a better theory?'

'I think he requested the scenario, but they each thought the gun wasn't loaded.'

'Who loaded the gun, then?'

'A third party at the agency who either wanted him dead or was paid to kill him. Possibly her pimp.'

'Sounds more ludicrous than my theory. Didn't the Old Bill explore the assassination motive?'

'Yep, but they didn't come up with any credible suspects. Doesn't mean there weren't any.'

'What does it all matter, anyway? If you find Urté, she'll shed light on the mystery. Easy.'

'The chances of me finding her are vanishingly slim.'

'That's the spirit, Jimbo—always looking on the bright side. Sounds like you need me there to cheer you up. Look, if you want to get inside someone's head and work out what makes them tick, do a Marlon Brando.'

'What?'

'Method acting. Tom Cruise. Robert De Niro. Daniel Day-Lewis. Take your pick. The idea is, you fully inhabit the role of the character you're portraying. So, it's simple: just imagine yourself as Geoffrey Fitzroy-Oojamiflip.'

James rolled his eyes. 'Of course! Why didn't *I* think of that?'

'Right, Sergio's back with my G&T. Got to go. See you on the Costa del Grime tomorrow.'

'Yep. Bye.'

'See ya.'

Well, that was useful. Not.

James threw the phone onto the bed. He paced the room with his hands jammed deep in his pockets, puffing his cheeks and slowly releasing the air, contemplating the case, demanding answers.

The crime scene photo caught his eye and he picked it up from the bed, studying it for the umpteenth time. Where exactly *was* the thrill? He just didn't get it. Perhaps he was too prudish, too conservative, too sexually repressed to empathise?

He lay down on the bed, flat on his back, and shuffled himself into a comfortable position, letting the photograph drop to the carpet. He took several deep breaths, trying to lull himself into a thespian trance.

Close your eyes. Breathe slowly. Real slowly. Imagine you're him.

What would he say? Absurdly, the first thing that came to mind was, —*Do you mind not making marks in my carpet with your heels?*

No, she's the boss. She'd be telling him to keep quiet. *Don't say a word or I shoot, okay?* He could do silence, no sweat.

The imaginary woman moves around the room, opening doors, clawing through drawers, hurling the contents around the room. Glass shatters. She strides towards him, the catsuit creaking between her purposeful, toned thighs. He can smell the leather; her pungent perfume. He feels her hot breath in his ear. *Where's the fucking money?*

—*I don't have any money!*

The woman laughs. A filthy, smoky, Russian assassin's laugh. *You have one more chance to tell me.*

She's dragging the barrel of the gun down his naked chest, pausing at his groin for a heart-stopping moment, then she brings it up to his face, pressing it hard into his temple.

Where's *the money?*
—*There is no money!*

Now, she's pushing the barrel into his mouth. The smart *snap* of her cocking the gun makes him jump. *I'm feeling it! I'm actually feeling it!*

'Shoot me, beautiful!'

'I'd rather not, Mr. Quinn.'

It took him a beat to realise that the voice did not belong to the sultry Russian assassin in his mind's eye, but a redoubtable guest house proprietress standing reproachfully in the open doorway.

James scrambled to his feet. 'Aren't you supposed to knock before entering?'

'I did,' Mrs. Elliott said unrepentantly. 'You couldn't have heard me.' She hesitated for a moment, then said, 'There is a "do not disturb" sign for'—she gave a small cough— '*private pursuits.*'

'It's not what it seems,' James pleaded.

'It never is, Mr. Quinn.' She stepped inside and placed a small object on the dresser. 'I came to return your driving licence.'

Her gaze shifted to the discarded photograph on the floor, then to James. 'If there's anything you need during your stay,' she said coolly, 'you know where to find me.'

'Thank you, Mrs. Elliott.'

She shut the door behind her, and James dropped to the bed, sinking his head into his hands in embarrassment.

Bloody Molly! That was the last time he was going to listen to one of her harebrained ideas!

THIRTY-TWO

IT WAS WELL past eight o'clock when James barrelled down the stairs, clutching his room key and the OS map. He was a mess: unshaven; bed hair; his shirt tails untucked. He hated tardiness in others and despised it in himself. The culprit: one Guinness too many, last night at the pub.

It had been a stupid idea to go back.

There was a nasty whiff about the place, and it took him too long to realise it was him.

Of course, Mrs. Elliott happened to emerge from the kitchen the moment he stepped breathlessly into the hall. She wore a cook's apron and wielded coffee and tea servers like they were weapons. The swing door behind her flapped violently in her wake.

'You're late,' she said bluntly as she hurried past.

'Is that your standard greeting?' he muttered under his breath.

He followed her to the breakfast room. Against the left wall was a sideboard on which were jugs of water; milk and orange juice; a stack of bowls; upturned drinking glasses; individual boxes of cereals; a plate of fruit; a bowl of grapefruit replete with ladle; and some yoghurts. There were about a dozen tables squeezed into the space, only two of which were occupied, one by a middle-aged couple at the far end, the other by a lone man in the bay window. The man—slightly overweight; dark hair; olive skin—flashed James a brief and awkward smile. He replied with a slight nod of the head, grateful to discover he wasn't the only solo guest. Mrs. Elliott busied herself attending to the couple.

James chose a table in the middle of the room and pulled out a chair.

'Not there, Mr. Quinn!' Mrs. Elliott called out.

'Oh?'

'I've set you this one, here.' She gestured to a table, adjacent to the couple. The gap between the two tables was a couple of feet at best.

James didn't feel inclined to resist or to question the logic. What was it about women of a certain age that made him so meek? It was the same with the woman at the pub last night.

He took his seat where he was told and unfurled the map, weighting it at each corner with his key fob, phone and the salt and pepper pots. The route to the first port of call—Seashore Holiday Park, on the northern side of town—would take him along the promenade. A quick walk would get him there in half an hour, he calculated. Quicker, if he jogged. Of course, he could drive, but what was the point in being at the seaside and not enjoying the sea air?

Mrs. Elliott left the couple and went over to attend to the man at the window table.

James sensed the woman at the next table looking in his direction, and he turned to meet her gaze. Late sixties, he guessed. Face heavily made-up. Hair lacquered into an almost spherical nest. 'Lovely morning, isn't it?' she said. Behind her, through the window, a watery sun was threatening to break through the clouds.

James smiled politely.

'I'm Elsie,' the woman continued. 'And this is my husband, Merv. Although you won't get much out of him. Deaf as a post.'

The man—a curmudgeonly-looking chap with an arched back and a paper napkin tucked into the collar of his yellow shirt—stabbed a fork at his breakfast plate, like his full English had done something deserving of punishment.

'I'm James. Pleased to meet you.'

'And what brings you to Yarmouth, James?'

'I'm here to see an old friend.'

'How lovely! We're here for our wedding anniversary.'

James's temple throbbed. He forced an interested smile. 'That's nice.'

The husband, Merv, picked up his cup of tea, brought it to his lips and slurped loudly. Elsie's eyebrows rocketed to the ceiling. 'The big day's actually tomorrow. That's if I don't shove him off the pier first! I fancied a Caribbean cruise, you know. But old misery guts here said he wanted a trip down memory lane. We honeymooned in Yarmouth, you see. Forty years ago! Can you believe it?' She lowered her voice and checked Mrs. Elliott wasn't in earshot before adding, 'It's not what it used to be. Gone to the dogs.'

'*Hmm.*'

Elsie tutted and said, 'Who would want to be lying on the deck of an ocean liner under a tropical sun, sipping a Coco Loco, when you can have all this, eh?'

'Quite.'

'These sausages, Else,' Merv complained, thrusting his

fork at his wife. 'They're those bloody Paul McCartney ones!'

'*Linda*, Merv!'

'What?'

'*Linda* McCartney makes the sausages. *Paul* writes the songs. And they're not vegetarian. I asked for Lincolnshires, especially.'

'Speak up, Else! I can't hear you.'

'Never mind, Merv.'

'What?'

'I said, "*Never mind, Mervin.*"' She turned to James and said indiscreetly, 'See what I have to put up with? The man's going to drive me to an early grave.'

Mrs. Elliott came over, and James was grateful for the reprieve. 'Tea or coffee?' she asked.

'Coffee, please.'

She poured it into his cup. 'I'll fetch your breakfast now. I've left it standing under a hot lamp, but it'll be past its best now.'

'Not a problem, thank you.'

'Everything all right, here?' Mrs. Elliott enquired, addressing Elsie and Merv.

'Oh, lovely, thank you, Pamela. Merv is *loving* his vegetarian sausages. Thank you for being so accommodating.'

Merv gave a confused smile, and Elsie winked at James, before returning her attention to her small portion of grapefruit.

To the irritating sound of her spoon clinking against the bowl, James returned his attention to the OS map, only for him to be further distracted by the presence of a figure to his left. He looked up to see that it was the other loner, pouring himself a glass of orange juice and, at the same time, squinting at James's map.

There was something vaguely familiar about the guy,

but James couldn't for the life of him put his finger on it. Perhaps their paths had crossed in his past life as a copper? In any case, he was flushed with annoyance, so he gave the man a look that soon sent him on his way.

'The Time and Tide Museum.'

James swivelled his head to find Elsie staring at his map. She pointed at the markings for the museum. 'If you're looking for somewhere to take your friend. It's wonderful. Set in one of the country's best preserved Victorian herring curing works.'

'Are there many?'

'What?'

'Victorian herring curing works.'

'I've no idea. Or you could try the Lifeboat Station at Caister?'

'I've got this in hand, thank you.'

'Your breakfast, Mr. Quinn,' Mrs Elliott said, standing over him like a teacher about to upbraid him for a poor effort with his homework. 'No eggs, as requested.'

Mrs. Elliott set his plate down, unceremoniously, on the map. A couple of baked beans spilled over the side.

'Careful!' he said.

'Maybe it's a sign,' Elsie chipped in. 'One of the beans has landed right on the Time and Tide Museum.'

Mrs. Elliott handed James a paper napkin, which he snatched from her and used to wipe the beans. He could sense everyone's eyes on him. Didn't like it one bit. 'Will you all please leave me to study my sodding map in peace?'

There were a few moments of awkward silence before Mrs. Elliott said, her tone clipped, 'There's no need for such rudeness, Mr. Quinn.'

'Don't touch the sausages, pal,' Merv bellowed. 'They're bloody vile!'

'Will you shut up about the sausages, for goodness' sake, Mervin!' Elsie reprimanded her husband.

Mrs. Elliott, affronted, swept out of the room, and James allowed himself a wry smile.

It was a cool morning, and the early promise of sunshine had been dashed by a moody sky now threatening rain. Nonetheless, rejuvenated after his hearty breakfast and a long, steamy shower, James strode purposefully along the promenade, breathing in the seaside air. He wore his runner's backpack, and in it, he'd stashed a bottle of water, his map, his notebook and pen and a sheaf of missing person flyers.

There were not many people about: a few dog walkers and the occasional jogger. The beach was deserted. He recalled something tucked in a forgotten corner of his brain long ago. His mother had bought him a bucket and spade set; impenetrably wrapped in yellow netting, so she'd had to use her nail scissors to help him retrieve the items. He also recalled his mother's bag—a huge blue and white striped canvas affair, permanently slung over her shoulder—that carried everything a family might need for a day at the beach, and more besides.

He carried on, passing a parade of colourful shops, cafés and amusement arcades, most of which were yet to open for the day. He continued on past the model village; the Sea Life centre; the adventure golf course; an unmanned lifeguard's pod; the landscaped gardens. He picked up his pace, settling in to a light jog. The exercise felt good.

A detour from the wide promenade pavement took him across a large grassland expanse, past an unsavoury toilet block, and closer to the beach. As he approached a shelter, he noticed a homeless person curled up, motionless on the bench within; a patch of black hair poking out from a dirty sleeping bag. James averted his gaze and ran a little faster, not wanting to gawp. Part of him wished he could do something to help, but he was powerless. The causes of homelessness were complex: poverty; unemployment; lack of affordable housing; mental and physical problems; substance abuse; escape from violence and physical abuse. The list was almost endless.

He ran faster, pushing those depressing thoughts from his mind, running until he reached Seashore Holiday Park, a sprawling complex. It had a bar; a restaurant; a coffee shop; an entertainment venue; a convenience store; a soft play centre; a swimming pool; an adventure playground; a wildlife nature trail; a 'woof park'; an amusement arcade; and much more. He knew all this because he was standing at a huge information board at the entrance to the park, catching his breath. The board was dominated by a site map, which showed the caravans, arranged in colour-coded clusters. How many units must there be? Hundreds, he wagered.

The park was clean and well kept but, because it was out of season and with very few holidaymakers around, it still felt bleak and desolate. James wandered around for several minutes, getting his bearings, peering into vans, furtively glancing at faces. Then he found the convenience store.

Just inside the door, there was a cork noticeboard with several white cards pinned to it, mostly comprising items for sale: kiddies bikes; garden furniture; a pram. And a lost pet—a three-year-old ginger tom called Sandy. A twenty-five-pound reward was being offered for his safe return.

What price would it take for the safe return of a lost human? Could you even put a price on that?

James gave the abridged version of Urtė's plight to the young, gum-chewing woman behind the counter. Late teens, early twenties at best. Face angry with acne. Hunched posture, typical of someone who spent mindless hours enthralled by their mobile phone. 'Can I put this flyer on the board?' he enquired.

'My manager says we can only put the white cards up.'

'Can't you make an exception, just this once?'

The woman popped a strawberry-scented bubble. 'Maybe if I fold it to the same size?'

'How's that going to work?'

'Yeah, I see what you mean.'

'Where's your manager? Can I speak with them?'

'It's Bev's day off. She'll be back tomorrow, if you want to talk to her?'

'There's a big gap on the board at the moment. Why don't you just put it up for now and then *you* speak to your manager when she's back?'

'Well, I dunno …'

The familiar sinking feeling was taking hold. How was he going ever going to make progress if he couldn't even get this airhead to pin a piece of paper to a board?

'And we charge five pounds a week for adverts.'

'It's not really an advert, though, is it? Just ask your manager.' He forced an affable smile and added, 'Please.'

He left the store, lacking any confidence that Urtė's picture was going to go anywhere other than the bin. He tried his luck elsewhere: the arcade; the guys manning the outdoor play areas; the swimming pool. He encountered varying degrees of receptiveness and courtesy, but the response was always the same: no one recognised her.

In the bar, he approached a friendly-looking barman and gave him the familiar spiel.

'Funny, it must be the season for missing persons,' the

barman commented. 'We had a bloke in here the other day, looking for a girl.'

'Really? The same person?'

'No, it was his daughter. Ran away from home. A teenager.'

'Right.'

'He was one angry man. I can understand why she wanted to get away.'

'Okay. If you could just spread the word about Urtė? My number's at the bottom.'

'Will do—and good luck.'

James checked his watch and realised he'd spent over an hour at this one park already. The thought of repeating this exercise—an exercise in utter futility, he was beginning to conclude—made him feel quite depressed. What had his life come to? A man old before his time, his body too broken for real work, traipsing about the country, handing out missing person flyers. He was a glorified leaflet pusher, with little prospect of glory.

He kept having to remind himself he was doing it for Ruth; to fulfil his sacred promise.

And to solve a murder.

Once outside in the fresh air, he reached into his pocket for his phone and dialled Roxie's number again. Expecting her phone to be off, he was surprised to hear the dialling tone. It continued to ring.

'Come on,' he cursed. 'Answer!'

Eventually, the call connected, but no greeting was offered.

'Hello? Roxie?'

No reply.

'Roxie?' He could hear breathing. 'It's James Quinn. The detective. Can you talk?'

There was a brief moment of silence before a deep male voice spoke. '*Detective?*'

'Who's that?' James asked, feeling a stab of concern in his gut. He knew the answer.

Andric Panchenko.

'Why is *detective* calling Roxie?' The heavily accented voice carried a gruff, intolerant tone. 'A private matter,' James replied. 'May I speak with her, please?'

'That is not possible right now.'

'Why not? Is she okay?'

There was a slight chuckle in response. 'Don't worry. She is fine. Sleeping like baby. But it is not really Roxie you want, is it, detective? I know you looking for Alexia.'

James stayed silent, concerned over where the conversation was heading. Panchenko continued. 'When you find her, give me call. Me and Alexia have business to finish.'

'What do you mean?'

'I need to tell her she is *bad* girl.'

'What, for killing your client? Fitzroy-Fergusson? Was killing him not part of the plan?'

Panchenko laughed for several seconds before stopping abruptly. His voice became loud and menacing. 'The fucking bitch kill my brother!'

The line went dead, the roar of Panchenko's fury echoing in James's ear.

THIRTY-THREE

ROSA WAS RUSHING to work along the promenade, hunched against a nasty headwind, casting occasional glances over her shoulder, her ears trained to any strange or sudden noises.

There was still no sign of Kayleigh.

Rosa had assumed she'd come hammering at the door, desperate to find her phone. Teenagers couldn't be without them for a second, could they? She wondered why Kayleigh hadn't come to the caravan, or to the arcade. Maybe she'd gone back home, only to be beaten by her monster of a father? Or worse. Had the girl actually killed herself this time?

Rosa told herself, over and over, that the girl wasn't her problem.

But she never quite managed to convince herself that was true.

She'd spent the days since the incident with Kayleigh's father in a heightened state of alert, sleeping fitfully, a baseball bat at her side, convinced he was biding his time, waiting for the moment to exact his revenge. The bat belonged to Clifford. She'd been over to his van to apologise profusely for her behaviour and told him that she was worried; that she feared she had a stalker. And Clifford was an absolute gentleman. Said he'd report the matter to the police; even offered her a bed in his caravan so she would feel safer. She told him that was all very sweet, but it wasn't necessary; she was probably worrying over nothing. A bit of extra security in her own van would suffice, to put her mind at ease. Bless him, he'd leapt straight into action, installing another deadbolt; said he was going to order some security cameras, too, and put them up around the site. What a lovely man!

Rosa felt a sudden pang of guilt for manipulating him over the rent, and she resolved to fully reimburse him that evening, even if it meant pushing back her plans by a few more weeks. Her mind wandered to the day he'd rescued her from despair; her knight in dirty corduroy.

She'd been in Great Yarmouth for three days, having alighted on the town for no other reason than that it was getting dark when the bus had pulled into the terminus and she was exhausted from all the travelling. It had been the last in a series of random journeys—by bus, train, car and truck—that had taken her away from London, across miles and miles of flat, agricultural landscape. She'd done her best to avoid CCTV cameras, but they were everywhere, so she'd also disguised her appearance, cleansing her face of make-up and stuffing her hair into a woollen beanie.

After trudging the dark streets for an age, she'd found a single room in a damp, dirty guesthouse, sandwiched between the railway line and a busy road. They took cash in advance and asked no questions, but Rosa was soon out of money and could not afford to stay any longer. Needing to find work, fast, she'd trawled cafés; market stalls; shops.

Most places at the time didn't have vacancies; those that did had required proof of identity; an address; a bank account; proof of the right to work. None of which a fugitive like Rosa could provide.

Facing a night sleeping rough, she'd pleaded with one particular pub landlord. She'd offered to work behind the bar; to serve food; to clean the place; anything. But the answer, again, had been a polite *"sorry, we can't help you"*. Desperate, she'd asked if she could use a phone. She'd call Roxie.

The man at the pub had taken pity on her and had let her use the landline in the upstairs apartment. She'd dialled the number and had put the phone to her ear, doubtful that Roxie would answer. She'd suspected her phone would be on silent or switched off, stashed away in her own secret hidey-hole. But she could leave a message: tell Roxie the truth about what had happened to the client and to Evgeni; let her know she was alive and well and not to worry. Perhaps, she'd thought, Roxie could get her some money, to tide her over until she found work. Rosa had slammed the phone down. Could she possibly have been any dumber? She'd risked giving away her location. And how the hell was Roxie supposed to get money to her without a bank account and without providing an address? Acting first, thinking later. Again!

She'd returned to the bar area, tearful, her options exhausted. The warm, fusty air had been full of chatter and laughter, and the wonderful smell of hot food. And that's when Clifford had said, 'You look lost. Can I help?'

He'd been sitting alone at the bar, with a plate of food and a glass of drink. Ham and chips and cola, if she remembered correctly. She'd regarded him warily; he looked odd, the type of man a mother would tell her children to avoid. But he'd offered her a kind, sympathetic smile. He'd introduced himself as Clifford and had patted the vacant bar stool next to him. Before she knew it, she'd finished his chips and had told him a convincing tale of how she'd fled an abusive relationship to start a new life from scratch in an unfamiliar town, with no money; no home; nothing. A sanitised version of the full, gory truth.

And that's how Clifford came to offer her the caravan. Said the owner of the site also owned an amusement arcade and was on the lookout for a reliable, friendly face to work in the change booth.

The wind subsided a little as Rosa hurried alongside the tall hedge dividing the promenade and the pleasure garden. As she walked, she heard a strange and sudden noise; a kind of distressed whimper. Through the thick foliage, she caught a flash of beige.

Rosa addressed the hedge doubtfully. 'Hello?'

'Rosa?' came the hesitant reply.

She smiled, recognising the voice, and made her way around into the gardens, where she found an out-of-breath and chaste-looking Clifford Snell. He had a pair of binoculars around his neck and an old-fashioned camera. The knees of his beige slacks bore dirt stains, and there was a fresh bruise over his eye.

'What happen, Cliff?'

'I-I-I …' he stammered. Unable to form the words, he pointed at the camera and binoculars.

'*Aw*, Cliffy! Have you been looking out for me?' she teased. 'My personal security man? That is so sweet, but is not necessary.'

'No, no! It's not that,' he said, throwing a thumb over his shoulder. 'I've been in pursuit of … of …'

'Yes?'

'A willow tit.'

'A *what?*'

'It's a very rare bird. It's making a nesting hole in a decaying tree stump, next to the shelter over there.'

'Right. Okay. That is good. But I need to be at work now.'

'There was a girl in the shelter. She must have thought I was spying on her, like a …'

'Pervert?'

'A Peeping Tom. I'm not a Peeping Tom, Rosa. You must believe me.'

'Of course I do, Cliff. You are gentleman.'

'I'm just a twitcher,' he said, holding aloft his binoculars by way of proof. 'I hadn't even noticed her. I had my Pentax trained on the stump, waiting patiently for the t-t-t-tit to arrive back from a foraging expedition. Then she emerged from the shelter, screaming *vile* words at me.' He raised a finger to his bruised eye. 'She did this to me.'

'A girl? On her own?'

'Yes. There was a sleeping bag on the bench. I think she's been sleeping *rough* …'

'What does she look like?'

'Very thin and pale. Black hair. P-p-piercings. Do you think I should call the police?'

'No! Is she still there?'

'I think so, yes.'

The girl was sitting upright on the bench, drinking from a two-litre bottle of cheap cider. There was a crumpled old sleeping bag beside her and a plastic carrier bag filled to the brim.

'Kayleigh?'

The girl was bedraggled and dirty, her hair plastered to the side of her face, her eyes puffed and watery.

A flash of recognition danced in the washed out eyes, but her tone was instinctively hostile. 'What do you care?'

'I have something of yours,' Rosa said and held out the mobile phone.

Kayleigh snatched it without a word of thanks and put it in the bag.

'How long have you been sleeping here?'

The girl shrugged.

'Look, I go arcade now. Start my shift. You come with me? You must be freezing. I will make you a hot drink, and you make yourself clean in the washroom.'

'Thought you said I was banned?'

Rosa smiled. 'I do not have the power.' She held out her hand. 'Come with me? Please?'

THIRTY-FOUR

JAMES WAS STILL REELING from the shock of his conversation with Panchenko when he arrived at the next site on his itinerary. Assuming the gangster was speaking the truth, what the hell had happened for Urtė to have killed Evgeni? Was that the real reason she fled London? Was that what Roxie had been trying to tell him?

The circling questions lent a fresh urgency to his investigation.

"SANDY BAY HOLIDAY P RK", the welcome sign announced. "F N FOR ALL THE FAM LY. GUARANTEED!"

It was James's fifth site so far and the bleakest by some distance. The static caravans were barely more than tired old tin boxes, lined up in uniform rows on a windy expanse of overgrown grass sloping towards the sea. Signs of life were few and far between: a parked-up family estate here, a rotary dryer cluttered with sopping towels there.

He passed a ramshackle children's play area with a paltry collection of equipment: three swings (one of which had no seat); a little merry-go-round covered with graffiti;

and a couple of sit-on animals mounted on rusting springs —a chicken and a frog, he'd say, if he were forced to guess. Thickets of dandelions, clogged with litter, sprouted from wide cracks in the tarmac. Not a child in sight.

James quickly located the site office but it was closed. A laminated sign taped to the dirty window informed him that the opening hours were 10:00 a.m. till 2:00 p.m. James checked his watch. Just gone two. Underneath the opening hours, the sign said, "FOR OUT OF HOURS EMERGENCIES, PLEASE CONTACT THE SITE MANAGER AT CARAVAN D14."

When he found Caravan D14, he saw that it had "PEDO" spray-painted in large, misspelt green letters across the door.

He sighed and rapped on the tin door.

Moments later, there was movement inside, then the sound of several deadbolts unlocking.

The door opened a few inches, the maximum allowed by the security chain.

'Yes?' a reedy voice said from the gloomy interior.

James craned his neck so he could see the owner of the voice: a tall, slim man, probably mid-to-late fifties. He was wearing the type of jumper your mother bought you as a birthday present, the sort you felt compelled to wear in her presence because you didn't want to hurt her feelings: a brown, oversized woollen garment with a zigzag pattern. His beige trousers sported stains of a dubious nature.

'Hello, sir. I saw the sign that said I could contact you out of hours?'

'And what is the n-n-nature of your emergency?'

'I'm a private detective, and I'm looking for a woman who's been lost for a long time,' James said, never one to beat about the bush. 'I'm hoping you might know her whereabouts?'

There was a short silence before he replied, 'A woman, you say?' The man wiped the underside of his nose with the back of his hand. 'There are a lot of them in this world. Nearly four b-b-billion, I believe. Perhaps you could be more specific?'

'I have her photograph. May I come in, sir? It's a bit blowy out.'

The man was reflexively hesitant. 'Your credentials?'

James shoved a business card through the gap. The man took the card and scrutinised it with a sceptical gaze. At times like this, James wished he still had his warrant card; wished he was still an *actual* detective. 'I used to be a policeman,' he said to the man, hoping that imparting the information would offer some reassurance.

Although … that's precisely what you'd say if you were a psycho, trying to con your way into someone's home.

Regardless, it appeared to do the trick. The man unlatched the security chain and beckoned James inside.

He was greeted by an overwhelming, acrid stench; the kind that called for a Trebor Extra Strong Mint. James used the fortuitous occasion of returning his business card holder to his pocket to surreptitiously tease a mint from the packet. He popped the little disc of minty reprieve into the side of his mouth and savoured the instant relief.

The man's tiny home was a panorama of brown: the carpet; the sofa; the curtains; the lampshades. Its occupant, too, if truth be told. There were piles of old newspapers, books and magazines on every surface. And what *was* the source of the smell? Yep, a grey parrot, in a cage by the front window.

The parrot squawked.

'That's Newton,' the man said, following James's eyes. 'He's saying hello.'

'Hello, Newton,' James said awkwardly to the parrot, before turning back to the man. 'I didn't catch *your* name?'

'I didn't state my name.'

'May I ask your name?'

'Yes, you may.'

James was beginning to not like this man. He bit down hard on his natural compulsion for sarcasm. Until he'd established whether the man was of any utility to the investigation, he'd have to humour him.

'What's your name?'

'My name is Clifford Snell.'

'Thank you. I'm James Quinn.'

'I know. I read your business card.'

'Well, I'm glad we've made our acquaintances before one of us died.' *Damn, couldn't resist.*

'Can I get you a d-d-drink, Mr. Quinn? Tea? Coffee?'

James's gaze switched to the kitchen area, where the sink and countertop were piled high with unwashed plates, bowls, cutlery, mugs, foil containers …

'Do you have anything in a bottle? Or a can? I've got an allergy to … er … you know… any drink that isn't hermetically sealed.'

Clifford screwed his face into a puzzled expression. Then, moments later, he appeared to have a lightbulb moment. 'Um Bongo?'

'Sorry?'

'I've got a box of thirty somewhere, in the other room.' He pointed a thumb over his shoulder. 'Never been touched. Let me see if I can dig them out.'

'O-kay.'

After Clifford disappeared through the internal door, James's eyes drifted around the caravan, eventually settling on the parrot's cage. Involuntarily intrigued, he wandered over, taking care not to step in the clumps of bird shit ground into the carpet.

He looked at the parrot.

The parrot looked at James.

James wondered if he ought to engage the bird in polite conversation. Perhaps it was easier to strike up a conversation when the interlocutor was an entirely different species? That felt daft, so James merely nodded.

The parrot took a small sidestep on its perch, then returned to its original position, cocked its head to one side and puffed the feathers on its head. Throughout the routine, the bird maintained its glare at James, as if it were evaluating him.

James was beginning to feel unnerved. '*Boo!*' he said, keen not to be psyched out by a foot-high exotic pet.

The parrot squawked and retreated to the far end of its perch.

'Gotcha!' James said, with petty satisfaction.

'*Wanker!*' the parrot hissed.

'*Newton!* How many times must I tell you about those f-f-filthy obscenities? We have a guest!'

Clifford had returned, and he was clutching a kiddies' drink carton.

'I'm terribly sorry, Mr. Quinn,' he said sheepishly. 'Newton must have picked up that *profanity* from one of our guests. Once they're learned, unfortunately, they can't be unlearned.'

Clifford went over to the parrot's cage and opened the hatch. The bird flew out and performed a quick, flappy circuit of the room, then executed a flawless landing on Clifford's shoulder.

James looked at the carton in Clifford Snell's hand. It had a cartoon picture of a pink hippo sitting astride a blue rhino. A stripy orange snake looked on with an angry expression.

'Oh, yes! Your drink, Mr. Quinn. Here. I'm glad to have finally found a taker. You see, I was asked to host a children's party down at the community centre. For little Barry Tyler's eighth birthday. I saw these on special offer at the cash and carry, and I thought the kiddies would like them. I'd planned a pirate theme, you see. I was going to be Long John Silver, and Newton—'

'Yes, I can picture it.'

'I even made myself a false wooden leg from an old b-b-broom handle. And it was quite fortuitous that the Sue Ryder shop had an old crutch in stock. But then, the night before the party, right out of the blue, Barry's mother cancelled. Said little Barry would prefer to play football with his pals.'

James broke off the little straw attached to the carton and unsheathed it from its plastic wrapper. He punctured the little foil hole, then took a tentative sip.

Clifford's mouth gaped, and his eyes twinkled with anticipation. 'Well? Is it *good*?'

The drink didn't taste quite right. Sweetened battery acid came to mind. James held the liquid in a suspended gargle for a few moments, then forced himself to swallow. 'When was this kid's birthday, out of interest, Clifford?' he enquired.

'*Ooh*, good question. Now, let me think …' The parrot pecked at Clifford's shoulder, as if it were sprinkled with invisible Trill. '… 1997. That's right. The year Tony Blair got in with his landslide. Remember?'

'*Things Can Only Get Better*?'

'That's right! Of course, things *didn't* getter better for little Barry Tyler. He grew into a six foot tearaway. Him and a couple of pals stole a car, the day after his sixteenth birthday. Crashed it into a lamppost during a high-speed police chase on Marine Parade.'

'Oh?'

'The car went up in flames.' Clifford threw his hands above his head in a dramatic gesture. '*Whoosh!*'

Newton squawked and mimicked the action.

'They had to identify Barry from his d-d-dental records.'

'Oh … Well, I'm sorry to hear that.'

'Terrible business.'

James looked at his watch. 'So, back to the purpose of my visit …' James reached into his pocket. 'Do you recognise the woman in this photograph?'

Clifford took Urtė's picture and scrutinised it. 'Missing, you say? For how long?'

'Over fifteen years.'

'*Fifteen* years?'

'Yes. Fifteen years.'

The parrot regarded the photograph from the vantage point of its master's shoulder, then started to rock with enormous enthusiasm, chanting, '*Pretty girl! Pretty girl! Pretty girl!*'

'That she is, Newton,' Clifford agreed. 'That she is.'

'Do you recognise her, though?' James asked, his patience wearing thin.

'What's her name?'

'*Rosa! Rosa! Rosa!*' the parrot squealed.

'*Rosa?*'

'Rosa was my former wife,' Clifford said sadly. Newton's never really reconciled himself to her departure. It was very sudden.'

Why on earth would a woman want to leave this fine figure of a man? 'Right, okay, but do you recognise this woman? Her name is Urtė Cuda. She came to this country from

237

Lithuania. I have reason to believe she may be residing in a caravan, somewhere in Yarmouth.'

'Lithuania? Sounds cold and somewhat grim to me. I don't think we'd fancy visiting Lithuania, eh, Newton?'

The parrot bobbed up and down. Was it indicating agreement or dissent? Who knew? Either way, James was starting to wonder if Clifford Snell had been a politician in a previous life, answering questions with questions. He tried again. 'Do you recognise her?'

'And what were the circumstances of her disappearance?'

'For *fuck's* sake, Clifford! Can you just answer my question?' James jabbed at the photograph. 'Do. You. Recognise. *Her?*'

'There's no need for such *disgusting* language, Mr. Quinn. Newton is a very impressionable bird.'

The parrot squawked a word. James was sure it was *arsehole*. 'Did your bird just call me an arsehole?'

'*Arsenal*,' Clifford clarified. 'We're avid supporters. He struggles to get his b-b-beak round the letter "n."' He handed back the photograph. 'Sorry. I've never seen her before in my life.'

'Well, thank you very much for your time, Mr. Snell,' James said perfunctorily. 'I'll leave you to it.'

James turned to the door.

'*Arsehole*,' the parrot hissed.

'Back at ya, bird brain!'

THIRTY-FIVE

FIVE SITES. Six hours. Thirty-three flyers. Countless caravans. One parrot with an attitude.

Number of promising leads? The square root of diddly squat.

Not a day for posterity, thus far.

James was at the rendezvous—a pay and display car park on the seafront—waiting, propped against the wall of a toilet block. She'd said she'd be here by 4:00 p.m. at the latest, but that was twenty minutes ago. He was now getting funny looks because he was standing right next to the entrance to the ladies, which was only because that end provided the best shelter from the incessant wind.

He took another look at his watch. *Come on, Molly, for Christ's sake.*

To think he'd once had feelings for her. *Ridiculous.* It never would have worked; they were chalk and cheese. *A momentary lapse in good sense, brought on by stressful circumstances*, he told himself, without much conviction.

The squeal of tyres and the beat of loud pop music

heralded the arrival of her white Range Rover Evoque as it turned, way too fast, into the car park. Molly parked carelessly, taking up two spaces, and turned off the engine. James went over to the driver's side to greet her.

'Have I kept you waiting long?' she breezed as she emerged from the car. The wind nearly took her words away, and she scurried to open the boot, retrieving a coat, which she hurriedly put on. She slammed the boot shut and slung her fancy handbag over her shoulder.

'Do you want to reposition the car?' James said.

'What?'

'Look. You're parked across two spaces.'

'Yeah, deliberately. I don't want some mindless arse-hole scratching my baby. Besides, the place isn't exactly inundated, is it? Now, where's the loo? I'm dying here!'

James gestured towards the toilet block.

Her nose wrinkled in disgust, and she handed James her handbag. He looked at it, puzzled. 'I'm not taking that anywhere near public lavatories,' she clarified. 'Won't be a minute.'

It was at least three minutes before she emerged, shaking excess water from her hands.

'Bloody disgusting!' she groused. 'No paper towels *and* the hand dryers are out of order.'

James allowed himself a small smile and returned her handbag. 'Fancy a walk along the promenade?'

The wind was whipping Molly's hair all over the place, and she was fighting a losing battle to restore a semblance of tidiness. 'Would it hurt your feelings if I said I'd rather die?'

James laughed. 'The sea air will do you good. And the ticket machine is out of order, so you get to park for free. Maybe it's a sign?' he added sardonically.

'Yeah, a sign to get the hell out of Dodge. Ten minutes —that's all I'm doing.'

They walked along the seafront for a few minutes while James updated her on the day's fruitless search activities. He got the feeling Molly wasn't paying one hundred percent attention, though. 'Fancy a hot drink? My shout,' he offered.

'*Ooh*, where are you going to take me? A boutique coffee house with a roaring fire …'

'How about here?'

They stopped at a kiosk that seemed to sell just about everything: sweets; crisps; chocolate bars; fizzy drinks. There was a huge tea urn at the back and, to the side, a stand housing newspapers and magazines, fastened with wire to stop them blowing away.

'How lovely.' Molly rolled her eyes. 'Make mine a non-fat latte with caramel drizzle, will you, Jimbo?'

A woman wearing a scarf and fingerless gloves stood behind the counter, and she seemed grateful for James's business when he asked for a couple of teas.

Molly pointed to a newspaper on the stand. The headline read: "LOBBYING SCANDAL ENGULFS GOVERNMENT". 'All in a day's work,' she said immodestly.

'Well done,' James murmured, not wanting to massage her ego.

'Sorry, speak up. Didn't quite hear that.'

'You heard.'

'In fact,' Molly said, 'think I'll take a copy. For my records. Don't mind treating me, do you?' Without waiting for his consent, she teased the paper from the stand and handed it to James.

The woman behind the counter handed over two polystyrene cups, and James gave one to Molly.

Molly fired back a banal smile. 'Why, you are spoiling me.'

'Anything else, love?' the woman asked.

James grabbed an assorted collection of mints and gave the woman a ten-pound note.

'Don't they give you a stomach ache?' Molly asked. 'All those mints?'

'Nope, but too many questions give me a migraine.'

'Here's your change, love,' the vendor interjected. 'Have a good day.'

'Thanks. You, too.'

James and Molly continued along the promenade, taking sips of tea.

'It's actually quite nice,' Molly said.

'The tea or the seaside?'

'This. Being here. With you.'

He followed her gaze as she looked out across the sea to the horizon, where grey sea and overcast sky merged.

'What's the other side?' Molly enquired. 'Holland? Belgium? France? I'm not much cop with geography.'

'Holland, I think. I came here on a family holiday once. Must have been about eight or nine, I suppose.'

'We never went on holiday,' Molly said ruefully. 'Not that I can remember, anyway. Well, perhaps we did before Dad was turfed out. She Who Will Not Be Named didn't approve of holidays. Said only the bone idle had time for them.'

'What did your dad do wrong?'

'*Breathe*, probably.' Molly laughed. 'Seriously, though, I don't really know, and that's the frustrating thing. I always assumed there must have been another woman involved, somewhere along the line. Who could blame him, really, for being tempted? Mother would just kill any conversation

I tried to start about him, so I eventually gave up asking. When I left home and went to university, I made some enquiries; set about seeing if I could track him down. Tried again a few years later when we got the internet. But I got nowhere. It was like he'd just disappeared into thin air. Guess you know what that's like, hey? And now I hear about him, one year after his death. Find out he was living under a different identity. It's all very curious.'

Molly looped her arm through his, drawing herself closer to him. The wind was billowing through her hair, and it occasionally made contact with James's face. She kept trying to tame it by tucking strands behind her ear.

'So, you never knew about this great aunt, then?' he asked.

'Nope.'

'When are you going to her house?'

Molly was uncharacteristically quiet for a few moments, then took a deep breath. 'I'm kind of putting it off.'

'You're scared, aren't you? I can see it in your eyes. I never had you down as the type.'

'She's not responded to my letter. What if she spurns me? What if she *does* invite me in and then tells me that *I* was the reason he left? I don't like rejection, Jimbo.'

'You're overthinking it, Moll. Do you want me to go with you? Would that help?'

'Aw, that's sweet of you, but I'd rather do it on my own. Besides, haven't you got some static caravans to be inspecting?'

'Another nine sites, yes. A bit of assistance would be appreciated.'

'You must be having a bloody giraffe, sunshine! Forget it! Mind if I smoke?'

Without waiting for his answer, Molly handed him her tea, then raked through her bag, eventually pulling out a cigarette packet and lighter.

'Been trying to give up for years,' she said, facing away from the wind and taking several attempts to light up. 'But it's my only vice. That is, if you don't count booze, junk food, gambling … and lousy men. I reckon it's all down to *her*, you know. If I'd had a normal mother, I'm convinced I'd be settled down now. House in the country. Aga. Husband. Kids. Labrador. The works.'

'You can't keep on blaming your mother for everything. At some point, *you're* going to have to take responsibility.'

'You sound like my therapist.'

'Reckon I'd make a good therapist.'

Molly gave him a dubious smile. 'Yeah, right. You have to listen, for a start.'

'Sorry, what was that?'

She jabbed him with her elbow. 'Smell that?' she said, taking a deep sniff.

'The sea air?'

'No, you prat. Fish and chips. I'm Hank Marvin. Come on, let's get out of this bloody gale.'

Inside, the fish and chip shop was hot and steamy, and the smell was intoxicating. There were perhaps a dozen dining tables, mostly occupied by elderly couples. The windowed front wall was fogged up. James cleared a circle in the condensation while they waited in the long queue so he could peer out. Ahead of them was a tiny old lady in a head scarf, resting against a tartan zip-up trolley-cum-walker thing.

'Cod or haddock?' Molly asked. 'What's your favourite?'

'Not fussed. They're pretty much the same, aren't they?'

'What? Hell, no! Haddock all the way for me. It's got a fishier flavour and a more tender texture. Cod's firmer. Holds up well to grilling.'

'Cod sounds like my kind of fish.'

'Now you're talking pollocks.'

'*Ha!* See what you did there.'

'Mushy peas?'

'No. Disgusting!'

'Agreed. Remind me too much of my own cooking. I aim for *al dente,* but it's more like *al denture.*'

The queue shuffled forwards, and James got out his wallet in readiness to pay. The old woman in front of them was giving her order.

'Put your money away, Jimbo. This is my shout. You got those speciality teas and the paper.'

'Don't be daft. I'm paying.'

'No,' she said firmly. '*I'm* paying.'

He prised a twenty from his wallet and slapped it down defiantly on the counter.

'Mate, this is the *twenty-first* century. A woman is enti-tled to treat a man. Or is that an affront to your masculinity?'

'Jesus! I just want to pay for two fish suppers. It's not like I'm laying down my coat over a puddle for you.'

Molly raised her voice. 'I've just received three hundred thousand quid from a dead father I hadn't seen for decades, and I have more money than I know what to do with. *I'm* paying.'

The place fell silent, and James sensed many sets of eyes looking in their direction.

'Sorry. Did I say that a little too loud?' Molly feigned.

'Fine, then. You pay.'

'Glad we got there in the end.'

James looked at the counter and frowned. 'Where's my money?'

'What?'

'My twenty-pound note. I put it on the counter.'

They looked about them, but couldn't see it anywhere. In front of them, the counter assistant handed the old woman her food, wrapped in a plastic bag. She opened up her trolley and placed it carefully inside. 'Thank you, dear,' she said, her voice as unsteady as her hands.

'You don't think *she* took it, do you?' James whispered to Molly.

'Well, why don't you go and interrogate her? Read her her rights? I reckon there's only a fifty percent chance she'll die of a heart attack.'

'What can I get you?' the counter assistant asked politely. He had a little name badge on his chest that said "NICK." A young lad, early twenties at most. He gave the appearance of someone who played competitive sport or spent his spare time at the gym. Not someone who indulged in anything as unhealthy as fish and chips. Still, he looked a prat in his white overalls and chip-shop hat, and in that, James took comfort.

'One cod and chips. One haddock and chips, please,' Molly said.

'Anything else?'

She raised her eyebrows flirtatiously. 'How about you and me hit the town after you knock off here, followed by a night of high jinks and no sleep?'

The assistant looked nothing short of the proverbial deer in the headlights. 'Er, I'm sorry …?'

'I'm joking, Nick. Relax. I'm old enough to be your mother. More's the pity.'

'Well … some of my mates are into that … MILF stuff.'

'Mate, I'm joking. Seriously.' Molly did her best to convey indignation, but James detected a hint of pride. She circled her finger over the condiments on the counter. 'Plenty of salt and easy on the vinegar.'

'Same for me,' James said. He felt an urge to crawl under a rock after being exposed to Molly's embarrassing banter.

'Eat in or take away?' the lad asked.

'Eat in,' Molly replied.

'Take away,' James said firmly. 'I'm getting too hot in here,' he added for Molly's benefit.

'Well, looks like we'll be eating out, Nick. I'm always happy to defer to a man.' She just couldn't help herself.

Outside, the wind seemed even fiercer than before.

'Great idea, Jimbo. *Al fresco* dining. Can't beat it.'

'We'll head to the town centre. It'll be more sheltered there, away from the sea.'

'Whatever you say, Jimbo. Just make it quick. I'm bloody starving!'

They walked briskly. James opened up the paper wrapping of his meal and jabbed at the chips with his little wooden spork. Above them, seagulls circled with intent.

They passed numerous bars, cafés and amusement arcades before they reached the centre, which seemed to have more than its fair share of charity shops. They turned a corner, and Molly gestured to an empty bench, which boasted a prime view of a branch of Cash Generator and a computer repair shop. She sat down and started to unwrap her supper.

As James sat down, Molly burst out laughing. She pointed at his shoulder with her spork. 'You've been shat on by a seagull. It's splatted all the way down your back!'

'*For God's sake!* How long have I been walking around with that on me?'

'It's meant to be a sign of good luck, right?'

'Sure. That's *exactly* what it feels like.'

'Give me a minute,' Molly said, and she commenced rummaging through her bag. Her hand emerged, clutching a packet of wet wipes. She teased out a wipe and started to rub at the shit.

'I'll wring their bloody necks if they come anywhere near me! What is it with me and birds?'

'That a philosophical question?'

'Not really. I encountered a grey parrot earlier. Called me an arsehole.'

'Sounds like a good judge of character.'

Molly stowed the wipes back in her bag, then returned to her supper, dutifully selecting a fat chip that she appeared to savour. Then her expression changed, as if something puzzling had just entered her mind.

'What is it?' James asked.

'Just thinking. Don't you think it's a bit weird, you being here to find Urtė, and me, looking for answers about my father? In the same place, I mean. It's like our stars are aligned or something.'

'Horse shit,' James scoffed. 'It's just a coincidence. Nothing more, nothing less.'

Molly set her supper to her side and motioned to the newspaper on James's lap. 'Pass me that, will you?'

'Why?'

She gave him daggers and snatched the paper. After thumbing through the pages, she alighted on the section she was looking for and her mouth split into a smug grin. 'Here we go. Gemini.' She read from the paper: '"*Hopefully, you have got your financial situation on firmer ground because the temptation to spend money may be too much to ignore today. If you must go on a spree, at least splash the cash on things that have lasting value."* Now, tell me that's just a coincidence, after my inheritance?'

James rolled his eyes. 'That's just generic shit that anyone gullible enough will interpret as being applicable to their particular circumstances.'

Molly looked at him reproachfully, then returned her attention to the newspaper. 'You're Virgo, aren't you?'

'Am I?'

'Figures.' She tutted. 'Ah, here we are. Virgo. *"You may not be the sort who shows your feelings easily"*—understatement of the century!—*"but with Mercury, your ruler, linked to passion planet Pluto, your emotions will go from freezing cold to burning hot in two seconds flat. The intensity of your response may shock a few people."* Uncanny, wouldn't you agree?'

A sudden commotion from the other side of the street spared James from the conversation. He looked across to see a girl emerging from Cash Generator, clutching a bunch of items; he couldn't make out what. She was laughing. A scrawny thing: fourteen, fifteen, perhaps. Jet black hair. Pale white skin. Everything pierced. One of those goth types.

A voice boomed from the dark interior of the shop. '*Hey!*'

The girl looked left, then right, then quickly took off along the pavement, shoving her way past surprised pedestrians. Soon after, the owner of the booming voice emerged from the shop: a bearded man in a sleeveless shirt. '*Thief!*' he hollered, before catching sight of the girl and giving chase.

There was no way he was going to catch her in his condition. James rose from the bench, poised to assist, but Molly grabbed his arm.

'Leave it, Jimbo. Think of your heart.'

'My heart's fine.'

Molly smiled sympathetically. 'It's not worth risking your life for the sake of a few old DVDs or whatever it is she's nicked. Come on, fella, let's finish these fish and chips, then you can walk me back to my car.'

THIRTY-SIX

Rosa checked the time again. Kayleigh had been gone for nearly an hour, but the smell still lingered in the change booth. She pinched her nose and sprayed the can of air freshener liberally around her. The girl was in desperate need of a hot shower to wash out the enduring stench from sleeping rough.

Supervising Kayleigh had proved to be exhausting. Like having a toddler to look after, Rosa couldn't take her eye off the girl for a second. Earlier, she'd returned from a toilet break to find Kayleigh unwrapping the cellophane packaging of an iPhone charger. She'd got it from the prize cabinet after unlocking it with the keys Rosa had stupidly left on the shelf in the booth. Some of the arcade machines gave out little yellow tickets, each worth a point, that customers could collect and exchange for prizes. The charger was priced at a thousand points; it was a stupid thing to offer as a prize, but still, Peter would be as mad as hell if he found out one had been tampered with. He'd probably make a deduction from her wages. Nonetheless, Kayleigh had begged her to let her use the charger, just for a few minutes so she could get the phone working. Rosa had relented, assuming Kayleigh needed to make urgent contact with her family or something—but no. When Kayleigh couldn't get past the four digit passcode on the lock screen, she'd admitted that the phone wasn't even hers. She'd stolen the damn thing!

Rosa had nearly blown her top, demanding the girl return everything she'd stolen to their rightful owners. Kayleigh had protested, saying she no longer had most of it. She'd sold it all on. 'Then get it back!' Rosa had shouted. 'I know you steal from that house—the one you pretend was yours. I know where you really live …'

'You're lying!'

'The house has a shark painted on front. I meet your dad—' Rosa stopped herself from saying any more.

Kayleigh had been quiet for a moment, before realising there was a bargain to be struck. 'I'll return everything,' she'd said, 'but only if you let me stay with you.'

The arcade was quiet; just a smattering of customers about. One of those days where time slowed to a crawl and you could end up just staring at the clock for hours on end, driving yourself mad. Days like this made Rosa fret about her job; Peter could easily decide to shut up shop until next year's summer season.

She supposed there was no point worrying about something that might never happen. Besides, something else would turn up. It always did.

The sudden sound of footfalls made Rosa look up. A man, puce with anger, was storming towards her. Startled for a moment, she composed herself when she realised it was a customer.

He jabbed his thumb in the direction of the coin pusher machines. 'Fucking machine's not giving me my prize!' His gaze shifted briefly to Rosa's chest and back to her eyes. 'It's a fucking swindle! I must have sunk more than five quid into it.'

'It is okay, sir,' she soothed. 'I can sort it.'

Rosa grabbed the big set of keys and accompanied the man to the offending machine. His prize—a pencil topped with an eraser styled like a panda's head—was jammed between the ledge and the glass. She opened up the machine and retrieved the jammed pen, holding it out for the man. He grabbed it thanklessly and pocketed it, like he was in fear that someone might otherwise steal his magnificent artefact. Without speaking another word, he left the arcade.

'Come back soon?' she shouted after him.

When she got back to the change booth, Kayleigh was sitting inside, smiling widely, her fringe damp with sweat.

'Well,' Rosa said, addressing the girl through the Perspex divide. 'Did you return everything?'

'Of course!'

'If you lie, I will find out. I can check with owner of house.'

Kayleigh shrugged. 'Be my guest.'

There was the sound behind her of someone clearing their throat, and Rosa turned to discover it was Peter McManus, her boss, standing with his arms crossed, looking particularly displeased. What were the chances? The man owned dozens of venues in town and rarely came to the arcade. When he did, he liked to make surprise inspections to keep everyone on their toes. He lowered his voice. 'Rosa, a word. *Now!*'

Taking Rosa to one side, he motioned towards Kayleigh with a flick of his head and said, 'What is that *thing* doing in there? I don't recall Dracula's love child being on my payroll.'

'I was going to call and explain,' Rosa lied. 'She is

friend in trouble and needs my help. She will only be here for one day, I promise. Her name is Kayleigh—'

'I don't need to know her name, Rosa. I just want her out of here. She reeks, and she's putting off the customers.'

Rosa looked around the arcade. 'What customers?'

'*Exactly!*'

Peter pushed back the sleeve of his coat with his finger, revealing an expensive-looking gold watch on his fat, hairy wrist. 'Right. I've got a business meeting now. But I'm coming back tonight to conduct a stock check. If there's anything unaccounted for, it's coming out of your wages. Got it?'

'Of course.'

Peter glared at Rosa for a few moments, then departed hurriedly.

'See, I tell you, you get me into trouble with my boss,' Rosa said to Kayleigh when she returned to the booth. Kayleigh shrugged in reply, not engaging eye contact.

They sat in awkward silence for several minutes until Rosa could bear it no longer. 'Do you want to tell me about your situation? Why you steal?'

'There's nothing to tell.'

'Why you not at school?'

'Got expelled.'

'You should finish school. Do exams. It is never too late.'

'Who are you? My Mum? I got less aggro from her.'

'What happen to her?'

'It doesn't matter.'

The more questions Rosa asked, the less responsive Kayleigh became, so in the end, she just gave up. Handing Kayleigh a duster and a can of polish, she told her to go and make herself busy. 'Do I have to?' Kayleigh whined.

'Why does everything have to be argument? If you want to stay with me tonight, go clean the machines!'

An old, shaky, familiar voice interrupted them. 'Daisy?'

Rosa turned to Nancy Patterson, standing there with her tartan walker, grinning broadly and brandishing a twenty-pound note.

'Miss Patterson, you make me jump! What are you doing here? It's not your normal day.'

'A nice young man gave me this. Will you change it for me, dear?'

'Of course.'

Nancy's gaze switched briefly to Kayleigh, then she leaned in to Rosa and whispered, 'Has the Jerry got you captive, Daisy? Shall I *neutralise* her?'

Rosa smiled, masking her confusion. 'She is here to help me for the day. Do not worry about her.'

'If you say so, Daisy.'

'Her name is Kayleigh. Say hello to Miss Patterson, Kayleigh.'

'Whassup?' Kayleigh murmured.

Nancy Patterson eyed Kayleigh with suspicion for a few moments before taking the pot of change Rosa had filled for her. She shuffled over to her preferred grabber machine.

'She's nuts!' Kayleigh said indiscreetly.

'*Shh!* Keep voice down. Nancy is lovely. I won't let you say anything bad about her.'

'She thinks I'm a German,' Kayleigh scoffed.

'Oh, is *that* what "Jerry" means? I always wonder.'

Kayleigh laughed. 'Have you never heard of World War Two? You know, Hitler, Churchill, the Blitz …'

Rosa felt wounded, embarrassed by her ignorance. Come to think of it, there was lots she didn't know. History.

Geography. Science. Anything academic. If only she'd paid attention at school, things might have been different …

She pointed to the duster and polish in Kayleigh's hands. 'If you do a good job, I will buy you dinner tonight.'

Kayleigh regarded the cleaning items contemptuously, then said, 'Something Italian?'

Rosa smiled. 'That your favourite?'

'Yep.'

'Mine, too.'

There was a sudden shriek, and their attention was snapped to Nancy Patterson at the grabber machine. 'Daisy! Daisy!'

When Rosa rushed over, the old woman had her hands pressed to the glass, and she was staring into the pile of sequinned unicorns.

'What is it, Nancy?'

'I've *found* her! I've *found* her! Will you get her for me? Be careful! She might be hurt.'

What is *going on in Nancy's muddled mind?* Rosa wondered. She thought it best to humour the old woman, and, smiling warmly, she checked over the machine and found one of the toys in the prize drawer.

A tear rolled down Nancy's cheek as she took the unicorn from Rosa and started to cradle it like a baby. 'There, there, darling. Everything's going to be fine now, I promise.'

Kayleigh slouched over. 'What the *fuck*?'

Rosa elbowed her in the side and flashed her a stern look, but Nancy was oblivious, in a world of her own, tickling under the unicorn's chin. She started to whisper a lullaby: *Amazing Grace.*

Kayleigh laughed, making Rosa cross. She motioned to the other end of the arcade. '*Go!*'

THIRTY-SEVEN

MAY 1941

NANCY WAS LYING on her back, something sharp pressing into her spine. She could hear creaks and groans all around her. The worst thing though was the smell: the stench of gas; the rancid stink of raw sewage; the bitter notes of cordite; damp plaster; brick dust; an odour like burnt toast.

So very cold.

Where was she?

Through a hazy fog of dust, she could see a patch of black sky and a smattering of stars. She couldn't hear a sound.

Nancy struggled to turn her head and look around. She could see no one. She was alone, trapped in a jumble of broken beams and smashed furniture. She was covered in dust. The dust congested her nostrils, and she felt a sneeze coming on. She tried to stop it, but her efforts to resist it just made the pain worse when it finally exploded from her.

How did she get here? She remembered climbing the stairs. Why was she going upstairs when Moaning Minnie was blaring, the guns cracking, the planes whining overhead?

It made no sense. It was far safer in the cupboard under the stairs. She'd taken to sleeping there, in the warm, instead of the cold Anderson shelter, now half-flooded and barely habitable after the atrocious winter. Grandma Ada had been in her armchair, of course, permanently rooted. She slept in it, ate in it …

Oh, God! Had she *died* in it?

Nancy tried to call out for her grandmother, but the words didn't form in her dry, filth-filled mouth. All she could force out was a pathetic *squeak*. Nancy found herself praying that the end, if that was the case, had been swift and painless.

Her head was a fug, and she wondered if she were fatally injured. She had a sharp headache—internal bleeding, perhaps? Strangely, that thought didn't worry her too much.

The blood.

She remembered. Seemed like gallons of the stuff. Gushing from her, all over the carpet, making a terrible mess. She recalled thinking her mother was going to kill her when she got home from her shift at the munitions factory, unless she could get it cleaned up in time …

But why had she been bleeding?

Grandma Ada had sent her upstairs. To fetch a towel. One of the big, fluffy ones from the airing cupboard on the landing, for the …

Baby.

Oh, dear Jesus. The memory hit her like one of Hitler's high explosive bombs.

Nancy had no idea, not the first clue, she'd been carrying a child all that time. Her stomach was as flat as a pancake; how was it even *possible*? Yes, she knew full well that the baby was the product of the night in the shelter, back in the autumn, with Jack. The night of the *act*. A stupid, irresponsible, reckless act, she knew, but it had just seemed so *right*. And, besides, why worry about tomorrow when tomorrow might never come?

One minute, she was experiencing terrible stomach cramps; the next minute, the baby was sluicing out of her onto the floor. It looked like an alien—a squirming, screaming alien, drenched in blood, fluid … gore … attached via the cord to that disgusting, bloody, veiny sponge thing.

Nancy recalled scooping up the pathetic creature into her arms and carrying it to Ada, who'd woken with a start when Nancy had started wailing at her. Oh, God, what must her poor grandmother have thought when she had dropped the baby—a little girl—and all the accompanying *stuff* into her lap?

Nancy had been halfway down the stairs with the towel when the bomb came screaming down. There was the giant thunderclap; the sensation of falling; the terrible feeling that all her organs were being sucked out of her body.

How long had she been lying here? Minutes? Hours? Days? Impossible to know. It felt like the bomb had destroyed time itself. Nancy started to panic. No one was coming to help her. She was going to die alone—before she'd even named her child.

Ivy? Gladys? Faith? Grace? None of them sounded right.

Had she imagined the baby; the shock; the fluids sluicing from her body; the violence of its arrival into the world? Perhaps she was delirious; hallucinating? The pain in her stomach felt real, though. The soreness, too. Nancy moved her hand painfully, awkwardly, and found her night-dress was slick and sticky.

She thought of Jack. If he were alive, he'd have been fighting to get her out; digging furiously with his bare hands. Nancy closed her eyes so that she could see his dirty, impish face once more. She thought, too, of Father, even Mother. She thought of all the things she needed to say to her mother. "*Sorry*", for one. "*I love you*", for another. In an instant, she felt her heart rate calming. *Just keep thinking of them all*, she told herself, to take her mind off her predicament; off the awful smell of gas.

Something shifted above her, and she was sprinkled with a shower of fine dust, forcing her to shut her eyes.

A deep voice boomed, close to her—a man's voice. 'Hello, Nancy. Got yourself into a bit of a scrape, eh? Never mind, let's get you out of here, shall we?' Nancy opened her eyes, painfully, and she could see Mr. Elmswick's grimy face smiling back at her.

'Baby …' she murmured, but she knew it had come out wrong.

'What's that? Ada, you say? Don't you worry about her, darling. I'm sure she'll be as right as rain.'

She fought to correct him, but Mr. Elmswick, seeing her struggle, pressed his finger to her dry lips.

'Don't try to speak, Nancy. Save your energy till you're out. There's a nice cup of tea waiting for you at the canteen. Plenty of sugar, just how you like it. Sod the bloody rations, eh?'

Mr. Elmswick, struggling to manoeuvre himself, turned to shout something unintelligible over his shoulder.

'We'll have you out in a jiffy, sweetheart. The lads have switched off the gas, so you don't need to worry.' He retrieved something from his pocket; it rattled as he brought it closer to Nancy. 'Saw this glinting in the moonlight. We might not have found you so quick if I hadn't. I'm guessing it's your old man's, eh?'

The cigarette case. She'd stowed a little photograph of Jack within, along with the awful emerald ring he'd stolen the night he died.

Nancy nodded weakly. Then a sudden pain shot through her stomach, and she screwed her face in agony. The pain passed quickly, and she felt calmer, but her strength was failing her. She was struggling to keep her eyes open.

'Don't fall asleep on me, Nancy,' Mr. Elmswick pleaded, squeezing her hand. His voice was becoming distant. 'Come on, girl. Not long to wait now.'

But Nancy could resist the lure of sleep no longer.

She was spent. She'd had a bellyful of this war.

THIRTY-EIGHT

WHILE KAYLEIGH SHOWERED and the cheap frozen pizzas cooked in the oven, Rosa set about creating the best Italian dining experience she could in the circumstances. The dingy caravan was a far cry from the pizzerias of Rome or Naples (not that Rosa had ever been). She dug out an old wipe-clean table covering from under the kitchen sink, shook it out and draped it over the table. Come to think of it, it was probably a ground sheet, rather than a table covering, but it had a red and white chequered pattern that served her requirements perfectly. She set down place mats, knives and forks, the salt and pepper pots, and a couple of glasses.

She switched on the old hi-fi in the lounge, twiddling the radio tuner until she found something fitting for the occasion: a classical music station.

Rosa surveyed the pathetically spartan table. What else do they have in Italian restaurants? A big jug of water. She didn't have a jug, but there was a dusty old vase, which she retrieved from the cupboard and rinsed under the tap, before filling with water. Something else?

Candles. She had no candles! And no bread! No salad! No flowers! And even if she did have flowers, there was now nowhere to put them because she was using the vase as a water jug!

This was turning into a disaster.

Calm down. You're being crazy. Breathe.

When Kayleigh eventually emerged, pink and wrinkled, from the shower, Rosa was sitting at the table with two cold, miserably thin pizzas.

The teenager burst into laughter. She sidled over, took the seat opposite Rosa and looked down at the cutlery, bemused. 'What's all this shit for? It's just pizza.'

'I want to make it special.'

Kayleigh tore a wedge from her pizza and stuffed it into her mouth. 'Why?'

'Because … I don't know. I'm on my own for so long, I guess.'

'You're pretty. Why are you on your own, in this shitty caravan? It doesn't make sense.'

'Would you like some water?'

'Don't you have anything stronger?'

'Only vodka.'

'Perfect.'

'I do not think so, young lady.'

Kayleigh continued to gorge on the pizza. Rosa sensed from the look in the girl's eye that she wanted to ask her something, but it took a few more mouthfuls of margherita before she managed, 'My dad. What did he say when you went round?'

A little dagger of fear stabbed at Rosa's stomach. She turned her face away from Kayleigh, uncomfortable under the glare of her enquiry. 'It doesn't matter.'

'He hurt you, didn't he? That's why you're not making me go home. You've seen what he's like.'

'He say something strange to me, about being a *dyke*. Why would he say that?'

Kayleigh scoffed. 'I told him I was a lezza to get him off my back. But it just made him more angry. He went schizo. That's why I left.'

'Has he … Does he … abuse you?'

Kayleigh flashed an irritated look at the Hi-Fi. 'Can you turn that off? It's doing my head in.'

'In a minute.' Rosa placed her hand on Kayleigh's. 'Tell me what he did to you.'

The girl shook her head.

'And your mum? You say she leave home. Did he hurt her? Is that why she leave?'

'I guess. She had a breakdown. The doctors put her in a mental institution.'

'Is she still there?'

'Don't know.'

'Do you want to find out?'

'That bitch left me on my own. With *him*. I don't ever want to see her again.'

A sudden noise startled Rosa. Kayleigh flinched, then looked nervously towards the door.

'Do not worry,' Rosa said, trying not to show her concern. 'The caravan moves in the wind and makes funny noises. You get used to it.'

'You don't look like you're used to it.'

Rosa smiled ruefully. 'Does your father know about this place?'

'Do I look stupid?'

'No. Not at all. I think you are very intelligent girl. Just like my friend, Rūta.'

Kayleigh frowned.

'She was my best friend.'

'*Was?*'

'We lost each other … when we came to England.'

Kayleigh laughed. 'How can you just lose someone?'

'Doesn't matter,' Rosa said sadly, and she pushed herself up from the table. She picked up her plate to take it over to the sink, even though she'd barely touched any of her food.

'What's that, on your arm?' Kayleigh enquired.

Rosa saw that her sleeve had ridden up her arm, exposing several centimetres of the scar beneath. 'Nothing,' she said and quickly pulled down her sleeve.

'See? You don't like all these questions, either.'

Rosa went to take Kayleigh's plate, but the girl stopped her and said, 'I haven't finished. And if you don't want the rest of yours, I'll have it.'

'Fine, take it.' Rosa pushed her pizza onto Kayleigh's plate, then went to the kitchen sink, dumping her plate in the bowl. She squirted some washing-up liquid and ran the hot tap.

'Have you got any games?' Kayleigh asked once she'd finished eating.

'Games? Like what?'

'I'm not fussed. Cards? Board games? I used to play with my mum, on holiday, before she went loopy.'

'There are some under the seat in the lounge. But I never play them.'

'I'll take a look,' Kayleigh said cheerfully and bounded from her seat over to the sofa. As she put her hand on the cushion, Rosa remembered the biscuit tin. '*Wait!*' she said and rushed over to intercept Kayleigh.

'What's the problem?'

'It is very messy in there,' she replied unconvincingly. 'I get the games. You sit back down.'

Kayleigh was many things, and astute was one of them. 'You're hiding something, aren't you? What is it?'

'Go sit down. Get a vodka, if you want.'

The girl's face lit up, and she returned to the kitchen.

Rosa lifted the sofa seat and hauled out the games, setting them down on the carpet. She made a mental note to transfer the biscuit tin to her wardrobe later. She examined the tatty boxes and read out the names in faltering English. 'We have, er … Battleship, Monopoly, Operation, Scrabble …'

'Scrabble!' Kayleigh called out.

'Okay. What is it?'

'You serious? You've never heard of Scrabble? It's simple. You just have to find words that score the most points. I'll show you.'

It didn't sound simple to Rosa at all. Nonetheless, pleased that Kayleigh had seemingly come to life, she took the game over to the table. Kayleigh had opened the vodka bottle and was pouring them each a large glass. The teenager took a mouthful of hers, wincing at the strength of the alcohol, then began setting up the game by laying out the board in the middle of the table and giving them each a little plastic rack. There was a score pad and pen, which she retained, then she took the cloth bag of tiles from the box, shook them and said to Rosa, 'Take seven and put them on your rack, then try and make the best word you can from them. You go first. Just put your word across this middle tile. You get double points on the first go.'

Rosa studied her rack of letters, taking a few sips of vodka to aid her concentration. Eventually, she found a word. 'Okay, what about this?' she announced proudly as she laid the tiles out on the board.

Kayleigh laughed, almost spitting out her drink. 'Is that the best you can do—"net?"'

'How much it score?'

'That's … *ooh*, I might need a calculator for this … six points.' Kayleigh jotted down the score on the pad. 'Take another three tiles. My turn.'

Kayleigh seemed to take forever contemplating the letters she'd been dealt, shuffling her tiles, changing her mind, drinking vodka. She rubbed her chin in deep concentration, then broke out in a broad grin and laid down her word.

It took Rosa several seconds get her mouth around it. '"Jezebels?"' she exclaimed. 'What does it mean?'

'Shameless women!'

'*Ha!* How much?'

'Ninety-four points.'

'What?'

'I get double letter scores for the "J" and the "Z" and fifty bonus points for getting all my letters out.'

Rosa frowned and glared sceptically at Kayleigh. 'Are you sure you not cheating?'

'*No!* I never cheat at Scrabble. I just know lots of words.'

'How?'

'Easy. I read lots of books. It's my favourite thing to do. When I'm reading, I get transported to a better place.'

Rosa liked the sound of that. She couldn't remember the last time she'd read a book. As a schoolgirl, probably.

'Your turn,' Kayleigh said, rummaging in the bag for replacement letters.

The game carried on in a similar vein. More vodka was drunk, more laughter spilled, mostly at Rosa's expense, and Kayleigh continued to produce words Rosa had never heard of, including some two-letter creations like "xu" and "qi", which Kayleigh absolutely insisted were genuine.

At the end of the game, Rosa asked, 'So, what is final score, then? Am I winner?'

Kayleigh totted up the marks on the score pad and said, 'Five hundred and forty to me and ... er, ninety-seven to you.'

'Close, then?' Rosa said, laughing.

'Do you want to play another game?'

'*No!* I need a break.' Rosa got up and took her empty glass over to the sink, filled it with cold water, then knocked it back. Too much vodka had made her lightheaded.

Kayleigh clumsily got to her feet, almost knocking over the bottle. She declared that she needed the loo and stumbled drunkenly through the doorway, giggling.

Rosa took herself to the lounge area, switched off the music, then slumped on the sofa. There was something she was supposed to do, wasn't there? The biscuit tin! It would have to wait; she didn't have the energy to get up off her lazy backside. Besides, she was pretty sure Kayleigh was her ally now and wouldn't steal from her. With luck, she'd seen the light and had put her thieving days behind her.

What was she going to do with her? As much as the idea of company appealed to Rosa right now, allowing the teenager to stay long term wasn't an option. Sooner or later, either that awful man she called a father would find them or, if not him, the authorities—social services; the police; the education department; whoever. No matter how good her intentions, Rosa thought, it must be a crime to harbour an underage girl. And, of course, she had to stay under the radar herself ...

What to do?

Her head was too fuzzy to deal with that question now. Leave it until tomorrow. Relax and enjoy the evening and make the most of the present. Her eyes drooped contentedly at that thought.

An awful, shrill scream flared from the other end of the caravan.

The sound cut Rosa to the bone, and she shot off the sofa and dashed to Kayleigh, finding her in the spare bedroom.

'What happen?'

Kayleigh pointed a shaky finger at the window. 'There's someone out there, in the dark. A man. He was staring right at me.'

Rosa's stomach lurched. 'Who is it? Your father?'

The teenager was terrified. 'I don't know.'

Rosa pressed her face to the window and peered out into the gloom of the night. 'I cannot see anyone. Are you sure?'

'Of course I'm sure!'

'It was probably nothing. Just another resident walking by.'

A sudden pounding at the door made them both jump. 'Stay here,' Rosa said, feeling her heart knocking against her chest. 'Let me see who it is.'

After grabbing the baseball bat from her bedroom, she cautiously approached the door. 'Who is it?' she shouted, tightening her grip on the bat.

'It's me. Clifford,' came the reply, which instantly calmed Rosa.

Sighing with relief, she opened the door. 'Cliffy! It is very late. You scare me. What is wrong?'

Clifford's gaze shifted to the baseball bat and then back to Rosa. 'I saw someone in your van. A stranger. I was worried … about, you know, your st-stalker.'

Rosa smiled. 'Aw, Cliffy, that is very sweet. Thanks for looking out for me. But is okay. It is just my friend. She stay with me for the night. That is not a problem, no?'

Kayleigh appeared at Rosa's side and said to Clifford with a slurred sneer, 'You're that pervert with the camera!'

Clifford started to protest, unable to form a coherent sentence.

'It was … misunderstanding,' Rosa said diplomatically, addressing Kayleigh. 'Clifford is very kind man. Just checking we are okay. Right, Cliffy?'

Clifford Snell nodded and Rosa smiled sweetly at him, before giving a kindly wave. 'Night, night, Cliffy,' she said and closed the door, bolting it securely.

Minutes later, Rosa and Kayleigh were settled on the sofa, watching a movie. Something must have triggered a thought in Kayleigh's mind, and the girl turned to Rosa to enquire, 'How exactly *did* you lose your friend? Rūta?'

Rosa contemplated the question for a few moments. Her instinctive reaction was to reveal nothing at all; to wave away the question; to tell her it hurt too much to travel to the past. But, in the end, she decided to tell Kayleigh everything. Where was the harm, really?

Rosa took a deep breath and began. She explained that her real name was Urtė and that she had come to England from Lithuania, where she had been living with her best friend, Rūta, in a tiny, decrepit apartment in the capital city, Vilnius. Urtė and Rūta had been inseparable since they first met in primary school, having formed an unbreakable bond because of their shared experience of an upbringing without parents. Rūta was brought up by her grandmother after her parents were killed in a car accident, and Urtė had gone into the care system at an early age.

They had been working long hours in shitty jobs with no prospects, earning barely enough to cover the rent and basic necessities. One evening, after a bottle of cheap white wine, Rūta had raised the half-serious suggestion of moving overseas, somewhere with better job prospects.

Urtė, ever the impetuous one, had clasped her hands together and squealed, 'Yes! Let's do it!'

So, that's how it happened. Of course, Rūta had made all the arrangements. She was far cleverer than Urtė, more sensible. Her English was much better, too. She'd found a specialist agency who promised them work in London and arranged their accommodation and their flights to the UK.

They'd landed at a place called Robin Hood Airport, in the north of England, a long way from London. Rūta had been worried, but Urtė wasn't. Their consultant at the agency, Jack, had told them it was a much cheaper option and he'd even arranged for a driver to take them all the way to London.

Exhausted after all the excitement and not long into that car journey, Urtė had fallen asleep on Rūta's shoulder.

It was only when she'd been violently shaken awake that the nightmare began.

THIRTY-NINE

JAMES WAS TRAIPSING AROUND YET another caravan park, getting nowhere, when Molly called. 'Well, how was it? With your aunt?' he asked.

'She wasn't in.'

'Did you even bother trying?'

'Of course I did! Hammered on the door like crazy. Tried the back. Neighbours must have thought I was casing the joint.'

'So, what are you going to do?'

'I popped a note through the letterbox with my details. If she doesn't call, I'll give her one last try tomorrow. If she's not in then, I'll take it as a celestial sign that I was never meant to find out about my father.'

'Tomorrow? Thought you were driving back tonight?'

'Change of plan. Got myself a last-minute booking at a gorgeous little boutique hotel.'

'Do such things even exist in this town?'

'I'm in the penthouse suite, would you believe? The place has got a bit of a retro vibe going on. Incredible sea views.'

'Right.'

'It's called Hillcroft House.'

James let out a big sigh, and Molly chuckled. 'I saw the name on your ridiculous key fob,' she explained, 'while you were fannying about in the fish and chip restaurant. Landlady's a bit odd, don't you think? Reminds me of my old headmistress.'

'Well, I can't stand around chatting …'

'Maybe we can make a night of it? What do you reckon? Come on! It could be such fun.'

'I was thinking of having an early night.'

'What are you, ninety or something? How about a comedy show? I saw a flyer at the guesthouse. I fancy a good belly laugh.'

'Who's performing?' James enquired. 'Anyone famous?'

'Dudley Mackenzie.'

'*Dudley Mackenzie?* As in the guy who used to be on telly in the eighties? Told those politically incorrect jokes?'

'The one and only.'

'Surely he's dead by now?'

'*Au contraire*, Jimbo. So, how do you fancy it?'

'I'd rather spoon out my own eyeballs.'

The warm-up act was a camp geriatric by the name of Barney de Silva. His material didn't seem to have been updated since the seventies, comprising predictable gags about Irishmen, sex and mothers-in-law. His comic timing was dreadful and, to add insult to injury, his microphone kept cutting out at all the wrong moments.

Now, the act had been paused to allow the backstage technicians to fix the sound problems.

The venue—a tired old music hall—was half empty. Or half full, if you were an optimist, which James wasn't.

It had the stale reek of old beer and poor ventilation. Members of the audience, scattered at small round tables, engaged in animated chatter while they waited for the warm-up to resume.

James took a sip from his glass, determined that he was going to make his pint of Guinness last the whole evening. Molly took out her bottle of sauvignon blanc from the ice bucket and filled her glass to the brim.

On stage, an exasperated Barney de Silva tapped the malfunctioning microphone with his finger, triggering a horrific screech of feedback.

'So glad we got here early,' James murmured for Molly's benefit.

'We've nabbed the best seats in the house. What's there to complain about?'

Plenty, James thought but didn't say. He'd have preferred a table in a back corner. Theirs was front and centre and spelled only one thing: trouble. The school pantomime trip of 1989 was forever seared in his memory. The whole year group had travelled by coach to see *Aladdin* at the Hackney Empire. They were barely ten minutes into the performance before Widow Twankey had decided to haul him on stage and force him to sing along to the wishy-washy laundry song. Child abuse. No other words.

'Can't believe you've brought that with you,' Molly said, her eyes elsewhere.

'Huh?'

She nodded at the Fitzroy-Fergusson file on the table beside his pint. 'My company not scintillating enough for you?'

'Take it that's a rhetorical question?'

'Unbelievable. Lucky for you, I'm thick-skinned. Discovered anything useful yet?'

James told her about his call with Andric Panchenko and the revelation of his brother's killing.

'Bloody hell, Jimbo! And you're only just telling me this *now*?'

'I was waiting for the right moment. Like, when you paused for breath …'

Molly raised her index finger while she drank more wine. 'So, what do you think happened? I know! Maybe she gets home all sheepish; creeps to the kitchen to make herself a strong coffee. He comes in for a beer from the fridge, sees the kettle shaking in her hands, the blood spattered all over her face, her clothes. "Good day at the office, dear?" he asks. "Not really, Evgeni," she replies. "I accidentally killed the client." He lets the words sink in, the implications, then gets a little angry; starts slapping her around, throwing her around the kitchen. In desperation, she grabs whatever's close to hand—a frying pan; a rolling pin; a meat tenderiser—and, *wallop!*'

James didn't get the chance to offer his thoughts because, right then, the microphone came back to life just as Barney happened to be shouting into the wings, 'Just get it fucking *sorted*, Kev!'

The audience fell silent and Barney cringed, before quickly resuming character. 'You just can't get the staff these days!' he said with a camp swat of his hand. 'Funny how it never happens in rehearsals!'

He made a series of lame jokes, provoking nothing more than a few embarrassed titters from the audience, before concluding. 'Anyways, ladies and gentlemen, boys and girls and what have you. It's time for the main act of the night. Now, in a *slight* change to our advertised programme, Dudley Mackenzie *won't* be performing tonight.' He motioned for the audience to quieten as it collectively groaned. 'I know, I know, but it can't be helped.

Dudley took a nasty fall in Asda this afternoon and put his hip out.'

Molly jabbed at James with her elbow. 'Maybe you should check it's not an insurance fraud, hey, Jimbo?'

James brought a finger to his mouth. '*Shh!*'

Too late. Barney cupped a hand to his ear and said to Molly, 'What's that, my love? Summat about fraud?'

'Nothing,' she called out breezily. 'Just banter with my friend. He's a private investigator, you see.'

'For Christ's sake,' James muttered. 'He doesn't need to—'

'*Ooh*,' Barney said, directing an exaggerated wink at James. 'A *private investigator*?' He planted his knuckles on his ample hips and started to gyrate. 'You can investigate my *privates* any day of the week, treacle.'

James felt scores of eyes boring into him. He feigned a game smile, then sank into his chair.

'Anyway, as I was saying, before I was *rudely* interrupted,' Barney continued, 'Dudley can't be with us tonight— but fear not, comedy fans, I'm delighted to announce that the show will go on as, fortunately, we have a stand-in for our stand-up.' He paused for laughter that never came. 'I promise, you're going to love 'im. So, without further ado, please bring your hands together and give a huge Great Yarmouth welcome to our very own, homegrown, comedy legend of the future, Michael Winterbourne.'

There was another screech of feedback from the microphone and Barney shot an angry look into the wings. As he exited stage left, he high-fived the clearly nervous Michael Winterbourne as the comedian edged towards the microphone stand, like he was approaching a precipitous drop.

Michael Winterbourne was a weedy-looking guy in skinny black jeans, white trainers and a loud Hawaiian shirt. Couldn't have been much older than twenty-five. Molly raised her hands above her head to clap and whoop encouragement.

As Michael fumbled in his back pocket, a bad feeling washed over James.

Well, as much as it pained him, he was proved correct. The act was a car crash. A catastrophe of epic proportions.

'That's two hours of my life I won't get back,' he groaned later, when he slumped into the back of the taxi. 'The guy was reading from a script, for Christ's sake.'

Molly giggled and slurred something incoherent, then quickly fell asleep on his shoulder for the journey back to Hillcroft House.

At the B&B, it took him an age to coax Molly from the cab and get her up the steps to the front door.

He checked the time: five past eleven. *Shit!* They'd breached Mrs. Elliott's curfew. He had a grim vision of hauling Molly up the emergency staircase and through his attic room window.

Thankfully, the door opened with a turn of his key.

Of course, Mrs. Elliott was waiting for them in the hallway, her judgemental hands clamped to her hips. She looked Molly up and down with contempt, then made a deliberate display of pulling back her sleeve to check her watch before enquiring prissily, 'Good night, was it?'

Molly, on his arm, slurred something, and James smiled awkwardly.

With Mrs. Elliott noisily attending to her locking-up routine at the door, they started their lumbering assent to the attic floor. Molly, in high heels and pissed as a fart after two bottles of white and three G&Ts (not that he'd been counting), kept losing her footing on the narrow treads, lurching each time for the handrail.

Eventually, they got to the little landing at the top.

Molly stole herself against the jamb of her door and caught her breath, then started to rummage through her handbag. She handed James a packet of cigarettes; a lighter; a lipstick; an eyeliner; a packet of travel tissues …

'There you are, you little bugger!' she said and pulled out her key, holding it proudly aloft. 'Coffee?'

James returned her stuff to her handbag, then looked into her eyes. Her pupils were dilated, and her make-up was smudged. A smoky-bar smell hung over her, and she did that thing with her hair: tucking a stray lock behind her ear. It was a tic she shared with Ruth, and it brought back all kinds of feelings for him. He wished, in a way, that he'd thrown caution to the wind and got smashed himself; loosened the shackles of his natural inhibition. But he was determined to keep a clear head for tomorrow, so he threw a thumb in the direction of his room and said, 'Going to get myself a good night's sleep. You should do the same.'

'Come on,' she said, walking two clumsy fingers up his chest. 'The night is young.'

He grabbed her wrist. 'No.'

'Suit yourself, Jimbo.' She turned, fumbled the key in the lock and disappeared into her room, closing the door with a bang.

James sighed heavily, then made for his room.

Inside, he kicked off his shoes, threw the key on the table and draped his jacket over the back of the chair. He was on his way to the bathroom for a glass of water when he heard his phone buzzing. He smiled. It would be Molly, begging him to come back. He could be such an insensitive prick sometimes. She'd just invited him in for coffee, he chastised himself. But when he retrieved his phone from his jacket pocket, he saw that it was a London number he didn't recognise. Who the hell was calling him at this time? Was it a lead? 'Hello?' he said hopefully.

'Is that Mr. Quinn? Mr. James Quinn?'

The formality unnerved him. 'Who's asking?'

'DC Baxter. Sean Baxter. I'm calling from the Met. I know it's late. Is it convenient to talk?'

'I'm guessing that no isn't really an option?'

There was a wry laugh and the officer said, 'This is an important matter, sir.'

James pulled out the chair from under the desk and sat down, a familiar sinking feeling coursing through him. 'What is it?'

'You're a private investigator, I understand?'

'Yes,' James replied, slightly puzzled. 'I used to be a DCI for Herts. Major Crime Unit. Until I—'

The Met detective cut him off. 'I don't need you to recite your resumé, sir. I'll get to the point. We've found a body.'

'A body?' James echoed.

'This afternoon, a member of the public called to report a suspicious object wrapped in plastic, floating in Regent's Canal. A possible human body, they said. Turned out they were right to be suspicious; we found the naked body of a woman inside.'

'*Jesus*. Description?'

'We estimate early-to-mid thirties. She's tall, about five ten, slim build, sixty kilos, long blonde hair.'

'*Fuck!*' James exclaimed. 'Roxie.'

'Care to expand, sir?'

'Of course. But you first. Why are you calling *me*?'

'Well, the thing is, sir,'—Baxter cleared his throat—'the victim's fingers were curled around your business card.'

FORTY

SHE WAS JOLTED awake by a sudden noise.

Rosa's foggy brain told her it was smashing glass, but she wasn't sure she could trust her brain. Perhaps it had happened in her dream?

There was total silence now.

What time was it? She looked at the digital display on the bedside clock: 2:00 a.m. She returned her head to the pillow, but she was wide awake now. Far too alert for sleep.

Better just check everything's okay.

It was cold in the van, so Rosa quickly dressed into warm clothes, slipped on a pair of comfortable pumps and stepped warily into the narrow hallway. She'd made up the bed in the other bedroom for Kayleigh and she didn't want to disturb her unnecessarily. Rosa pressed her ear to the door, but she couldn't hear anything.

Another noise startled her. The noise sounded like it came from the bathroom: a pained groan, followed by splattering.

'Kayleigh?'

More splattering. Rosa smiled. The girl had clearly

drunk too much vodka and was now suffering the consequences.

She rapped on the door. 'Need a hand in there?'

'*No!*'

'Some water? Coffee? Paracetamol?'

'Leave me alone!'

'Okay, sweetheart. Just shout if you need anything.'

Rosa had a dull vodka-induced headache herself. She wouldn't be able to get back to sleep unless she took the edge off with some pills. There was a packet in the kitchen. She started for the door, then halted when she registered an unpleasant, chemical smell.

Then she noticed the whisps of grey smoke seeping through the gap under the door.

O Dieve! she thought. *The oven.*

Had she forgotten to turn it off after the pizza?

Hesitantly, she opened the door.

The heat struck her first, then the blinding yellow light. At the lounge end of the caravan, flames were licking the walls, stretching to the ceiling and crawling along the carpet. The curtains were ablaze. Thick, choking smoke everywhere.

'Kayleigh!' she shouted. 'There is *fire!* Get out! Get out! *Now!*'

Rosa turned back, intent on collecting Kayleigh and shepherding her from the caravan, then she stopped herself, remembering the stash of money under the bench. No way could she let the fire destroy it and send her back to square one. Not after all her hard work; her sacrifices.

She took a deep breath, covered her face with the crook of her arm and pushed herself through the smoke. The smoke was too thick, so she dropped to all fours. Better. She stole a deep gulp of air, which made her cough, then started to crawl towards the sofa, across shattered glass. The heat became more intense the farther she crawled.

'*Kayleigh!*' she shouted again. '*Get out!*'

A sudden scream erupted from behind her. Rosa stole a look over her shoulder, and through the blur of smoke, she could make out Kayleigh's outline. She had something wrapped around her head; a towel, she guessed. 'Get out!' Rosa croaked. 'I will be there in a minute.'

Kayleigh paused for a moment as if in shock, then scrambled to unlock the door, eventually getting it open. She gave one quick look at Rosa, then fled from the van.

Thank God, she's safe.

Coughing uncontrollably now, Rosa groped for the sofa seat, swung it open and fumbled inside for the tin. She grabbed it, tucked it under her arm, then leapt to her feet and hurtled through the flames and smoke, out through the open door, into the cold night.

She doubled over, coughing.

'Kayleigh?' she tried to shout, but the word stuck in her raw throat.

Her eyes stung and were streaming with tears.

Flames leapt from the van and Rosa moved farther away, fearful that the gas might ignite and cause an explosion.

A muffled scream snapped her attention to the distance. She blinked furiously and wiped her eyes. Through her blurred vision, she could make out the figure of a person—a man—tall, and large framed. He was half-carrying, half-dragging an object—something heavy and awkward, Rosa judged from the manner of his lumbering gait.

Except it wasn't an object. It was Kayleigh.

Rosa took off after them, and as she got closer, she saw the man was dressed in dark clothing and a balaclava. He held Kayleigh around the waist, in the crook of his arm. She guessed his other hand was clamped to her mouth to stop the girl from screaming.

It had to be her father. But how had he found the van? How did he know Kayleigh was inside? Had he been watching them? Waiting for an opportunity? What was he going to do to his daughter?

The answers to those questions could wait. The most important thing now wasn't *why* it was happening, but *stopping* it from happening.

Rosa swallowed the urge to cough. She needed to take the piece of scum by surprise.

She was now a couple of metres behind them. She held the biscuit tin in both hands and raised her arms aloft, poised to pummel it down on his skull.

An almighty explosion erupted behind her.

The force of the blast threw her to the wet grass, making her drop the tin. Clumps of burning material thudded into the ground around her, clattered on tin roofs. Instinctively, her hands flew up to protect the back of her head.

Rosa lay for a few seconds, disoriented, trying to work out if she'd been injured (not so far as she could tell). She lifted her head and saw that Kayleigh and her abductor had also fallen. The girl was trying to scramble away, but the man grabbed her leg. She let out a scream.

Where was the biscuit tin? Rosa got up and looked about her, quickly locating it on account of the metallic surface reflecting the light from the fierce flames consuming her home. She snatched the tin and clambered towards the man.

'*Hey!*' she screeched before realising in an instant she should have stayed quiet. No matter, she still had the upper hand, so long as she acted fast.

The man released his grip on Kayleigh, and as his head snapped towards her, Rosa smashed the tin into his face. Again and again. He howled in protest and flung desperate hands up to shield his face, trying to protect himself. She lifted the tin above her head and slammed it against his head. The brute force caused the lid to come off and the contents spilled out. The wind caught the notes —dozens and dozens of them; tens, twenties, even fifties— and scattered them amid the smoke.

The man slumped to the ground, groaning.

Rosa hastily set about collecting the cash, stuffing it back in the tin, in her pockets. Within moments, Kayleigh joined in, her voice groggy and confused. 'Where's all this from?'

'It does not matter. Just help me.'

Then there came the distant sound of sirens.

'We must go!'

Kayleigh held a huge fistful of cash, but between the two of them, they'd only salvaged a fraction of the stash. Rosa snatched the cash from Kayleigh and stuffed it into the tin, fastening the lid. She stole one last look at the man, at the abandoned cash, then took the girl by her wrist.

'Come! We must leave!'

She noticed that lights had come on in a few surrounding caravans; she could hear doors opening. Voices. Panic.

They took a route that avoided any unwanted attention: around the dark edge of the park, along the overgrown pathway, and into the neighbouring housing estate.

They ran through empty streets for several more minutes before Kayleigh complained. 'Stop! I can't run anymore.'

Rosa was breathless, too, and her coughing fit was back with a vengeance. She sat on a low garden wall and patted the space to her side. Kayleigh joined her on the wall, dropping her head into her hands while she caught her breath.

'I feel sick,' Kayleigh said eventually.

'We need to find water,' Rosa wheezed.

'Do you think he's dead?'

Rosa shook her head. 'No. He will live.'

'Shame. So, what do we do now?'

'We need to get out of town. Go as far from here as we can.'

'How? Look at us! We look like a couple of tramps.'

Rosa laughed. Kayleigh wore one of her grey track-suits, and it was covered in vomit stains. Rosa's clothes were blackened with soot. The laughter triggered another coughing fit.

'There are no trains or buses now,' Kayleigh continued. 'And no one's going to give us a lift like this. Unless they're a psycho.'

'You are right. We must find somewhere for the night, to get washed and change our clothes.'

Behind them, there was a sound and then a man's voice boomed, 'Hey! Do you know what time it is? Fuck off from my property!'

Rosa look around to see a bare-chested man at an open first-floor window.

'Sorry,' she said.

'Look at the state of you two!' the man continued. 'Fucking dykes.'

'Keep your hair on, *mate*,' Kayleigh shouted defiantly, jumping to her feet.

Rosa put her arm on Kayleigh's. This was no time to make a scene. 'Come on,' she muttered. 'Let's get out of here.'

They walked away, to the sound of the man slamming

the window shut. They trudged the cold, empty streets aimlessly for several minutes. The keen wind was making Kayleigh's teeth chatter. Rosa looped her hand through the girl's elbow, holding her tight.

They turned into a street and Rosa instantly recognised Nancy Patterson's house, looming large and incongruous with its neighbours. She stopped abruptly.

'What is it?' Kayleigh said.

'The house, there. It's Nancy Patterson's.'

'I know,' Kayleigh said. 'Everyone knows Nancy. Do you think she'll put us up?'

'I don't know. Maybe we should not scare her at this time of night.'

'She's probably awake. You know old people. They sleep during the day and stay up at night, don't they?'

'I'm not sure that's right? And what will we say to her?'

Kayleigh's face broke into a big, devious smile. 'I have an idea …'

FORTY-ONE

Nearly three a.m. and James was lying in bed with a filthy headache brought on by too much thinking and not enough sleep.

None of the facts were confirmed, but the explanation was too compelling: the body in the canal had to be Roxie. He'd established from his conversation with DC Baxter at the Met that she'd been severely beaten, then strangled and dumped in the Regent's. Purposely not weighted down so her body would rise and be discovered.

It wasn't an exact science, and it depended on a whole host of variables, like the depth and temperature of the water, the contents of the woman's stomach, the amount of air trapped in her clothes, and the bag she'd been dumped in, but if the body was dumped soon after death, then his best guess was that it had risen to the surface within twelve to forty-eight hours.

James wondered if there was anything he could have done to save Roxie? He, of all people, knew the danger women like Roxie lived under each day. Worse than the feeling that he should have done something to help her was the feeling that he had inadvertently set in motion the events that had led to her death. There was no point, however, in dwelling on it. There was nothing to be gained from pondering *what if*s. The best thing he could do for Roxie—and for Urtė—was to uncover the truth.

What, then, was Panchenko's next move? Did he now have new information that would help him track down Urtė, the woman who killed his brother? The worst case scenario, he deduced, was that, just as he had, Panchenko had discovered the number of the Sailor's Tavern in Great Yarmouth. He hoped Roxie had told the truth when she'd told him she knew nothing more about Urtė's location.

But James had to face a hard truth. Both he and Panchenko had the same mission: to find Urtė. James just had to make sure he found her first.

A gust of wind buffeted the rickety sash, distracting him from his thoughts but compounding his headache. He swung his legs from under the duvet and sat upright on the edge of the bed, rubbing his eyes. After switching on the bedside lamp, James stepped as lightly as he could over to the bathroom, conscious not to disturb the occupants in the room below, or Molly, on the other side of the wall.

The strip light above the bathroom mirror cast him in a harsh, white light, illuminating every blemish; the grey-flecked stubble; the deep creases of his brow. The whites of his eyes looked a sickly yellow, riddled with red veins.

What a state you are, James Quinn.

His medication crowded the shelf. Statins; anti-platelet agents; blood pressure lowering tablets; calcium channel blockers; chest pain relief; anticoagulants; pills to help protect the lining of the stomach … You name it, he took it.

He found a blister pack of co-codamol and teased out a couple of pills, popped them on his tongue and threw back his head to swallow them. Hopefully, they'd dull his brain and allow him some sleep so he could attack his mission with fresh vigour in the morning.

He returned to the bedroom and dropped onto the bed. The light cast by the lamp cut across the picture on the wall, leaving half of it in sinister shadow. James hadn't really paid any attention to the picture before. It was a reproduction oil painting of a pretty young girl with her hands clasped around an ornate cage. Inside the cage was a sad-looking bird on its perch. No doubt the original artist was famous; James didn't have a clue, being ignorant where art was concerned.

The picture triggered a childhood memory long tucked away. His brother, David, had been entrusted with the custody of his friend's budgie for a couple of weeks, to cover a family holiday. The bird was a timid little blue thing called Lucky. David had quickly grown bored of Lucky, so James, always the more conscientious of the brothers, had taken on the responsibilities: filling his feeder; replenishing the water dispenser; clearing the droppings from the bottom of the cage. One morning, as usual, and before the rest of the family were awake, James had gone into the living room with the box of Trill and removed the cover from Lucky's cage. The budgie had looked so sad and dejected, alone on his wooden perch. *What better way to cheer him up*, young James thought, *than to release him from his little cell? Let him fly around the room, give him a taste of freedom, if only for a few minutes?*

He'd made sure the doors and windows around the room were all shut and then he'd opened the hatch, coaxing Lucky from his cage with some encouraging whistles. The bird had hopped to the ledge, stretched his wings, checked the coast was clear, chirped a happy chirp and had then taken flight—straight into a window and a premature death. Shocked, but possessing the clearheaded decision making that was to stand him in good stead in later life, James had scooped up the limp-necked corpse, placed it gingerly on the bottom of the cage, closed the hatch, replaced the cover and crept back to bed. The truth had never emerged.

The memory of Lucky made James think of the weirdo in the caravan and his pet parrot. Clifford and Newton. No wonder the wife had run for the hills. What was her name? The parrot had chanted it. Rosie? Rose? *Rosa!* Nice name. Brought to mind an English rose: wind-flushed cheeks; plump lips; flawless complexion. Whatever had possessed her to marry such a man in the first place? None of his business. People probably asked the same question of Ruth.

Rosa.

James stiffened.

Was the parrot *really* chanting the name of the wife? Or was it the alias of a resident, whose identity Clifford was protecting? The man had seemed guarded, but James had put it more down to personality than intention.

Made sense, though. Or was his imagination getting the better of him?

There was only one way to find out.

James's mind went into overdrive. He threw open the wardrobe and grabbed a pullover. Put on his jeans, a pair of socks, his jacket and grabbed the keys.

He was halfway down the stairs when he realised he'd be better off taking the fire escape route instead. Why risk the wrath of the redoubtable Mrs. Elliott?

Like a cat burglar, he slipped noiselessly out of the window, leaving a finger-width gap so he could get back in later. He scurried down the metal staircase to the small courtyard at its base, then hurried along the path to the car park.

FORTY-TWO

THE SPEED LIMIT WAS THIRTY, but he was edging forty. Speeding didn't seem like such a big deal right now; the streets were deserted, and there were no cameras about. Thank God he'd stayed sober.

The Audi rounded a bend and, out of nowhere, James was blinded by oncoming headlights. His forearm flew up to shield his eyes. The vehicle, its engine roaring, hurtled past him. Christ only knew what speed *he* was doing! A boy racer in a souped-up Corsa, no doubt.

He reached Sandy Bay Holiday Park and parked by the entrance. As he emerged from the car, he felt the heat of the flames immediately, and he could hear the crackle and spit of fire. Ash and debris everywhere; burning embers swirling in the wind.

As he dashed towards the source of the heat, he encountered a small crowd gathered near a burning caravan. 'Is there anyone inside?' he shouted at no one in particular.

'Don't know.' A man's voice. 'The door's open. Maybe she got out?'

'Or maybe the explosion blew the door open?' a woman said, before adding, 'These bloody vans are a death trap!'

'Who lives there?' James asked.

'Rosa,' the woman replied.

Knew it.

James covered his mouth and nose with the crook of his arm and edged towards the open door, but it was hopeless; the heat and smoke beat him back before he could get within a couple of metres.

'Rosa?' he yelled. 'Are you in there?' The smoke triggered an awful coughing fit, and he had to turn away from the fire.

Scanning the faces of the gathered crowd, he demanded, 'Has anyone seen her?'

Silence.

He noticed a couple of kids squatting on the ground nearby, scooping up pieces of paper and stuffing them into their coat pockets. When he drew closer, he saw that the scraps of paper were bank notes. *What the hell?*

He spun back to the adults, shouting, 'Has anyone called the fire brigade? Police?'

'My wife's calling now.'

Anger surged in his chest. The residents were just standing, gawping. No one was *doing* anything to help. 'Anyone got an extinguisher?'

'Cliff'll have one,' an elderly man said, pointing to the distance. 'The site manager. Van D14, at the far end. I'm surprised he didn't hear the explosion. He's normally the first to …'

The man's words trailed off as James charged towards Clifford Snell's caravan. He was livid. If he'd just told him the truth yesterday …

The caravan was in darkness, and there was no

response when he rapped hard on the door. James pressed his face to a window, but he couldn't make out anything inside.

He knocked the door again, then tried the handle. The door opened.

He hesitated for a moment, instinctively reaching into his pocket for his phone. A career investigating major crime told him that it was rarely a good idea to enter a property via an unlocked door in the dead of night without backup. An inner voice offered the counterview that delay can be just as costly. Potentially deadly.

'Mr. Snell? You there?'

James took a cautious step inside, knowing that he could be walking into a crime scene. Precisely what crime, he didn't know. His remote detective brain was now drawing faint dotted lines between the explosion, Roxie's murder and Fitzroy-Fergusson's death.

He put the light on. The flickering fluorescent light overhead illuminated a trashed interior: chairs thrown about the place; smashed glass and crockery; pots and pans; paperwork; foil cartons everywhere. The parrot's cage had been knocked to the ground. The hatch was open, and there was no sight or sound of the bird.

Or its owner.

'Mr. Snell?' James called out again, advancing into the kitchen area. 'Clifford?'

No response.

The wail of sirens heralded the arrival of the emergency services. He hoped to God that Urté hadn't been killed in the explosion; that she'd somehow escaped and was safe somewhere, unharmed.

A cutlery drawer had been pulled out and upended, its contents strewn over the countertop. He groped through the mess, quickly locating a carving knife. He trained his ear for any sound that might indicate the presence of another human. Nothing.

The door rebounded off the wall when he kicked his way into the inner hallway. He flicked the light switch and tentatively crept farther into the claustrophobic corridor, calling Clifford's name, the knife raised before him.

A door to his right, half the width of a standard door, was open. James stole a look inside: a tiny, disgusting bathroom comprising a shower cubicle, toilet and basin. Bizarrely, the shower cubicle was being used for storage of all kinds of random stuff: tins of paint; mops; boxes piled waist-high. Perched on top was the bulk pack of *Um Bongo*, ripped in one corner, a carton removed.

There was a sudden *bang* that made the entire caravan judder. His stomach lurched before he realised it was the wind slamming the main door shut.

Two further rooms at the back, both doors shut. Bedrooms, presumably. He opened one door and squeezed his way inside. The light switch didn't work, so he side-stepped to allow light to spill in from the hall.

There was a flicker of movement in the corner of his eye. Some kind of material hung, flapping, at the window. On closer inspection, he found that it was a large sheet of black cardboard made from smaller pieces held together with Sellotape. The sheet had come away from its fixing at the top of the window and the wind was blowing in, exploiting a small gap in the ill-fitting single glazing.

A line of string hung from one wall to its opposite like a washing line, but instead of items of clothing, there were pieces of paper pegged to the line. Black-and-white photographs. He couldn't make out what they depicted in the dim, residual light. There were several lone pegs, and James looked down to see that he was treading on more photos.

A narrow workbench stretched the length of the interior wall, housing the paraphernalia of a photographer's darkroom: bottles of chemicals; sheafs of paper; archive boxes. An old-fashioned Pentax camera hung by its strap from a hook on the wall. Who the hell still developed photographs this way?

James snatched some of the photos from the carpet and returned to the hallway. Standing under the light, he flicked through the pictures. A bird feeding its young in a nest. The same bird, departing the nest. The bird, again, this time on a tree branch, silhouetted against a moody sky, grubs poking from its beak.

The next picture caught him off guard.

The photo had captured a woman standing at a caravan window, presumably at the kitchen sink. She wore a tight-fitting top, with her ample cleavage on display. From the compressed perspective, James could tell that it had been taken from a distance, with a telephoto lens.

Was it her? Urtė?

There was a reasonable resemblance—the right kind of age and build. James discovered more pictures of her: emerging from a caravan door; walking along a path; in an amusement arcade. Jesus, was the guy *stalking* her?

For a moment, he'd forgotten where he was, and what he was supposed to be doing. James dropped the pictures to the floor and tightened his grip around the knife handle.

Only one door remained. Had to be his bedroom.

He rapped loudly on the door and said, 'Clifford? It's James Quinn. The detective.'

When there was no answer, he cautiously opened the door.

It was the smell—the stench of a violent death—that struck him first, making him gag.

Clifford Snell, naked except for his underpants, was

sprawled on the bed, blood spattered everywhere, coating the Arsenal-themed duvet cover.

James put two fingers to the site manager's neck to check for a pulse. Nothing. He wasn't sure why he'd bothered; it was glaringly obvious that Clifford was dead.

James had seen his fair share of dead bodies in gruesome circumstances, but this one was up there. No painstaking forensic investigation was needed to piece together the puzzle of this death. The hole in Clifford's chest told James the cause of death was a bullet to the heart. The cuts, scratches, lacerations, welts and bruises covering his torso and face spoke of torture over a prolonged period. The objective of the assailant's torture? Surely to get Clifford to give up Urtė's location. He'd clearly resisted, but every man has his limit.

And what was the straw that broke the camel's back?

The answer was skewered to the wardrobe door with a kitchen knife, next to an Arsenal-themed calendar: the lifeless body of the grey parrot, slick with blood, its head lolling unnaturally, limp and twisted.

James took a few moments to steady himself, called 999 to report the homicide, then raced back to the scene of the explosion.

The caravan was now a burnt-out, smouldering shell, dripping with water.

A fire officer emerged from the wreckage, and James was the first to accost him. The officer gestured for him to step back.

'Anyone in there?' James asked impatiently.

The officer removed his helmet and wiped his brow with a gloved hand. 'No, it's clear.'

'Thank God for that! What happened?'

'And you are?'

'James Quinn. I'm a detective,' he said, fumbling in his pocket for a business card.

The guy motioned for him not to bother. 'Petrol bomb, mate,' he said laconically, then went off to join other members of the fire crew.

James turned to inspect the wreckage of the caravan. Panchenko had to be responsible. He'd either wanted to kill Urtė outright or flush her out. With no body at the scene, he must have taken her. But where?

He turned back to interrogate the residents milling about, choosing anyone who'd engage eye contact.

'When was the last time you saw Rosa?' ('Can't remember.')

'Are you sure you haven't seen anyone suspicious lurking about? ('The only suspicious person's *you*, mate!')

'Where are the fucking police?' (Silence.)

God, the speeding vehicle he'd passed on the way over! Was that him? Panchenko? The car had passed by in such a blur that James didn't even clock what make of vehicle it was, let alone its colour, model or registration.

There was nothing to be gained from hanging around here any longer, so he ran back to the Audi. While he ran, he pulled out his iPhone and started to input 999, but, on cue, a squad car turned the corner. He flagged the vehicle down. Inside were four uniformed officers. As they got out and hurried towards the scene of the fire, James addressed the one who was clearly in charge, an overweight man rapidly becoming out of breath.

'You need to declare a critical incident and send out some urgent transmissions over Airwave. A woman has been abducted. The suspect is a man named Andric Panchenko, and he's highly dangerous. Known links to organised crime.

He petrol-bombed the missing woman's caravan. Her name is Urtė Cuda. I can give you a description. She's in grave danger. I believe Panchenko intends to kill her. We might already be too late. Are you *listening* to me?'

The officer addressed one of his colleagues. 'Crawford, you and Barnsey take the explosion. Secure the scene. Speak to the fire crew. Take witness statements. Smithy, you and me will handle the alleged homicide.'

'*Hello!*' James erupted. 'Did you hear what I was saying about the abduction?'

'Are you the individual who reported the homicide, sir?'

'Yes,' he snapped.

'Then take us to the location. Constable Smith will take the details regarding the missing woman there. Got that, Smithy?'

'Sarge.'

James flashed a look at Constable Smith, who returned his gaze with a timid smile. In his ill-fitting uniform, the guy looked about twelve.

The officers split into the two groups.

'I didn't catch your name?'

'James Quinn.'

'Sergeant Lawson. Who's the victim?'

'Clifford Snell. The site manager.'

'And he's definitely deceased?'

'Yes. Shot through the chest. The nature of the scene indicates he was tortured to give up information on Urtė Cuda's location—'

'You don't need to concern yourself with motive right now. Leave that to the professionals. Unless'—he looked James up and down—'you *are* a professional?'

'I'm a detective.'

Lawson stopped walking for a moment and raised a doubtful brow.

'Private,' James added, by way of reluctant quali-fication.

'I see.'

James detected the familiar look of scorn in the sergeant's expression.

Lawson was well into his fifties, James guessed. Sergeant was clearly the highest rank he was ever going to achieve. 'I used to be a DCI ...' He was about to put Lawson in his place when he noticed a security camera fixed to a telegraph pole. It was a cheap, amateurish model, but it looked new.

By the time they got to Snell's caravan, Lawson's breathing was ragged.

'Here,' James said. 'The body's in the bedroom at the back. Left-hand side. You won't miss it. And while you're inside, see if you can find a computer; a laptop, probably. Anything. I think the deceased recently installed security cameras.'

Lawson flashed James an annoyed look, then stepped through the doorway, quickly turning around on the threshold and holding out a palm to indicate to James that he and Smith were to remain outside.

'You'll need to get the forensics team out, obviously,' James said.

'Gee, I hadn't thought of *that!*' Lawson paused to gulp down air, then continued. 'Smithy, take down the details of the abduction from Jessica Fletcher here while I check out the body.'

Constable Smith took out his notebook and pen, licked a finger and painstakingly located a blank page.

'Are you on work experience, son?' James asked.

'Eh?'

'Doesn't matter.' James handed him Urtė's photograph and began to explain the story of her disappearance. He hadn't got very far when Lawson hollered from inside, '*Jesus H. Christ!*'

James winked at Constable Smith. 'That'll be the parrot.'

FORTY-THREE

Kᴀʏʟᴇɪɢʜ ᴘʀᴇssᴇᴅ her thumb on the bell for the third time.

'Come on, let's go,' Rosa said. 'Is not fair to wake her.'

'*Shh!* I hear something. She's coming!'

Moments later, the door creaked open. Nancy Patterson stood before them like a geriatric phantom, in her ankle-length nightgown and cosy slippers. 'Daisy?' she said, her face a picture of concern. She glanced briefly at the biscuit tin Rosa held tightly to her chest before enquiring, 'Whatever's the matter?'

Not entirely comfortable with Kayleigh's plan but with no other alternative, Rosa blurted, 'A bomb fell on my home and we have no place to stay.'

'Oh my goodness! Are you hurt?'

'No. But my house is destroyed.'

'Those blasted Jerrys! Come inside, dear, at once.'

'Kayleigh, too?'

The old woman hadn't registered Kayleigh's presence, and she turned to her, eyeballing her with great suspicion.

'It's okay, she is not the enemy, Nancy. Remember?'

'All right, Daisy. I trust you.' Nancy motioned for them to move into the house. 'Quickly now!'

Nancy closed the door behind them, sliding across several bolts.

The temperature inside was cool, but it was at least a relief to be out of the bitter wind. The capacious hall was lit by a totally inadequate candle wall sconce, which threw flickering shadows to the ceiling. Rosa was struck by the musty, old house smell.

'You poor things,' Nancy cooed. 'I didn't hear the air raid warning. Must have slept through it. Have they sounded the all-clear?'

'Yes,' Kayleigh chimed in.

'We do not want to be trouble,' Rosa added.

'Nonsense, Daisy! We're all in this together, aren't we? You both look chilled to the bone. You need hot drinks. Sugary teas? Perhaps something a bit stiffer? I could add a drop of brandy? That'll warm you up; get the blood flowing again.'

Kayleigh puffed her cheeks as if she might throw up.

'Tea is good, Nancy. Thank you.'

The old lady gestured to an open doorway. 'You go through to the sitting room and make yourselves comfortable. I won't be a moment.'

Kayleigh flicked on the ceiling light as they entered the room.

'*Wow!*' Rosa exclaimed. It was like stepping into the past; a museum display. The room was a feast for the eyes: walnut display cabinets; chunky leather armchairs with curved arms and gold cushions; a tiled fireplace with an art-deco mirror hanging from a picture rail above it; a bureau in the corner, covered in papers; a sideboard bearing a gramophone and a frosted-glass table lamp; bare floorboards; and a huge, geometrically patterned rug.

Against the length of one wall were floor-to-ceiling shelves, crammed with old books. Thick, dark curtains hung at the window, blocking out any light from outside.

Kayleigh moved to the fireplace, where framed photographs cluttered the mantelpiece. Pointing to one, she said, 'This must be her, before she was ancient.'

It showed a smartly dressed young woman at a glamorous reception, receiving an award from an official-looking man.

Kayleigh shifted her attention to the bookshelves. As she ran her finger over the spines, her face lit up in awe.

'Do not touch *anything*!' Rosa demanded.

There was the sound of rattling china behind her, and Rosa turned to see Nancy struggling with a laden tea tray.

'Let me help,' Rosa said. She put the biscuit tin on the floor and took the tray from her, setting it down on a side table.

Nancy shuffled back towards the door and pressed the light switch, plunging the room into almost total darkness.

'Nancy?' Rosa said, perturbed. 'I can't see.'

Seconds later, a small table lamp flickered to life.

'It must be the shock of the bomb, Daisy dear. You know we can't be letting out the light! Please, sit down. Both of you.'

Rosa took two cups of tea from the tray and handed one to Kayleigh, then they both sat in an armchair each. Nancy shuffled over to another chair and, with a great amount of effort, dropped herself into it.

Rosa took a sip of tea and winced. '*O Dieve*, this tea is sweet.'

Nancy tapped the side of her nose with her crooked forefinger and lowered her voice. 'Don't tell anyone, Daisy, but I have a great stash of sugar under the kitchen sink. For occasions just like this. *Bugger* the rations, hey?'

Rosa smiled through her confusion. She swallowed the tea without further fuss.

'You're quiet…' Nancy said, addressing Kayleigh, before turning to ask Rosa, 'What's her name?'

'Kayleigh.'

'Hayley? That's nice, I suppose.'

Kayleigh yawned extravagantly, then said, 'I'm tired.'

'Of course, it's late. What am I thinking?' Nancy forced herself from the chair. 'You must get yourselves to bed. I haven't been upstairs for a long time, but I think the beds are made up. Pick a room each, girls. There's plenty of space. There's a bathroom up there, too, if you'd like to take a wash. And help yourselves to any of my clothes in the wardrobes. I think my frocks will fit you perfectly well, Hayley.' Nancy's gaze shifted to Rosa's chest. 'Although for you, Daisy dear, they might be rather tight for comfort.'

'Where do you sleep, Miss Patterson?' Rosa enquired.

'Downstairs, with Lottie, of course. I need to be able to get out of the house fast whenever duty calls. Don't you remember anything? That bomb has *clearly* done you some damage, dear.'

Upstairs had the feel of somewhere no human had occupied for years. The rooms—spartan, dusty, draughty and full of cobwebs—echoed with the sound of footfalls as they tiptoed their way around on the bare floorboards.

Kayleigh, ignoring Rosa's protest, clambered up the steep staircase to the attic floor.

Rosa sighed and left the teenager to it. She was exhausted and was desperate for a wash. She found the bathroom and tried to turn on the basin taps, only to find they were stuck fast. Eventually, after strenuous effort, the cold one gave out. The water ran an awful rusty colour for a minute before it became clear, and Rosa splashed her face, wincing at the icy discomfort. She did her best to clear her face of the grime from the fire, then dabbed herself dry with a crusty towel that hung from a rail under the window.

An awful taste lingered in her mouth, and she searched amongst the dusty pots, packets and lotions in the vanity unit above the basin for toothpaste. She found what she was looking for and, in the absence of a brush, squeezed a small ball of paste onto her fingertip and ran it over her gums. It was gritty and had a funny taste; not at all like any toothpaste she'd previously experienced. For a horrible moment, Rosa wondered if it was even toothpaste at all.

She returned to the landing and examined each of the three bedrooms leading off it from their doorways. The one at the front of the house was her preferred option because it had twin beds, each neatly made up. She flicked the light switch, but nothing happened. Fortunately, there was a streetlamp on outside, exploiting a small gap in the curtains, so she needn't face the prospect of total darkness. Rosa was hopeful that Kayleigh would want to join her in this room. She didn't fancy the idea of sleeping alone in a creepy old house like this.

The sodium glow of the streetlamp illuminated a small wardrobe in one corner. Rosa opened it, and a powerful mothball stench hit her. The rail was tightly packed with garments, which she walked her fingers through, finding a long cotton nightgown. Shucking her dirty clothes to the floor, she quickly changed.

The room was cold, and Rosa could feel a draught coming from the window. She found the window slightly ajar and tried to close it, but, like the bathroom taps, it was stuck fast. As she stared out at the deserted street for a few moments, fear rumbled in her gut, so she turned away from the window and climbed into bed.

Above her, she could hear Kayleigh's roaming footfalls. Doors banged and drawers opened. There was a minute or so of relative silence before she heard the sound of the girl trudging back down the stairs. Rosa called out to her quietly but firmly, 'In here.'

Kayleigh came into the bedroom. 'Is this where we're staying, then? Cool!' She wore a huge grin.

Rosa looked at her sternly. 'What were you doing up there?'

'This house is *amazing*. It's full of books and old stuff. Loads of things from the war, like you wouldn't believe.'

'And what is that I see, in your hand?'

Kayleigh held out an object. 'Check it out.'

Rosa ran her hand over the shiny, metallic object. It was a container of some description, covered in scratches and indentations.

'It's an old cigarette case with a bullet hole in it. Look!'

'I say no touching Miss Patterson's things! Put it back!'

'I'm going to ask her about it tomorrow. It must be something important as it was locked in a safe.'

'A safe? Then how did you open it?'

'She'd written down the code in a notebook. It took me, like, two minutes to find it!'

'Kayleigh! Get washed and changed. We must sleep. There are many clothes in cupboard.'

Kayleigh rummaged through the hangers and pulled something out, then left the room. Rosa could hear her cursing at the bathroom tap, then yelping with displeasure. She couldn't help smiling to herself.

When she returned to the bedroom, Kayleigh was wearing what could only be described as dungarees. She went over to the front window and gripped the curtains in her hands.

'Do not close the curtains!' Rosa cried out.

'Why not?'

'Because I hate the dark.'

As Kayleigh laughed, Rosa stared at the high, cobwebbed ceiling for a while, then turned to face Kayleigh. 'Why are you so cheerful? After all that happen?'

'Dunno.' The girl shrugged. 'Suppose it feels like an adventure.'

To Rosa, the girl's attitude and demeanour seemed so naive; so immature. She smiled inwardly. It was no different to how she would have been at her age, she supposed. 'An adventure?' she repeated. 'Like one of your books?'

Kayleigh climbed into the other bed. 'Yeah, I guess.'

Rosa let out a huge yawn. 'Right, I go to sleep now. Night!' She turned to face the wall, closed her eyes and wondered to herself what tomorrow had in store for them.

FORTY-FOUR

JAMES HAD RETURNED to Hillcroft House shortly after five o'clock, once he'd provided his statement and the police had made clear he was of no further use to their enquires. They'd promised to keep him updated with any developments, but James didn't trust their word so he'd forced a very reluctant Sergeant Lawson to give him his mobile number.

After a fitful sleep of less than two hours, he took a long, hot shower, shaved, dressed and went down for breakfast early.

In the hallway, the other lone guest was shouting into his phone, pacing up and down and waving his hands all over the place, totally oblivious to James's presence. He sounded Spanish. What on earth brought a Spaniard to Great Yarmouth?

The morning sunshine streaked into the unoccupied breakfast room. Clear blue sky. The scent of cut flowers and fresh orange juice; bacon wafting from the kitchen. James helped himself to a plain yoghurt and a glass of freshly squeezed orange juice and took a seat at his allotted table.

There wasn't much he could do other than wait for news. He checked his phone for any messages. Still no word from Norfolk Constabulary. *Urtė could be anywhere by now. Possibly dead already.* If there was nothing in the next couple of hours, James decided, he'd call Lawson for an update.

The Spaniard ended his call and left via the front door, slamming it angrily. The place fell completely silent. What time was it? Nearly eight. He spooned the last of the yoghurt and turned his head towards the sun. Closed his eyes to feel the warmth on his eyelids.

He realised he'd dropped off when a terrible commotion jolted him awake, causing him to knock over his glass. Luckily he'd already finished the orange juice. He righted the glass and turned to the doorway as a group of women piled into the room, dolled up to the nines and giggling like schoolgirls, even though they were clearly pensioners. He counted six of them and soon clocked that it was a hen party. One of them—cream frock; high heels; combed auburn tresses plunging dramatically to her waistline; and skin like a rhino's hide— wore a pink bride-to-be sash and a tiara. A waft of booze struck him. Christ, they were starting early.

A flustered-looking Mrs. Elliott followed the women into the breakfast room and shepherded them towards two adjoining tables in the back corner. One of the women asked for Buck's Fizz all round, and Mrs. Elliott explained she didn't have a licence to serve alcohol. Another of the geriatric dollybirds caught James in her crosshairs and gave him a seductive wink. He quickly averted his gaze and took a sudden interest in his fingernails.

It was nearly eight thirty when Molly finally made an appearance, waltzing into the room like a low-rent Jackie Onassis with her handbag on her arm and oversized sunglasses. She hoisted the glasses and surveyed the room with dismay before alighting on James. She frowned when she noticed his table was set for one, and before he could explain, she snatched the cutlery, place mat and coffee cup from another solo table and joined him.

'She won't like it …' he warned.

'Won't like what?'

On cue, Mrs. Elliott swept into the room, coffee server in one hand, tea in the other. She motioned to the correct table with her elbow. 'Please, Miss Tindall, I laid a place for you there.'

'No, I'm going to be sitting here with my friend, thank you very much.' Molly turned to James and laughed. 'Reminds me of that supper at the Murdochs' house. Remember? An evening with Hyacinth Bucket …'

'How could I forget.'

Mrs. Elliott cleared her throat. 'I am still here, you know.'

Molly twisted her neck, looked up at her and, after a brief hesitation, said, 'You don't look like you're enjoying this. What's the point of working in hospitality if you can't be hospitable?'

Mrs. Elliott's face twitched, then she quickly rearranged her expression into an inscrutable smile. 'Tea or coffee, madam?'

'Coffee, please. If it's not too much trouble?'

'Not at all, madam.'

'There, that wasn't too bad, was it?'

James cringed.

'I'll bring out your breakfast shortly. I've been keeping

it warm under the hot lamp,' Mrs. Elliott said pointedly. 'But in the meantime, please help yourself to anything on the side table there.'

'Actually, you can forget the cooked breakfast.' Molly palmed her stomach and grimaced. 'My belly's doing somersaults after last night. I'll stick with the continental.'

Mrs. Elliot looked on the verge of rage. 'You might have forewarned me, Miss Tindall. To save me from wasting perfectly good food. I won't be offering a discount, you understand?'

'Of course. Now, if you don't mind …'

Mrs. Elliott retreated huffily from the room. James imagined a lioness licking her wounds.

The hen party rabble were getting raucous now, and James had to keep repeating himself to be heard. 'Sleep well?' he asked again.

'Like a baby,' Molly replied. 'You?'

'Same,' he lied. Now was neither the time nor the place to explain the events from last night. 'You going to keep those stupid glasses on?'

Molly sighed. 'I'm in crisis mode. Panda eyes. And I only packed my essential make-up kit.' She rubbed her temple. 'I don't know what was in that wine last night …'

'So, it was all down to the quality, not quantity?'

Molly picked up a fork and harpooned the delicious sausage he'd been purposely saving. She took a large bite.

'Hey! Thought you couldn't face a fry-up?'

'Changing her mind is a woman's prerogative, don't you know? So,' she continued, 'same routine for today, is it? How many caravan parks are on the itinerary?'

'Three, four maybe?' James shrugged, concealing his deceit.

'Michael Palin must be quaking in his boots.'

'*Hilarious.* And what about you? All set to visit your aunt? Not going to chicken out this time?'

'Of course not, Jimbo. You know me. Ready for whatever life's about to chuck at me.'

FORTY-FIVE

Rosa woke with a start to the smell of burning. Panicked, she looked about her.

In the other bed, Kayleigh lay fast asleep, snoring gently.

The smell was just the lingering effect of the fire, Rosa told herself, and she tried to get back to sleep. She was still tired, but she couldn't settle; kept tossing and turning. Perhaps she should make herself a hot drink? That might help.

She crept out of the room, keen not to wake Kayleigh. She had no idea what the time was, only that it must be morning as bright sunshine flooded the house.

The burning smell lingered—stronger, if anything—as she padded down the stairs.

When she got to the hallway, Rosa saw smoke coming from a door at the back.

'Nancy?' she called out, rushing towards the smoke. 'Miss Patterson? Are you okay?'

She covered her mouth and pushed open the door. Smoke billowed from the oven. Rosa found a cloth and opened the oven door. Smoke wafted out, making her cough. She flapped the cloth around to disperse the smoke and then turned off the heat. Inside the oven were two charred pieces of toast. She took hold of the oven tray using the cloth and transferred it to the sink, dropping it with a clatter when the heat seeped through the threadbare fabric.

'Nancy?' she called out. 'Where are you?'

Rosa opened a window to help clear the haze. As she turned back, she nearly jumped out of her skin when she saw Nancy standing in the doorway.

Nancy was holding the unicorn toy from the arcade against her shoulder, gently patting its back. The old woman's gaze shifted to the oven; to the sink; to the open window. 'Daisy! What have you done?'

'The bread … It was burning. There was smoke everywhere …'

'Oh, Daisy, dear, you must take more care! Never mind, there's no point crying over spilt milk, I suppose. Let me make you some breakfast. How does a nice boiled egg sound?'

'It's okay, I'm not hungry anymore.' She wasn't even hungry in the first place, but there was no point in confusing Nancy. Besides, the thought of Nancy boiling water filled Rosa with dread.

'Nonsense! You've had a big shock, Daisy, after the bomb. You need sustenance. Nothing better than an egg! I'll do soldiers, too.'

'*Soldiers*?' Rosa queried, puzzled.

'Oh, Daisy, you are in a tizzy!' Nancy chuckled. 'Go and get yourself dressed while I sort out breakfast. But first, I'll need to get poor Lottie settled. She's all out of sorts this morning. I hope her crying didn't wake you in the night? She can make such an awful racket.'

'No, she did not wake me.' Rosa smiled. She knew it was for the best to go along with Nancy's fantasy world. 'I find Kayleigh now. See if she is hungry.'

'Hayley?'

'My friend, remember? You let her stay, too?'

'Of course, dear. I'll fetch three eggs from the pantry. Now, off you go.'

Rosa noticed the biscuit tin in the lounge as she passed by the door in the hallway. She went in to retrieve it, then returned to the bedroom, finding Kayleigh still in bed but stirring. 'Time to get up, lazy bones. Nancy make us breakfast.'

Kayleigh let out an enormous yawn and shifted position, turning to face the wall. 'Ten more minutes.'

Rosa smiled. *Teenagers!*

She opened the wardrobe and stashed the biscuit tin inside before looking for something to change into. She quickly opted for a khaki green pussybow swing dress, wrapped in protective plastic. The dress was perhaps sixty or seventy years old, yet it had been perfectly preserved.

She slipped out of the nightgown and folded it neatly on her bed, then unsheathed the dress and, holding her breath, squeezed herself into it. It was at least one size too small, pinched around the waist and particularly constricted about the chest, but Rosa didn't care—the dress was beautiful. *Although*, she thought, her nose wrinkling in disgust, *I absolutely stink*.

She remembered there was a dresser in the largest of the bedrooms and made her way there to rummage through the drawers. It felt horribly intrusive, but she supposed Nancy wouldn't mind.

She found a gorgeous vintage crystal perfume atomiser, which she shook gently, expecting its contents to have long since evaporated, but she was pleased to discover there was still scent within. She squeezed the nozzle into the air and inhaled the mist. Beautiful. Notes of rose; violet; iris.

After applying the perfume liberally to her neck and the insides of her wrists, Rosa returned the atomiser to the drawer. A beautiful little box embossed with "STRATTON OF LONDON" caught her eye. Teasing off the lid, she found that it contained a silver compact and lipstick set.

Rosa seated herself at the dresser and deferentially took out the lipstick. With the assistance of the compact mirror, she deftly painted her lips. The shade she'd selected was a stunning red-orange which instantly lifted her whole face—and her self-confidence, to boot.

There was a freestanding full-length mirror in the corner of the room, and she went over to stand in front of it, regarding her reflection for a few moments. She puckered her lips and raised her hair, imagining it styled as a gorgeous Sophia Lauren 1950s bouffant. Then, giggling, she lifted herself onto her toes and performed a pirouette; the skirt flared and swirled in reply.

A vivid memory of an old black-and-white movie struck her. On the stage, the band played with great fervour and, on the polished dance floor, a young couple danced the jitterbug. Rosa found herself tapping her foot and clicking her fingers to the imaginary beat.

A noise from the ground floor jerked her from the daydream, and flushed with sudden concern, she rushed to the stairs.

The noise was Nancy Patterson, rocking a huge, old-fashioned pram back and forth in the hallway. The old lady gave a backward glance as Rosa came down the stairs and broke into a warm smile. 'Don't you look a picture, dear,' she said.

Nancy returned her attention to the pram and rocked

it a few more times. She brought a gnarled finger to her lips and whispered to Rosa, 'She's finally dropped off. The poor mite's exhausted. This damn war has a lot to answer for.'

Rosa didn't really know what to say, so she just gave a smile, then followed Nancy as she led her to the kitchen, where a pan now rested on one of the cooker rings. Three eggs were floating in the water.

The old lady gestured to a chair at the table. 'Sit yourself down, dear. I'll make us a nice cup of tea.'

'Let me do it,' Rosa pleaded.

'No, I won't have it, Daisy. You must rest and gather your strength. You'll need it in the days ahead.'

Reluctantly, Rosa sat down at the table and watched Nancy shuffle over to the kettle, which sat on a cluttered work surface. After flicking on the kettle, she set about locating some cups amongst the clutter, then fetched milk from the fridge. Every movement, every action, took an age.

'Do you have anyone to help you, Miss Patterson?' Rosa asked. 'You know, with the house? It is very big.'

'*Help?* Why on earth would I need help? I can manage perfectly well on my own, thank you very much. Now, dear, I'm putting three sugars in your tea. That will see you right.'

Loud footfalls sounded above, and Nancy raised her eyes to the ceiling and frowned.

'Kayleigh,' Rosa reminded her.

'What is she doing upstairs? It's much safer to be on the ground floor. She must know that?'

'But, Nancy, you tell us—' Rosa stopped herself, then continued, 'It does not matter. It sounds like she is coming now.'

Kayleigh barrelled down the stairs and came into the

kitchen. Her hair was a tangled mess, but she seemed bright and breezy, all things considered. 'Morning!' she said cheerfully.

'Are you on duty, dear?' Nancy asked. 'I wish I could join you, but I have my hands full with Lottie.'

Rosa could now see, in the light of day, that the dungaree thing Kayleigh had put on last night was, in fact, some kind of uniform: a green overall, buttoned from collar to hem. Sewn onto the breast was a badge bearing the letters: "WVS".

Kayleigh smiled sweetly at Nancy, then left the room without saying anything.

'Where are you going?' Rosa called after her. She got no response. The thought of Kayleigh roaming about in Nancy's big house unnerved her.

'You know, dear,' Nancy said as she placed Rosa's tea cup unsteadily on the table, 'you can stay for as long as you like. Until they repair the damage or the council find you new accommodation. It will be nice to have some adult company.'

'Aw, that is very kind, Miss Patterson, but I do not want to be burden—'

Rosa's words were interrupted by the sound of loud music. 'Kayleigh!' she exclaimed as she got to her feet. She rushed to the living room and found the girl standing at the front window—the curtains slightly parted—next to the old record player.

A clicking sound and the smell of burning dust made Rosa snap her attention to a large radiator. Kayleigh must have turned it on, she guessed.

Rosa returned her gaze to Kayleigh. 'Turn the music off!' she shouted above the crackly voice of the male singer.

'*What?*' Kayleigh mouthed, cupping a hand to her ear and laughing, pretending not to hear.

'Turn it *off.*' Rosa repeated. 'And close the curt—'

'Oh, lovely.' Nancy's voice, behind her. 'Would you like to dance, Daisy?'

'Well, I, er …'

Nancy took Rosa's hand in hers and rested the other on her shoulder. Instinctively, Rosa placed her other hand gingerly around Nancy's waist. It was the closed dance hold position, which she remembered from the ballroom dance lessons she'd had many, many years ago in Lithuania, with Rūta. Mrs. Petreikis, a terrifyingly strict, upright old woman, had run the classes. Rosa—then Urtė, of course—had got into such terrible trouble for not paying attention to her instructions. She'd been carried off in the arms of a good-looking boy. Couldn't think of his name, but she certainly remembered the boy's hand slipping from her waist and taking a cheeky squeeze of her backside. And she also didn't remember protesting.

She could picture Rūta, in the arms of her partner, looking over at her, rolling her eyes.

Innocent times.

O Dieve, why hadn't they just stayed in Lithuania?

Rosa pulled Nancy closer to her, and they soon settled in to a slow foxtrot. *Slow, slow, quick, quick …*

Rosa took a deep intake of the distinctive scent of old people: a mild sweetness and mustiness; a very faint hint of lavender.

Nancy croaked along to the words. She was trying to throw back her head, but she couldn't quite manage it.

The music stopped abruptly, and Kayleigh, standing at the window, shouted, 'There's a man in a car parked out front, pointing at us!'

'What? Who is it?' Rosa asked.

'I don't know.'

'Is it a Jerry?' Nancy asked.

'Someone wants to hurt us, Nancy,' Rosa said. 'Kayleigh, move away from the window and close the curtains.'

Kayleigh obliged, and the room fell into semi-darkness.

They were frozen, each staring at the other in the low light, unsure of what to do.

Then there came the hammering at the front door, so loud that it made Rosa's insides crumple. 'What should we do?'

'Quick,' Nancy said, 'follow me.'

Rosa and Kayleigh trailed Nancy into the hallway. A stolen glance at the front door caught the outline of a figure through the obscure glass.

Nancy pulled open a door under the stairs and stepped to one side. 'The cellar,' she said, calmly yet assertively. 'You must stay down there while I sort out the situation.'

'No, no, that is not fair …' Rosa began to protest.

The person at the door hammered again, making her physically jump. She took hold of Kayleigh's cold, bony hand.

'Quickly now,' Nancy said, opening her arm to encourage them through the cellar door. 'Just do as I say and everything will be as right as rain.'

Rosa stepped hesitantly through the door. 'But it is so dark. I cannot!'

'There's a light switch to your right.'

Rosa flicked the switch and an exposed bulb came on, illuminating a steep wooden staircase.

'Quickly, girls!'

Rosa took Kayleigh's hand and led her gingerly down the shallow treads, ducking under the light bulb that hung from the low, sloping ceiling.

At the bottom, the light from the weak bulb didn't reach very far into the cellar, but it was enough for Rosa to see that the room was full of accumulated junk: old furniture; boxes; tins; piles of books; appliances; stacks of yellowed paper. Everything was caked in dust and spiderwebs. The smell was awful. She turned her head and cried out, 'Miss Patterson! I can't do this!'

Too late. The door slammed, and the key turned in the lock.

'Nancy!'

Kayleigh squeezed Rosa's hand. 'It's okay,' she said soothingly. 'We can do this.'

Rosa sniffed at the air. Was that gas she could smell?

Kayleigh encouraged her to advance into the cellar.

Crouching in the restricted space, Rosa swept an arm before her to clear spiderwebs as they inched forward, dodging obstacles about their feet.

Above them, the joists were stuffed with insulation, through which they could hear Nancy's muted shuffle.

'Look.' Kayleigh pointed. 'We can sit on those.'

Stacked against a large chest storage box were some foldable garden chairs. They took one each, unfolded them and positioned them against a wall.

They sat silently for several moments. Rosa trained her ear to the dull sound of muted chatter above them, desperately trying to discern what was happening, but it was a hopeless task.

She was mad with herself for allowing this situation to happen. Here she was, cowering in a cellar, while a frail old woman with a mental impairment put herself in harm's way to protect two people she hardly knew. Rosa should never have imposed on Nancy like this. It wasn't right or fair. If Nancy got hurt, she would never forgive herself.

A door slammed shut above them and Rosa's hand flew

to her mouth, stifling an involuntary squeal of fear. She kept her hand in place, listening for sounds from above. First, there was silence, then Nancy's distinctive shuffle, followed by the unmistakable *tap, tap, tap, tap* of a second pair of feet.

Nancy and Kayleigh looked at each other in silent, wide-eyed terror.

Just then, the cellar light bulb blew, plunging their claustrophobic, subterranean world into total darkness.

FORTY-SIX

At Hillcroft House, James hung back at reception while Molly checked out.

'I shall be writing an *honest* review on TripAdvisor,' she said, taking great pleasure in telling Mrs. Elliott and obviously trying to provoke a reaction. When that didn't work, she tried again. 'I'm a journalist, I'll have you know. Investigative. My pen is mightier than the sword!'

Mrs. Elliott smiled primly. 'And there was me thinking people used computers these days. Would you like a *handwritten* receipt, Miss Tindall?'

'No, thank you, *Mrs. Elliott*. I'd like to be home before the sun sets.'

James shook his head. Why did she always have to make such a scene?

He checked his watch. Should really check out himself, he supposed. Nothing to keep him in Yarmouth now. But, as his third night was free, he figured he might as well try and make something of it. Perhaps he could go back to the caravan park and speak to the residents. Find out what they knew about "Rosa". How long she'd been there.

Where she worked. Any friends they knew of. He needed to be doing *something* to distract him from the feeling of helplessness.

'I do hope to see you again soon,' Mrs. Elliott said, disingenuously.

'I think that's *very* unlikely, don't you?' Molly glanced down at her travel case, then at James. 'Carry that to the car for me, will you?'

'What did your last slave die of?'

'Disobedience.'

The case weighed a ton. Christ only knows what she had in it. By the time he'd hefted it to the car, he was out of breath and sweating buckets. Molly was waiting for him, hands on hips, her face like thunder. 'Look,' she said, pointing at her car.

Her white Evoque was completely hemmed in by the wall on one side, a BMW X1 on the other and a garishly pink Fiat 500 to the front.

She threw her arms over her head in exasperation. 'It's Miss Havisham and her gang of geriatric floozies, isn't it? Inconsiderate slags!' She kicked the Fiat's front tyre. 'I'll get them to move this monstrosity, for starters. If they've so much as *scratched* my paintwork, there'll be hell to pay.'

'Leave it,' James said as Molly turned on her heel. 'I can take you to the house. We can come back for your car later.'

Molly's anger dissipated. 'Aw, you sure, Jimbo? Would you do that for me? That's so sweet.'

James zapped the central locking on the Audi and hoisted the case into the boot. 'Let's cut the soppy crap. Come on.'

. . .

Molly was uncharacteristically quiet on the five-minute drive to Nancy Patterson's house. She simply kept staring out of the window, away with the fairies.

He contemplated breaking the news about Urtė but thought better of it. Right now, Molly needed to focus on herself, rather than helping him.

James pulled up out front and switched off the engine. The house was tall and narrow, crooked in places, deeply set back from the road and clad in decaying weatherboards. 'Jesus! Looks like something out of a horror movie.'

'Doesn't it just,' Molly said, unbuckling herself with a trembling hand.

'Can't believe you're so nervous. What's the worst that can happen?'

Molly smiled uneasily, then opened her door and stepped out onto the road.

James was just about to unbuckle himself when his phone started buzzing. Surely it had to be news about Urtė? But it wasn't Lawson's number. The lazy bastard had probably delegated the task of relaying any messages to his drippy sidekick, Smithy.

'Let me just take this,' he called out to Molly. 'You go in. I'll follow in a minute.'

'I'll wait.'

'No, this is confidential. It's my doctor. Only be five minutes or so. Go.'

'Right, okay. Deep breath, Molly.' She smoothed down her coat, adjusted her glasses, then closed the door.

James waited until she had started down the path. She glanced back at him, and he waved at her impatiently. 'Go on!' he shouted. 'And take those bloody sunglasses off! You'll frighten the old dear to death!' But, of course, she didn't hear him.

The phone continued to buzz, and he took the call. 'Hello?'

'That James Quinn, the detective?'

A man's voice. Gruff and impatient.

'Who's asking?'

'I've seen one of your flyers. The missing woman.'

James was momentarily poleaxed. 'Right. And …?'

'Have you found her yet?'

'First, you need to tell me who you are and why you're calling.'

'I know her.'

'Okay. How?'

'I don't want to talk on the phone. Are you in town? Can we meet somewhere? I'll explain everything.'

'Well, yes, sure. Like when? Can you meet later today?'

'How about right now?'

'Well I'm tied up where I am at the moment, but … Can you come to me? I'm on Sycamore Road, in a silver Audi A4, and I'm parked in front of a big, old, ramshackle house. Don't know the number, but it looks like something out of the Addams Family.'

The caller chuckled. 'That'll be Nancy Patterson's place.'

'Yes, how do you know?'

'Everyone in this town knows Nancy, mate. She's a legend. Stay where you are. I'll be there in twenty minutes.'

'Right. Okay.'

The man hung up.

Well, well, a turn-up for the books. Probably too late, but you never know. Might have some useful information to impart.

James sighed and looked across to Nancy's house. Molly was still there, at the front door, hopping from one foot to another, smoking a crafty fag and looking in his direction.

He hastily clamped the phone back to his ear and pretended to still be in discussion. He made a "knock knock" gesture with his hand, and she pettishly stubbed out her cigarette underfoot and turned on her heel to rap at the door.

James noticed something from the corner of his eye: curtains twitching at the front window. The old woman *was* in, then. There was no excuse for Molly to pretend she wasn't. He watched Molly for what seemed like an eternity, mentally hurrying the old woman along so he could remove the damn phone from his ear. Eventually, the door opened. He couldn't see the woman because Molly blocked the view, but it seemed they were engaged in a conversation that lasted for ages. *Come on, please!* Eventually, Molly stole one more glance over her shoulder before disappearing into the house.

Feeling slightly guilty, but mostly relieved, James threw the iPhone onto the passenger seat.

Knackered from the lack of sleep and the mental and physical exertion of the previous night, he rubbed his eyes. The sun was streaming through the windscreen, threatening another headache. Now the air-con was off, the car's interior was getting stuffy, so he pulled down the visor and wound down the window an inch or two. Despite the welcome influx of cool, fresh air, his heavy eyelids drooped.

Lacking the energy to fight his own body, he reclined his seat, folded his arms and permitted himself a restorative power nap.

He woke with a jolt.

A little bit of drool was snaking its way down his chin, and he wiped it with the back of his hand.

Completely disorientated, he checked his watch. How

long had he been out for the count? Thankfully, no more than ten minutes.

A sudden sound startled him, a noise like screaming. He looked about him, trying to identify the source, but now there was nothing. Probably just kids. *Chill, James.*

He yawned and looked over at his phone on the passenger seat. He picked it up. No further calls or messages. He knew he really should join Molly, to give her his support. He had promised, after all.

Maybe he should just give Lawson a quick call first? He'd started to dial the sergeant's number when he heard another scream. More alert now, he could tell that it was not the scream of child's play.

It was a woman, her voice shrill and haunting.

And it was coming from Nancy Patterson's house.

James pocketed the phone and leapt out of the car. After hotfooting it down the garden path, he hammered on the opaque stained glass door insert. 'Molly? Nancy?' he hollered. 'You okay?'

He sank to a squat, pushed his fingers through the brass letterbox plate and peered inside. The stench of gas struck him, making him recoil.

'Molly?'

'James!' Molly shouted from deep inside the house. 'Help me!'

He tried the door, but it was locked.

Retreating a few steps, he scanned the exterior of the house for an alternative means of entry. There was no route to the back, and all the windows were shut.

He went over to the large ground floor window, which, bizarrely, was crisscrossed on the inside with masking tape. There was a small gap in the curtains, and he pressed his face to the glass. Scanning the gloomy interior, he saw

Molly seated on the floor, her back to the wall. No sign of her aunt.

He knocked on the window to get her attention. She thrashed about, yelling something unintelligible at him. What the hell had happened?

Back at the front door, James did a quick mental count-down, steeled himself, then hurled his shoulder at the frame. After half a dozen attempts, panting like a dog and with his arm dead, he realised he was getting nowhere. Plan B, then.

He needed a heavy object. Scanning the ground around him, he soon found the perfect candidate: a piece of edging stone that had come loose from the path.

James hurled the stone through the glass insert, then teased out the jagged shards that remained in place. After reaching inside to turn the lock, he was in.

The stench of gas was overpowering, so he covered his mouth and nose with the crook of his arm.

There was an ancient pram in the cold hallway, against one wall. James stole a look inside: a sequinned unicorn toy, tucked under a blanket. Perfect sense.

'*James!*' Molly screeched.

He advanced through the capacious hall, putting his head around the first open door on the left, into the living room. Molly was on the floor, next to a radiator, surrounded by smashed fragments of something. Crockery?

'What the hell are you doing down there?'

She yanked her hand, making a jangling noise, revealing that she was cuffed to the radiator. 'Is it not obvi-ous? I'm recreating the Terry Waite experience, dummy! Just for the sheer thrill of it.' She shook her fist. 'Get me out of these bloody things!'

James scratched his head. 'What is it with you and cuffs?'

'That's below the belt, Jimbo.'

'Who did it to you? And why?'

Molly hesitated, then shook her head. Her hair was limp, her forehead glistening with sweat. 'Turn the bloody radiator off, will you? I'm boiling alive here.'

As James turned down the valve, Molly continued. 'I know this is going to sound ridiculous, but it was *her*.'

'*Nancy?*'

'Yes, Nancy. The woman's off her bleedin' rocker!'

'I don't understand. Where is she?' He wrinkled his nose. 'And what's with the gas?'

'I don't know; just get these off me! I knew I should have just let sleeping dogs lie. Should have just trusted my instincts; not let you convince me—'

James pressed his forefinger to her lips. 'Just wait there. I'll be right back.'

She jangled the cuffs again. 'Not going anywhere, Jimbo.'

He retreated to the hall, then, advancing through the house, he peeked into each room: a dining room and another small room, laid out as a bedroom. It contained a chest of drawers, on the top of which were laid out various pill bottles. Old photographs lined the walls. Books and papers were scattered everywhere.

'Nancy?' he called out, not too loudly, wary of frightening her. 'Miss Patterson?'

No reply.

The kitchen was at the back of the house. In here, the smell of gas was strongest, and he soon realised that the source was an old upright cooker. There was a pan on one of the burners and its control dial was turned to the maximum setting, but the gas hadn't been ignited. After turning off the ring, he peered into the pan. It was filled almost to the brim with water. He dipped his finger in to check it was cold, then performed a quick inventory of the contents. Three hen's eggs. A large door key. A pair of sunglasses. A mobile phone.

He fished out the key, the glasses and the phone and dried them on the tea towel that hung on the oven door. He put the key in his pocket and left the phone and glasses on the side.

Surveying the dishevelled state of the room, his thoughts raced to his mother and his memories of the first signs of her dementia. He'd noticed she kept repeating things; kept getting anxious over trivia. She'd tell him that she couldn't remember things that had only happened moments before. At first, they'd adapted; found ways for her to live an independent life despite her deficits. It was a life of post-it notes and memory aids. Labelled pill dispensers. Batch-cooked meals delivered weekly.

Mary Quinn had plateaued for so many years, retaining her autonomy, that when the decline finally came, it hit James hard. She had become so increasingly impaired that it was no longer safe for her to live at home. She'd forgotten how to use the shower. Didn't know how to use the oven. Forgotten she had to eat.

James took a moment to take in Nancy Patterson's kitchen. It was a museum piece. Skirted cabinets. Formica worktops. Open shelving. Vintage weighing scales. An old oak table dominated the room, cluttered with pots, pans, bottles, recipe books, piles of mail and old newspapers. The newspapers fluttered in a cold draught, which James realised came from the partially open window. He opened it to its full extent to help the gas dissipate.

The window offered a view of a long, narrow, over-grown garden. His eyes followed a meandering path through tall grass and weeds to the far end where, amongst a small orchard, he could just about make out a ramshackle wooden building; a shed of some kind. He wondered if that was where the old woman had disappeared to. Better check, he supposed.

He stopped himself. *Don't scare her.*

'James?' Molly's voice startled him. 'Where are you?'

He went back to the living room, and she looked at him with hopeful eyes. 'Well, did you find the key?'

'Well, I found *a* key,' he said, smiling, and reached into his pocket.

'Oh, for Pete's sake!' Molly said when she saw it.

'It was in a pan of water on the stove, with some eggs. There was a mobile phone in there, too. Some sunglasses. Yours, I presume?'

Molly shook her head in dismay. 'My day keeps on getting better!' She looked down at the cuffs. 'Can't you just cut through the chain?'

'Oh, yes, of course. How could I be so stupid?' He patted his pockets. 'Damn, sorry—it seems I've left my bolt croppers at home.'

Molly rolled her eyes to the ceiling.

James knelt down and examined the cuffs. They were heavy duty backstop Darby style handcuffs. Military issue from the war, he wagered. Built to last. No way would the old bent-paperclip trick work with these bad boys.

Molly wiped her forehead with the back of her free hand. 'Wake me up from this nightmare, will you?'

'How did she manage to do this to you? At her age?'

Molly sighed heavily. 'She disarmed me with her "sweet old lady" act. Brought me in here; told me to make myself comfy while she went to make the tea. While I waited, I had a little nosy around the place. I got absorbed in all the little knick-knacks; the books; the pictures. Next thing I know, she's shuffling in with a rattling tea tray and I turn around to help her, only the bloody thing falls from her hands. Crashes to the ground. Everything smashed to pieces. "Don't worry, I'll sort it," I said and dropped to my knees. Started picking up all the pieces and returning them to the tray. Somehow she managed to squat down, too, and joined in. "That's a nice watch, dear," she says. "Why, thank you," I say. "It's a Cartier Tank Francaise."'

James rolled his eyes.

Molly continued. 'Anyway, Nancy starts pointing to a spot under the radiator. "Couldn't just pick up that piece, dear?" she says. "No problem, Nancy," I say. Next minute, she's snapping these bloody things round my wrists and fixing me a steely glare. Removes my glasses and tells me she knows *exactly* who I really am.'

'And who's that, then?'

'Why, a Nazi collaborator, of course.'

'*Obviously*. Stupid of me to ask, really. So, after she cuffed you, what did she do?'

'She rummaged through my bag, confiscated the phone, then left the room. Haven't heard a peep since.'

'She gave no hint of where she was going? What she was intending to do?'

'Perhaps she's out looking for Captain *sodding* Mainwaring of the Home Guard?'

'It's not funny, Moll. It's sounds like she has advanced dementia. She shouldn't be living alone in a big house like this.'

'Do I *look* like I'm laughing?'

James took out his phone. 'I'm ringing social services.'

A sudden crashing noise broke beneath the floorboards. He looked down at the floor, then back at Molly. 'Oh, God, there's a cellar … What's she doing down there? She might have hurt herself.'

Molly, speechless, just offered him a puzzled look.

James set about looking for the cellar entrance.

In the hall, there was a door under the stairs. Locked. But why? Had she turned the key from the inside? James imagined his mother faced with the same scenario and shuddered at the thought of her cowering down there, frightened out of her wits. He rapped lightly on the door. 'Are you down there, sweetheart?'

There was no reply.

Wait. The key!

James retrieved it from his pocket and tried it in the keyhole. It worked, but, of course, nothing now made any sense. If Nancy was responsible for putting the key in the pan, then who—or what—was in the cellar?

Perhaps it was a pet, he rationalised. A dog or a cat? Maybe there were rats down there? A shiver rippled down his spine at the very thought. Then a ludicrous image flashed through his mind: the gasman held hostage, bound and gagged.

He banished the ridiculous thought and tentatively opened the door. Inside, he could make out a few steps of a steep wooden staircase that led down into the dark cellar. He groped at the wall, quickly locating a light switch, but when he flicked it, nothing happened. 'Hello?' he called out, into the gloom.

No reply.

He switched on the torch feature on his iPhone and gripped the handrail. Took cautious, creaky steps down. The treads were so narrow, he had to twist his feet almost at right angles to ensure he kept a tight footing.

At the bottom of the stairs, he held up his phone and shone the torch into the room. The light bounced about, revealing all manner of junk: boxes; chests; ladders; old appliances; garden tools; narrow shelves crammed with bric-a-brac. In a far corner, there were two unfolded garden chairs.

'Hello?' he called again.

Nothing.

Down here, there was a very obvious change in atmosphere: the temperature was colder, the humidity higher. A pervasive damp, stale smell.

He advanced further into the cellar, stooping to avoiding clouting his head on the ceiling joists.

His foot struck an object on the floor, sending it flying. A tin can clattered across the stone floor, its contents strewn everywhere. He flashed his light to the floor and saw countless rusty nails, screws, tacks …

He discerned a sudden noise from the back of the cellar. He looked up, registering a blurry figure barrelling towards him.

The figure wielded a weapon.

Something like an iron bar, James deduced, in the split second before it slammed into his collarbone. In agony, he slumped to the ground.

FORTY-SEVEN

SHE WAS bloody livid with him. It was all *his* fault. She would never have encountered the psycho-biddy if he hadn't cajoled her. Molly should have trusted her instincts and left well alone.

Pah! Who was she trying to kid?

What *was* he up to down there? She could hear such an awful commotion.

'James?' she bellowed. 'What the hell are you playing at?'

He didn't answer, of course. As per. She wiped her brow and let out a frustrated sigh. She felt herself cramping up. What she wouldn't give to be able to stand up and stretch her legs!

When, moments later, she heard the sound of feet pounding the stairs, she was ready to give him a piece of her mind.

But, to her surprise, it wasn't James who burst breathlessly into the living room. It was a woman in an olive green pussybow swing dress. Her hair was dyed a shocking shade of scarlet, and her lips were tangerine. It was such a technicolour ensemble that Molly wondered if she might be hallucinating.

They exchanged a look of mutual bewilderment.

Then, from behind the woman, a vampiric creature appeared: a girl with jet black hair and skin so pale, she looked like she'd grown up in the dark, like a mushroom. Just about everything above the neck was pierced: ears; lips; eyebrows. She was dressed in what could only be described as a green romper suit. Molly soon realised she had seen such an outfit before, in history books, on TV dramas: it was a uniform from the Second World War.

There was something familiar about the girl, and it took Molly a few beats to place her: the thieving toerag they'd seen legging it from Cash Generator yesterday!

Who exactly were this pair? Some kind of modern-day Fagin and Dawkins? Fugitives? Confidence tricksters, conning their way into the lives of confused old ladies trapped in wartime fantasies? Seemed a very niche criminal enterprise, in Molly's opinion. And what were they doing in the cellar, for Pete's sake?

'Morning!' she said affably, fixing a smile. 'Lovely weather.'

The redhead and the vampire exchanged looks, as if imploring the other to come up with something plausible to say.

Molly noticed the girl was holding her hand behind her back. 'What's that you're hiding?'

The girl sheepishly brought out her hand to reveal a length of metal. What was it? A candlestick? Lead piping? Molly immediately felt like she was in a game of Cluedo. Had James become Dr. Black, his corpse lying in the cellar? Molly let out a gasp of horror. 'Have you hurt him?'

The absence of a response answered Molly's question. 'James?' she bellowed. '*Jimbo?*'

There was no reply, and Miss Scarlett frowned. '*Jimbo*?' she repeated. 'You mean, the man in the cellar? We thought he wanted to hurt us.' Her accent was mildly Slavic. 'Who is he?' she asked.

'He's a … a friend. He was looking for Nancy Patterson. Do you know her? Where is she?'

Miss Scarlett looked down briefly at Molly's cuffed hand, then said, 'I don't understand.'

'You and me both, love.'

The woman's eyes roamed nervously from Molly to the cuffs and then to the girl.

'Look,' Molly said, deciding to play a straight bat, 'let's just start from the beginning, shall we? My name's Molly and I've recently discovered that Nancy is a relative of mine. I came here to meet her for the first time, but it seems she got a little confused.'

'She thought you were the enemy?' the vampire ventured.

'Exactly. She's clearly living in the past. The war. And you two? You look like extras in a bloody period drama. Who are you? And what the *bloody hell* were you doing down there?'

'Miss Patterson let us stay here after'—the woman paused and gave an embarrassed smile—'someone burn down my house.'

'Burned down your house? Of course, *that* sounds perfectly plausible …'

'We thought the man who did it follow us here,' the redhead explained. 'Nancy tell us to hide in cellar while she sort him.'

'Again, makes perfect sense. Who better to resolve the situation than an old woman with dementia? What are your names?'

Molly half expected them to say Thelma and Louise,

but instead Miss Scarlett said, 'I am Rosa. This is Kayleigh.'

'Very pleased to make your acquaintance, ladies.' Molly rattled her cuffs. 'Look, can one of you go and find Nancy, please? She can't have gone far. Get the key to these things. And will someone please check James is okay down there? Call an ambulance. He's got a dodgy heart, for Christ's sake.' Then, shouting into the space beyond Rosa and Kayleigh, she hollered again, 'James? You okay?'

There was no reply from the cellar.

'Go!' she shouted at the women, annoyed by their apparent lack of gumption.

But then there was a sound in the hallway: footsteps. They were far too quick to be the old woman. *Who, pray tell, is this?* Molly wondered. A concerned neighbour? The police? A man in a white coat?

'Hello?' a gruff male voice called out uncertainly. 'Nancy? You there? What's going on?'

Neighbour, then, Molly reasoned.

Rosa and Kayleigh exchanged panicked glances, then Rosa took the girl's hand and led her further into the living room.

'There's something you're not telling me, isn't there?' Molly called after them.

Before either could offer an answer, the owner of the voice appeared in the open doorway. He had the look of a casual labourer: dirty, tanned skin; scruffy hair; soiled t-shirt; a smattering of indistinct tattoos on his forearms. He looked like a Dwayne. The sort of fella that pitches up at your house when you call for an emergency plumber.

"Dwayne" looked down at Molly and scratched his temple. His mouth fell open, but no words came out.

'Hello?' Molly said genially. 'Are you from next door? You probably heard the kerfuffle, and now you're wondering what I'm doing down here on the floor, shackled to a radiator? It's a long story, but—'

'Dad?' Kayleigh interjected, her voice laced with fear.

Dad? Molly thought, perplexed. This was beginning to feel like a farce. Who would be next? The vicar? The local bobby? The French tart?

"Dwayne" stepped into the room and turned to look in the direction of the window, registering the presence of the women. Rosa pulled Kayleigh into a protective embrace.

Seemingly lost for words, "Dwayne" looked at Kayleigh, then at Rosa. Then, consumed by sudden rage, he jabbed a finger into the air and said, 'You disgusting *skank!*'

To whom might you be addressing that charming endearment? Molly pondered. She couldn't tell from her vantage point. Rosa? He did have a point, she conceded; the woman's heaving bosom was nearly bursting out of her dress. Or was it his daughter he was referring to? "Disgusting skank" was no way to address family, no matter the truth of the accusation.

"Dwayne" marched over to them, and then, in the blink of an eye, it all took off. Fists and bitch slaps flying everywhere. Hair pulled. Insults hurled. Books and trinkets and keepsakes lobbed.

A book landed near Molly's leg. She read the spine upside down: *Little Women*. One of many overrated classics, in her not-so-humble opinion.

When she looked up from the book, Kayleigh was swinging wildly at her father with the metal weapon. He snatched her by the wrist and forced the pipe from her grip.

Molly felt like a voyeur in a domestic argument; like she was on the front row in the studio audience of *The Jeremy Kyle Show*. What was the gig? Was the girl pregnant?

Had she just received news of the positive test result? She pondered who the father might be. Some lowlife urchin, no doubt. A lad from school? A cousin? Or maybe it was an older relative. An uncle? The girl's own father? Nothing surprised Molly these days.

She felt like she should have been pumping her fist above her head and whooping. *Fight! Fight! Fight!*

When "Dwayne" took hold of Rosa by her dyed red hair and started to drag her, screaming, from the room, Molly was snapped out of her voyeuristic trance by a sudden pang of female solidarity. '*Hey!*' she yelled, yanking the cuffs in another impotent attempt to break free.

Kayleigh retrieved the pipe and threw herself at her father, striking him on the back and forcing him to release his grip on Rosa.

Go, girl! Whoop, whoop! Molly was enjoying the fracas a little more than she should.

"Dwayne" shook off his daughter's attack and shoved her into a nearby bookcase. Molly was beginning to wonder whether this was a custodial tussle. Was Rosa the girl's mother? She seemed too young, nor could Molly see any familial resemblance between the two women, but that didn't exactly mean much. Molly looked *nothing* like her mother, thank God.

The scrapping continued unabated. Such an unedifying spectacle, yet Molly was rapt. *Somebody pass the popcorn! Bad Molly.*

James was missing out. God, was he all right?

As if on cue, she sensed the presence of someone in the doorway and turned. 'James?'

Nope. A great brute of a man, his frame virtually filling the doorway. Thick black jacket. Neatly trimmed goatee. A wild look in his eyes. Chiselled features; not unattractive.

She blew her moist fringe and said, 'Hello, young man!

Welcome to the party! I would get you a drink, but, as you can see, I—'

The man gave Molly the most cursory of glances (the story of her life), sniffed and stepped a few slow, silent paces into the room. He stopped and crossed his arms against his huge chest, casually observing the ongoing tussle for several moments before coolly enquiring, 'Alexia?'

Alexia? Now, this was getting interesting. Molly's imagination—febrile at the best of times—went into hyperdrive. She was thinking abusive relationship; been going on for years. Then, suddenly, something happens that makes the wife snap and pluck up the courage to flee the marital home. She changes her name; dyes her hair. Starts a new life in a new town (*Yarmouth, of all places? No accounting for taste*) under a new identity. Only now the husband has finally tracked her down; has come to seize back his assets; to show her the error of her ways. And to mete out punishment on the new beau. An overweight plumber with anger issues, no less.

Alexia. The name now triggered a new thought. *Was* it? It couldn't be, *surely*?

Molly took another good look at Rosa. If this was Urtė, wasn't she supposed to bear a strong resemblance to Sandra Bullock? Molly couldn't see it one bit. It was a coincidence, pure and simple.

'Alexia?' the newcomer called again, this time emphasising each syllable as if he were beckoning a cat inside for its tea. That thought made Molly think of Freddy. She wondered how he was, the little munchkin. Probably missing his mamma. *Back soon, little man. Mwah.*

A sudden silence informed Molly that the latest arrival's presence had been noted. She could almost sense the collective intake of breath.

'Andric!' Rosa exclaimed, breaking the silence.

Andric! Holy shit, Molly thought. *Looks like none of us are having a particularly good day.* She looked at his left hand, clocking the missing fingers James had told her about. How could she have not noticed before?

Rosa continued, 'How … How did you find me?' The poor woman sounded out of her mind with terror.

Andric gave a sinister laugh. 'You gave away your location when you tried to call Roxie, you stupid bitch. She told me everything.'

"Dwayne" turned to face the visitor. He grabbed Rosa's wrist and took a step forward. 'And you are?'

'Let her go,' Andric said, his tone measured.

'And who's asking?'

'I am not asking. I tell. Let go.'

'Gonna make me?'

Boys! It was like a playground spat. *Keep it classy, lads.*

Andric gave a mirthless laugh, then said, 'You are detective?'

'What are you fucking talking about?'

Yes, Molly concurred. *What* are *you talking about? Wait! Did he think "Dwayne" was James? Please! What an insult!*

Andric made a beckoning gesture to Rosa. 'You come with me. *Now.*'

"Dwayne" stepped forward to place himself between Andric and Rosa, standing his ground like an alpha male defending his territory. Andric gave an indifferent shrug, then, lightning fast, shoved "Dwayne" in the chest, sending him barrelling to the floor. He grabbed Rosa by the arm, and she squealed in pain.

Now, the teenager was getting in on the act. She jumped over and took hold of Rosa's hand. Not to be outdone, "Dwayne" scrambled to his feet, now brandishing the metal pipe.

Andric gave another of his sinister chuckles and released his grip on Rosa so that he could reach inside his jacket. *What do we have here?* Molly wondered. *What surreal twist will be thrown up now?* Perhaps it was the results of the DNA test (*Surprise, darling! I'm the father!*).

But Andric didn't bring out a paternity certificate; he pulled out a gun—a pistol, replete with one of those silencer attachments that Molly had only seen in films.

Andric aimed the gun at the other man's forehead.

Shit!

"Dwayne", not unreasonably sensing the game was up, dropped the pipe and threw up his palms in surrender.

"Dwayne" and Andric stared at each other fixedly for several moments.

'Andric,' the redhead beseeched. '*Don't.*'

He ignored her.

Andric shifted his aim to the man's knee and fired the gun. Molly had braced herself for an ear-splitting *bang*, but of course, the gun had a silencer. The only sound was a much more pathetic *pfft*. Such an incongruous sound, considering the impact. "Dwayne" buckled and fell heavily to the floor, howling like a stricken stag.

Molly had determined the family arrangements of those present were dysfunctional at best, but she expected some kind of reaction from Kayleigh to the sight of her father being shot—a piercing scream; an urgent dash to attend to his wound. But no, the girl just stood there with a strangely detached look on her face, staring at him as he twisted and contorted in agony. Andric coolly fired a further shot into the other leg. *Pfft.*

Andric switched his attention to Rosa, waving the gun at her. 'Come. Now. We go.'

The redhead appeared frozen with horror.

It occurred to Molly that she herself was feeling

strangely numb and unconcerned by this violent escalation. Why was she so blasé? She supposed the answer to that question was her abduction by a depraved serial killer, Troy Perkins.

Kayleigh—foolhardy, plucky, brave, call it what you will —stepped in front of Rosa and spread her arms. 'Leave her. She's done nothing wrong. You've got the wrong person.'

'Kayleigh,' her father groaned as he writhed on the floor. 'Help me.'

Andric gave an exaggerated sigh and blithely fired another shot into the man's stomach before returning his attention to Kayleigh. 'Step out of way,' he commanded above the sound of demented cries.

The girl stole a cursory glance at her father. Standing her ground, she hissed at Andric, 'No!'

Andric flicked his gun. 'Out of the way. Now!'

'Do what he says!' Molly shouted.

'*No!*' the girl said assertively. 'He doesn't scare me.'

Jeez, Molly thought, *this girl has some steel. Either that, or a screw loose.*

Andric tilted his head to one side, almost in admiration.

'Shoot me,' the girl invited, slamming her palm into her chest. 'I fucking *dare* you.'

'Kayleigh, *no!*' Rosa pleaded, trying to move Kayleigh out of harm's way. But the teenager forcibly stood her ground.

'As you wish,' Andric said impassively.

'*No! Stop!*' Molly hollered.

Pfft.

Kayleigh dropped to the floor, and Molly's stomach lurched.

'What have you done?' Rosa screamed as she sank to

her knees. She tugged at the fabric of the girl's overalls. Slapped her cheek. 'Kayleigh? Kayleigh?'

'It is your fault, Alexia.'

Rosa looked up briefly, tears streaming down her cheeks. 'How did you find me? Have you hurt Roxie?'

Andric adjusted his features to show mock distress. 'I'm afraid Roxie went for walkies and fall into canal, darling. After I find her secret phone.' He glanced briefly at Kayleigh, at Kayleigh's father, then his pistol, before casually shrugging his shoulders.

Molly's mind was performing somersaults. How many bullets did the gun hold? Six? It was always six in the movies, right? And he'd fired four already. Another to dispatch Rosa. Leaving one more for the last remaining eye witness to his massacre …

Andric shrugged. 'You don't want to come with me, Alexia? No problem, I am bored now anyway.' He levelled the gun at Rosa's heart and smirked. 'Goodbye, darling.'

FORTY-EIGHT

HE WOKE with a start into a semi-dark world of vague shapes and peculiar smells.

His cheek was pressed into something cold, hard and damp. He was racked with pain, radiating from his shoulder.

The realisation that he was lying on the ground of a dank cellar came seconds before the memory of being struck with a heavy object.

James got unsteadily to his feet, careful not to whack his head on the low ceiling, and heaved himself groggily up the cellar steps, clutching the handrail for support. His head throbbed like the mother of all hangovers.

There was some kind of a commotion going on upstairs, and as he staggered through the open doorway into the hallway, he found a man, his face drained of colour and contorted in pain, dragging himself by his elbows through the living room doorway towards him.

'Help me,' the man groaned, pawing at James's shins. 'I've been shot.'

The trail of blood behind the man certainly backed up his claim.

Things had definitely escalated in his absence. How long had he been out for the count on the cellar floor? Minutes? Hours? Days?

'Who shot you?' he asked.

'James. In here!' Molly's voice. The living room.

'Wait here,' James instructed the man.

Molly was where he'd left her, tethered to the radiator, as white as a sheet. She spoke with her wide, dumbstruck eyes, inviting him to survey the room.

When he did so, the tableau before him was so grisly that he needed to grab the back of a nearby armchair to steady himself. He struggled to process the information his eyes were relaying to his brain. A huge guy, dressed in black, lying prone on the floor, stock-still. A red-haired woman in a green dress, on her knees, rocking back and forth as she tended to a black-haired girl whose head lay on her lap. The girl was moaning dully. Blood spatter every-where. The redhead greeted his gaze in wide-eyed terror.

'It's okay,' he offered calmly. 'Everything's going to be fine. Just stay where you are for now.' James scratched his head, then turned to Molly. 'What … What the …?'

She spluttered something unintelligible and motioned with her head towards the armchair he was using to keep himself upright. When he looked down, he saw a mop of wiry grey hair.

Nancy Patterson.

He went around to the front of the chair and dropped to his knee to examine her. She was breathing shallowly and staring straight through him, her eyes glazed over. He gingerly took the old woman's hand in his and whispered, 'Are you all right, sweetheart?'

Stupid question. Of course she wasn't all right.

There was something in the gap between her leg and the chair's arm—a metallic object. He tentatively prised it out to discover that it was a gun: an Enfield No.2 revolver, one of the standard Commonwealth sidearms in World War Two.

He regarded the frail old woman before him in bewilderment. Surely *she* wasn't responsible for this carnage? Irrespective, he needed to disengage the firearm before any more damage could be wrought. After releasing the cylinder latch, he pushed the ejector rod and a single spent shell casing fell out. He checked the chamber and the cylinder to ascertain that the gun was completely empty, then he set it down carefully on the floor.

'Molly,' he said, 'what the hell's happened?'

She began to babble something, but a groaned complaint from the hallway drowned her out. 'I'm dying. I'm dying! Help me.'

In James's experience of major incidents, it wasn't the talkers you had to worry about. It was the silent ones.

His gaze flitted between the groaning girl and the huge guy on the floor. Deciding the girl was not in need of immediate attention, he went over to check out the man, squatting next to his chest and putting two fingers to his neck.

Dead.

It took James no time to establish the cause of the death: the large exit wound in his chest evidenced that he'd been shot at close range from behind.

Examining the space around the man, James discovered another weapon, a Glock 17 handgun. It was only when he was disarming the gun that he noticed the man's left hand was missing two fingers. 'Panchenko!' he gasped. 'What the hell!?'

Wait? If this is Panchenko, does that mean …

He turned to study the redhead. Her pleading eyes, rimmed with tears, bored into his. *Was* it her? He wasn't at all sure. 'Help her, please,' she pleaded. 'He shot her.'

'Has anyone called an ambulance?' James asked as he moved to attend to the girl.

'My hands are tied,' Molly responded sardonically. 'And besides, the old girl wrecked my phone, remember?'

As he scanned the girl for signs of gunshot wounds, James enquired, 'What's her name?'

'Kayleigh,' the redhead replied. 'Please help her.'

'And what's your name?' he asked, preparing himself for the response.

'Rosa.'

He was momentarily paralysed by the confirmation before remembering there were more pressing matters to attend to: the girl.

He could see no obvious gunshot wound. Certainly no blood. 'Can you hear me, Kayleigh?' he said, scrutinising the fabric of her outfit. Her eyes were closed, and her breathing was laboured. Her cheek, though pale, was warm to the touch. She was groaning with pain, trying to speak. 'Where does it hurt, Kayleigh? Show me.'

She moved her hand, grimacing, to hover briefly over her breast pocket.

James examined the pocket and found a small puncture in the fabric. He gingerly poked a couple of fingers inside and teased out a metallic object. An antique cigarette case: pockmarked; scratched; heavily damaged. There was a deformed 9mm bullet embedded within the twisted metal. '*Jesus*,' he murmured, before smiling at Kayleigh. 'You must have a guardian angel.'

She muttered incoherently in response.

'What was that, sweetheart?'

'It fucking *kills*,' she rasped. Straining, grimacing, she

shuffled herself onto her elbows. Rosa put a protective arm around her shoulder.

'Careful,' James cautioned. 'You'll have bruised ribs, at least. Possibly fractured. And there could be internal bleeding. We need to get you to the hospital. Let them check you over.' He dug into his pocket for his phone, but it wasn't there. Then he remembered: he'd dropped it in the cellar. 'Do you have a phone?' he asked Rosa.

She shook her head. Same response from the girl.

Who didn't possess a phone these days, for Christ's sake? He'd have to see if Nancy had a landline.

On his way out of the room, he cast his eyes around again, clocking the component parts of the hellscape and trying to stitch them all into a coherent narrative. His head throbbed.

At the doorway, Molly called out, 'James?'

He shot her a look. 'What?'

'The cuffs, please.'

He rolled his eyes. She was the least of his worries right now.

In the hall, he found the wounded man was sitting against the wall, his head slumped, his chest heaving with the exhaustion of breathing. Who was he? 'Hold on there, fella. I'm calling for an ambulance right now.'

There was no sign of a landline, so James concluded that it would be quicker to retrieve his mobile from the cellar rather than searching the house.

He struggled to find it in the dark, and by the time he'd emerged back into daylight, Kayleigh had made it to the hall and was screaming blue murder at the man in the hall. Although clearly in pain herself, she managed to swing her right foot and slam it hard into his stomach. His pathetic protest was nothing more than a groan.

James was about to intervene when Rosa emerged from the kitchen to shout, 'Kayleigh! We must go, now!'

Kayleigh screamed at the man, 'I fucking *hate* you!' and she spat at him, before limping painfully to the kitchen.

'Wait!' James demanded. 'Kayleigh needs to be checked out. I'm calling the ambulance now—and the police, of course.'

'*No police!*' Rosa asserted.

'I have to. This is a crime scene.' But he understood her hesitancy over not wanting the police involved. 'Look,' he said, pulling out his room key from his pocket and showing her the name and address of Hillcroft House, 'Go here. You'll be safe. My room's on the top floor. There's a fire escape at the back. Go up the staircase there; the window's open. Wait there until I get back. Do you think you'll be able to manage?'

Rosa looked at him with evident suspicion. 'How can I trust you?'

'Yeah,' Kayleigh concurred. 'Who are you?'

He hesitated then, purposefully succinct, he said, 'Because I know your real name is Urtė. Because I married your best friend, Rūta. Because I promised her I would find you, no matter how long it took. Because I know what happened to you since the two of you were separated and I want to make things right.'

Rosa was shaking her head wildly as he spoke these words, her hand covering her mouth. She started crying and said, 'But they told me Rūta was dead! They killed her!'

James inhaled deeply, appreciating the shock of his revelations. There wasn't time now to explain everything, nor would she be able to process it all. He shoved the keys into her hand and closed her fingers around them. 'I'm afraid Rūta is dead, sweetheart, but it didn't happen how they told you. She escaped the traffickers. We had a happy life together. Let me explain everything later. I'll tell the police that you ran off, terrified out of your wits.'

'*James!*' Molly again, with her knack for exquisite timing.

'I'd better see what she wants,' James said, smiling.

A sudden panic flashed across Rosa's face and she looked to the ceiling.

'What is it?' James said.

'My money. I hide it in wardrobe. In a tin. I get it.'

'No time!' James asserted. 'I will find it and bring it to you. I promise.'

Rosa hesitated for a moment then relented. As she and the girl left through the back door, James returned to the living room. 'What's the matter?' he asked Molly as he simultaneously dialled the emergency services.

'It's Nancy. She's trying to say something. Ask her where she put the keys, will you?'

His 999 call was answered and he gave the relevant details. The ambulance and police crew would be there in minutes, the call handler advised. He hung up, knelt down in front of Nancy and placed a hand gently on her knee.

'Nancy, sweetheart? Can you hear me, darling? Can I get you something? Cup of tea? Nice warm blanket?'

No response.

'The key, James! Does she have the sodding key?'

Nancy's lips parted and life sparked in her eyes. She whispered something.

'What was that, sweetheart?'

'I … love you … Jack.' The effort of speaking was seemingly so great, she closed her eyes.

'Well, does she?' Molly said, exasperated.

There was a pocket in Nancy's woollen cardigan, and

James felt inside. He pulled out a set of keys attached to a large loop fob and threw them to Molly.

Nancy Patterson's breathing became progressively shallower. Her chest rose and fell, each action barely perceptible. Instinctively, he held her hand.

When the movement of her chest finally stopped, James put his hand to her mouth and felt no breath against his skin. He checked her wrist for a pulse.

Nothing.

He bowed his head.

'What is it?' Molly asked, desperately fumbling with the keys.

'She's gone.'

FORTY-NINE

MAY 1943

THE PIERCING CALL of the air raid siren came at a fortuitous moment, cutting off her dream.

Most nights, it was the same dream. Nancy was alone, the night so bitterly cold, so desperately quiet, a crescent moon the only witness to her desperate attempts to dig her way out. Clawing at the rubble—bricks; broken joists; shards of glass—she yelled dementedly for help.

But no one ever answered her call.

Lottie? Lottie! Where are you, darling?

It had been two years since she'd lost her to the bomb, and there hadn't been a day that had passed when she didn't think about her daughter. Apart from Grandma Ada, who died the very same night, the only other person who knew of Lottie's existence was Mr. Elmswick. 'Don't worry, Nancy,' he'd told her, holding her hand while they were waiting for the stretcher party to arrive. 'It's probably for the best. It can be our secret.'

Could it ever be "for the best" for a baby to die? To save its mother the shame of giving birth out of wedlock?

Nancy knew such questions would haunt her for the rest of her life.

As the siren wailed, she leapt out of bed and threw her greatcoat over her pyjamas, forcing her bare feet into her boots. Then she dashed out of the Nissen hut, sprinting across the grass to the gun park as fast as she could.

By the time she reached the height and range finder, Daisy and Pamela were already in position. They were her best friends in the world. The friendships would never have happened—would never have worked—under different circumstances. The girls were like chalk and cheese. Daisy was the flame-haired beauty: easy-going; game for a laugh; forgetful. Drove the men crazy! Pamela was the dowdy one: serious; bookish; intense. Nancy fitted somewhere between the two extremes, she supposed.

'What kept you?' Pamela asked.

There was something about Pamela's voice, about the intense atmosphere, that told Nancy this was no false alarm. She cast her eyes to the sky, tracking the beams of the searchlights criss-crossing overhead.

And then she saw the formation: three shining dots. As they passed directly through the glare of the beams, they flashed silver for a second, and Nancy could make out the outlines of a Focke-Wulf Fw 190.

'Engage!' the captain roared, and the three women flew into action, as per the drills they'd practised countless times. Nancy and Pamela swivelled the height and range finder until they had the lead plane in their sights.

'Read!' Pamela shouted.

'*Read!*' Nancy echoed.

'Seven-nine-hundred!' Daisy hollered. In response, the predictor girls began working the controls to swivel the giant base. 'Fuse two-four!' came the call.

Nancy watched as the men loaded the shells into the

guns. A mounting frustration fizzed inside her. Why were the women not allowed to touch the guns? It was absurd. She was perfectly capable.

The moment they were ready, the captain boomed, '*Fire!*'

In the stillness of the night, the noise of the guns was like a thunderclap, but they were all hardened to the sound. The shells burst thousands of feet overhead and Nancy studied the lead German plane, watching for any sign of damage. She held her breath in anticipation.

And then it happened. The plane, silhouetted in the piercing beam of the searchlight, burst into flames and a fireball plunged from the heavens, landing seconds later in the sea. The remaining planes in the formation swerved, deviating from their course, which meant there was now little chance their bombs would land on target. Then they passed beyond the searchlight beams, disappearing into the inky blackness.

Back in the dormitory that night, reflecting on the morning's excitement, Daisy said to Nancy, 'That was good, wasn't it?'

'Yes!' Nancy replied in an instant. And then, as she drifted off to sleep, she wondered if she was developing a thirst for blood.

FIFTY

Poor old Nancy's body had just been carried out when Sergeant Lawson–the first responder, once again–told James and Molly they could leave.

The house was swarming with paper-suited CSIs, going about their business. Photographing the scene. Collating samples. Bagging evidence.

They'd been kept there for a good hour at least, providing witness statements, consenting to DNA samples and so on. But at least a few pieces of the puzzle had now slotted into place.

The wounded guy in the hallway had been rushed to the James Paget hospital. Widely known to Norfolk Constabulary, he was Dean Bridger, a wannabe criminal overlord, but in reality, a petty crook: burglary; theft; extortion. Bridger lived with his daughter, Kayleigh—a chip off the old block, by all accounts; expelled from school for disruptive behaviour and a serial shoplifter, to boot. Seemed she had run away from home and Dean had been keen to track her down. The police weren't the least bit surprised that she'd fled the scene. The attending officers said they'd put an alert out for her and Urtė. They were also able to match Dean's number to the call James had received earlier, when he'd dropped off Molly. James had inadvertently reunited the pair.

There were still big gaps in the puzzle, however. Like how did Panchenko discover the caravan site, then Nancy's house?

At the end of the garden path, the uniformed officer hoisted the blue and white police tape to let them through.

James got out his phone and opened up his photographs. He scrolled to the one he'd taken inside of Panchenko lying dead, then copied it to WhatsApp and composed a pithy message: "Job done." He found Alf Kealy's number, hit send, then pocketed the phone.

Molly rubbed at the livid red marks the cuffs had left on her wrists, then lit a cigarette.

James, retrieving his car keys, looked at the cigarette and tutted. He was keen to get back to the B&B.

'Don't judge me,' Molly said, blowing smoke into the sky. 'Is it any wonder I need nicotine after my morning in the bloody House of Horrors.' She jabbed a finger at the house. 'It's all *your* fault. And why didn't you tell me Panchenko was in town? Or about the torched caravan? Kind of important details to keep from me, don't you think?'

Molly didn't allow James time to speak. She continued her diatribe. 'And as for that Sandra Bullock bollocks, that red-haired hussy looks *nothing* like her!'

'I was waiting for the right moment to tell you.' James rolled his shoulders and worked his neck. Something clicked unexpectedly, and pain ran down his arm.

'You should go to A&E,' she said, calming. 'Get your-self checked over. You could have concussion. Feeling confused? Nauseous? Bothered by light or noise?'

'All the time,' he snapped. 'Stop fussing over me. I'm *fine.*'

He took the opportunity of waiting for Molly to finish her cigarette to hold his face to the sun, close his eyes and feel its warmth on his eyelids. After a deep intake of crisp air, he opened his eyes and looked around. Farther up the road, a dozen or so houses away, he spotted a grey Chevrolet, parked at a lazy diagonal. Had to be Panchenko's. The plates were familiar.

He turned to shout at the cordon officer, 'Tell your gaffer the Chevrolet over there needs to be checked out. Think it's Panchenko's.'

The officer nodded, then spoke into his radio.

James turned to address Molly. 'Come on, finish that thing. We need to get back to Urtė and Kayleigh.'

She took a long drag on the cigarette, exhaled and threw the butt to the gutter. She glanced back at the house and shook her head. 'Mental,' she murmured.

Seemed a fair summary of events.

They got in the Audi and buckled up. Molly gave an exaggerated shiver as James turned the key in the ignition. 'Do you want the heater on?' he asked.

'It's not that. Just been thinking, what was going through Nancy's head when she went looking for the gun? If Dean and Andric hadn't turned up when they did … Don't think she would have shot me, do you?'

'Can't imagine anyone wanting to shoot you, Moll. What *I* can't understand is why she was left on her own in that house. Surely someone of authority must have realised she was a danger to herself.'

'I guess she was just fiercely independent. Probably fought tooth and nail to stay put. Anyway, she's gone out in a blaze of glory, don't you think? A *heroine*. If I had to choose my own ending, it would be something like that.'

'Suppose.' James released the handbrake and put the car into gear.

'And talking of guns, why didn't Panchenko just break into the caravan and shoot Rosa? Why go to the effort, take the risk, of petrol bombing the van?'

'Guess he wanted to scare the wits out of her. Flush her out. Take her some place else—maybe his home patch—to torture her, inflict a slow, painful death. Make her pay for killing his brother. Who knows what goes on in the mind of a psychopath?'

Molly gave a knowing nod. James continued, 'Anyway, time to solve the next riddle: what happened to Fitzroy-Fergusson?'

'Want me to drive?' Molly asked. 'Not sure you're in a fit state.'

'No. I've seen you behind the wheel of that Evoque. You're a bloody menace.'

'I'm an *excellent* driver, thank you very much! In twenty years, I've not had a single accident—' She stopped herself. 'Sorry,' she said sheepishly. 'Wasn't thinking.'

James smiled wryly. 'No worries,' he said and set off.

Red lights at some roadworks on the return journey tested his patience beyond endurance, so he took an impromptu detour through an industrial area. Various businesses slipped past: warehouses; a self-storage unit; a double glazing outfit.

'So,' Molly asked, 'how's it feel, after all this time, to have finally found her?'

Feel? God, he hated that kind of question. How do you even begin to answer it? Truthfully, he supposed. He *felt* knackered. More importantly, he *felt* damned responsible. His obsession with finding Urtė had put her life at risk. It had also set the ball rolling on so many deaths. Roxie. Nancy Patterson. Clifford Snell. Even a bloody pet parrot.

He should have left everything well alone.

They were passing a grotty-looking MOT centre, its forecourt crammed with clapped-out vehicles, when he became aware that Molly was talking to him. 'Jimbo? Speak to me. You've gone a deathly shade. And slow down, for Christ's sake!'

He jammed the brakes so hard that Molly was thrown violently forward.

'*Bloody hell!*' she shouted. 'You nearly broke my neck! What's got into you?'

He was looking through her, barely registering her words. The MOT centre had sent his brain elsewhere—to Alf Kealy's crash repair outfit. 'The scratch,' he uttered. 'It was just a useful decoy.'

'What are you talking about, man?' Molly released her seat belt. 'Right, I'm driving. No arguments.'

James switched off the engine and unbuckled himself. Opened the door and got out.

When Molly came round to his side, he was crouched beside the front wheel. He ran his fingers under the wheel arch and found what he was looking for. Curling his fingers around the magnetic tracking device, he yanked it free and showed it to Molly.

'I don't understand,' she said.

'Alf Kealy's played me for a fucking fool.'

FIFTY-ONE

HE'D RELENTED and let Molly drive the remainder of the journey. James had his fingers curled tightly around the grab handle, watching her like a hawk.

Kealy wasn't answering his phone, of course. Why would he?

The whole thing about the warehouse fire, the drugs, Panchenko tampering with his brakes and causing the accident that had killed his wife …

It was all bullshit.

And James had fallen for it. Hook, line and sinker. Kealy hadn't wanted James to bring him Panchenko; he'd wanted *him* to lead Panchenko to Urtė.

The consolation that the plan hadn't worked in the Eastern European gangster's favour offered James a crumb of comfort. Urtė was alive, and Panchenko was dead. But Kealy had blood on his hands. And James would see to it that he paid for it. Whatever it took, however long it took him.

At Hillcroft House, Molly turned into the gravel lane. They were halfway along it when a vehicle exited the car park to face them: the red Mondeo.

Surprisingly, the driver didn't reverse; just continued towards them.

'Back up, arsehole,' James murmured.

Molly hit the brakes. 'Who is it?' she said. 'A Beverley sister? Probably doesn't know her reverse from her elbow.'

As the Mondeo drew closer, James realised it was the Spaniard, looking particularly grumpy. He reached over and slammed his palm on the horn.

'That'll show 'em, Jimbo.'

The Spaniard honked back and revved his engine, lifting his hands from the steering wheel to gesture—in stereotypical Continental exuberance—his impatience for Molly to submit to his will.

'Stand your ground, Moll. We're in the right here.'

'I don't need your advice.'

The Mondeo continued towards them—if anything, speeding up—then its driver slammed his brakes at the last moment. Their bumpers came to rest inches apart, the Spaniard gesticulating wildly.

One minute passed in a similar vein. Two.

Time was, to break stalemates like this, James would play the ace up his sleeve: his warrant card. Not anymore. But he wasn't going to stand for this nonsense any longer. Time to give the guy a piece of his mind; to teach him a thing or two about the Highway Code. Rules 200 to 203, if the memory from his brief and unhappy stint in Traffic served him correctly. He unbuckled his seat belt and reached for the door handle.

'Oh, for Pete's sake, man!' Molly snapped. 'Life's too short to waste on petty standoffs like this.'

'*Petty standoffs*? That's rich coming from you!'

She gave him one of her looks and put the car into reverse, hooked her hand around the back of his seat and floored the accelerator. The gravel crunched and the transmission whined as she barrelled down the lane. As the Audi emerged onto the road, she threw the steering wheel a quarter turn to the left and brought the car to a shuddering standstill.

James dared to open his eyes.

The Spaniard emerged from the lane moments later. Did he show any gratitude? A tip of the head? A small wave of the hand? A mouthed "thank you"?

Did he hell.

They parked up without further incident and breezed into the B&B. Thankfully, no sign of Mrs. Elliott inside.

As they reached the top of the stairs, Molly, breathing raggedly, rasped, 'What are the chances they're not even here? Probably scarpered.'

James put his ear to the door. He couldn't hear a thing.

He turned the key in the lock, pushed open the door and entered his room. 'God's sake!' he exclaimed.

Molly, behind him: 'What?'

'They've turned the place over. Look.'

The room was a bombsite: drawers and wardrobe doors gaping open; clothes flung everywhere; papers strewn over the floor.

The net curtains fluttered in the open window, and James went over to peer out. Couldn't see a soul.

'Did you leave anything valuable here?' Molly asked.

'No.'

James sat on the edge of the bed and pressed his palms into his eye sockets. He'd totally misjudged them.

Then there was a sound from the bathroom.

Molly put an ear to the door, then turned to tell James, 'Think someone's in the shower.' She rapped on the door.

'Hey! It's James and Molly. We're back.' She knocked again, louder.

A minute or so later, the door opened and Kayleigh emerged, wrapped in a bath towel, her face pink. Behind her, the bathroom was swamped with steam. She looked about the room—at the mess; at James; at Molly. Puzzlement, then concern flickered across her features. 'Where's Rosa?'

'How would we know?' Molly asked. 'We assumed she'd be here?'

'She was, before I went in the shower. She was lying on the bed, dozing.'

'Think she's done a runner, I'm afraid, love. Left you for dust. Is there anyone we can call? Your Mum? A relative? You must be in shock, you know, after earlier …'

'How long were you in the bathroom, Kayleigh?' James interjected.

'Dunno. Five minutes, maybe six?'

He went over to the window, parted the net curtains and looked out. Scanned the car park. 'And you didn't hear anything?'

'No.'

'What is it, James?' Molly said.

It couldn't be *him*, could it? He knew there was something vaguely familiar about the guy; he'd just never been able to put his finger on it. 'That fucker's taken her! And we just let him do it.'

'Who?'

'The bloody Spaniard in the Mondeo!'

'I'm not following. Where, exactly, does he fit into the equation?'

James slammed his fist against the wall with such force that the bird picture bounced off its nail and crashed to the floor.

'James? Jimbo?'

He turned to her. 'What if it wasn't when the scratch was being repaired?'

'Eh?'

'What if it was when the pissing scratch was made in the first place?'

'What on earth are you wittering on about?'

'The maid's son, Molly! Rodríguez. That's who followed me to Yarmouth!' He made for the door. 'Stay here with Kayleigh. I'm going after him.'

'Oh, no, no, no,' Molly said, moving to block his path. 'Don't you dare pass me that hot potato! It was *your* idea to send them here, not mine. You need to own the consequences. God knows what offence we're—*you're*—committing here! Harbouring a minor? Child abduction? Kidnap?'

James turned to Kayleigh. 'How old are you, sweetheart?'

'Sixteen.'

Really? 'We're fine, then. Assuming, of course, we have your consent?'

Kayleigh nodded. 'I'm coming with you,' she said. 'To help you find her. You need someone with local knowledge, right?'

James smiled. He was warming to the girl. 'How are your ribs? Still hurting?'

She pointed over her shoulder. 'Took a load of pills. Can't feel a thing now.'

'*Which* pills, exactly, did you take, Kayleigh?'

She shrugged. 'Just a selection.'

Christ, he thought. 'Fine, we're good to go, then. Get yourself dressed, quickly.'

'Well, I'm not getting changed with you watching me!'

'You've got one minute.'

'I've got some stuff in my car, love,' Molly said, putting her hand on Kayleigh's arm. 'If you fancy a change from that romper suit. I've got blouses, jumpers, jeans … you name it.'

'Jesus, Molly! We've not got time! The car park. Fifty seconds.'

He stormed out of the room. As he hurried down the stairs, he pulled out his phone and dialled Sergeant Lawson's number. It rang several times before it was picked up. 'Lawson? James Quinn. I need your help. Urgently.'

There was a pause before Lawson replied wearily, 'Look, mate, I've just got through the front door after the shift from hell. Fifteen hours straight. I'm famished, filthy and fucking knackered. I need to get something to eat, then go to bed before I drop dead from exhaustion.'

'Do you want Urtė Cuda's death on your conscience?'

Lawson sighed. 'Fuck's sake, man! You've got ten seconds. This had *better* be good.'

'I have reason to believe she's been abducted within the last ten minutes.'

After a couple of beats of silence, Lawson exclaimed, '*Abducted!?* Are you taking the piss? Wasn't the Panchenko guy meant to have been her abductor? Last I checked, rigor mortis was setting in!'

James pinched the bridge of his nose hard, and began to explain.

Lawson cut in, 'You're sounding like the boy who cried fucking wolf. Look, this Urtė woman, *she's* not my problem. Call the station. 999 …'

'Come on, man! The clock's ticking. Every second we waste—'

'I'm pressing the button to end the call, right now.'

'You've heard of Geoffrey Fitzroy-Fergusson, right?'

'What?'

'You find Urtė and her abductor, and you solve his murder. Imagine that? You'll be inspector before the week's out.'

There was a pause, followed by a long sigh. By this time, James had reached the reception desk. 'So, you're going to help?' he asked.

'Give me everything you have.'

'Get a call out. The guy you're after is driving a red Mondeo. Last known location: exiting the gravel lane to the side of Hillcroft House B&B. Approximately'—he checked his watch—'11:55 a.m. Heading west. Male. Mid thirties. Five eight, five nine. Heavy build. Colombian nationality. Get someone looking at CCTV, traffic cameras—'

'Don't tell me how to do my job, matey. Any hint on the suspect's name? The vehicle registration?'

James was looking at the empty reception desk. Specifically, through the open door into the back office. 'Give me a moment. I'm just getting you them now.'

There came the sound of heavy treads on the stairs. He turned to see Molly and Kayleigh emerging from the staircase into the hall. Kayleigh was wearing one of his favourite sweaters; way too large. It hung on her skinny frame, hem at mid-thigh, the sleeves turned up.

'Why didn't you just go down the fire escape?' he asked Molly.

'What, you think I'm going to climb out of a window and scramble down that rickety old staircase in these shoes?'

'Keep your voice down! We don't want to disturb—'

Too late.

The door to the private quarters swung open and out bustled Mrs. Elliott, her face pinched with indignation. She looked at the three of them, then honed in on James. 'Would you care to explain, Mr. Quinn?'

James placed the phone against his chest. 'This is really important, Mrs. Elliott. I need the name and registration number of another guest. I know you keep records.' He nodded in the direction of the office.

She gave a superior little laugh and moved to stand behind the desk, planting her palms, spread well apart, on the counter. 'And *why* would I do something like that?'

'Because I have reason to believe he has just abducted a young woman and her life is in grave danger. Please. We can't afford to waste time.'

Her brow twitched minutely and she blinked several times before she tilted her head and said, 'Are you a police officer, Mr. Quinn?'

'Yes. Well … not anymore.'

'I see,' she said and folded her arms. 'Then I'm afraid I can't help you. My hands are tied. There are laws I must obey, as I'm sure *you* are well aware.'

James held out his phone. 'I have a police officer on the line right now.' He pressed the phone to his ear. 'You still there, Sergeant?'

'What's going on? Where are you?'

'Going to put you on speaker. Give me a tick.' He fumbled at the screen, trying to find the speaker setting. Turning to Molly, he said, 'How do you get this bloody thing on speaker?'

Molly rolled her eyes. 'Give it here,' she said and went to snatch the phone.

'Just show me,' he said, tugging it back. Somehow, he managed to lose his grip and the phone fell to the floor. He crouched down to scoop it up and pressed it to his ear. 'Hello? Sergeant?'

The line was dead.

'Hey!' Mrs. Elliott squawked. 'You can't do that, young lady! *Out!*'

James leapt up to see Mrs. Elliott retreating into the office. Moments later, Kayleigh emerged, shoving past Mrs. Elliott and brandishing a red hardback notebook.

'Sorry,' James said to Mrs. Elliott, snatching the notebook. On the front was a white sticker, labelled in neat handwriting: "GUEST VEHICLE REGISTRATIONS". He smiled, then, addressing Mrs. Elliott, said, 'Gotta go. We'll return the book, I promise.'

They raced along the lane to the car park, Kayleigh alongside, Molly some way back.

At the car park, James unlocked the car and jumped into the driver's seat. Kayleigh took the front passenger seat.

He hooked the iPhone up to the USB cable and started leafing through the records in the notebook. He quickly located the subject of his search. Santiago Rodríguez. 'I knew it!' he exclaimed.

He dialled Lawson again. While it rang, Molly appeared, pressing her face to Kayleigh's window. James threw his thumb to the rear seats.

'See I've been relegated,' Molly grumbled as she climbed into the back.

'Just buckle up.'

'How lovely.'

James had manoeuvred the Audi out of the tight car park and was on the lane when Lawson answered. The sergeant sounded like he was eating. James held the notebook open against the steering wheel and relayed Santiago Rodríguez's details. Registration. Home address. Then he hung up.

They reached the end of the lane and turned right. He sped towards the junction with the busy trunk road, slamming his brakes on at the last possible moment. He looked left, then right.

'So, what's the plan, Jimbo? I'm thinking needles … haystacks …'

'Got to get into the mind. Occupy his skin. Isn't that right, Moll? So, which way?'

'Right,' Kayleigh said in a heartbeat. 'Quickest way out of town. Out of the county. That's where I'd take someone if I was abducting them.'

In the rearview mirror, Molly's features pinched into a scowl.

James smiled and activated his right indicator.

FIFTY-TWO

Rosa opened her eyes in the screaming dark. Her body was hunched, contorted, her cheek pressed against rough and scratchy fabric. She tried to alter her position, to flex her cramping legs, but there was no give.

The constant hum made no sense until the realisation struck her: she was in the boot of a car!

The car accelerated, and the hum became a shrill whine.

She screamed.

Screamed until there was no sound left in her throat.

FIFTY-THREE

'Ease off the gas, Jimbo.'

James glanced at the speedo; saw that he was pushing fifty in a thirty zone. He slowed to thirty-eight. Seemed a reasonable compromise, in the circumstances.

'So, what exactly does Rodríguez want with her?' Molly asked from the back. 'Do tell.'

'I don't know. What's the point in us postulating now? The priority is finding her before it's too late.'

'Well, maybe you should leave that for the police to deal with. It is their job, after all.'

'I can't just sit around, doing nothing.'

Molly said something in reply, but he couldn't hear her. He looked at her in the rearview. 'What was that?'

'*Speed!*'

Was he speeding? Yep. Fifty-four, fifty-five …

He eased off and the car quietened.

'You're going to kill us all at this rate,' Molly continued. 'Don't you think there's been enough collateral damage already?'

James didn't say anything. He hated it when she was right.

'And think of your blood pressure. Your heart.'

James scowled. 'I don't want to hear you utter that word again. Got it?'

'Fine. Whatever.' A pause. 'How about *pump-like organ for circulating blood*?'

'God's sake!'

'Are you two married?'

The question came from Kayleigh. He'd almost forgotten she was there.

Molly scoffed. 'Credit me with some taste!'

Something seemed to catch Kayleigh's attention in the storage compartment at her side. She shoved her hand inside and brought out a packet of sugar-free Polos. She teased one from the packet and popped it into her mouth. 'Neither of you have a Scooby what happened, the day of the politician's murder, do you?'

'She told you?' James said, surprised.

Kayleigh, sucking noisily on the mint, shrugged. 'Of course.'

'*Everything*?' Molly added.

'Guess so.'

James exchanged a look with Molly in the rearview, then pulled up on the side of the road and demanded that Kayleigh tell them everything she knew.

FIFTY-FOUR

THE RELIEF of daylight and cool air soon gave way to fresh horror.

Rosa could see the edge now. Beyond it, only blue. Impossibly blue. The sky. The sea.

She glanced over her shoulder at the abandoned car. The driver's door was open, as was the boot, after he'd hauled her out. Tyre marks trailed back across the expanse of grassland to the road. If she screamed, would anyone hear her?

No, she shouldn't scream. That risked enraging him; making him act in haste. She didn't even know if she was capable of screaming. She needed to bide her time. Stay calm. Keep her wits about her. Someone would have seen or heard something. They'd come to her rescue soon.

Wouldn't they?

'Who are you?' she asked again, her voice cracking. There was something vaguely familiar about her abductor, but she couldn't place him. 'One of Andric's gang, right?' she ventured. 'You don't need to hurt me now. You know he is dead, right?'

Her abductor jabbed the gun into her side. '*You're lying! Move!*'

Gripping her harder around her upper arm, he forced her to keep walking. Towards the cliff edge.

She was skidding on the damp grass, her weak legs buckling. 'Please, you're hurting me …'

There was no barrier. No wall. No fence. Just a poxy little wooden sign hammered into the ground that said, "DANGER".

Rosa was still staring at the sign when he released her arm and shoved her forward so hard that she crashed to the ground. The edge was so close that she could see over it. The drop was almost vertical, culminating in huge rocks at the base, far below. She felt the awful sensation of blood rushing to her stomach; the anxiety; the fear that the ground would give way beneath her.

She scrambled to her feet and turned to him, holding out her hands, palms forward. She took a tentative step away from the edge.

He raised the gun towards her and she halted. 'Evgeni,' she croaked. 'I didn't mean to kill him. I had to get away because I knew Andric would be mad and he wouldn't believe me.'

His reaction surprised her: a brief flicker of confusion. Her abductor lowered the gun to rest against his thigh.

'You believe me, yes?' she said.

Silence.

'Let me go. *Please*. I won't go to the police, I promise.'

It didn't make sense. Nothing made sense. Why bring her here to such an exposed position? Why the urgency? Had something happened to thwart his plans? Was he panicking? He did have a vague look of panic about him; she could see it in his shifting eyes, his twitchy movements. She could talk him round, calmly. Make him see sense.

Rosa went to open her mouth, but the man spoke first. '*Jump!*' he demanded.

'What?'

He aimed the gun at her chest. 'Jump off the cliff or I shoot.'

What kind of a choice was that? 'Please,' she begged.

It was when he took a step towards her that she saw it in his green eyes; in the faint tremble of his hand. She could hear it in his hesitant, stammering voice.

Fear.

She could even smell it.

Just like she did a year ago in Notting Hill.

The realisation of his identity struck her with a sudden, cold force. 'It's *you*,' she said. 'You killed him. The client.'

His face contorted with rage. '*Jump!*' he hollered impatiently.

'No!' Her own assertiveness almost caught her by surprise.

'I'm going to count down from five, and if you don't jump, I shoot.'

'Why did you kill him?' Rosa calmly demanded.

He stole a look around him, then started, 'Five … four …'

Rosa took a bold step forward, keeping her eyes fixed firmly on his. 'You couldn't shoot me then, and you can't do it now.'

Another step took her to within inches of the man's weapon. She looked at the gun. At him. And smiled. A kindly smile that she hoped wouldn't betray the crater of broiling fear inside. She gently rested her fingers on the barrel of the gun, but he recoiled.

'You have to die …' he said, his tone almost apologetic.

'Why?'

He didn't answer, but the torment of the question was etched in his features.

'Has somebody order you to kill me?' she persisted. 'Who?'

He paused briefly, shook his head and resumed his countdown. 'Three … two …'

'You won't do it!' she scoffed, though now she wasn't so confident.

He cocked the trigger, and the *click* made her jump.

'Let me go!' she begged, her voice rising in panic. 'I will disappear. You can say that I drown in the sea.'

'No! She needs proof.'

'*She?* Who?'

He didn't respond, but gave the impression that he'd already said too much. He raised the gun to her head and said, '*One!*'

Her eyes snapped shut, and she braced for the inevitable.

What came next surprised her. A distant noise. It took a few beats to register what it was: a dog, barking. She opened her eyes to see it haring towards them. A big, brutish thing. No owner in sight.

The dog was soon upon them, jumping up at the man, barking and snarling like a deranged wolf. The man kicked out, waving the gun and bellowing at the hound, all to no effect. He raised the gun, poised to administer a pistol-whip, when they heard a distant voice. A woman.

'Oscar! Oscar! Here! *Now!*'

From the corner of her eye, Rosa noticed her abductor stowing the gun in his back pocket, and by the time the stout, middle-aged woman arrived, he'd adopted an innocent posture.

The dog-walker was somewhat breathless by the time she got hold of the beast by its collar and wrestled to clip on its lead. 'I'm so sorry,' she said, raising her voice to be heard above the dog's continued barking. 'I don't know what's got into him. *Be quiet, boy!*'

The dog calmed slightly, allowing the woman to take stock. Her gaze switched between Rosa, her abductor, the abandoned car, and then back to Rosa. 'Everything okay here?' she enquired.

The man gave Rosa a faint nod and a knowing look, and Rosa said to the woman, 'We are fine, thank you. We look for something. My necklace. We lost it here earlier.'

'A necklace? You must let me help you find it. It's the least I can do after Oscar's behaviour. What are we talking? A choker? Pendant? Gold ch—'

'No!' the man said. 'We'll be okay on our own.'

The woman ran a hand through her tousled grey hair and eyed the man with a degree of suspicion. She turned to look at Rosa, who subtly attempted to mouth the word "*help*".

Unfortunately, the man must have noticed.

In a flash, he pulled the gun from his pocket and fired a shot into the sky.

The woman screamed and, of course, the dog went totally berserk.

'Leave! Now!' Her abductor commanded the woman, aiming the gun at her. She retreated swiftly, dragging the baying beast along with her.

He turned to face Rosa, and she swore there were tears in his eyes. 'I'm sorry,' he said, and for the second time in one day, Rosa had a gun levelled at her heart.

FIFTY-FIVE

A MASKED INTRUDER, then. Who would have thought it? Not him. Nor the Met, it seemed. If James had got a pound each time a dim-witted criminal had tried to pin the blame for their dastardly deeds on a masked intruder, he'd have been a very rich man.

To be fair, the clues were all there in the case file. Santiago Rodríguez had a criminal record for burglary and theft. And traces of his DNA had been found everywhere.

So, that was the *what* and the *how* resolved. Just the tricksy matter of the *why* to fathom. It was quite the leap from burglary and theft to cold-blooded murder …

'It's obvious,' Molly said from the back, as if reading his thoughts. 'The murder was payback for Fitzroy-Fergusson not settling his debts. You saw his dire finances. The quantities of cocaine they found at the house. And who was supplying the coke? Rodríguez. Had to be. Urtė was the only witness to the murder, so she needed to be eliminated. Only he bottled it on the day. Typical weak male. Now, he's here to finish what he started. Don't you see? It all fits.'

James raised his brow at the rearview. 'You were equally as certain it was an elaborate suicide before.'

'Well …' Molly shrugged. 'I'm reappraising my view in light of new evidence. That's how it's supposed to work, is it not?'

'So,' James said, addressing Kayleigh, 'what do you reckon?'

'I reckon we need to find them, fast.'

'Agreed.'

James dialled Lawson, who picked up after several rings. 'What is it?' Lawson asked gruffly.

How refreshing to be conversing with someone who dispensed with pleasantries. 'Urtė Cuda. Any sightings yet?'

'Can't really talk.' The sergeant sounded breathless, the line crackly. 'There's been reports of gunfire in Corton. Suffolk Constabulary have requested our assistance. Heading there now.'

'Gunfire? Is it connected?'

'Who bloody knows? All I know is, if there hadn't been bloody budget cuts, Suffolk wouldn't be requesting our assistance and I'd now be sound asleep.'

James started the engine. 'Corton, you say? Whereabouts?'

He didn't get an answer, as Lawson had already hung up.

Corton was a small coastal village, just the other side of the county border. 'Keep your eyes peeled, everyone,' James said as he drove past the welcome sign.

They passed a church and took a sharp bend to join a road running parallel to the coast. The sun streamed into the car, dazzling him. He flipped down the visor.

They continued through the village.

'Not seeing anything,' Molly said.

'Perhaps you could change the habit of a lifetime and only speak when you have something useful to say?'

'*There!*' Kayleigh exclaimed. She was pointing across an open expanse of grassland to a set of tyre tracks leading to a Mondeo, seemingly abandoned, its boot lid open.

James slammed on the brakes and turned the wheel sharply, mounting the kerb. The Audi bumped and bounced and skidded over the uneven ground.

'This brings back some happy memories!' Molly chirped.

'What's she talking about?' Kayleigh said.

'Just ignore her.'

He drew alongside the Mondeo and jumped out. Stuck his head through the open driver-side door. The key was still in the ignition, so he took it out and pocketed it. The interior was a state: fast food wrappers; discarded cans; an ashtray filled with butts. The sickly sweet reek of cannabis. Paperwork littered the passenger seat and the footwell. He rifled through the papers and found nothing of interest, except for a couple of his own missing person flyers. The open glove box was empty.

'James!'

He closed the door and looked over to Molly. She was at the cliff edge with Kayleigh, wildly waving her hands above her head.

He ran over to join them. 'What is it?'

'Can you hear it? A dog barking. Down at the bottom.'

James peered cautiously over the ledge. How far? Forty, fifty metres, he supposed. He could hear the dog, but he couldn't see it. What he could see was a wide concrete path. The sea wall. Beyond, a narrow stretch of beach. A calm sea. Partially submerged groynes. Seagulls squabbling in a brilliant sky. 'How do I get down?' he asked Kayleigh.

She pointed. 'There's steps, that way. Let me come with you.'

The girl was breathing in shallow, pained breaths, her palm pressed against her ribcage.

'Stay here with me, love,' Molly said, putting an arm around the girl's shoulders. 'Keep me company. There's *no way* I'm clambering down there.'

'Wait in the car,' James said, giving the keys to Molly. 'And make yourself useful. Call the police and tell them we've located his vehicle.'

The steep concrete steps snaked a haphazard course down to the path below. As James descended, the furious barking grew louder. He followed the sound to a small cluster of people, gawping at the rocks.

The dog was a German Shepherd; an awful, feral-looking thing, snarling and lurching. Its owner—a middle-aged woman—was struggling to restrain it. They stood at some distance from the other onlookers.

'What happened?' James enquired as he got to the gathering.

'Looks like they jumped,' someone said. 'Poor bugger.'

An icy cold hand clutched at James's heart and squeezed hard.

'I can't bring myself to look,' said another.

'Then don't. Out the way.' James shoved his way irritably through the gathering so he could see who had fallen.

'Are you a medic?' an elderly man enquired. 'I'm afraid there's nothing that can be done now,' he added. A statement of the bleeding obvious, considering what was now in plain sight: Santiago Rodríguez's body, lying battered and twisted on the rocks, spatters of blood everywhere.

Thankfully, there was no sign of Urtė. What on earth

had happened? Had they tussled and fought, with Urtė emerging victorious? Where was she?

He turned to the crowd, addressing no one in particular. 'He was with a woman. Has anyone seen her?'

The woman with the German Shepherd raised her hand. 'A woman, you say? Red hair? Green dress?'

'Yes, that's her. Where is she now?'

The woman nodded in the direction of the clifftop. 'They were up there. I was taking Oscar for a walk when he suddenly bolted. Totally out of character.' (*Yeah, right*, James thought, as the hound acknowledged him with a volley of monstrous barks. *That thing should be muzzled. Preferably, put down.*) 'I chased after him and came upon this couple. Having an argument about something or other, I assumed. The woman gave me some cock and bull story about a missing necklace. Anyway, next minute, he was pulling a gun on us; told us to scram. We were halfway back to the road when I glanced over my shoulder, only to see him throw himself off the cliff. Madness.'

'And what did the woman do next?'

'She ran to the car, went inside for a few moments and emerged with something. I couldn't see what. I was shouting at her, asking if she needed help, but she ignored me. Maybe she didn't hear. Then she ran to the road. A bus came along and she waved it down; jumped on board.'

'Which bus?'

'There's only one that runs along this road. The X101.'

'Direction?'

'South. Next stop, Lowestoft.'

James was about to leave with a crisp "thank you and goodbye" when the damned dog bolted from the woman's grip and scrambled, its lead trailing, over the rocks in the direction of Rodríguez's corpse.

Yelps of horror spewed from the crowd.

'Oscar! *No!* Get back here! Now!'

Of course, the German Shepherd ignored the repeated commands of its owner. It was too interested in the body, subjecting it to an extensive amount of sniffing. Next, it was tugging at an arm. Then a leg. And now it was grabbing something in its mouth. Whatever it was the dog had found appeared to satisfy its curiosity because it bounced back to them, its tail wagging, all happy and smug.

For a horrible moment, James thought it had retrieved a severed body part—a hand; a foot; an ear—but no, the dog opened its mouth and dropped a gun at its owner's feet for her admiration. Surely only cats did that? Or was it expecting her to lob the revolver into the distance? A game of fetch with a lethal weapon? Either way, it probably wasn't expecting what came next: a clip round the ear and a vicious reprimand.

Before he'd even picked up the gun, James could tell it was a revolver that had been converted from a blank-firing pistol. He knew this because, some six years ago, he'd led the covert cross-county operation to smash an organised criminal network that had smuggled a huge cache of them into the country.

There were five live cartridges left in the chamber, which James quickly emptied. Now, he needed somewhere safe to stow it and to prevent any more contamination of the evidence. Time was, he'd carry evidence bags everywhere he went, but he'd long since dropped the habit. 'Do you have something I could put this in, please? A bag?' he asked the woman.

'Only for dog mess. Will one of those suffice?'

'Lovely. Clean, I hope?'

She rummaged in her coat pocket, pulled out a little black turd sack and handed it to James. He placed the gun and cartridges inside, then secured it with a double knot.

'Oscar has a thing about guns,' the woman said. 'You see, he's ex-police. Three years in Specialist Operations before they retired him.'

James looked at the dog in a new light, one crime fighter cut off in his prime to another. Gave it a wink. The dog growled softly and curled its upper lip, which James interpreted as reciprocated respect.

'Got to go,' he said to the woman, and he made briskly for the steps.

Halfway there and, behold, who was this fine specimen of a man huffing and puffing in his direction? Why, Sergeant Lawson of Norfolk Constabulary, of course. Flushed with exertion and his forehead beaded with sweat, he met James's eye and sighed wearily.

'Always late to the party?' James said chirpily, then stepped to one side to allow Lawson a view of the body on the rocks.

Lawson rolled his eyes and took a deep draw from his inhaler. 'Is it him? Rodríguez?'

'Got it in one, Sherlock.'

'Just him?'

'Yep. The woman back there, with the dog, says she witnessed Urtė flee the scene and board a bus. After Rodríguez threw himself off the cliff, apparently. Suggest you speak to her first.'

Lawson's attention switched to the bag in James's hands. His nostrils flared. 'That what I think it is?'

'Are you thinking it's one of hundreds of starting pistols smuggled through Felixstowe by a ruthless criminal enterprise and converted to a revolver to be sold on the black market at an extortionate profit?' James pushed the bag into Lawson's chest. 'Thought not. Get it properly bagged and itemised. Contact the Met and have them compare it to the forensic evidence from the Fitzroy-Fergusson case. If it's not the murder weapon, I'll eat my hat.'

While Lawson stood there, speechless, staring at the bag, James looked over Lawson's shoulder. 'Just yourself, is it? Seems a bit light. No offence.'

'Cavalry's up on the clifftop, checking over the Mondeo.' Lawson took out his radio and spoke into it. 'Smithy, get your arse down here now!'

'Right,' James said, spotting his opportunity. 'Got to dash.'

'Where to, exactly?'

'To find Urtė, of course. What are you looking at me like that for?'

'You know, a sergeant more cynical than myself might think that a layman being present before the police arrive at one crime scene is unfortunate, but *three* in less than twelve hours might be cause for suspicion.'

'Well, thank goodness you're not a cynic,' James said, patting Lawson on the shoulder. 'Catch you later.'

On the way back up the steps, he passed Smithy and a pair of paramedics, then found the clifftop busy with emergency services personnel. Hordes of uniforms; a firearms unit; an ambulance. A gathering crowd of onlookers circled the cordoned Mondeo.

After returning the Mondeo's keys to a surprised-looking constable, James went to find Molly and Kayleigh but found the Audi had gone, and there was no sign of either of them. When he checked his phone, he found several missed calls from Molly. She hadn't left a voicemail, so he called her. After an age, it was Kayleigh who answered. 'Where are you?' he asked.

'On our way to Lowestoft. There was a witness who told us they saw Rosa get on a bus.'

'Hope you don't mind us taking the car, Jimbo,' Molly shouted. 'We didn't think you'd want us hanging around, doing nothing.'

'Tell her if she prangs the car, I'll wring her bloody neck.'

'Heard that, Jimbo! Kayleigh's put you on speaker. Meet you there, yes?'

'Can't you just swing back and pick me up?'

They hung up.

That would be a no, then.

FIFTY-SIX

HE HAD to wait twenty bloody minutes for the next bus to Lowestoft. He was fit to burst with irritation by the time he boarded.

James paid the fare and flopped onto a window seat, a few rows back. In his judgemental opinion, if you had to travel by bus, it was a sign you hadn't made it in life. As if to prove his point, there were only three other travellers, and all of them were ancient. If one of them didn't die before Lowestoft, it would be a miracle.

When had he last been on a bus? He'd have been about fifteen, he guessed. He recalled the excitement of catching the double-decker to Martins the newsagents in town to spend his paper round money on penny sweets and Panini football stickers, or a game for his Sinclair ZX Spectrum. The bus had been an old boneshaker that belched out dirty clouds of pollutant from its exhaust. He could picture the chequered fabric; the seat-back ashtrays clogged with rubbish; the hardened globs of discarded chewing gum everywhere you looked. If it was available—and it rarely was—he'd take the front seat on the top deck so he could pretend to be driving. And there was that intriguing little periscope thing where you could peer into the actual driver's cabin below. Sometimes he'd pressed his face to the square of glass and the driver's angry voice would bellow up the stairwell. Happy days.

The buzz of the phone in his pocket cut through his thoughts. A mobile number he didn't recognise. 'Hello?'

After a beat of silence, a voice whispered, 'James?'

'Urtė?'

'Is Kayleigh okay?'

'She's fine. Where you are? And how'd you get my number?'

There was no response.

'I know who took you,' James continued. 'And I know what happened. You weren't responsible for any of it. Everything's going to be fine. Just tell me where you are.'

'I want to see Kayleigh. Please.'

'Sure. Just tell me where you are.'

'No police.'

James hesitated. 'I don't think you're their priority right now. They have their hands full with other matters.'

'Just promise. Please.'

'I promise. Now, give me your location.'

He rendezvoused with Molly and Kayleigh at a town centre pay and display. Thankfully, the Audi appeared unscathed. Molly threw him the keys, and they made a dash for the café.

Abutting the promenade, the café was a cheap and cheerful place: green plastic tables and chairs out front and busy with patrons inside, enjoying the simple fair on offer —donuts; bacon rolls; milkshakes; tea and coffee.

Urtė stood up nervously from her corner table when

they went inside. A smile formed when she saw Kayleigh. Kayleigh dashed over and the pair held themselves tightly in a tearful and silent embrace for long enough that James started to feel almost voyeuristic. Finally, they all sat down, except for Molly, whose offer of a round of teas was gratefully accepted.

On the table was a bunch of plastic flowers in a pink pot, an empty tea cup, a folded piece of paper and a mobile phone. Urtė must have noticed James looking, and she unfolded the paper to reveal one of his flyers. She told him she'd found it in Rodríguez's car.

'My money,' Rosa said, suddenly anguished. 'Where is it?'

Shit, James thought. He'd forgotten all about it. 'It's safe in my car,' he lied. 'I'll fetch it for you later.' He switched his attention to the mobile on the table. 'The phone. Is it his?'

'Yes. I find it in the glove box.'

James picked up the phone. An old smartphone, not passcode protected. 'Amateur,' he tutted.

'Messages keep coming,' Urtė said. 'But I do not understand the language.'

'Spanish,' James said, by way of explanation, as he casually scrolled through the message inbox. All he could discern was that the person trying to get hold of Santiago was Gabriela ("Mamá"). 'I don't speak a word, either. I'd better keep hold of the phone. The police will need it as evidence.'

'Spanish, you say, Jimbo?' Molly said breezily as she arrived with a tray of teas and an assortment of donuts. She distributed the teas and invited everyone to select a donut of their choice. Kayleigh wasn't shy about going first, opting for one with pink frosting and sprinkles.

James wasn't hungry. Nor, it seemed, was Urtė.

As Molly sat down, James showed her the phone and explained its importance. 'Give it here,' she said. 'I got an A in GCSE Spanish. And I've spent many a happy holiday in Spain. Been to Chile, too. Although that trip wasn't *quite* so happy. You see, I met this monk, or at least that's what he *claimed* to be. Turned out he was a—'

'Spare us the details, Moll. Just read the messages and tell us if there's anything interesting.'

While Molly studied the phone, James said to Urtė, 'I really should let the police know you're safe. They'll want to hear your side of everything, but from what I understand, you've got nothing to fear. We know who was responsible for Fitzroy-Fergusson's death. As for Evgeni, you'll be able to plead self-defence. You fled because you feared for your life, not because you were guilty.'

Urtė's spine stiffened, and her face crumpled with fear. She reached out for Kayleigh's hand and squeezed it tightly. 'Is it true what Andric say about Roxie? Did he kill her?'

'That's what it looks like. I'm sorry.'

Urtė chewed her lip, trying to stem the tears. 'I can never go to the police. Andric and Evgeni may be dead now, but there are others in the gang. Every girl that ever try to go to the police is killed. That is how it works.'

'But if that's the case, they'll put you in a formal protection scheme. Then you can supply names of the gang members still out there. They'll be arrested, stand trial and get sent to prison for a long time.'

'And where does that leave me?' Kayleigh mumbled through her last mouthful of donut. 'I'm not going back to live with my dad. Hopefully, he'll be dead soon.'

'You don't mean that, love,' Molly said. 'It's the shock talking—'

James cut in. 'You always have the option of Urtė

applying through the courts to be your guardian, till you reach the age of eighteen.'

'Yeah, right,' Kayleigh murmured. 'Like that's ever gonna happen.' She religiously licked her fingers one by one, then reached for another donut.

'Christ Almighty!' Molly suddenly exclaimed.

'What?'

'*She's* behind it all. The bloody mother. There's text after text after text from her, demanding to know if he's done the deed yet. He keeps on making excuses, but she's having none of it. The woman's absolutely relentless. You can see from the call list, too, that she's been calling him day and night. With a mother like that, is there any wonder he put himself out of his misery?'

'I do not understand,' Urtė said. 'Who is she?'

'You know her. Gabriela Rodríguez. Fitzroy-Fergusson's housekeeper.'

Urtė's expression moved from puzzlement to shock, to acceptance. Then her brow furrowed once more and she asked, 'But why does she want me dead?'

'Because,' Molly said, 'you were the only witness to the crime and—'

The phone in Molly's hand suddenly started ringing and she jumped, almost dropping it. Other customers turned to look for the source of the god-awful ringtone. 'I'm going to answer it,' Molly said.

'*Don't!*' James interjected, and he snatched the phone. 'We can't tip her off.' He fumbled at the phone, trying to turn down the volume, but managing to accept the call on speakerphone instead. After an uneasy pause, Gabriela's manic voice sang out. 'Santi? Santi?' Another pause, then a barrage of words, indecipherable except for a repeated phrase that sounded very much like "abort the mission." 'Santi?' she cried, one more time, and hung up.

They stared at each other, dumbfounded, before James enquired of Molly, '"Abort the mission"—that's what she said, right?'

'Yep. That's what I got. Couldn't make out much else as she was speaking too fast.'

'The Met clearly haven't informed her of her son's death yet,' James said. 'What's the sudden panic?' He turned to Urtė. 'I can't sit on this knowledge of Gabriela's involvement. I must inform the police, you understand?' Urtė's eyes widened and she started to shake her head. 'Don't worry,' James continued, trying to assuage her. 'I won't give you up against your will.'

He dashed outside and found a private spot to call Lawson. Lawson didn't pick up so he tried the Met via 101 instead, where he was transferred between umpteen individuals before eventually someone was prepared to listen— a detective sergeant by the name of Franklin. James relayed the details as efficiently as he could.

When he returned to the table in the café, the conversation between the three women suddenly fell silent and Molly turned to him, grinning oddly. 'What have you been plotting?' he asked.

'Nothing!' she said. 'Just been trying to fill in some of the blanks. Everything okay with the cops?'

'The Met are sending a couple of detectives round to Gabriela's house to break the news about her son and to ask her to account for her actions. I'll need to drop the phone in at Yarmouth Police Station.'

'Perfect,' Molly said. 'You can drop me at Hillcroft House and I can collect my car. That's if the old crone hasn't already had it sent to the wrecker's yard. But first, Kayleigh and I are going to nip out for a bit of retail therapy. Give the two of you a bit of quality time to catch up.' Molly stood up and held out her hand to Kayleigh.

James looked at his watch. 'Don't be long,' he said, then, once they had departed, he turned to Urtė. Strange, he'd spent so long working towards this moment, imagining it, but now that it was finally happening, it almost felt like it wasn't real. There was so much for them to talk about that he didn't even know where to begin.

Urtė, clearly sensing this, helped him out. She put her hand on his, glanced briefly at his wedding ring, then said, 'Tell me how you met Rūta.'

Molly and Kayleigh eventually returned, laden with shopping bags. Kayleigh was dressed in new clothes, head to toe in black, of course.

They'd been gone for well over an hour, but for once, James wasn't annoyed. He'd relayed his life story and Urtė had reciprocated. She was exactly the sweet, kind-hearted woman Ruth had always described. That she had remained so was amazing given the ordeal she'd been subjected to for fifteen years. He rarely wished death on people, but, God, was he thankful that the Panchenkos were already dead. If they weren't, he couldn't be sure he'd be able to resist seeing to it himself. What a pair of evil, sadistic bastards. Rotting in hell now, if there was any justice in this world.

Molly handed Urtė a huge plastic bag. 'We found a gorgeous little boutique down a side street,' she said. 'I wasn't sure of your style, so I got a selection. Trust I got the right size?'

Urtė opened the bag and stole a quick look inside, her mouth dropping in surprise. She closed the bag and tried to return it to Molly. 'I cannot take this. I don't have money to pay you.'

Molly flicked her hand in the air. 'My treat, love. It's the least I could do after all you've been through.'

'Thank you so much!' Urtė said, clasping the bag to her chest.

'Trust the two of you have caught up on everything?'

Urtė smiled at James, and he nodded.

'Why don't you go and get changed into one of those outfits?' Molly continued. 'I'd love to see what it looks like on your gorgeous figure. I'm *so* jealous! There are public loos just around the corner. You'll just need to hold your nose while you change. Kayleigh, you help her while James and I get another round in.'

James glanced over his shoulder to the door again. Raised his sleeve to check his watch. Twenty minutes now.

He turned to Molly. 'They're not coming back, are they?'

Molly raised her tea cup to her lips and took a long sip. The look in her eye answered his question.

FIFTY-SEVEN

THE TWO WOMEN stood at the railings, the sun warm on their backs, looking out to the boats in the harbour.

'Which is your favourite?' Urtė asked Kayleigh.

Kayleigh pointed to a sleek white yacht, much larger and shinier than any other. 'That one, there. *Endless Summer*.'

'Perfect. Mine, too.'

They stood for a few more minutes without speaking, before Urtė asked, 'So, would you have jumped?'

'Jumped? When?'

'You know, the night I find you at the pier.'

'Oh, that,' Kayleigh said.

'Yes, *that*. Well? Would you have jumped?'

Kayleigh gave an extravagant teenage shrug. 'Maybe. Maybe not.'

Urtė smiled as a guy emerged on the deck of *Endless Summer*. He wore blue shorts and a smart white polo shirt, a dark sweater slung casually around his shoulders. He had a wonderful sportsman's physique. Late twenties, she guessed, and beautifully tanned.

She dug her hand deep into the pocket of the gorgeous cashmere cardigan and curled her fingers around the fat envelope. Kayleigh had told her there was twenty thousand pounds inside, the most Molly could withdraw from the various banks in town at short notice. Urtė hadn't yet dared to take it out of her pocket to count it. She had no reason to doubt the amount, though.

Twenty thousand, she mused to herself. The exact same amount the Panchenkos had paid for her fifteen years ago. She flicked her head in the direction of the guy on deck. 'Shall we ask him where he sails to next?'

'Why not?' Kayleigh replied nonchalantly.

FIFTY-EIGHT

'GABRIELA RODRÍGUEZ CONFESSED WITHIN MINUTES, APPARENTLY,' James said as Molly sank another pound coin into the machine. She plunged the lever, and the huge wheel began to spin. A blur of coloured squares and numbers flashed before his eyes, making him feel queasy. 'How much more cash are you going to piss away like this?'

'Get over it, Jimbo! It's *my* money, and I'll spend it how I like. So, what did she have to say for herself?'

The news of the housekeeper's confession had been conveyed to him by a kindly DS when he'd handed in the phone at Yarmouth. With her only son now dead and her beloved sister too frail for any new treatment, it seemed Gabriela Rodríguez had concluded there was no point in continuing to live a lie.

'Well, according to her, it all started when Felicity Fitzroy-Fergusson turned up unexpectedly one day at the London pad and caught Santiago red-handed, stealing cash from her husband's bureau. Geoffrey was hopeless with money and too stupid to ever twig that he was being

401

habitually fleeced by the no-good son of his housekeeper. Gabriela begged Felicity not to shop him to the police; told her he was a good boy really, just trying to help raise funds for his beloved aunt's life-saving cancer treatment. If she reported him, he would face a certain prison sentence, what with his previous convictions. Felicity was having none of it, of course—'

'Course not. The hard-nosed, upper-class bitch.'

'So, Gabriela played her trump card and revealed that Geoffrey had been conducting illicit cocaine-fuelled sexual liaisons for months with a mystery woman. Gabriela knew because she'd listened at the door; smelled the exotic perfume; discovered their "equipment" when she cleaned the bedroom.'

'Kinky buggers. Did she say what kind of equipment?'

'No. Funnily enough, I didn't ask. Anyway, back to the point. She said she was perfectly prepared to go to the tabloids with all the sordid details, reckoning they would pay her handsomely, far more than the cost of her sister's treatment. You still listening?'

'Yep. Carry on, Jimbo. I can sense it's going to be a big one.' Molly drummed her fingernails on the glass in excited anticipation, transfixed by the machine. 'Maybe the jackpot.'

'Where was I? Yes … Felicity, enraged by her husband's betrayal and determined that she would never again be humiliated by him, hatched a plan. She would pay for the treatment if her husband and his lover just so happened to be killed in a burglary gone wrong.'

'Oh, for Pete's sake! *Forty* tickets? That'll barely cover a penny chew.'

Molly crouched to retrieve the line of yellow tickets spewing from the machine.

'Shall I bother telling you any more?' James asked. He

was almost shouting to be heard above the cacophony of beeps and whistles. Another headache was brewing.

Molly got up and threw a tangled collection of tickets at him. 'A burglary gone wrong? Sounds like a genius plan to me. Go on.'

James, reorganising the tickets into a neat roll, continued, 'Initially, Gabriela, the God-fearing Catholic, was reluctant, but eventually she came round to the idea. It was easy to discover the date of his next liaison because Geoffrey kept a day planner. His trysts were always disguised as "private constituency work". Felicity gave Santiago the money to buy a pistol from his drug-dealing associates and all was set. The "burglar" would enter the house via a first-floor window at the back, believing it to be unoccupied, only to "discover" Geoffrey and his lover *in flagrante*. There'd be a struggle; a fight. The burglar would let off two shots and make his escape ...'

'Only that's not quite how it worked out.'

'Indeed.'

'Never does, does it? Assume Felicity's denying it all?'

'Of course. Sure they'll find something to prove her involvement in due course, though.'

Molly's face creased into a frown. 'There's one thing that puzzles me. Why did Santiago fling himself off the cliff? I get the fact he couldn't bring himself to kill a beautiful woman and, as a consequence, he'd incur the wrath of his mother for not going through with the plan. But still, *suicide*?'

'Well ...' James said, his lips curling into a smile. 'It turns out there's more. I took a sneaky look through some of the older messages on Santiago's phone. Guess what I found?'

'Surprise me.'

'I found extensive conversations conducted in basic

English between him and Andric Panchenko. Seems Santiago was one of Panchenko's drugs pushers. It was probably him supplying Fitzroy-Fergusson with cocaine and quite possibly how Fitzroy-Fergusson became acquainted with Roxie and Urtė in the first place. You know, with them being part of the other side of Panchenko's business. Anyway, Santiago was indebted to Panchenko to the tune of twenty thousand quid and he was under huge pressure to repay him. Perhaps he didn't believe Panchenko was really dead. Or he knew that another gang member would take his place to pursue the debt …'

'Told you he was the one supplying the coke, didn't I?' Molly said smugly. 'Twenty thousand, you say? That's a lot of money.'

'Nearly as much as you're sinking into these machines,' James teased. 'Oh! Just thought—there's something else I haven't told you.'

Molly rolled her eyes. 'Not like you to keep information to yourself.'

'How did Panchenko track down Clifford Snell's cara-van, I hear you ask? The cops at Yarmouth looked at his phone records and discovered he'd been repeatedly hitting last number redial. The number was Roxie's mobile phone. Eventually, someone took his call—'

'Let me guess,' Molly interjected, 'Urtė went round to use his phone at some point, attempting to contact Roxie. Clifford was lurking in the background, jealous, infatuated, trying to establish if there was another fella on the scene …'

'It's the most logical explanation.'

Molly sighed ruefully, then cast her gaze around her. 'Now, what's next?' She set off, James following her like an obedient pet as she roamed the arcade, absently shaking

404

her plastic pot of change. 'Fancy a game of air hockey?' she asked.

'No.'

'Hot hoops?'

'*No!*'

'You're such a bore. Lighten up, man! *Ah*, here we go!'

She stopped at a grabber machine filled with sequinned toys and pressed a finger to the glass. 'Look! Unicorns. They're the spit of the one Nancy had in the pram.'

'You're not thinking of—'

Yep. She was. She sank a pound into the slot, thrust the pot into his hand and grabbed the little red joystick to set the claw off on its doomed foray.

'You do know the machines are pre-programmed, don't you, so you only win once in a blue moon? It's called the payout rate.'

She turned to him with a look of mock horror. 'No way?'

'And why would anyone want this tat, anyway?'

Molly pressed the button and the claw plunged, tanta-lisingly grabbing a toy for a fleeting moment before it fell back to join the others.

'See!'

Molly fed the machine another pound. 'What *was* going through her mind, do you think?'

'Who? Nancy? Reliving a childhood memory, I guess.'

'The stuff that happened at her house—I'm taking it all as a sign. Leave well alone when it comes to my father. Let sleeping dogs lie. Pandora can take her bloody box and shove it where the sun don't shine.'

'I don't believe you for a second, you know.'

Molly bit her tongue in concentration as she manoeu-vred the claw. 'I'm deadly serious.'

'Let me help you discover the truth.'

She hesitated, then turned to look at him. 'You'd do that for me?'

'Well, I've got nothing better to do.'

Molly smiled and returned her attention to the machine. 'I'm not paying you, you know.'

'Wouldn't dream of charging a friend.'

'A *friend?* Is that all I am to you?' She pressed the button and the claws dropped to grasp a unicorn firmly by its head, then hoist it from the pile. They both watched, rapt, as the toy was carried to the near corner and dropped ceremoniously into the collection tray.

Molly retrieved the unicorn and handed it proudly to James. 'What was that you were saying about blue moons? I'd say it was written in the stars. But you don't believe in all that rubbish, do you?'

James smiled and took the toy. 'What shall we call it?'

'Well, it has to be either Urtė or Nancy, don't you reckon? Can't decide which, though. Maybe I should try and win another?'

Molly went for another coin, but James pulled the pot away from her. 'Come on, let's get out in the fresh air. This place is giving me a headache.'

She looped her arm into his. 'Let's cash in those tokens first. Then I'll treat you to an ice cream. Might even ask for a flake. How's that sound?'

'Sounds perfect.'

READERS CLUB

I hope you enjoyed this book and are keen to follow James Quinn's next adventure.

Join my Readers Club to be among the first to hear about the release of the next book in the series and also to receive a free copy of one of my novels.

On an infrequent basis, I send an email telling readers when a new book is launched, or when I have something else that I think you will want to hear about.

It's completely free to sign up to the Reader's Club and you will never be spammed by me, and you can opt out easily at any time.

To join my Reader's Club and see which novel is available as a free download, visit my website at www.dpjohnsonau thor.com.

PLEASE LEAVE A REVIEW

Please do tell others what you thought about *Lost Souls*. I hugely appreciate each new review and read every one of them. If you wouldn't mind sharing your thoughts on any e-store, your own blog or anywhere else, that would be also hugely appreciated.

Thank you!

ALSO BY D.P. JOHNSON

Lies That Kill

A teenage insomniac yearning for adventure. An oddball neighbour accused of murder. Secrets waiting to be unearthed.

Lies that Kill is a standalone young adult / crossover psychological thriller set in the London's East End. If you like gritty adventure filled with twists and turns, then you'll love Kevin's story.

Stolen Lives

James Quinn – a flawed detective with a kind heart and a noble quest: justice. Or is it vengeance?

It's been two years since a young sex-trafficked woman fell victim to a sadistic murderer sensationalised in the tabloids as the "Dell Ripper".

The case remains cold, but no one particularly cares.

Except DCI James Quinn of Hertfordshire Constabulary.

James is convinced the Ripper is Troy Perkins – sex pest, stalker, petty criminal. His tormentor. The man who stole his happiness.

When the Ripper strikes again, James is determined to catch his man, whatever the cost to himself. Or the people he loves...

Printed in Great Britain
by Amazon

14874377R00239